Pretty in Ink

Pretty in Ink

LINDSEY J. PALMER

KENSINGTON BOOKS
www.kensingtonbooks.com

KENSINGTON BOOKS are published by

Kensington Publishing Corp.
119 West 40th Street
New York, NY 10018

All Kensington titles, imprints, and distributed lines are available at special quantity discounts for bulk purchases for sales promotion, premiums, fund-raising, educational, or institutional use.

Special book excerpts or customized printings can also be created to fit specific needs. For details, write or phone the office of the Kensington Special Sales Manager: Kensington Publishing Corp., 119 West 40th Street, New York, NY 10018. Attn. Special Sales Department. Phone: 1-800-221-2647.

Kensington and the K logo Reg. U.S. Pat. & TM Off.

ISBN-13: 978-0-7582-9433-3
ISBN-10: 0-7582-9433-6
First Kensington Trade Paperback Printing: April 2014

eISBN-13: 978-0-7582-9434-0
eISBN-10: 0-7582-9434-4
First Kensington Electronic Edition: April 2014

10 9 8 7 6 5 4 3 2 1

Printed in the United States of America

For Mom, Dad, Seth, and Adam

1

Leah Brenner, Executive Editor

On May 1, the *New York Post* makes the news official: Mimi Walsh has been appointed editor in chief of *Hers* magazine, to replace the recently deposed Louisa Harding. "Mayday!" I say under my breath, a private distress call that will eventually resound throughout the office. I estimate I have one month, tops, remaining in my post. As the former leader's second-in-command, I am by default a relic of the old regime. I can feel the target on my forehead: mortifying and unmistakable, like a pulsing red zit.

Mimi starts the very next day. It's a Wednesday, usually one of my work-from-home days, but I make a point of being on-site for the grand debut. A 5:00 a.m. alarm shocks my body awake, and I stumble through thick darkness to my mewling triplets for feedings. One by one I cheer them to suck, suck, suck, like some kind of demented stage mom. When all three are sufficiently sated, I make frantic (and mostly futile) stabs at turning the house into slightly less of a disaster zone. Then Maria, the girls' nanny and my personal savior, arrives. She humors me while I prep her on the latest baby info that she's likely known about for days. Next, I devote approximately ninety seconds to yours truly, racing to get myself to look somewhat presentable (I hope) or at least charmingly disheveled (I like to think). On my way out the door, I dig through my purse and replace toys and pacifiers and rice cereal with work folders and my planner and the breast pump. Gunning the gas on the way to the Westfield train station, I pray to dodge traffic cops and then—thank God!—I dash and manage to catch the 8:12 train. The fifty-six-minute ride to Manhattan, cramped with groggy bodies and smelling of burnt coffee, is the most peaceful hour of my day. Then it's a subway ride and a short walk to the office. By the time I've made it to my desk at 9:30, I'm ready for a full night's sleep.

At 9:45 sharp, the new boss calls the whole staff into the conference room. Physically, Mimi is the opposite of Louisa—big and broad and blond, where the old boss was petite and brunette and birdlike. She is imposing at the front of the room, like a gorilla who's already staked out and claimed this new territory as her own.

"I can't tell you how thrilled and excited I am to lead this team in the transformation of *Hers* magazine," Mimi trills. No one points out that "thrilled" and "excited" are synonyms; it's the type of thing Louisa would've had no tolerance for. "This title has such great potential. I can't wait to share my vision for change, and to pool all of your fantastic ideas and create a sparkling new hit of a magazine." We plaster on smiles and shift uncomfortably in our wedges and strappy sandals as Mimi casually dismisses the magazine we've proudly been producing month after month for years— we are a team that has stuck together.

Mimi continues: "A little birdie told me this office is known for—how shall I say it?—a laid-back schedule." If by that she means working from nine-thirty to six instead of nine-thirty to midnight like many publications, then she's right. "There's nothing wrong with laid-back, of course, but that's what weekends are for, right?" Mimi emits the first of what we'll come to know as her notorious "Ha!"s, a staccato syllable closely resembling a real laugh, but lacking the latter's underlying sense of humor. "Although the truth is, weekends might become a bit of a mirage this summer, too. We'll be working hard to prep the relaunch for the

November issue," she says. "I hope you're prepared to have your lives turned upside down for a while." Nervous titters all around.

"OK, now introductions!" We go around the room and state our names and titles. "I'm Leah Brenner, executive editor," I say with as much authority as I can muster, but I fear I sound like a fraud. Plus, I'm worried my heavy eyelids are drooping dangerously low, so I keep pinching my thigh; I can feel the beginnings of a bruise. To my left is Louisa's old assistant. "I'm Jenny," she says, "and I hope to be your assistant." Mimi lets out another one: "Ha!" followed by, "You're funny." Within hours Jenny will be a goner.

I scan the room—everyone smiling anxiously—and I feel a surge of pride, marveling at this team of capable and decent workers, all of whom are clutching at the last threads of their jobs. We've all heard the urban legend about the new editor in chief who took over a publication—which one, who knows?—and didn't fire a single person from the old staff; it's apocryphal, of course, along with the Montauk monster and the chronically single New Yorker who on the night of her thirty-fifth birthday meets the man of her dreams, a rich doctor with a penthouse on Central Park West, and within the year has a giant rock on her finger and a fetus in her belly. Fairy tales. In my head I sing a doom-spelling ditty—*dum, dum, dum, dum, DUM!*—a handy distraction from the rest of the meeting.

That afternoon, I force myself across the threshold of my new boss's office to introduce myself privately. I feel as if I'm walking off a cliff's edge, until Mimi surprises me by inviting me in. "Sit down, make yourself comfy," she says. "We'll chat and get to know each other."

I nod and nod as Mimi rambles on about how easy her new commute is, and how nice it is to finally work near an express train. "Where do you live?" she asks, but before I can answer she barks out, "Jenny, grab me a coffee," and then starts in on the total gridlock that is Manhattan and how hailing a taxi these days is pretty much a request to sit in traffic and listen to honking horns and a man babbling in a foreign tongue and meanwhile to pay for the privilege. I'm just beginning to make out my thoughts over my buzzing anxiety when Jenny arrives with coffee, and Mimi says, "Thanks, dear. Oh, I should tell you—because there's no point beating around the bush—I've already hired on my old assistant to take over your job."

I gasp, then pray it wasn't audible. I avoid Jenny's eyes, fearing I might tear up. Jenny, always the professional, nods once and straightens her spine, doing her best to act as if Mimi just told her about a new filing system. "It's nothing personal, of course," Mimi says, then sips at her coffee. "Ooh, that's way too hot. I nearly burned my tongue! Anyway, you're welcome to stick around and collect a paycheck until the new girl arrives, or you can cut and run today. Totally your choice." She smiles at Jenny as if she's just offered her a pick between a trip to Paris or Rome.

"I'll clear out my things by the end of the day," Jenny says, then makes her exit. I silently cheer her bravery.

"All right, then." Mimi turns to her e-mail with a level of focus that lets me know I'm dismissed, too. I slink out of her office, guilty with relief that the first ax has not fallen on me.

It would have been a different brand of cruelty had Mimi insisted Jenny stay on to train her replacement. But the result of Jenny's swift departure is that when the new assistant arrives a week later, the girl's job initiation falls to me. "You know the most about *Hers*, right?" Mimi asks me in a way that an undiscerning person might interpret as flattering. But I know what's coming. "Please be a doll and fill Laura in on the workings of the office." I nod. What else can I do?

Mimi introduces a girl a full head taller than me with the posture of a weeping willow. "Laura Maxwell, pleased to meet you," she announces, extending a hand as broad as a basketball player's. Her grip crushes my own.

With as much grace as I can muster, I show Laura around, introduce her to Ed, the mail manager, and explain the e-mail server and copy routing system. I notice that Laura has frizzy hair and visible panty lines. I know I'm being unkind, but I believe I deserve to. I can feel all the editors' eyes on me as I parade around the new assistant; she's like some honorary guest and I'm her lowly tour guide. I'm trying hard to hide my humiliation.

In the kitchen, I demonstrate how to work the finicky coffee machine, jiggling the button that gets it up and rumbling again. "Mimi mentioned she likes her coffee black," I offer, trying to be helpful.

"Oh, I've assisted Mimi before," Laura says. I think I catch the hint of a smirk. "Back at the old office." Right.

So then Laura knows what she's in for. She knows and, with free will and open eyes, has signed on. She's chosen to deal with the unreadable requests that Mimi scrawls in blood-red ink on Post-its and then drops onto our desks dozens of times a day. She's chosen to field the endless list of ridiculous requests (yesterday Mimi complained of blisters caused by her teetering heels and sent our sweet intern, Erin, off to a pharmacy deep in Tribeca for a special brand of bandage). And she's chosen to endure what I've officially named The Mimi Diatribes—those one-sided conversations that last up to half an hour, and make you feel like you're on the dark side of a two-way mirror. During my seven days of service so far as Mimi's deputy, I doubt my new boss has taken one real look at me. I keep waiting to be informed that she's already hired my replacement, too.

Laura knows all of these quirks about Mimi, and still she's chosen to saunter with her scuffed-up flats and unflattering T-shirt dress right into this battle zone, where I suspect the bloodshed has barely begun.

Rewind four months, back to January, to what should be a season of new beginnings—though for Louisa it's the beginning of the end. On a day marked by the latest in a long stint of snowstorms, I face the morning marathon with my ten-month-old daughters, and then wrestle against a wall of sleet and wind to make it on time from New Jersey suburbia to midtown Manhattan. But my car takes forever to start, the streets are slippery, and the subway stalls; when my office computer blinks awake it flashes 9:37 like an accusation—*late*. I suspect my always-punctual boss has beaten me to work, a premonition confirmed when Louisa wanders by my office and drops her glance to my snow-soaked boots. Busted. I refuse to wear the sleek, heeled ones that are trendy this winter—I've seen several of the fashion-y girls go slip-sliding across the ice while wearing them, and I'm horrified that any company would design winter boots with no traction. Still, I prefer to change into my heels before Louisa's arrival, to always look the professional part.

"Morning check-in?" I chirp. Louisa nods, but there's something—a twitch of the upper lip, perhaps?—that betrays anxiety. After three years as her number two at *Hers*, and many years before that as teammates at other titles, I can read my boss's face like the pages of a magazine. I can also read her outfit, the way she parts her hair, and her decision to leave the office door closed or open or slightly ajar. I've memorized her favorite adjectives and most de-spised adverbs, her children's birthdays, and the two perfumes she likes to spritz simultaneously to blend into her signature scent. Sometimes it's occurred to me that I myself possess neither a sig-nature scent nor a list of my favorite adjectives, but usually I'm too busy tending to Louisa to focus on such details.

As I sit with my boss, reviewing the status of the next issue's features and watching her sip her hazelnut dark (Louisa likes Dunkin' Donuts, but drinks it from a Starbucks mug—the one chink in her armor of self-esteem), I consider that she has a meet-ing this morning on the thirtieth floor, the Schmidt & Delancey corporate suite, otherwise known as Head Honchos Headquarters. We've just completed *Hers*' third redesign in a year, and today Louisa will introduce the newest vision to Corporate. I imagine the PowerPoint through its soundtrack—I compiled it, so I know it by heart. The presentation will encapsulate *Hers* magazine's con-ception of the modern thirty-something American woman. As with everything I work on with Louisa, I can't help but feel proud.

The story is, several years earlier, Louisa inherited a title so tired and frumpy that she had to search a dozen New York City news-stands before finding one that stocked a recent issue. *Hers* had be-come a suburban midwestern magazine, most of whose readers inherited subscriptions from their mothers. (My own mother, the consummate snob, scoffed when I accepted the job at *Hers*, but then her own editorial career took place exclusively in the elite echelons of only the highest-brow magazines.) Back then, the *Hers* covers offered promises that seemed ripped from 1950s home economics course catalogs—"Secret tips to whip up your best chocolate soufflé!" "Pretty patterns for your sharpest holiday outfit!"—and the people pictured on the pages were plain and doughy, the theory being that readers would prefer to see women who looked like them rather than beautiful, intimidating models.

Until this past year, each of Louisa's redesigns has nudged *Hers* a bit sleeker, more sophisticated, upmarket. Recently, in response to readers' ongoing economic woes, she's reverted a bit to the magazine's roots, including more bargain items and money-saving tips. I can tell it pains my boss to commission stories on supercouponing and bargain-basement items that can pass for designer, but she's submitted, admitting it's the way the wind's blowing. For this most recent transformation, she's been worrying about including a $250 Club Monaco blazer in the PowerPoint (she hasn't said as much, but I've seen her add and then remove and then add the blazer again while tweaking the slides).

"The final cut," Louisa says now, loading up the completed presentation on her laptop. I crouch next to her chair, thrilled as always to be in such close proximity to my boss. Not only has Louisa kept in the Club Monaco blazer, but she's displayed it on the first slide; the sight sends a shudder of fear down my spine. Louisa flips through the rest of the presentation, and I notice she's made some changes since I last saw it: slides of socialites and runway fashion mingle with those of gourmet meals prepared in lovely, aspirational kitchens.

"It's stunning," I say, because it's too late to change anything. I feel a premonition of doom.

"Oh, good. Abby wanted me to lead off with the budget dining piece, but good lord, how depressing." I nod like an idiot. "I'm going for sparkle and magic and drama—the kind of magazine that makes you dream." Louisa makes eye contact, her irises shining with excitement, and—I can't help myself—it's contagious.

Even as a young girl, I had dreams of scaling the ladder of career success. My twin sister, Cara, teased me mercilessly, but I found her tree-climbing, tag-playing notions of fun to be frivolous. My favorite way to spend a Sunday was dressing up in my mother's silk blouses and pencil skirts and then sitting at the kitchen table—my makeshift desk—with a big stack of paper (blank) and a coffee mug (empty), and shouting out orders to my minions (pretend). My mother would marvel at my corporate setup and call me her little child in chief. Cara would roll her eyes at this display of affection, but I noticed that my mother didn't coin a pet name for her. While Cara busied herself converting the contents of our recycling bin into her latest costume for a play, I pored over Pottery Barn and Crate & Barrel catalogs, admiring all the sleek trappings of what I imagined to be success. I pictured people oohing and aahing when they saw Adult Me: "What a brilliant, powerful woman," they'd whisper, just as I knew they did about my mother. I couldn't wait to grow up.

In my senior year at Columbia, I made it my mission to read the memoirs of all the world's most powerful women—including the CEO of Schmidt & Delancey—and to memorize all their secrets to success. Nearly every woman talked about the importance of attaching yourself to a star in order to rise along with her and get genius guidance along the way. When I first interviewed to be Louisa's assistant fifteen years ago, back when she was a senior editor at *Modern Woman Today*, I knew I'd found my star. Here was a person who could help me launch the big, ambitious career I'd always dreamed of. So far that instinct has served me well.

But I'm not the only one who's in awe of Louisa. When she gathers the staff together to unroll a fresh vision or explain a new direction, she inspires like a preacher. She's not a perfect editor, or boss, but she commands respect and admiration, and everyone believes in her. Or rather, they did until recently. I fear even my own faith in our leader is slipping.

* * *

When Louisa returns from the thirtieth floor, she breezes past my office without a word, and I suspect the head honchos might not share my boss's confidence in the redesign. Louisa's assistant, Jenny, calls me and, in a voice so calm I can tell our fearless leader must be frantic, says, "Will you kindly come down to Louisa's office, and please pick up Abby and Mark along the way?" The managing editor, creative director, and I file into our boss's office on tiptoe. Jenny gently replaces the door in its frame.

Louisa's workspace is rimmed on three sides by floor-to-ceiling windows, which means only thin panes of glass separate us from a raging snowfall outside; we're surrounded by storm. "It's not good," Louisa says, the wind howling and whipping against the glass. I feel desperate to flee.

"The problem is obvious," says Mark, our creative director, his voice like shards of glass. "This magazine is schizophrenic. Over the course of one year, we've altered the fonts, the logos, and the colors three separate times. Our fashion has gone from runway to bargain bin and back. You've renamed the health pages 'Monthly Checkup,' then 'Rx for a Healthy You!' then 'Doctor's Appointment.' You've made us move beauty from the front of the book to the back of the book, then back to the front. The changes are manic!"

Louisa sighs, and I feel a bit sick. It's true what Mark's saying: Someone who picked up a copy of *Hers* at the hair salon last June and then bought another issue at the airport over Christmas might not have known she was reading the same magazine.

"OK, let's all just relax," says Abby, our always calm and reasonable managing editor.

"We'll work it out," I say, my conviction weak despite my words.

"Hey, Jenny," Louisa calls out to her assistant. "Grab me lunch, will you? One California roll, one spicy tuna, and a seaweed salad"— her usual—"and, um, four Peppermint Patties." Candy—a definite sign of trouble.

Leaving Louisa's office, I feel the attention from the trenches hot on my cheeks. Though they're trying to hide it, it's obvious that every staff member is staring from her respective cubicle, desperate to glean a glimpse of the goings-on behind Louisa's door. As far as I'm concerned, they're lucky to be spared the details. Jenny is off fetching Louisa's food, and on her desk I spot a prescription for Ativan. It's in Louisa's name. I discreetly tuck it under a folder, which I notice is labeled, "Any decent public schools in NYC?" I shove both documents into Jenny's top drawer, then retreat to my office.

As the wintry days drag on, heavy and cold with dread, I savor even more than usual the two days a week I work from home. My home office is far from glamorous; unlike my roomy space at *Hers* that looks out onto Central Park, my basement work area is cluttered and windowless. But it's quiet and calm, a temporary escape from Louisa's naked looks of need and the worry that she now wears on skin's surface. Plus, at home I'm treated to occasional visits from a daughter who manages to escape Maria's watchful eye and clomp-crawl her way past my door.

"Hello, love," I say, bending down to pull Daisy onto my lap.

"Ma-ma." I grin with pride at this word that she's recently learned to say, her first. Daisy's tiny fingers go right for the gold—a 14-carat hoop hanging from my right ear. I swat her away. Thankfully I've honed laser-fast reflexes during my ten months of motherhood, and so far my daughters have failed to inflict serious injury in pursuit of my baubles. My husband, Rob, believes my refusal to stop wearing dangly earrings around our babies' grabby fingers is masochistic and insane. In truth, it's vanity; I haven't managed to kick the last ten pounds of baby weight, and damn it all if I'll be denied my shiny jewelry, too.

Maria swoops in and reaches for Daisy. "You're not allowed in there, chica," she says, pinning me with accusatory eyes. She's right; I preach "Do not disturb" during office hours, but half the time I'm alone at the computer I pine for the particular company of my three squirming babies; sometimes I go so far as to snatch one up. (Inconveniently, as soon as Maria is out the door for the day and I am inundated with nothing but baby time, I long for sweet solitude.)

My phone rings, three p.m. on the dot, my husband as reliable as a clock. "Baby," he says. "How's the editing?"

"Hey, apple of my eye. Peachy as pie. How's the designing?"

"Fruitful. Very fruitful." I still love this silly routine that we've developed over nearly a decade as partners. "I'll pick up a rotisserie chicken on the way home. How's it going really?"

"Oh, I dunno. I Skyped with Louisa earlier to review page proofs, and I'm worried she's losing her knack, like she can't tell what's good and what's not, what matters and what doesn't. Or maybe I'm just going a little crazy myself."

"I'm telling you, it's too much time spent holed up with all those crazy women." I roll my eyes, knowing what's next. "You need some distance. I signed up for subscriptions to a few Vermont papers so we can check out the listings."

"Oh, goody," I say, not bothering to mask my sarcasm.

"Just to look, Leah. Just to dream. Picture it, you and me cozied up under a blanket with a fire going in a big old farmhouse, the girls running around some giant swatch of land, all of us planting vegetables and raising chickens—we'd have fresh eggs!"

"Newsflash, Rob: We *have* fresh eggs here, from a lovely little place called Stop & Shop. No shitting chickens, either."

"Just think about it, OK? Imagine all that extra time you'd have with the girls."

I feel a pang. Rob can be good at this, and sometimes I even fall for his fantasy of what my freelance writing career out in the country would look like—batting around great ideas with enthusiastic editors, interviewing brilliant experts about fascinating topics, and pouring my heart into groundbreaking features for big, important publications. In reality I know freelancing is 90 percent hustling and churning out rehashes of the same articles over and over and 10 percent fighting against the spiral down into derangement due to lack of human interaction. Rob is lucky he can do his web design job from anywhere.

"If we moved to Vermont, we wouldn't have Maria," I say. "I'd keel over and collapse within a week."

"Baby, you can bring Maria in your luggage. Just poke out some air holes."

"You are terrible," I say, picturing our white family packing away our Colombian nanny in a suitcase and tossing it in the back of our station wagon. God, somebody's probably done such a thing. "I have work to do. Bye, sweetheart."

Through my office door, I hear Maria singing, *"Hasta mañana, nos vamos a la cama,"* a tune the girls love regardless of whether it's actually bedtime. Maria is a gift. When she gets finicky Rose to go down for a nap or tickles Lulu's belly and makes her explode into hiccup-y laughs far more excited than I can elicit, I feel not at all wistful in the ways I've heard some working moms talk about their children's caregivers. I'd clone Maria if we could afford to shell out double her salary.

It's around the time the frozen ground begins to thaw (when you may as well face it that whatever shoes you wear will end up matted with mud) when Louisa's and my private language starts deteriorating. It used to be, we could maintain an entire conversation with glances and gestures. Louisa would conclude a meeting and offer hearty assurance to some VIP and then shoot me a split-second peek that meant, "No way in hell!" or "Thank the Lord that's over," and I'd nod politely and understand just the right way to dismiss the visitor. But lately Louisa's looks have become garbled. Now she fixes on her Competent Editor mask and forgets to remove it when we're speaking privately.

The day it proves to be all over is one of those unseasonably warm days in April. Ed the mail guy enters Louisa's office bearing a bouquet of lilacs; I wonder who's sent them and why: her husband as a gesture of support? a public relations rep eager as always to woo? the corporate suite as some kind of final offering?

"Thanks, those are my favorite." Louisa's voice is wooden, like she's reciting lines, like she doesn't remember that of course both

Ed and I would know what her favorite flowers are. She stares per-plexedly at the bouquet, looking as if she's aged about a decade.

"We'll have Jenny put them in water," I say, going to grab a vase.

I'm still sitting in Louisa's office, awaiting instructions from our formerly fearless leader who's now putzing around her space like she's lost, when Jenny patches through a call from the teacher of Louisa's five-year-old son. "She claims it's urgent," says Jenny, who knows closed-door meetings are usually noninterruptible. Louisa puts the phone on speaker.

"Hi, Ms. Harding," we hear over the line. The teacher sounds nervous. "We had a double recess today. You know, because of the nice weather. So we stayed at the playground through what would have been reading. I know, I know, reading is important. But the kids were excited, and—" I start to zone out, wondering if the $40,000 sticker price for the private school where Louisa sends her kids includes this kind of mundane daily update from the teach-ers. My ears perk up when I hear the words "sprained ankle."

"Is Jasper OK?" Louisa gasps, her voice shrill.

"Yes, he's fine. He fell from the monkey bars, but he's all right. The nurse set him up with an ice pack and a cherry Popsicle, but we do need you or your husband to come fetch him immediately and take him to a doctor."

"I'll be right over," Louisa says, then hangs up.

"Shit," she shrieks. "Shit, shit, shit." She shrinks in her seat and her eyes go misty and brim over with tears. The fact that I've never heard my boss curse, never mind seen her slump or cry, makes me want to break down, too. I manage to maintain my com-posure, and offer Louisa a tissue. She draws me in for a hug, which shocks me into silence. With her mouth inches from my ear, she whispers, "An hour ago they fired me."

At first I say nothing. Still pressed up against her body, I can feel the narrow fragility of Louisa's frame—my shoulders are a good six inches broader than hers. She's like a frail kid. This realization stirs up my anger. My boss is like a child, delicate and innocent. *How could they do this to her?* "But, but . . ." I stutter idiotically.

"I know." Louisa plucks the tissue from my hand and blows her nose, a horrible honk. "They're morons."

"I'm so sorry."

"I'm sorry, too." Louisa inhales deeply and looks up at me. "I'm really sorry." She smoothes out her skirt, sighs, and then emerges from her office into the maze of cubicles.

"Louisa, what's wrong?" I hear Mark ask. "Are you OK?"

"Jasper broke his foot," she responds, hurrying out of the office. Jenny has to chase after her with her purse.

Louisa doesn't return that afternoon. Our managing editor, Abby, calls a staff meeting. We shuttle into the conference room, and everyone seems restless. I overhear Zoe and Jane chattering about *Hers'* poor newsstand numbers and flagging subscriptions; Mark and Debbie are murmuring guesses at Louisa's latest crazy scheme to save the magazine; Drew is telling the intern that some people are concerned *Hers* isn't making the transition fast enough to tablet technology. I stay on the sidelines and give my stomach a silent pep talk to stop its lurching.

I see the looks of shock as, instead of Louisa, Mrs. Winters, Schmidt & Delancey's editorial director, enters and takes her place at the front of the room. Mrs. Winters is known for her thick gray bun and her formidable poker face, though privately I suspect a wig is responsible for the former and Botox for the latter. A halo of hush surrounds her at all times. Mrs. Winters delivers the official party line: "Ms. Harding is stepping down from her position as editor in chief of *Hers* magazine in order to pursue other interests.

"Are there any questions?" she quips.

No one dares speak up. I hear Zoe mumble, "Is that what we're calling unemployment these days? 'Other interests'?"

"OK, then, that's all for today," says Mrs. Winters. "We'll give word as soon as there's any further news." Filing out of the conference room, we all flash our fake "No hard feelings" smiles at Mrs. Winters. I catch Drew, our photo editor, staring at me with a look of uncensored pity. Then Abby pats me on the back in a "Keep your head up" kind of way. Accustomed to being envied and admired and looked up to, I feel totally out of my element—and scared. That's when I understand. Louisa wasn't saying she was sorry about her own situation; rather, she was apologizing to me. Because I will soon be out of a job, too.

2

Jane Staub-Smith,
Associate Editor

As any decent (and anxious) reporter would, I begin preparing for my Mimi meeting as soon as we get the e-mail. It's from Laura, the new assistant: "Hi all! I'm scheduling each person fifteen-minute time slots with Mimi so she can get to know you and your roles at the magazine." In other words, so we can defend our jobs with everything we've got. My appointment is on Friday, two days from now, which leaves plenty of time for due diligence.

A morning's scroll through LexisNexis reveals that Mimi hails from Kansas farm country (which may as well be Uzbekistan, as far as I'm concerned); she attended the state school, then bartended in St. Louis for two years before shipping out to New York and working her way up at the big tabloids, meanwhile marrying and divorcing two men, first a nurse and then a doctor. Most recently the executive editor of the lowbrow celeb rag *Starstruck*, she's earned herself a reputation for being smart (despite the mediocre pedigree), ruthless, and impulsive. I uncover a decade-old photo of Mimi with her arm slung around our very own recipe creator, Debbie.

I make my way to *Hers'* test kitchen, and then hover outside until Debbie invites me in, as is protocol. "So you know the new boss from before, huh?" I ask.

"Diligent digging," Debbie says. "What, did you hire a PI to get the scoop before your meeting?"

"Guilty as charged, minus the PI. I'm nervous! So is it true?"

"Yeah, Mimi and I worked together at *VIP*, although I don't like to advertise the fact. That was the brief blip I spent hounding celebrities' every move. I reported on what they ordered in restaurants, how much of their meals they actually ate, and whether or not they requested doggie bags. A very fulfilling job, as you might imagine."

"Jeez. So what's Mimi like?"

"If I remember correctly, she's notorious for never using the bathroom—even after downing venti lattes and on late nights. Total freak. Also, she adores purple."

"Huh."

"I'd love to keep gossiping, but I'm neglecting my risotto, and I fear if it dries out the new boss will have my head." Debbie flashes a wicked smile.

"Return to your stirring, then." I swipe an apple on my way out.

On the day of my meeting with Mimi, I'm dressed smartly in eggplant capris and a lavender button-up, a manicure to match. But my scheduled time slot comes and goes, and then the appointment is pushed back three more times. I struggle to come up with three more just-right outfits. When it's finally my turn, I enter Mimi's office with as much confidence as I can fake. For my first real-life encounter with the woman who's already become a myth in my mind, I'm wearing my fourth and final purple getup, a lilac silk sheath I picked up at a BCBG sample sale (unfortunately by this point I've bitten my magenta nails down to the quick). I've brought with me a long list of my responsibilities, plus a longer list of ideas for revamping the magazine. I'm genuinely excited at the prospect of transforming *Hers* into a more impactful, serious-minded publication. I'm anxious to finally show off my journalistic chops.

The first thing I notice in Mimi's office, perched on a ledge behind the desk, is a portrait of the old boss Louisa's children, the boy gap-toothed, the girl squinty-eyed—some sort of joke or just an oversight? My research revealed that Mimi is not a mother. I feel the kids eyeing me accusingly from within the frame, like I'm on trial.

"I hear you work on our marriage coverage," Mimi says, pronouncing the word "marriage" like it's "cancer."

"Yes, for three years I've been writing the love, sex, and relationship pages." I'm proud of the stories I've written for *Hers*, especially the marriage ones; it's thrilling to receive dozens of letters each month from readers praising my work and thanking me for helping their relationships. "I actually have some ideas for—"

"Are you married, then?" Mimi interrupts.

"No."

"In a relationship?"

"Well, until recently, yes."

"So then, no?"

"Um, I guess not." I flash on an image of Jacob, and my eyes blur with tears. I blink until they recede.

"So, where do you get your ideas, Jane? How do you put yourself in the shoes of our readers?"

"I do research, of course. I know plenty of people who are married, so I talk to them, and I pay close attention to our reader mail." I'm trying to hang onto Mimi's wandering attention, secretly fuming that marriage has apparently become a prerequisite for my job. Never mind that I graduated top of my class from Medill School of Journalism. "I don't pretend to be an expert, but I have a dozen real experts on speed-dial, and their knowledge—"

"Oh, Jane, I think the reader is bored to death of hearing how to spice things up with her slob of a husband, how she should buy lingerie to impress him, how she needs to schedule sex to stay intimate, blah blah blah. I think she'd rather die than read another article about the Holy Grail of date night." I'm making an effort to maintain a neutral expression as my new boss insults everything I've covered at the magazine for three years. It's a particularly cruel prelude to firing me, I think, but at least it will soon be over. She adds, "Don't you agree, Jane?"

"Uh, I guess so." Mimi nods, like we're now collaborators. Maybe this is a game, and she's egging me on to see if I'll wither under the pressure or stand up for myself. I take a breath to calm my racing heart. "I will say, I've gotten lots of mail from women grateful for our sex and marriage advice. And Dr. Sharon Hellerman—"

"Oh, Christ, Dr. Sharon Hellerman!" Mimi emits a strange sound that may or may not be laughter. "Do you think that old bag has had sex once in the past decade? I picture Sharon and her husband of a thousand years sitting down to watch reruns of *Love Boat* each night, then chastely kissing each other on the cheek and tucking themselves in to twin beds, Bert-and-Ernie style. Marriage expert, ha! Please don't let me catch her name in the magazine again."

I jot down, "No more Dr. H," wondering how I'll cancel this afternoon's phone interview without rescheduling.

"Listen, Jane, you're a young, attractive, unattached girl. If you showed up at a dinner party full of our readers, you'd be the star of the show. The rest of them would be coupled up and likely bored to death of their partners, dying to hear your stories from the fun, exciting single life. They'd hang on your every word about your latest first-date catastrophe or the mind-blowing sex you had with the guy you met out at the bar last night. And believe me, I've been on both sides of the fence, so I know what I'm talking about."

I'm nodding furiously, as if I have a clue about what it's like to have a wild one-night stand, and like it's no big deal to chat about it with my new boss.

"So how about this?" Mimi says. "What I'd like you to do is to start a blog on our Web site. We'll call it something like 'Sex and the Single Girl: Having Her Fun Before She Snags the Ring,' and you can chronicle the highs and the lows of your dating life. OK?"

"Jeez, well . . ."

"All right, then. Good talk. We'll get to the rest of your pages as we go along. Great to meet you, Ms. Jane Staub-Smith." Mimi clicks her red pen, shakes my hand, and then calls Laura in to usher me out of her office.

Back at my computer, I neglect my e-mail and instead load up a game of Tetris. I think of Marjorie Dawson, the woman I've invented to be the face of our eight million readers, the one I picture when I come up with story ideas and the one I write to. There Marjorie is returning from her dental hygienist gig to her home in the suburbs of Minneapolis, a bag of groceries tucked under each arm, a golden retriever lapping at her feet, and an eight-year-old son answering her greeting without peeling his eyes from the newest Pixar flick playing on the screen. I imagine Marjorie starting dinner, then taking a break to log on to HersMag.com, where she's confronted with the latest post on "Sex and the Single Girl," a recounting of my botched make-out with that awful chubby guy after I downed one too many margaritas last Friday night. I shudder at the thought.

"Jane, are you *trying* to get yourself fired?" Leah appears in my cubicle and reaches across the keyboard to close out my Tetris game.

"Hey, I was about to beat that level." Leah's *I'm-disappointed-in-you* look is the worst; nothing makes me feel guiltier. "So, Mimi wants me to start a blog."

"Oh, yuck." Leah shares my disapproval of the oversharing epidemic that's infected our culture; still, we're careful to keep our reproach under wraps, for fear of becoming office pariahs. "Well, do you think you impressed her? Did she like your ideas?"

"I honestly have no idea," I say.

Leah nods, betraying nothing, but I imagine she's mourning the loss of her power. As executive editor, Leah was in charge by default during that strange, rudderless week post-Louisa and pre-Mimi, although we all understood that her authority had an expiration date.

"Jane, we have a problem." I can identify that high-pitched whine anywhere, and I feel myself breaking out in blotch: Sylvia Rogers, *Hers'* research chief, marches up to my cube.

"What's wrong?" I ask, not really up for a Sylvia confrontation after my dress-down with Mimi.

"We have a red-alert situation." To the research chief, a red-alert situation is a first draft that says an apple contains four not five grams of fiber. No doubt this attitude is a result of her past life as a fact-checker for the *Los Angeles Times*, where incorrect information could mean a source suing or a threat to national security. I respect Sylvia's dedication, but it's my opinion that a story about healthy snacks does not need to be treated like an investigative report on Guantánamo Bay.

Sylvia points her talon-like finger to a stack of papers. "In this article, 'Fit in Date Night—Fast!' one woman alleges that her minigolf outing with her husband lasted forty minutes, but the gentleman who runs the golf course just told me it should take only thirty minutes to complete." *Oh, jeez*, I think. Sylvia's most frantic freak-outs are usually caused by he-said, she-said disputes.

"This is from the woman's quote, right?" I ask. Sylvia nods soberly—she's bone thin, but somehow still has a double chin. "If she said it took forty minutes, let's say it took forty minutes."

"But the man who knows the course best says it takes only thirty."

"If it would make you feel better, then we can say thirty. That's fine by me."

"Well, that wouldn't be accurate, since the woman made a point of saying it took forty minutes. Apparently the couple hired a babysitter for an hour and, taking into account travel time, she mentioned they didn't have time left for lovemaking after the date." I smile at Sylvia's reference to sex. Our research chief is older than my mother. I sometimes imagine her sharing a bed with several cats, although in fact she has a rather dapper-looking husband.

"Should we compromise, split the difference?" I ask. "How about we say thirty-five minutes?"

"Then we're being doubly inaccurate. No one said it took

thirty-five minutes!" Sylvia emits a snort, as if my idea is ludicrous.

"What exactly do you suggest we do, Sylvia?" I sense my composure begin to crack.

"Can we eliminate the time reference altogether?"

"The premise of the story is that parents have very little free time, so we're sharing ideas for short date nights that they can actually squeeze in."

"I understand. But . . ."

"Why don't we say, 'It took us forty minutes' and then put something in parentheses like, 'Some people can get through the course in half an hour'?"

"I don't know. Maybe we should check with Mimi."

"I guess if you think that's the only solution, but I know she has a crazy schedule today." I'm trying to help Sylvia out. If Mimi is fed up with Dr. Sharon Hellerman's quotes about marital harmony, then she certainly won't have the patience for a nitpicky concern from our research chief. "What if we add the word 'about'?" I suggest. "As in, 'It took me about thirty minutes'?"

"Hmm. I'm not thrilled with the idea, but it may work."

"Great." There, I nailed it, striking that note of finality that's the only way to shake Sylvia. She skulks away, off to harangue someone else about the facts.

I hear Zoe, our web manager, cracking up from the next set of cubicles. "Now, I'd estimate that that conversation took about five minutes," she says, masterly aping Sylvia's voice, "but my high-tech, specially synchronized watch recorded an exact time of four minutes, thirty-two seconds. How might we rectify this discrepancy?" I giggle, and glance over my cubicle wall to Laura, thinking maybe I can draw the new girl in; collectively ridiculing a target is such an easy way to bond. But Mimi's assistant won't catch my eye. She's staring at her screen, pretending she hasn't heard a thing.

I know I'm in denial that Jenny is gone when, for the second time in a week, I lean over my cubicle and say, "Listen to this," primed to read my friend a letter from a prison inmate requesting more brunettes in the magazine. Laura looks up from the other side of the divide. "Oh," I say, startled.

Earlier, I'd begun reciting a press release for a contraption that measures the blood alcohol level of breast milk, "so Mommy can booze *and* feed baby." I'm freshly disappointed each time I spot Laura in place of my old friend.

I remember when Mimi told me about the girl who would become my new cubicle-mate, describing her as "our illustrious new team member, Laura Maxwell"; she hadn't realized Jenny was still within earshot, packing up her stuff. That's when Jenny dubbed her replacement, sight unseen, "Whore-a Maxwell." I'm glad Jenny never had to see how said illustrious new team member has transformed her former cubicle—the walls now plastered with cheesy *True Blood* posters and photos of herself among gaggles of lame-looking girls clutching neon cocktails.

Still, I know it's smart to buddy up with the people you're cooped up with all day. And the assistant to the editor in chief is a useful friend to have, privy to all the boss's comings and goings, a key source of office information and gossip. So I will myself to make an effort. "Hey, Laura," I say, leaning over the divider again. "Did you hear at the August cover shoot, Georgina Sparks scarfed down an entire plate of cookies and then made a beeline to the bathroom?" It's been rumored the actress is bulimic.

"Is that so?" Laura says, and then drops her eyes back to her screen. She's clearly uninterested in my friendship.

My phone rings, and when I answer, Jenny launches right in: "This morning's *Jerry* was, hands down, the best episode ever. He had on pregnant moms and their pregnant teenage daughters, all competing to show off their sexiest dance moves, and each family's winner got a full baby wardrobe and nursery. Totally genius! Who comes up with this stuff?"

"Jenny," I say. "Have you gotten dressed today?" It's clear my former coworker is suffering a quiet breakdown, having morphed within two weeks from an ambitious go-getter to a sad, talk-show-addicted shut-in. Still, Jenny has listened to me moan and obsess over my ex, Jacob, for months, so I decide to give her another week's grace period before I'll start bugging her to get her act together.

"How's Whore-a?" Jenny asks, ignoring my question. I don't condone this mean moniker, and Jenny knows it. "How's Mimi? And everyone else?"

"Oh, you know, humming along." As time goes by, I'm finding it more difficult to explain the nuances of the office to someone who isn't with us in the trenches day in and day out. I miss Jenny as Coworker. I miss our elevator game of guessing which floor each person would get off on; it's a company-wide joke that everyone in the building dresses like the readership of their respective publications, and Jenny and I had a near 90 percent track record of accurately ID-ing them. On Jenny's last descent—both of us weighed down with her boxes—we nailed it: At the cafeteria level two people stepped on, a man who looked as if he'd just returned from a fishing trip and a woman who appeared to be a grown-up version of the high school queen bee; just as we predicted, the rugged guy exited at Floor 8, *Man Outdoors*, and the adult teenybopper got off at 6, *Teen Fashionista*. Jenny giggled before returning to somber. I tried to cheer her up by pointing out that she'd probably be earning more on unemployment than she'd made at *Hers*.

"You think?"

"Yep. That's the sad truth about the pathetic assistant salary at Schmidt & Delancey."

"Ugh, I never thought I'd have to apply for unemployment," she said.

"Are you serious?" I replied. "You know we've been in a recession going on four years now. I worry about getting fired approximately fifteen times a day, and that's not just since Louisa got the ax. You do realize the unemployment rate is at like 80 percent." There, I thought; I succeeded in making Jenny laugh. Then I watched my friend watch the floor numbers drop on the elevator's digital screen, imagining what was running through her head: *the last time I'll pass 3, the last time I'll pass 2.* "You shouldn't feel too bad," I said. "Every editor in chief gets fired eventually, and then half the staff gets canned, too."

"Well, good luck to you, I guess," Jenny said. The elevator opened to the lobby, my coworker stepped off, we waved good-bye, and then—poof!—she became an ex-coworker and I began ascending to a world that was no longer hers.

"Yoo-hoo, Jane, are you there?" Jenny's voice through the phone receiver snaps me back to the present. I realize Laura is shooting me a dirty look.

"Jenny, I've got to go." I slam the phone into its receiver. I'm terrified Laura is keeping a log of my use of office time and report-ing back to Mimi. Several times a day I watch the two of them with their heads together, whispering. I'd kill for a wiretap.

Mimi walks by: "I'm looking forward to your ideas in the mar-riage and sex brainstorm this afternoon," she says, and I nod clue-lessly. When she's gone, I turn to Laura: "What's she talking about?"

"Didn't I add the meeting to your Outlook calendar?"

"Um, no."

"Oh, I'm still getting used to the company's scheduling sys-tem," she says without apology, and it takes all my energy to mask my private panic with a sweet smile.

Mimi reaches for a banana from the pile on the conference room table, peels it suggestively, and cackles. "Let's start brainstorming, shall we?" Zoe, our Web manager, is the only other person to take a banana, and the rest of us stare. "What?" she whispers. "I'm hungry."

Laura's hand shoots up. "How about we get women to share the details of their best orgasms," she says. I notice her notepad is chock-full of scribblings; everyone else's is blank. With Louisa, we all typed up our pitches and routed memos to her, which she then marked up with careful notes and returned to us—our ideas re-jected or approved. Apparently Mimi's system is to gather together all the editors in a competitive free-for-all in order to pitch ideas

for my section of the magazine. Perhaps it's an informal group interview to identify my replacement.

"Great thinking, Laura," says Mimi. "Jane, will you round up
some of your friends' accounts of their best orgasms and we'll see
what we get?" Before I can react, we've moved on. Zoe *psst*s from
across the table and mouths that she can contribute a great anecdote. I feel the blood rush to my cheeks. Sure, I've had countless
conversations with researchers about the science of sexuality, positions that bring women the most pleasure, and tips for surviving a
dry spell, but these are my coworkers—and *my boss*—and I feel humiliated for all of us. Over the course of the next fifteen minutes,
I've recorded in my notebook, "Ask friends about orgasms,"
"Road-test G-spot vibrators," "Go on date wearing stripper heels,"
and "Attend swinger party." This can't be real, I think, but then
again, I figure as long as I'm pegged as the guinea pig for these
ridiculous stories, I won't be fired.

"OK, I always find the best source of inspiration is my own relationships," Mimi says. "Every position I tried with Steven, my
first ex, ended up on the pages of whatever publication I was
working for at the time. We got to where we were inventing con-
tortions just so I had new material for the magazine. Ha! So who's
got something to share—what's going on in your bedrooms? Give
us the dirt."

I can sense Zoe on the edge of her seat. Too Much Information
is practically her motto, and this is her big chance. "Well, my husband really likes to picture us having a threesome," she says. *Here
we go*, I think. During the workday Zoe seems to possess a radar for
when people are at their busiest and then she plants herself beside
their desks to accost them with long stories in which she's always
the hero and everyone else is to blame. I've actually already heard
this threesome story, and I wonder which details she'll alter this
go-around.

"So last week, when Graham and I were going at it, and he was
narrating his fantasy, I figured, 'What the hell?' I'd tell him about
the real threesome I had back in college." (Rumor is, Zoe attended
community college, didn't even finish, and landed her first job at

Schmidt & Delancey through some hotshot cousin in Human Resources.) "So I start describing what happened—all of us leaving a party together and heading back to my dorm. Thing is, it was me and *two guys*. Well, I figure out pretty fast that Graham likes picturing us with another woman, but just me and two men? OMG, forget it. He goes, um, slack, and then just flops over and falls asleep, snoring like a sailor. Sex fail! We haven't done it since—a full two weeks ago! FML! It's sexual jealousy, and of people I was with before I even met Graham. It's totally cray-cray."

"Very juicy," says Mimi. "It could be an interesting angle. Jane, why don't you look into that?" *Look into what, exactly?*

"We should definitely do a piece on reclaiming your sex life after baby," says Leah. "My girls are over a year old, and I still don't understand how mothers can muster up the time or energy to get it on. It's pathetic."

"Wow," says Mimi, nodding in agreement that it is indeed pathetic. "That's certainly a story there. How about you, Abby? You're married, right?"

Abby, our managing editor, *is* married—to a woman, and I'm not sure if Mimi knows this and is deliberately trying to stir up something or if she's oblivious. I've never heard Abby utter the word "sex," let alone share with a group personal tales from her bedroom; now she does her best impression of Violet Beauregarde, her cheeks swelling up and coloring a deep crimson. The managing editor is most comfortable talking about workflow and time sheets and budget issues. As a joke, whenever public relations companies send me ridiculous contraptions—edible underwear and mojito-flavored lube—I give them to Abby; she always camps out under her desk in protest until I remove the offensive object from her workspace.

"Well," Abby says, "so many of my friends have young kids, and they describe how difficult it is to be romantic, even when their kids are years older than Leah's triplets."

"Oh, great," says Leah.

"The thing is," Abby continues, "they can't seem to get the kids to stay in their own beds at night. I have friends whose seven-

and eight-year-olds still sleep with them. Some believe it's natural to cosleep, but for others it's because they can't get the darn kids out of their room. It's like this dirty little secret of parenting. That could be an interesting story." Leave it to Abby to keep it classy in a sex brainstorm meeting.

"Brilliant," says Mimi. "Let's assign that immediately. And find out if any celebrities are doing it, too. OK, who else?"

I force myself to speak up. "Well, I have this friend—"

"Oh, please, Jane," says Zoe. "We're all pals here, you can let loose and open up." She rolls her neck and shoulders, and I wonder how she managed to acquire the self-confidence of Superwoman.

"Really, it's my *friend.* She recently got diagnosed with HPV and is now freaking out about who gave it to her and how she can avoid passing it on. Let's get a roundup of women to talk about their experiences with what I think is the most common STD, and we'll have a doctor weigh in and clear up any misinformation, like is it really as harmless as people think it is?" Probably everyone knows I'm rehashing a recent plotline from *Girls.* This group brainstorm format makes me nervous, and I fear if I bring up one of the many real issues that actually arose in my relationship with Jacob, my eyes will well up.

"Or how about we profile women who've slept with like fifty guys?" Laura blurts out. "They can share their experiences, and talk about whether or not they feel like sluts."

"Ooh, fun," says Mimi. It occurs to me that Laura may be a virgin.

"Here's another one," says Zoe. "My husband really wants to stick it in where the sun don't shine, if you know what I mean, and it totally creeps me out. But I'm thinking of telling him that if he gets me these over-the-knee Prada boots I've been eyeing, I'll bite the bullet and do it. LOL. What do you guys think?"

"I think it looks like we've got ourselves another sex blogger," says Mimi. "Jane, you can handle the single-girl stuff, and, Zoe, let's have you write up the trials and travails of married sex."

"Yippee!" Zoe reaches across the table for a high-five.

I leave the meeting feeling as if I have food poisoning. Mark, our creative director, must see me clutching my stomach as I walk by his office. "Are you all right?" he asks.

"Thanks, I think it's indigestion. Or maybe consideration of my new responsibilities." A hint of a smile from Mark. I wonder if Mimi's going to enlist the only straight man on staff to participate in some of this sex story research. Or maybe she'll seduce him after hours and then make me write about it. Shoot me.

On our new blog, Zoe begins logging the details of her husband's threesome jealousy and of her backdoor sex negotiation, and I write about dating trends: the types of profile photos that garner the most responses according to OK Cupid research, how condom sales have spiked during this down economy, and a new kind of birth control that may also lift libido. My posts get hits, but nowhere near Zoe's numbers.

In the cafeteria one morning, Mimi sidles up to me by the toaster. "Listen, Jane," she says, "I know you're shy—"

"I'm not shy," I protest. Jacob accused me of the same thing. I thought my retort was a good one—*Would a shy person write an investigative series on the quality of life of Chicago's strippers, a series that won Medill's top journalism award, no less?*—but he just laughed me off. And then broke up with me the following week.

"OK, well, whether or not you're shy," Mimi says, "believe me that the only way the *Hers* brand will survive is if we all step up and embrace the gossipy, confessional, scandalous stuff that's currently de rigueur. That's what our readers crave."

I grab my toast, hoping I can duck away, but Mimi takes my arm. "I don't know if you're privy to the fact that *Hers*' ad sales have been plummeting, and that newsstand numbers are way down, too, and it's precisely because we're writing about"—she does air quotes and changes her voice to a droning monotone—"the number of women heading online to date postdivorce," which is the subject of my most recent blog post.

"We should be covering the passionate, sexy stuff, the juicy tidbits that readers can't wait to call up their best friends to share. Sex sells," she says loudly, shocking a woman who's reaching for her bagel. "Zoe gets this. I understand that you have journalistic aspirations that may or may not align with this reality, but you cover love and sex, for Christ's sake. You need to get with the program." Mimi saunters off, and I stand there watching pieces of bread at various levels of char pop out one after the other. I eventually chuck my breakfast and leave the cafeteria empty-handed. My stomach rumbles all morning.

That afternoon, I stare at the computer screen and think of Jacob. It's been six months since he confessed he'd fallen out of love with me. I begin typing:

> Title: The peculiar behaviors of the broken-hearted.
>
> Main text: My morning routine: J's Facebook profile, his Twitter feed, his Tumblr, his Instagram, Google alerts for his name, the card he gave me last year on my birthday that I still keep in my top desk drawer.
>
> J is my ex-boyfriend. Half a year post-breakup, I'm ashamed to confess I'm still deeply in love. I crave the minutia of his life without me. I figure, if I can't wake up next to him and text and IM with him all day and meet him after work for drinks and cuddle up with him in bed each night, I'll settle for all the dinky consolation prizes: his 140-character opinion of last night's *Daily Show*, his race time in the 5K for the heart disease foundation, a snapshot of the lemon roast chicken he cooked for Sunday dinner, so gorgeously browned that the sight of it slays me with pangs of lust.
>
> I seek out these artifacts with a maniacal devotion. I know it's sick because afterward I have that

same shameful, headachy hangover I get after a
boozy bender. Yet, everything J and I shared
when we were together is now untouchable. I
can't listen to our music, or eat at our restaurants,
or wear the clothes he once peeled from my body.
So I occupy this strange non-space, renouncing
everything he touched—*and after dating for four
years, what didn't he touch?*—yet hunting down
every trace of him now that I can't have him, now
that he isn't mine.
   I wonder, when will I get to be *me* again?
—Jane

Though it's not even so deep down that I know this embarrassing confession belongs only in a private diary with a secure pad-
lock, I consider Mimi's morning pep talk. And although I hate to
admit it, part of me hopes that Jacob cyberstalks me in the same
way I do him, and that he'll happen upon the missive. I wince and,
with trembling fingers, press "Submit post."

I watch with fascinated horror as the comments pour in—
"OMG I hear you!" "Totally went through that last year. It'll get
better, I promise!!! Just keep your head up. And get OFF-LINE!"
"Web stalking is the best, right? LOLZ." "Get a life, loser.
YOLO." Thirty comments in fifteen minutes. I've never gotten
such a response to a piece of my writing. I suspect I've unleashed
a monster, and when Mimi races up to my desk a few hours later, I
know it for sure.
   "*Daily Scoop* wants Zoe and you on the air tomorrow for the
morning gossip roundup," she squeals. "They called you two—
what was it?—'the hot new sex bloggers for a flagging brand that
may just be turning over a new leaf.' That show gets seven hundred thousand viewers. Congrats, this is huge!"
   In terms of activities that would make me proud of myself, talking about my love life on national TV ranks at about the same
level as prostitution. But I understand I'm not allowed to say "no."

My only consolation is a pang of hope that Jacob will see me on the show all dolled up with my hair and makeup done and then decide he wants me back. I know how pathetic this sounds. I also know Jacob would register Republican before he'd sit and watch the inane banter of *The Daily Scoop*. He doesn't even own a television.

"So I drag my husband to Prada and show him the to-die-for boots," Zoe says. "The moment he turns over the price tag, I slink up next to him and whisper my proposition in his ear." I'm marveling at how, in the space of four minutes, Zoe has established what appears to be an actual friendship with the *Daily Scoop* hosts, Kelly and Shelly. They're tilted toward her, gasping and cooing at her every word. The live audience is rapt.

Kelly interrupts: "So how much would your dear hubby actually have to spend before you'd, um—"

Shelly cuts in: "Do the nasty?"

The audience erupts into laughter. They sound like mad hyenas. I zone out Zoe's chatter and instead watch her face; it's animated with the excitement of sharing intimate details of her marriage. But it strikes me that her story is oddly impersonal, as if she and her husband are characters in a bad rom-com. I start remembering all the movies Jacob and I watched together, curled up in my bed or his.

"What?" I yelp. I realize everyone's eyes are on me, and my heart pounds. Although our entertainment director, Regina, didn't specifically give me the tip in my media training, I imagine you aren't supposed to daydream while on live TV.

"I said, exactly how heartbroken do you feel in the wake of your breakup with your ex, Jacob?" Kelly cocks her head, awaiting my answer.

I begin to laugh. It's the first time I've realized that "breakup" rhymes with "Jacob," and it seems absurd, like of course dating a guy named Jacob wouldn't work out. "Oh, I'm sorry," I say, remembering where I am. "Sometimes if I don't laugh, I know I'll cry."

Kelly and Shelly nod in unison, looking like very understanding marionettes. "I've been there," says Shelly. "We've all been there, right?" She turns to the audience, and they burst into applause. "Now, tell us, do you feel like Jacob was The One?"

"Um . . ."

And then Zoe, sensing a comrade in need, heroically comes to my rescue. "You should've seen Jane and Jacob," she says. "They were the perfect couple, totes adorbs. He was always sending flowers and chocolates to the office." (Not true.) "He would drop by all the time just to say hey." (Sort of true—he did this twice.) "Everyone was seriously jealous. We all wanted a guy like that, so sweet and sensitive, plus smoking hot." (Very true.) "And the breakup came out of nowhere. One week flowers, and the next—bam!—he peaced out. It just goes to show that love is unpredictable and that heartbreak can happen to anyone." Zoe rubs my shoulder, and I feel genuinely comforted. I'm so thankful I want to kiss her on the lips.

"Wow," the hosts chime together, offering me their most TV-friendly looks of pity. "Breakups are hard." I plaster a smile onto my face, wanting to punch them both in their perfectly rhinoplasted noses.

Back in the office after the segment, my coworkers make the required fuss over my fancy newscaster coif. "You look incredible," Regina squeals. "You could be a movie star," says Erin, the intern. Only Ed, the mail manager, winces at my appearance. "Go a bit easier on the war paint next time," he says, winking.

I smile at the joke, but my stomach actually feels like it's a war zone. I dash to the bathroom, lean over the toilet, and empty the contents of my gut. Emerging from the stall, I catch my reflection in the mirror. My hair is shellacked stiff as straw and my makeup resembles a clown's; it's horrifying how little I resemble myself. My image makes me think of the magazine, how Mimi wants to dress it up in garish, unnatural colors, obscuring any substance with a glossy sheen.

I splash water onto my face and attack the layers of gunk with a handful of rough paper towels. The caked-on colors run and smear, transforming my skin into an abstract painting. After scrubbing for a full five minutes, my real face begins to emerge in the mirror. My relief is immense.

I stare at my reflection. When I decided to become a journalist, I wanted to uncover truths about the world and to help people by disseminating valuable, important information. My goals never included offering up my heartbreak as fodder for entertainment television, or capturing the lowest common denominator's attention by any means necessary. I spit a heavy globule of phlegm into the sink, and then exit the bathroom, knowing exactly what I need to do.

I stride into Mimi's office. "I have to tell you something," I say, talking quickly so I can get it all out before I lose my nerve. "I understand what's happening to the industry with the competition from the Internet and people's shortened attention spans and the terrible economy and all of that. And I get why you're changing *Hers* the way you are. But—"

"Jane, stop," Mimi says. "I can see where this is going, and I'm not going to let you do it."

"I just don't think—"

"You have such great potential." Always a sucker for a compliment, I feel something soften inside of me. "I admire your gumption, Jane, I really do. In fact, it makes me even more confident that you'll continue to thrive and excel here at *Hers*."

"But . . . what about that speech in the cafeteria? What about—"

"You heard what I had to say, and you responded. You got on board. Listen, do you really think you'll be able to find another job in this crappy economy? How much money do you have saved up? Have you really thought this through?"

Mimi is right, and she knows it. Less than a month's rent remains in my checking account. My boss's smile is a haughty, triumphant one. I feel her might encasing me like tentacles. I know I'm powerless to resist.

"Fine, I'll stay," I say, barely audibly. "But I don't want to do the blog anymore."

"Oh, all right. Zoe can tackle it all for now. But enough of this nonsense. Back to work."

I retreat from Mimi's office, feeling ridiculous. But as I stride the length of the floor, I consider that the editor in chief called me brave and then fought for me to stay. She actually *wants* me here. I pass by Laura's desk and wave hello. She and I now have something in common that no one else in the office has: security.

3

Victoria LaRue,
Food and Diet Director at Starstruck

Mimi's phone number flashes up on my call waiting, and since I'm on the line with Dr. Harris, I stifle my squeal. Ever since Mimi left her executive editor post here at *Starstruck* and fled for *Hers*, I've been on high alert, awaiting her call. After nearly a month, I sense my patience is about to pay off.

I try to hurry Dr. Harris along: "Georgina Sparks's publicist says she's now a size 2, so what do you think that is, fifteen pounds down?" I ask.

"I'd estimate the weight loss as eighteen pounds. Her cheeks have really hollowed out, and check out that collarbone."

"Thanks as always, Doc," I say, disconnecting and clicking over. "Well, hello Ms. Fancy-Pants Woman in Charge. How's the new gig?"

"Divine," says Mimi. "I've finally adjusted my desk chair to the perfect height."

"That's an important step."

"What are you up to at the old haunts?"

"The usual," I say. "Covering a starlet's gaunt debut at her Cannes premiere. Dr. Harris says she's dropped eighteen pounds."

We quip in unison: *"Though he hasn't personally treated her."*

"What's the total tally now?" Mimi asks. She knows I keep score of celebrities' collective weight gain or loss for the year.

"Let's see, up 379 pounds since January."

"They're obese, those celebrities." Mimi, a perpetual yo-yo dieter, has probably gained and lost as much weight during the time I've known her.

"Maybe they should try that juice fast you're a fan of," I say. "Although we are entering summer—bikini season—so I expect a major reversal any day now."

"Listen, I know how attached you are to chronicling the weight loss triumphs of actors and reality TV stars. But what would you say if I tried to lure you away from Celebrity Mecca to the slightly more glamorous world of the midmarket mommy mag?"

"I'd say, when can I interview?" I perform a celebration dance in my seat, pumping my fists until I notice coworkers staring. Working at *Hers* has always been my dream; I grew up worshipping my mother, who worshipped the pages of *Hers*. Of course I'd never admit such an earnest desire to Mimi, the least sentimental person I know.

When Mimi landed the *Hers* gig, she hinted at bringing me on board, but she also made it clear she'd have to learn the lay of the new land before making any decisions.

"Great," says Mimi. "I hate to ask you to do this—"

"No, you don't. What is it?" For Mimi I've gone on full-day stakeouts at restaurants where an A-list celeb was rumored to have a reservation.

"You're right. Can you come in on Monday? Yes, it's Memorial Day, and yes, you probably have some big, celebratory, start-of-summer plans, but—"

"I don't," I say, cutting her off. I promised Jesse a beach day, but we can go lie on the sand and soak up cancerous rays another time.

"Fabulous. This way none of the staffers will be there to throw darts at you as you walk through the office." She emits her signature cackle, and I wonder how bad it really is over at *Hers*.

"Perfect." I picture breaking the news to Jesse, and his mocking impression of Mimi: *Victoria, I'll need you in the office Saturday morning to watch the cartoons with me and my precious puggle*, he'll say in an uncanny version of my former boss's voice, flipping his pretend curls. Then in a chirp that's supposed to be me, he'll add, *I'll be there at the crack of dawn*, at which point I'll wrestle him down to the couch with a tickle attack.

A security guard lets me in to the abandoned Schmidt & Delancey building and, alone on the elevator, I have a sneaking suspicion I'm being sent on a sting operation; I imagine the doors opening, and then out pops *Starstruck*'s editor in chief to say she knew I was a traitor all along. But when I step into the *Hers* lobby, all is still. I let myself into the office and search for Mimi, paranoid about the click of my heels amidst all this hushed sleekness. Nearly every surface is made of glass, without a fingerprint in sight, an environment designed to make people feel like they've truly made it. It couldn't be more different from *Starstruck*'s open-plan maze of clapboard cubicles, an office we joke was built out of discarded materials from the set of some sleazy reality TV show.

I spot Mimi in the corner office—of course—spinning like a child in her oversized chair. "Knock, knock."

"Don't mind me, I'm just playing." She slows to a stop. "Come on in."

I obey, struck silent by the space. It's nearly the size of my apartment. Floor-to-ceiling glass separates us on three sides from the outdoors; we're hovering directly over Central Park.

Mimi catches me gawking. "Amazing, right? I've instated a rule that people must use Purell before entering. Ha!" I've missed that laugh. "Check you out, so chic!"

"Thanks," I say. Mimi is well aware that my usual work look involves more elastic and pleather than cashmere and silk, but today I jumped out of bed at six a.m., pumped to pick out the perfect interview outfit. A very groggy Jesse was less thrilled to be awakened so early on a holiday and then quizzed about all my different getups. When I finally decided on a look it was nearly eight-thirty and I had to book it to the train. I was almost at my destination before realizing I'd left without taking my basal temperature. I'll initiate sex tonight, just in case.

"So listen," Mimi says. "I want to warn you, it's going to be rough going for a while around here." I nod. I've been through several redesigns before, so I know the late-nights-and-weekends drill. "You'll be the new executive editor—a big job. You'll be coming in and shaking up the staff's cozy complacency, forcing them to get off their lazy butts and raise this magazine from the grave."

"I'm prepared and willing." I perform my best military salute.

"They're not going to like you."

I doubt this—I'm very likeable—but I concede, "They're in a hard position, having their jobs on the line."

"Whatever. The truth is I have it harder, and you will too if you sign on. Believe me, it's much more difficult to handle the burden of other people's resentment than it is to fear being fired." I'm still nodding, though I'm not so sure.

Mimi says she has to make a call and that I should show myself around. I weave my way through the rows of workspaces and run my fingers over the nameplates, wondering which ones will still be here in three months. I pass Laura's cubicle—she was Mimi's first poach from *Starstruck*—and then a desk labeled "Zoe Lewis," piled so high with papers and take-out containers that I literally can't see the surface. As executive editor I'll be able to mandate that desks be kept clean, and people will have to listen (unlike how Jesse ignores my pleas to put his dirty laundry in the hamper, not on the floor).

"Shit!" The shout comes from behind. I swivel around and see a woman squatting on the floor surrounded by the contents of her purse. She looks up, startled. "Oh, sorry, I didn't think anyone would be in today."

"That's OK," I say, not sure what to add.

"I work here. I'm Leah Brenner."

"Victoria." I wave at her, like an idiot. "I'm, uh, Mimi's friend." I see her eyeing the outfit I was so proud of just a few minutes ago: a French Laundry belted number that makes my figure look fantastic but requires me to take small, ladylike steps (which means I hardly ever wear it), plus Jimmy Choo sling-backs. Now I wish I were in jeans and sneakers. This woman looks scared; she knows I'm not here just to visit.

"Nice to meet you." She extends a hand.

"Here, let me help." I bend down and begin gathering objects—a compact, a picture book, a strange-looking contraption with tubes and suction cups.

"Sorry, that's my breast pump. How mortifying." She snatches the object from my hand and finishes recovering the scattered stuff.

"So then Mimi's here too?" she asks. I nod, and she smoothes down her hair. "God, I'm a wreck. I didn't think anyone would be in, but I guess I should've known that *that one* would work on a holiday." She rolls her eyes, and then glances up nervously to check if I caught her doing so.

"I was on my way to this barbecue with my family, but then one of my babies started throwing a fit in the backseat, wailing for her Petey the Penguin. That stupid stuffed animal is the only thing that'll soothe her, the monster. I remembered I'd left it in my office. God knows how these things end up in my workbag. So here we are, driving from Westfield to Hoboken via midtown Manhattan. Very convenient. The whole gang—my husband, the triplets, the nanny—they're all outside in the car idling by the curb, and here I am spilling the entire contents of my Mary Poppins purse like a complete klutz. Thanks for your help, really."

"It's no problem at all." I find myself following Leah down the hall to her office. It looks lived-in. Her bulletin board is plastered with photos. I point to one. "Is that your family?"

"Oh, that's our Christmas card from last year. My husband, Rob, and the little troublemakers, Daisy and Lulu and Rose, just nine months there. Now, where on Earth is that freaking penguin?"

As Leah rummages through drawers, I can't stop gazing at the photo that seems like it could be the stock one from a picture frame—the well-scrubbed family posed in a Pottery Barn living room, Leah pretty in a hunter green wraparound, her handsome husband a good sport in his reindeer sweater, and the three little

ones practically edible in matching elf onesies. I've been designing the LaRue family Christmas card in my head for years. Last
year Jesse suggested we pose just the two of us with Floppy the
Cat, but the idea seemed too pitiful.

"So do you have kids?" Leah asks. I quickly shake my head.
"Lucky you. Doing the working mom thing is a total mess ninety
percent of the time, even though they let me work from home
part-time. You can't even imagine."

"Sounds hard." I picture her and the husband and the slew of
kids hanging out in a grassy backyard behind their big house in the
suburbs. It doesn't seem fair that she has all that and this beautiful
office, too.

"There you are, you little twerp," she says, freeing a threadbare
stuffed animal from between two file cabinets. "Thank God. Now
we're only going to be, let's see, an hour and a half late. Ridiculous. OK, I'm running. It was nice meeting you. . . ."

"Victoria."

"Right, Victoria. Take care."

I hang back in Leah's office after she's gone, scanning the photos and knickknacks, the mug full of pens, and the tabs on her file
folders: "The Rise of Gun-Toting Mothers," "Natural Treatments
for Postpartum Depression," "Style Solutions for America's
Busiest Women."

I see another snapshot; it's Leah in a hospital bed holding the
three infants, each as small as her hand. For a period of time I fantasized about this very scene; I was considering in vitro, which
everyone knows often leads to multiples. But after I researched
the price, the image receded from my mind. Ditto with picturing
myself the mom of an African or Asian baby, and then discovering
the exorbitant cost of adoption. When I confessed to Jesse that I'd
always assumed adoption was free or nearly so—someone wants a
baby, someone else has one that she can't care for, what's so complicated?—my husband looked at me like I'd been adopted from
outer space. "Hey, maybe one of us has a long-lost aunt who'll
croak and leave us with an enormous inheritance," he joked; I
silently seethed, not for the first time, over his sculptor-slash-

waiter career that seems to cost us more in supplies than it brings in. (I imagine Jesse has suffered his own moments of resentment about my slightly out-of-control online shopping habit, but these are topics we tend not to discuss.) I've since started a savings fund that Mint.com tells me will take a decade to accrue the funds needed to adopt.

"So this is where you've been hiding," Mimi says, poking her head into Leah's office. "Leah Brenner is our executive editor—for now."

"Oh."

"Total mommy mush brain, that one." She rotates a finger by her ear, making the cuckoo sign. "Anyway, I need you to write out some story ideas—a few features and front-of-book items, a couple of new sections, nothing too involved. It's a formality, but I have to include it in your application file. I'm heading out for a shopping spree with the company's stylist—poor me! ha!—but feel free to linger in the records closet for as long as you like. You can page through back issues for inspiration."

We trade cheek kisses and I watch her leave, thanking the universe for Mimi Walsh. Gratitude is key to happiness, according to countless articles I've read in women's magazines. Jesse rolls his eyes at it, but lately each night I've been trying to list all I have to be thankful for (along with bemoaning my lack of luck, a habit I can't seem to kick). Mimi has been like my fairy godmother, hovering over my shoulder and waving her wand to sprinkle fairy dust on me throughout my career. Years ago, when I wanted to try my hand at writing a novel, it was Mimi who cheered me on and gave me the courage to quit *Yummy Weekly*. And then my literary aspirations devolved into daylong TV marathons and crippling despair, which led to a six-month dry spell between Jesse and me and a conversation where we flirted with the idea of separation. Meanwhile, our meager savings dwindled to nothing and were fast replaced by four- and then five-figure credit card debt. All of that happened to coincide with the economy's implosion that sent shockwaves of layoffs and magazine shutterings through the publishing world. It was Mimi, of course, who miraculously found me a job at *Starstruck*, rescuing my self-worth, my marriage, and my credit score all in one fell swoop. I practically owe her my life.

Sitting among the back issues in the records closet is like rewinding twenty-five years to my childhood in Oklahoma City. Rather than page through recent issues of *Hers* to spark story ideas, I've pulled out nearly every issue from the eighties and fanned them out around me.

As a child, I remember the thrill when I'd return home from school and see a new issue of *Hers* peeking out of the mailbox. My friends all read *Girl Talk*, then later *Teen You*, but I cherished the *Hers* ritual I shared with my mother each month. She would prepare our afternoon snacks—Oreos and milk for me, nut mix and a gin and tonic for her—and together we'd pore over the pages. The fashion tips and home decorating tricks seemed like magic wisdom from a faraway land, and I was in awe of my mother's cool when she successfully pulled off the chic outfits and executed the projects in our own home. Each month we'd study the cover model, and Mom would try her hand at replicating the makeup and hairdo on me. All done up, I'd gaze at myself in the mirror for hours, trying to mimic the model's glamorous, sophisticated expression.

I locate the November 1987 issue in the records file and I flip back to the recipe pages. There it is, Festive Apple Spice Pie. I remember I was in fifth grade, and it was the day before Thanksgiving break when my mother announced she would teach me to bake a pie. Even at age ten I fantasized about someday passing along this lesson to my future daughter. I'd share the secret trick of adding nutmeg to the crust dough for extra flavor, Mom's personal touch.

The whole of my mother's dinner repertoire came from the pages of *Hers*—turkey meatloaf, buttermilk mashed potatoes, pineapple upside-down cake. After my third miscarriage last year, I dredged up Mom's recipes and spent the entire afternoon cooking pot roast and cinnamon bread pudding. Jesse thought it was endearing, my stick-to-your-ribs meal, and he cleaned his plate. He didn't even complain that I'd transformed our studio's matchbox kitchen into what looked like the aftermath of an earthquake; he washed and dried and put away every dish. Jesse likes bi bim bop; Jamaican spiced patties; and other hip, eccentric fare that he carries home in brown take-away bags (and which costs us a fortune, I often complain), but I secretly prefer Mom's *Hers*-inspired, totally uncool home cooking, pure comfort on a plate.

I begin sketching out a story idea based on vintage *Hers* recipes—how to cook the magazine's classics in less time and with healthier ingredients (Mom used to spend the better part of each evening in the kitchen, preparing the rich, artery-clogging food). Everyone's always rushing around these days, and who wouldn't love to prepare sweet potato casserole in just fifteen minutes and have it be nutritious, too?

I'm feeling that familiar tingle of discovery, the ideas popping up in my mind like soda bubbles. It's that delicious thrill of creation that makes me feel like I'm perpetually winning a medal. Another article could take a fun, kitschy look at which old *Hers* advice is worth reviving versus which advice should remain buried in the past. We could run a series on women's biggest dreams and disappointments; we'd get celebrities to pen personal essays describing what they imagined their lives would look like and how their actual lives measure up. I'm scribbling down thoughts like a maniac, my notebook filling up with ink. Before I know it, it's five p.m. and I've put in a full day's work.

Back at *Starstruck* the following day, the editor in chief assigns me a piece on the cravings of middle-aged, knocked-up celebrities, which is how I find myself sitting across the table that afternoon from a six-months-pregnant, forty-five-year-old movie star and getting very drunk. At first I order a single glass of merlot, but then I think, *What the hell?* and ask the waiter to bring over the bottle. This is the type of not-so-brilliant idea that Mimi would have talked me out of if she still worked at *Starstruck*.

"So what do you find yourself eating late at night?" I ask listlessly, notebook in hand.

"Pickles and ice cream. I'm a total classic," the actress says, and

I'm tempted to point out that sporting a baby bump when you're on the brink of menopause is not at all classic. "And when I want ice cream, there's nothing getting between me and Ben and Jerry. My husband runs out to the store at all hours of the night. It's so adorable."

She's probably told this anecdote—invented, most likely—to a dozen other sources, and I know my boss will want me to dig up something fresh. "What brand of pickles?" I ask.

But I don't listen to her answer. I swig the rest of my wine and pour myself another glass. "Let me ask you something, off the record," I say, leaning across the table. "How did you do it? I mean, really: Was it special vitamins, a certain sex position, some kind of miracle worker gyno, what?"

I'm thinking that maybe she'll be honest. Maybe she'll admit she got an egg donor or is faking the whole thing, or she'll reveal some other strange truth; I'm always hoping these celebrities will cast aside their P.R.-approved talking points for one second and say something real. But to no avail: The actress shrugs, smiling smugly, and takes an infuriatingly small sip of her green tea. "My beloved and I figured if it was meant to be, it was meant to be. I went off the Pill and—boom!—one month later I was with child." She giggles, and I take too much pleasure in noticing the deep, crinkly lines that frame her eyes and mouth. My mother would be ashamed of me. I gulp down my wine and excuse myself, ending the interview.

I'm still more than a little tipsy when Mimi calls to officially offer me the executive editor job at *Hers*. I accept in five different rambling forms before she tells me to shut up or she'll rescind the offer.

I dial Jesse. "I got the job," I squeal, not caring that I'm surrounded by my *Starstruck* coworkers.

"That's amazing, babe. It's a big step up."

"That's right. I'll practically be at the top of the masthead."

"I know you've wanted a change for a while, and this might be just what you need." I find I'm suddenly irritated. What my husband knows is that I've hoped for a change along the lines of cutting back at work to focus on being a mother. He continues: "There's a new Indian place that just opened down the block that looks great. Let's go tonight—just me and you hitting the town to toast your big achievement."

"OK." I know Jesse is just trying to help me celebrate, and maybe it's on account of the pint of wine sloshing around my bloodstream, but my mood goes sour. This is supposed to be my big, special moment, but it doesn't feel like one anymore. I consider my typical day: Every morning it's a battle with the alarm clock over whether I'll force myself up to face the treadmill or catch another few winks, then it's off to the office for nine or ten hours of the grind, and then Jesse and I hit up happy hour or the latest blockbuster or some gallery exhibit, after which we return home to our tiny apartment to watch crappy TV or have crappy procreation sex; finally we collapse like zombies onto our pillows, and within several hours it's up and at 'em for the same thing all over again. Jesse seems content with this life (though I'm sure he wishes for hotter sex). I, on the other hand, swing like a mad pendulum between restlessness and lethargy, rage and despair. I'm terrified that one day soon Jesse is going to suggest we stop trying for a baby. The thought makes my eyes pool with tears. I blink them back furiously.

"I love you, babe," says Jesse. "I'm so proud of you."

"I love you, too," I say quietly, then hang up. I glance at my computer's screen saver, a shot of Jesse and me dressed up as Mario and Luigi from last year's Halloween party. The costumes were a hit, all the guests admiring our twin mustaches and reminiscing about their own favorite Nintendo games from back in the day. Jesse and I had stuffed our matching overalls with cotton and entertained ourselves throughout the night by bumping each other's potbellies, increasing our gusto as we downed more and more drinks. I had a blast at the party, but looking at the photo now fills me with shame. How pathetic I look with my drunken smile and fake belly paunch. I flash on Leah Brenner's Christmas card—her gorgeous Norman Rockwell family.

I shake my computer mouse, and the screen saver vanishes, pixilated Jesse and me and our comically distended stomachs instantly replaced by my Internet browser. I remind myself that I am getting Leah's job. Her perfect life will soon be less so, and it makes me feel sinfully happy. I load up the menu for the new Indian restaurant on our block and begin planning my order for the celebration meal.

4

Deborah Rosser, Recipe Creator

All morning I've been tweaking the cream cheese-to-sugar ratio in the frosting, and I've finally found the sweet (but not too sweet) spot. "Mmm," I announce to the empty kitchen, seducing the spoon with my tongue. The phone begins blaring—I set it loud so I can hear it over the hand mixer. I peek at the lemon cupcakes rising in the oven—fluffy and golden, gorgeous—then grab the receiver.

"Mimi would like PB&J, but they're out of it in the cafeteria."

"Hello, Laura."

"Hi. So can you make it up there?"

"Are you asking if I am able to construct a peanut butter and jelly sandwich?" I ask, trying to affect the patient but stern tone I use with my four-year-old grandniece.

"She prefers chunky, and she has a meeting in twenty minutes, so please aim for sooner rather than later."

"Yes, ma'am." I put my work on hold and set out the bread and the jars of peanut butter and jelly on the counter. I wonder how the French Culinary Institute, a graduate degree in nutrition, and twenty-five years' experience as a food editor and recipe guru have landed me here, personal chef to a forty-year-old with the tastes of

a kindergartener. I consider cutting off the bread crusts, but re-
frain.

I pull the cupcakes from the oven and set them on the cooling
rack, and then arrange the sandwich and a glass of cold milk on a
tray and walk from the test kitchen down to Mimi's office. "You're
a lifesaver," she says when I present her lunch. She gulps at the
milk and flashes me a drippy white mustache, proud like she just
invented sliced bread. I humor the display with a lackluster
thumbs-up.

I'm grateful to escape back to my kitchen. I suppose the space
is technically the property of Schimdt & Delancey, but for the past
two and a half decades I've reigned over it—stocking it with state-
of-the-art supplies, filling it with the aromas of thousands of delicious concoctions, tending to it with the love of a mother. This is
my home, where I can cook and experiment and eat and listen to
whatever kind of music I want, with little disturbance. I've truly
struck gold: I live in New York City with access to the world's best
restaurants, and because of this sprawling, state-of-the-art facility I
haven't had to settle for the typical Manhattan apartment kitch-
enette with one square foot of counter space and an oven more
finicky than a vegan with a gluten allergy. The appearance of
Mimi on the scene has been a mild annoyance, for sure, but I've
weathered such storms before.

I start in on the red velvet batter. When I pitched ideas for summer recipe packages a couple of months ago, it was pre-Mimi, and
Louisa nixed a hot dog taste test. Too many nitrates, she said. So
it's desserts again, for the third year running. The twist this year is
cupcakes for birthday picnics, since apparently August is the most
popular birth month. I've gone through twenty pounds of sugar so
far this week. Let's hope Mimi has a sweet tooth.

In the afternoon I set the cupcakes out on the free table and
then step away to avoid the staff stampede. I discovered long ago
that if you feed people, you remain on their good side no matter
what else you do.

"OMG, delish," says Zoe, spitting crumbs from a mouth full of cake.

"The frosting is to die for. How do you do it?" Jane asks, reaching for a second serving.

"It's nothing," I say, deflecting the compliments. Most of these people can't tell the difference between a halfway-decent dessert and a divine one (I can't believe the junk tourists line up for at the trendy bakeries in the city). It's true of our readers, too, who count cream of mushroom soup and freeze-dried stuffing as kitchen staples. Nevertheless, I hold our recipes to a higher standard. Louisa mostly shared this sensibility and gave me free reign, though after I ran a recipe for beef bourguignon with an ingredient list a page long (in my defense it was for the Christmas special), she called me into her office to read aloud all the complaint letters; after that, I had Ed pass the food mail directly to me so I could selectively share reader comments with the big boss.

I spot Drew, photo editor by trade, but a serious cook, too. "What do you think?"

She's nibbling on a red velvet variety. "Is there a hint of cinnamon in here?"

"There is!"

"It's tasty. Though I'd lose a bit of the cocoa—it overwhelms the other flavors."

"Interesting." I take a bite. She's right. I snag the last cupcake from the platter and carry it into Mimi's office.

"Oh, thank you, but I'm off sugar this month."

Yeah, right, I think, glancing at her hips; she must be at least a size 12. "Just a taste? We're planning to run these in the August issue. The pages have to ship this week."

"See what Laura thinks—I trust her opinion."

I nod. Laura, the new assistant, informed me on her first day that she's a very picky eater and doesn't care for cheese, most sauces, or legumes; no way am I going to ask for her opinion.

I spend the rest of the day tweaking the red velvet recipe and dreaming up ideas for the autumn issues: We could do Indian stews, or root vegetables in potpies and ragout, or a whole Greek feast from olives to baklava. It's hard to remember during a June heat wave, but when the weather cools, people recommit to spending time in the kitchen and creating sumptuous meals for their families. Fall is my favorite season for food. If the new boss isn't going to weigh in on the recipes, I'll take that as a blank check. Hopefully her next diet will involve those preportioned meals sent to her doorstep so she won't want to taste anything I prepare.

At the end of the workday, Mimi and I catch the same elevator down. I refuse to participate in the stick-around-until-after-the-boss-is-gone game that everyone else is playing these days; when I'm done with my work, I leave. I notice a glob of cream cheese frosting on the lapel of Mimi's jacket. "That stuff will stain," I say, pointing to the white dollop. "Don't rub at it. Mix bleach with warm water and soak it overnight. Have a good evening!" And then I flee.

The next day, a woman with long red hair appears in the office, looking adrift until Mimi runs up to her and they hug as if they were separated at birth. They spend the entire next hour holed up in Mimi's office, huddled in conversation.

"Who is that, her sister?" I ask Zoe, who's visiting my desk for her usual afternoon raid of my chocolate stash. I save the cheap milk kind for her; I've given up trying to convert her to high-quality dark.

"That's the new executive editor," she says. "Victoria LaRue. She's from *Starstruck*, too."

"Oh, great, another celeb-o-phile. Does Leah know?" We've never before had two executive editors on staff.

"Probably not. I already spied Victoria sizing up her office." After Leah had triplets and shipped out to the suburbs last year, she convinced Louisa to let her telecommute two days a week. So far Mimi has let this arrangement fly, too, but I predict Leah misses one big meeting and either she has to start schlepping into the city every day again or she gets the pink slip. Leah edits the food pages and, even though she's now usually covered in baby spit-up or changing a diaper as we Skype, her talent remains for transforming the language of my recipes into poetry.

* * *

"Ladies and . . . ladies," announces Mimi, winking at Mark, our brilliant creative director and the only man on staff. She's called us all to the conference room. "I want to introduce the brilliant Victoria. Victoria began her career at *Yummy Weekly*, where she covered snacking trends and kitchen gear with great skill and dedication, and then moved on to *Starstruck*, where she distinguished herself as one of the top reporters on celebrity diets and meal plans. I'm bringing her on deck as an extra hand to help us for the November relaunch, and I couldn't be more thrilled. Please join me in welcoming our new co-executive editor."

"Yay!" yelps Victoria.

"Yay!" echoes Laura, and she, Victoria, and Mimi embrace with a degree of dedication I've only previously seen on reality TV, usually when former friends-turned-foes reconcile (I'm ashamed I've seen enough of that trash to know this). I suppose since all three of them come from *Starstruck*, that is their world. Mimi opens one arm and pulls in a reluctant Mark, who is not the type for group hugging. I sense this will become problematic.

At first I don't notice anyone standing there, since I've got the food processor going and I'm singing my heart out to that cheesy new Helena Hope song: "We'd be lying in the sun, boy, I really thought we'd won. But, oh how I was wrong, how you strung me right along, told me I gotta be strong, left me with nothing but a song."

But when I wheel around and see Victoria in my door frame, her facial features contorted into what I suppose is an expression of amusement, I freeze. In one motion I flip off both my radio and the food processor.

"I guess you didn't hear my knocking," she says. She's violated the unspoken rule that no one comes up to my kitchen uninvited, and now she worsens the offense by entering the space before I grant her permission. She eyes a fresh batch of pistachio pesto. "Looks delicious."

I can't resist the urge to feed—I hand her a spoon. "Here, try. It's for the weeknight dinner series. Pesto orecchiette."

"Delectable," she says. "I'd reduce the oil a bit, and maybe go with orzo or some other pasta people have actually heard of." I make an effort to lift the corners of my mouth. "So, listen. I had a conversation with Mimi about our food coverage, and I wanted to relay the main points back to you." I'm already fuming that a discussion of *Hers'* recipes happened in my absence, and Victoria ratchets up my rage by initiating a self-guided tour of my space, sniffing at a bag of basil, then squeezing an heirloom tomato. I wonder when she last washed her hands. "First off, from now on we want to limit recipe prep time to twenty-five minutes. No one has the time to spend hours slaving away in the kitchen."

I'm surprised to find I'm prepared for this argument: "The average American watches four hours of TV per day," I say bitterly. "I think they can spend forty minutes now and then making dinner. A twenty-five-minute limit means we won't be able to include braised meat or pies with homemade crusts or even some soups. What about for special events?"

"I hear you," says Victoria. "But Mimi's point is, we should be giving our readers permission to spend holidays relaxing and hanging out with their loved ones instead of slaving over the stove like they're repressed housewives from two generations ago. Especially in this day and age, when everyone is so busy and we all have so little quality time with our friends and family. Those complicated, labor-intensive recipes aren't realistic for the life of your average busy mom."

This is all bullshit, of course; everyone has always been busy, and just because these days people would rather spend their free time scrolling through Facebook and stuffing their faces with Cheetos than cooking actual food for their families is not my problem. But there's something about how Victoria's speaking—a hollowness, maybe a lack of conviction?—that stops me from grabbing a butcher knife and chop-chop-chopping away my anger. It makes me think I can work on her, sway her from the party line.

"People connect through food," I say. "It's the glue of our gatherings. That's as true today as it was back when cavewomen got together by the fire to gossip about the cute barbarian in the next cave as they roasted the wooly mammoths or whatever the hell their men brought home from the hunt." *Where do I come up with this crap?* "Cooking is not some sort of throwback *Feminine Mystique* symbol of unfulfilled housewives; it's a way to bond with the people you love, and a means to enjoy and savor something delicious together. At least that's how I've always presented it in *Hers*. Are you familiar with the food coverage in *Hers* magazine, Victoria?"

She ignores the question and takes it upon herself to open my refrigerator. She buries her entire head in the cold air, as if she's in her own home jonesing for a late-night snack. If she reaches for anything, I'll pounce. "Another option we talked about," Victoria says, shutting the fridge, "and this might help you include the kinds of recipes you want but cut out some of the steps, is to rethink what we mean by homemade. My idea is, let's make readers feel great that they're cooking, but also give them some shortcuts, some little cheats to minimize the drudgery of doing it all from scratch. So, we'll make half of our ingredients ready-made. I've prepared a list of foods for you."

She passes me a typed-up memo, and I scan the items—bagged lettuce, instant rice, precut vegetables, jarred pasta sauce, canned whipped cream, and then the clincher—*cake mix*. "Maybe we should just give the readers a list of restaurants to go to instead?" I say, my tone chilly. "Applebee's, Chili's, McDonald's?"

"I see you have a sense of humor," Victoria says flatly. "I think we'll get along well."

"Oh, I'm sure."

"Last, I've been studying the reader mail, and they all want lighter options. Many of them are trying to lose weight."

"If they eat reasonable portion sizes and limit sweets to special occasions, as we encourage in *Hers*, then our recipes fit very nicely into a healthy lifestyle."

"Yes, but people like sweets and they tend to overeat," Victoria says. "And who can blame them? Let's give them options where they can eat large quantities and not feel guilty, rather than having to stick to measly little portion sizes." This is the problem with America, I think; our readers are fat pigs. "Have you heard of the popular personality Ravenous Rhee?" Victoria asks.

My anger, previously at a simmer, now dials up to a boil. Last week when I found out the Food Network was giving that silly twit her own show, I actually threw my remote at the television; my cat cowered. Ravenous Rhee must have been raised on TV dinners and Ho Hos. "You mean the woman who thinks freeze-dried bananas, a bag of gummy vitamins, and three packets of Splenda equal a square meal?" I ask.

Victoria laughs. "I mean the woman whose newsletter has three million subscribers, whose cookbooks have topped the bestseller lists for six months straight, and whom Oprah has dubbed 'the regular woman's Martha Stewart.' "

"Touché." I can respect Victoria's feistiness, if nothing else. I know we're not supposed to talk directly about what's happening on staff, but I decide to challenge her: "Mimi's replacing me with Ravenous Rhee, is that it?" I don't actually believe it, since that woman would command a fortune in salary.

"That would be quite a coup," Victoria says, then quickly backtracks. "I mean, no, no, not at all. She's getting a monthly column in the food section is all, and we want you to oversee it."

I clutch at a paring knife and begin aggressively mincing a clove of garlic. "So Rhee will pitch me ideas and then I'll give the yay or nay?"

Victoria shakes her head. "More like, she'll share whatever trend she's spotted in her niche of the culinary world or she'll cook up new recipes, then you'll test them out to make sure they work."

"So I'll be her assistant?" I ask.

"I wouldn't describe it that way."

"Of course you wouldn't." I steady my hand, still wielding the knife. "Victoria, I appreciate your stopping by. I'm going to get back to the weeknight dinners story, if you don't mind."

"Sure," she says. "I'm glad we're on the same page here." On her way out Victoria's hair swings behind her, the unnatural tint of cherry food coloring.

* * *

"What in the hell is this?" I slap Mimi's latest memo down on Abby's desk.

"Would you like me to read it aloud to you?" The managing editor smirks. I think she secretly enjoys my griping.

I read: " 'Starting tomorrow, *Hers* employees will set the example at Schmidt & Delancey of what it means to look polished and professional. To that end, we will no longer wear shorts and we will limit our donning of denim to Fridays.' " I look up at Abby. " 'Donning of denim'—is she *serious?*"

"The point is, Mimi would like to dress up the office a bit."

"No shit." I keep reading: " 'The ladies will make an effort with our hair and makeup, and wear high heels on a daily basis. If we choose to wear flats during our commutes, we will change into our heels before we enter the building.' Um, I haven't owned a pair of high heels since 1989."

"Would you like me to take you shopping? We can slip out to Barneys at lunch." I don't laugh at what must be a joke.

"Abby, our dictator in chief is pretty much mandating the shortening of our calf muscles and deterioration of our knees. Plus she's increasing the risk of falls. Does she really want to deal with a lawsuit when someone takes a face-plant in her stilettos and breaks a bone?"

"Debbie, I know you're upset, but the truth is, Mimi has a right to instate a dress code."

"What's next—she'll require Ed to wear a tux to deliver the mail?"

"Listen, why don't you just keep a pair of comfortable wedges on hand and change into them when you come down to the office or visit the cafeteria? Use your company card for the shoe purchase; you can expense it."

"Ugh, how come you're always so goddamned reasonable?" I storm out of Abby's office, clutching the offensive memo.

Back upstairs, I have an idea. I search through my back issues of *Professional Chef*, certain that what I'm looking for appeared sometime in 2011. I flip to the fall issue, and freeze: The cover features

Eileen Houtt, my partner and closest friend from back in culinary school; her big smile is familiar, only a bit crinkled with age and with an added dash of smugness. The coverline reads: "Houtt Commodity: Chicago's most inventive chef makes a splash with chic new seafood restaurant." I roll my eyes and toss it aside, then turn to the winter issue, where I find the story I want.

"Excuse me, she's busy," Laura says as I breeze by her cubicle and march into Mimi's office. I slap the *Professional Chef* article down on her desk.

"Jesus Christ, what is this?" Mimi wails. I forgot just how gruesome the story's images are. The burned, mangled foot looks like it belongs to some freakish monster, and the bruises span the colors of a painter's palette.

"What this is," I say, "is a story about people who wore improper footwear in the kitchen and then suffered the consequences: boiling Alfredo sauce splashed on the foot of a chef in open-toed shoes, and a prep cook who wore fashion boots, slipped on spilled olive oil, and fell flat on her back. She's probably now paralyzed from the neck down."

"Ah, I see what this is about," says Mimi. "You're upset about the memo."

"Damn right I am. How dare—" I stop myself. I consider what's at stake: my gorgeous, spacious kitchen, my Eden.

"Deborah, you've made your point loud and clear," says Mimi. "How's this? You may wear what you wish while cooking, but otherwise it's time to step it up a bit from the white Reeboks. The rest of the staff needs some extra polish, too. I assume you know that *Hers* has become the frequent butt of jokes in the building. We're known as the frumpy mom-types who haven't updated our wardrobes since the Clinton administration."

"Who cares what we're wearing as long as we're putting out a quality publication?"

Mimi smiles, and pauses before she speaks: "Would you say that's what you've been doing, Deborah? Putting out a quality publication?" Crap, I walked right into that one.

"Listen, Mimi, I have been working at *Hers* for longer than you've been in this industry. You know as well as I do that I am a grand bargain for you; you'd have to shell out double or more to get another recipe creator with my experience and expertise. And if you did let me go, my severance package would be—let's see, four weeks for every year at the company—two full years of my salary."

"You've thought this all through, haven't you?"

"Just the facts, ma'am. And another thing: I've got a full work-load already, so you'll have to find someone else to assist this Ravenous Rhee character. How about your assistant, Laura, whose taste you revere so much?"

"Deborah, I admire your willfulness."

"But?"

"But, you will have to work with Rhee. Unless of course you want someone else using your kitchen to test out her recipes?"

Ugh. My mind flashes on the *Professional Chef* profile of Eileen Houtt's hip new restaurant, an article I never bothered to read. Eileen and I had lost touch for years, but shortly before that story was published, I ran into her at a conference. When I told Eileen I worked at *Hers*, she said she wasn't familiar with it, but asked if I knew the editors at *Gastrome*, that snooty rag for rich foodies; apparently her sous-chef used to head up their kitchen. I shudder to imagine my old friend happening upon an issue of *Hers* and seeing so-called recipes created by Ravenous Rhee. "Fine, I will test out that phony's recipes," I say to Mimi now, "but if the result is inedible, I claim veto power."

"You may veto one out of every four recipes, and only if the *Hers* staff reaches a consensus on the decision."

"How about, I can nix one out of two recipes, and I only need staff majority?"

"One out of three, and fine. Anything else?"

"I'm not buying new shoes."

"Ha! I guess I know what I'm giving you for Christmas."

"Hanukkah, you mean. You should watch those kinds of assumptions. Religious intolerance is a serious offense at Schmidt & Delancey."

"Noted, Deborah."

"Please call me Debbie."

"OK, Debbie. Now, will you please remove these horrifying images from my desk?"

"Gladly." I snatch up my copy of *Professional Chef* and march out, feeling triumphant. I decide I'll treat myself to truffle oil mac and cheese for dinner.

The next morning I board the same up elevator as Mimi. She gives me the once-over, eyeing my usual sneakers, jeans, and T-shirt. I take out the tube of lipstick I nabbed from the beauty closet, the same crimson as Mimi's editing pen. I apply the dark stain carefully to my lips, and then smile flirtatiously at my boss. I wink and bat my eyelashes. Mimi's laugh is the hoarse hack of a smoker's; it sounds terrible. I decide I'll go up to the kitchen and brew her some herbal tea. Hibiscus flower with honey is very healing.

5

Leah Brenner, Executive Editor

I'm distracted as I enter my office, so when I go to fling my bag onto my chair, I nearly knock Victoria in the head. "God, I'm so sorry." One peripheral glance reveals that all of my belongings have vanished, replaced by stuff that is similar, but not the same. I feel a pang for my stapler, of all things. "What's going on in here?"

"Didn't you get the memo?" asks Victoria. "Laura was supposed to e-mail you." I nod like I know what she's talking about. The truth is I haven't checked my messages since yesterday afternoon, one of my work-from-home days. My husband surprised me by coming home early with a bottle of good champagne and takeout from my favorite Italian joint. I was wary of a catch, but Rob insisted he simply thought I deserved a break, then he powered down our computers and phones and poured us each a flute of bubbly. One evening a week Rob and I pretend we're living in a pre-Internet age; it's the closest thing we get to date night. (We derive all too much pleasure from the name we've come up with for the ritual: "Brenner Unplugged.") As a result, unread e-mails have been colonizing my inbox for the past eighteen hours, undisturbed by the predatory Delete button, and Victoria has managed to blindside me with this humiliating switcheroo.

"The thinking was," she says, chipper as ever, "we're co-executive editors now, but since you're only in three days a week, it makes more sense for me to have the office, since I'm here every day. You understand, right?"

To prevent my fist from delivering a right hook to Victoria's cheek, I practice the relaxation technique I mastered during my triplets' colicky stage: a long, deep breath; hold for one, two, three, four—*Oh, forget it,* I think, releasing the inhale in one defeated burst. My eye catches on a new photo on the wall: an altar shot at what must be Victoria's wedding. The guy's cute, but Victoria's dress is a horrendous layer-cake ordeal. The realization that my office has been usurped by someone who would pick that gown for the most important day of her life sets me spinning with vertigo.

"So where do I sit now?" I ask, trying to sound unfazed.

"The intern has been relocating your things to that large space over there." Victoria points to a cubicle next to the beauty closet, where I spot Erin propping my Christmas card up against the divider.

"But that's Liz's spot. She'll be back from maternity leave in less than a month."

"I'm sure we'll figure it all out when she's back." Victoria ushers me out of what I can't help still thinking of as my office.

Seated at my new desk, I smell Regina before I see her: tobacco mixed with her Calvin Klein perfume. I look forward to the frequent visits from our entertainment director; her gossip is always first-rate, plus her kids are grown, which is a reminder that some people really do survive motherhood. "Hey, Reg," I say. She leans down for a double-cheek kiss. "You're looking fabulous." An ikat-printed wraparound hugs Regina's surprisingly taut middle-aged curves.

"Oh, shut up. I'm straight off a red-eye from L.A.," she says. "And um, forgive me if I'm missing something, but what the hell are you doing sitting in this crappy little hole?"

"Gee, thanks for your tact. I had to clear out my office to make way for my new co-executive, Ms. Victoria Perfect, so it's back to cubicle-land for me."

"That's fucked up."

"Tell me about it. I'm picturing junior staffers perched up on my desk when we go over stories. That'll give me quite the air of authority."

"If you ask me, you should blow this joint for good, ship out of New York once and for all."

"I gather you've been talking to my Vermont-obsessed husband?"

"Seriously, with all the craziness that goes down in this town, it's best taken in small doses. Palm trees and the Pacific are what do a body good." Regina's permanent post is in Los Angeles; she visits the New York office a couple of times per month.

"This happy arrangement might not last for long, anyway," I say. "I saw the latest masthead, and "Victoria LaRue" and "Leah Brenner" don't even fit on one line—Mark had to shrink the font to ID us as co-executive editors."

"Well, shit." Regina smoothes down my hair, and I notice her discreetly removing a Cheerio from a strand. "Everyone around here does kind of look like a bully stole their lunch."

"Yeah, and the bully is our new boss."

"Mimi stole your lunch, huh? Speaking of which, tell me, is she a big eater?"

"More so than Louisa."

"Well, Louisa was permanently on the herbal tea and cottage cheese diet. I've seriously seen celebrities with bigger appetites. I'd prefer to do without the new boss's judgment, but you know I don't do plane food, and what I really need right now is a big old chocolate chip muffin before our little executive rendezvous."

"Ooh, get me one, too."

Regina has flown in for a meeting to discuss the November cover star. Mimi hasn't yet shared her vision of an ideal candidate, but I've taken it upon myself to compile a list of actresses I think would set the perfect tone for the *Hers* relaunch. I'm gunning for Dina Monahan, the breakout success and critics' darling from this year's Sundance Film Festival; she has a new indie movie coming out in November that's predicted to be a crossover mainstream hit. Plus, Dina Monahan's career is in the sweet spot for *Hers:* She's right on the cusp of fame, meaning she'd likely agree to an interview, and probably even divulge some real info about herself, not just the boilerplate, publicist-approved drivel all the bigger stars have learned to spout.

The senior staff—Victoria, Mark, Abby, and I—file into Mimi's office, where we discover that all of the chairs are already occupied by a small group of young women, spines like rods. We remain standing, awkwardly shifting our weight. "Don't mind the whippersnappers," says Mimi. "They're all recent grads from my alma mater, good old Kansas State. They're here for the day so we can hear their ideas and find out if any of them would fit in at *Hers.*" Oh, great, so now Mimi plans to replace all of us with twenty-one-year-old know-nothings whom she can pay slave wages. When I was their age, I drew confidence from the fact that this industry tends to value youth over experience. Now, I want to Fed-Ex all of their fresh faces directly back to campus; I couldn't care less about their youthful ideas.

As Laura carries in chairs for the editors, Regina struts in and throws her arms around Mimi. "We finally meet up in the flesh," she says. "What fun!"

"Welcome to the East Coast, dear."

Regina must have treated herself to a triple espresso (or an alternative I don't want to consider), because she launches right in, speed-talking like she's been given a time limit: "I was just at the September cover shoot, and Liliana Line cannot be more of a nightmare. She hasn't been in a hit movie since the nineties, yet she's kept up her diva routine with full force. I had my assistant running all over the Valley trying to locate tropical Starbursts and Cherry Vanilla Coke for Her Highness. The upside is, we did get some killer shots that we can all look at today; Drew's manipulating them now. I'm sitting down with Liliana next week for the interview, and I hear the trick is to get a couple glasses of merlot in her and then she talks."

"Whoa, let's hold on a minute," says Mimi.

"Oh, I just assumed you'd want to get straight to business. I'll start again. Hello, I'm Regina Peck, entertainment director of *Hers* magazine. It's a pleasure to see you."

"Hello, Regina. Mimi Walsh. Of course you know Leah, Mark, and Abby, and this is Victoria, our new co-executive editor. My assistant, Laura, was the one who showed you in. So how long has it been?" I had no idea Regina and Mimi knew each other.

"I don't know, a decade?" says Regina.

"More like a century," Mimi responds.

"My daughter's actually planning to intern at *Starstruck* this summer. You'd think having a mom like me would be enough to turn her off of celebrities for good, but she did grow up in Santa Monica, so what could I expect? I was hoping she'd get to work with you over there."

"You don't mean the daughter I remember you being pregnant with? You're telling me she's a *teenager* now?"

"Actually, in her last year at NYU."

"A college senior?!" Mimi says. "Christ, you're ancient!" Regina forces a smile. She often jokes about her flagging memory and sagging everything (and then happily passes around cards for her plastic surgeon—for the referral discount, she says), but no one else dares poke fun at her age. It occurs to me that she must be at least a decade older than Mimi.

"Regina's daughter is both beautiful and brilliant," I say.

Mimi ignores me. "So, I want to talk reality," she says.

"Wow, OK, let's do it," says Regina, with an artificial laugh. "So, tell me the situation. I sincerely hope you're not planning on shopping around my job, because I've got ears all over this business."

"No, not *reality*-reality," Victoria interjects. "She means reality TV." I wonder if Mimi and Victoria have already discussed the November cover in a premeeting prior to our meeting.

"Oh, obviously," says Regina. "What a relief."

"That's what our readers watch on the boob tube, so those are the stars I want on our covers," says Mimi.

"Really?" I say. "Because I am hearing amazing things about Dina Monahan, and I know she might not be a superstar quite yet—"

Mimi sighs, cutting me off. "Let's all make a deal. We'll agree to stop featuring B-list, artsy-fartsy actresses on our covers and filling their interviews with highfalutin, pseudointellectual bullcrap, while in the meantime we pine away for the A-listers and wish we were *Vanity Fair*. OK?"

I manage a nod. I can feel my cheeks burning red. I crumple up my dossier of the Dina Monahan info I've compiled. The crunch of paper in my fist is oddly satisfying.

Regina, meanwhile, has bounded up out of her seat and is literally shaking her booty. "Mimi, you've just made my week," she says. I catch Laura peering in at Regina as if she's from Mars rather than just the West Coast. "I have to tell you, I've been pushing to include reality stars in the magazine as far back as the third season of *Survivor*. Those loonies give the best interviews—you practically have to shut them up before they blurt out their ATM code."

"One thing to consider," says Mark, who is always considering and reconsidering everything, "is that reality stars don't quite look like models, or even actresses. The camera does love a train wreck, but not exactly in the way we're going for."

"That's a good point," I say, glad to have an ally. I glance at Abby, who's staying judiciously silent.

"Well, that's *your* job, isn't it, Mark? To make them look pretty," says Mimi. "I have faith you can work your Photoshop magic." I see Mark clench his teeth.

"So who should we snag for the November relaunch?" Regina says, her mind clearly motoring away at possibilities.

"How about one of those horrifying housewives?" suggests Victoria.

"I was thinking everyone's loving Janine, that disaster from *Worst Moms in the World*," says Regina. "We could pair her Q&A with some tongue-in-cheek parenting advice, and she could share her favorite Thanksgiving family traditions."

"That would be perfect." Mimi engulfs Regina in a bear hug. Victoria's jealousy is almost palpable, like a toxic gas emanating from her pores. I wonder if my own dismay comes off so obviously.

* * *

Later that day, I corner Regina. "So you know Mimi from before?"

"Oh yeah. I first met her through her then-boyfriend, soon-to-be-husband, now ex-husband, Steven, when he was my attending nurse in Lenox Hill's maternity ward. Even at nine months pregnant I was a pro at the art of bedside flirting."

"I bet you were. So give me some dirt."

"He and I became friendly, and when I mentioned I was an editor, he said his girlfriend—that was Mimi—was looking to break into magazines. In the interest of racking up some career karma, I set her up with a friend at *Persons of Interest*. And the rest is history. Her star has been rising ever since."

"So then you're responsible for the unleashing of the monster," I say. Regina laughs her great big guffaw.

"Shhh." We both hear it and wheel our heads around. It's Laura.

"Excuse me?" says Regina.

"Can you please be a little quieter? Your speaking voice is quite loud, and you've been on the phone making a racket all day. I can hardly hear myself think."

Regina mouths to me, *"Who does this girl think she is?"* Aloud to Laura, she says, "And why exactly do you need to hear yourself think? Is it that complicated to slot in appointments and schedule dinner reservations? You may be interested to know, I'm busting my ass over here, trying to book our November cover."

Laura sighs loudly. Regina gives her the finger from behind her screen, and I stifle my giggle.

That evening after the triathlon feat of getting my three girls to sleep, I'm detailing our November cover-girl options for my husband. "Janine from *Worst Moms in the World* is our top pick, but apparently she's knocked up again. If we can't get a pre–three months shoot, we'll have to wait for post–six months."

"No one wants a cover girl who just looks fat," says Rob, "even if she *is* pregnant, right?"

"Correct, sweetheart. So you *have* been paying attention all these years." I pat my husband affectionately on the head. "The second choice is Eliana from *Trapeze Rehab*. Victoria went on about how she's captivated everyone with her brave let-go-and-catch performances even as she tweaks out in heroin withdrawal."

"How very inspiring."

"Yeah, right. Regina also nailed down Brandy from *Make Me a Cake, Bitch!*"

"Oh, I know that show," Rob says. "I got the recipe for the girls' birthday cake from the season finale."

"You're kidding me. Well, apparently Brandy's lemon meringue tart was key in reuniting her with her estranged mother, and Regina claims that episode sparked a ten percent spike in lemon sales nationwide."

"That cannot be a real statistic."

"Sadly, I think it is. Mimi envisions a heartfelt interview alongside the contestant's latest cake recipes. Our food guru, Debbie, will have a conniption, but that's pretty much a new job requirement at *Hers* HQ."

"Oh, baby." Rob grabs my sleeve and leads me into the living room, where he's set up our projection screen. "I have something to show you," he says.

I experience a brief swell of hope that Rob has secured an advance copy of Dina Monahan's forthcoming film; Rob's brother works in the movie business and often sends us screeners. But when my husband dims the lights and presses play, my hopes are dashed: The screen flashes awake with an image of a moss-colored house well past its prime. If the house were a human, I think, it would be my ninety-year-old grandma slowly deteriorating in a nursing home upstate. Like my grandma, I learn this house also resides in the country. Up by its chimney, in the spot where a child's drawing would feature a curlicue of smoke, floats a sentence: "Discover the seductive charm of Putney, Vermont."

"Oh no, what is this?" I plead.

"It's a slideshow. A realtor sent it to us when I asked about a property listing." I groan. "Oh, come on, Leah. You adore Power-Point presentations."

"Yeah, PowerPoints about demographics and brand strategy. Not about decrepit farmhouses in the middle of nowhere."

"Actually, Putney is just ten miles from the bustling town of Brattleboro."

"Ooh, the big, bad urban center of Brattleboro, huh? How many Indian restaurants are there? How many movie theaters? How many people, Rob—are we talking a population of three or four digits here?"

"Oh, shut your trap and just watch the damn slideshow." He chucks a pillow in my direction.

"Fine," I say. "But I'm steeling myself with snacks."

When I return from the kitchen with a bowl of popcorn, Rob has changed the slide to an interior image, a living room that opens out onto a screened-in porch. The furniture is terrible—all wicker and paisley print—and the walls are lined floor-to-ceiling with a celestial scene of dancing cherubs. But when I imagine the space stripped of its owner's terrible taste (not to mention the slide's accompanying copy: "If you lived here, you'd be home now, relaxing on the comfortable sofa, enjoying the company of your loved ones, perhaps indulging in a delicious, wholesome meal. . . ."), I can glimpse the space's promise. Sunlight floods the large rooms, brightening the blond wood, and exposed beams lend the space a rustic hominess.

Rob clicks to the next slide, and now we see the grounds: The hills literally roll, purple flowers dot the lush grass, and a postcard-worthy stream winds its way through the panorama. "Can't you picture the girls when they're a little older sledding on these hills in the winter?" he asks.

"Ah, yes. *Winter,*" I say, and then poof goes my fantasy of Vermont as a place of permanent fresh-aired, light-breezed summer. No wonder the realtor doesn't show the landscape buried in snow and ice, a cold so bone-chilling you could probably feel it through the photo.

Click. The screen animates with a dozen squawking chickens. "We wouldn't have to keep them," Rob says, "but the owners have offered if we want."

"Fresh eggs," I say. "Just like you wanted."

"Yep." Rob clicks, and the hills appear again, only this time we're peering down at them through an oversized set of bay windows. The slide reads, "Breathtaking views you'd think you have to travel hundreds or even thousands of miles to experience."

"That's right, we *would* have to travel hundreds of miles to experience them," I say.

"The bay windows are in the master bedroom," says Rob, ignoring my comment. "Next we'll see the rest of the room." He clicks. I gasp, then collapse into giggles. There on the four-poster bed in the center of the room are two etched stick figures: a woman crouched on all fours, and a man penetrating her from behind. The man wears a Yankees cap. "And that there is the two of us christening our new home," says my husband.

"That realtor's a real gem, including this touch of personalization. It's so thoughtful of him."

"And romantic."

"Very."

"So what do you think, baby? I mean, just look at how much fun we're having already!" Rob points to the stick figures on the screen.

"I can't deny that. Here's what I think: How about if we put the kibosh on the Vermont talk for the night and we have some of our own fun right here in suburban New Jersey?"

"It's a deal."

Rob chases me up to the bedroom. As the two of us peel off our clothing, I'm suddenly struck by how small our windows are. I've never noticed it before. I can't help imagining how dramatic it would feel to make love against a backdrop of rolling green hills.

The next morning, Victoria intercepts me on my way to the November concepts meeting. "Mimi would like you to supervise today's beauty shoot." We've gotten the stars of the sitcom *Office Jungle* to showcase the fall's trends in makeup for the October issue.

"But what about Regina?"

"She had to fly back to L.A. last night for a meeting with that terrible mother from the reality show."

"Oh. How about Abby, then?" Abby, queen of managing over-sized personalities, has always been a staple on our celebrity photo shoots.

"Mimi wants Abby in the morning meeting." This is a first, the managing editor but not the executive editor getting invited to a brainstorm.

"OK. I suppose if Mimi felt I was the best person to handle the responsibility, I've got to go." Victoria gives me a pitying look.

"Hey, Leah," Mimi calls out from inside her office. "Just an FYI, I absolutely abhorred all the makeup artists who were booked for the shoot, so I made a few calls and hired new ones." I wonder if Abby knows about this; I imagine the first batch already got paid. "We'll still have the actresses show off the season's hottest colors, but I want them done up in the style of leopards and zebras and tigers and giraffes—you know, as a play on the title, *Office Jungle*."

"Um, so all of those animals actually live in the jungle?" I ask, playing dumb.

"Oh, whatever. We're just having fun, and our readers are too dense to think about whether zebras belong in the grasslands, or whatever. Ha! You can relay the new plan to the girls at the shoot."

Seriously? So then Mimi hasn't cleared this nonsense with the actresses or, more important, their publicists. My heart begins clanging at my chest like cymbals, and it continues doing so for the entire cab ride to the photo studio.

When I arrive on set, a little wisp of a man is coating his eyelashes in blue mascara. He bounds over to me and leans in for a kiss. "You must be Leah. I'm Jonathan, and I'm here to help with the shoot. I've done Mimi up for special events for years. Isn't she fab?"

"A pleasure," I say, wondering, *Help out with the shoot how?* He isn't one of the new makeup artists—they're over by the mirrors setting out their pots and palettes. It soon becomes clear that Jonathan will be art-directing the shoot, a job usually handled by Liz, our beauty editor who recently had a baby. I'm curious if

Mimi knows the danger of trying to oust a staffer while she's out on maternity leave.

Only one actress cries when I explain the new vision for the shoot. "So I have to wear a giraffe costume?" she asks through weepy sniffles.

"You'll still be modeling the saffron eye shadow, and believe me it will look beautiful against your olive skin, but we'll just be finishing off the look with a few giraffe spots and a yellow turtleneck. No big deal."

"Is it because I *look* like an animal?" she wails. Her publicist dabs de-swelling cream under her eyes and shoots me looks like daggers.

I want to scream out that she's getting paid bucketloads just to freaking smile for a camera, so she should really just suck it up. Instead, I assume my patient mother mode. "No, no, it's artistic," I assure the actress, imagining I'm speaking to a stubborn baby Lulu. "The other women will be made up as animals, too. You're lucky because the giraffe is the tallest, and the long neck represents power and vitality. You'll have a real presence."

I'm not sure how much more of this bullshitting I can handle. It's a good thing my daughters have been stuck lately on books about the zoo, so I'm up on my game. I've already made a case for the quiet grace of the zebra, the kick-ass prowess of the tiger, and the stealth charm of the leopard. At one point Jonathan suggests featuring one of the actresses as an elephant, and I tell him that, no, that will absolutely not be possible. Even my powers of persuasion are not up to that task.

The actress is still whimpering, but less hysterically, as her publicist keeps cooing about her client's neck—how it's lovely and perfect and, no, not at all too long. It's the first moment of the day when I'm not actively dealing with a crisis, and I realize my temples are pounding. And whatever that sappy crooning is coming from someone's iPod is making it worse.

Jonathan ducks his head in. "Everything peachy keen in here?"

His bright expression conveys no awareness of the crying model in the corner. "Good, good."

I head over his way. "Hey, my head's about to explode. I've got to take five." I notice Jonathan has started bouncing in place. "What is that godawful music, anyway?"

"You're kidding, right?" he says. "That's Helena Hope. It's *the* song of the summer." He starts singing along: " 'We'd be bound forever, joined as one, the two of us so young and fun.' "

"OK, enough, I'm ducking out for coffee. Want to come?"

"Nah, I'm rushing to catch my ballet barre class," he says, adding, "I'll see you tomorrow," which is how I realize he's now a member of the *Hers* staff.

In Starbucks, I order a skim cappuccino and carry it to a stool by the window. The air conditioning is arctic, and it's disconcerting to shiver while watching passersby sweat in the ninety-degree heat outside. I cup my hands around the warm drink and think, that actress will be fine. In fact, I will be, too. All I have to do is get through the workday; just four more decent shots for the beauty story, probably a handful more meltdowns from the celebs, and two more hours until end-time, tops. After that, who knows? Probably more countdowns to countless more endpoints. For this moment, though, I push aside the urge to look ahead and ahead and ahead, and decide to sit here, right now, sipping at my drink's hot foam, savoring its bittersweet taste.

6

Abby Rollins,
Managing Editor

I'm wading through stacks of invoices and receipts and contracts when Mimi flies into my office. "Great news," she announces, a statement I've come to realize could mean anything coming from her. "Lucia What's-her-name, the author of that superhot, best-selling zombie series, has agreed to write a short story for the November relaunch. Regina's hammering out the details, but I'm thinking some kind of Thanksgiving tale. Picture it: A housewife whose biggest everyday excitement is a visit from the mailman returns to her hometown for the holiday and, over turkey and cranberry sauce, discovers that all of her awful relatives are actually undead zombies. Cue the total life shake-up, followed by a few thrilling action scenes, and finally a life-affirming, zombie-embracing catharsis in which the protagonist suddenly understands that her ho-hum, dull-as-dirt existence is actually the happiest, most fulfilling life ever."

"Oh boy, that's an idea," I say. I'm worried not only that Mimi has insisted the writer pursue this particular plotline, but also about what she's promised her in return. That kind of hotshot author probably commands far more than the standard $2.50-per-word we offer our top-notch freelancers. "Do you want me to draw up the contracts?" I ask, hoping to have a hand in the payment.

"Nah, Laura's on it." Meaning, Mimi doesn't want me in the loop.

"OK, well, I'm finishing up the August cost record today, so we should go over the budget—"

The way Mimi simultaneously winces and dismisses me with a wave, it's as if she's allergic to the word "budget." More likely, she knows something I don't about *Hers'* finances. "I've got to run to a meeting," she says, "but I dropped by to let you know we're taking on four of those girls from my alma mater as freelancers. They'll help out during the transition. So please get the paperwork going." Mimi can tell that I'm doing the math, calculating the thousands of dollars in extra wages I'll have to factor in to the next cost record.

"They'll be worth it, you'll see," she says, then makes a fast exit. It's in my best interest to trust her, even if her sense of what's worth it seems fairly skewed; this morning I had to distract her so she'd forget about the Bloomingdales.com shopping cart she'd filled with three thousand dollars' worth of jewelry, about to be charged to her corporate credit card, no doubt.

My phone rings, and I pick up. "I just saw quite the sick puppy."

"Hey, Jule," I say into the receiver. Some veterinarians probably take notes between patients, but Julia prefers to call me to debrief. I've told her at least a hundred times that I'm not free to chat at hourly intervals throughout the work day, but her calls keep coming. And I always pick up.

"That poodle must've gotten into one very emotional eater's stash of chocolate," my wife says. "Seriously, his owner weighed like three hundred pounds."

"Julia, I'm really kind of slammed right now." I take in the pileup on my desk, a paper trail of everything we've paid out for the August issue: writers, photo shoots, clothing and props, models, intern stipends, and a dozen other things. "I can't really talk."

"Oh, come on, did I offend you? I'm just joking. I resuscitated the little doggie, I promise. And this morning I extracted a penny from a cat's stomach."

"Yuck."

"So how's the tabulation going?" It's Julia's usual question; she likes to poke fun at what she views as my very dull job. It just so happens I *am* midcalculation. I'm only halfway through the issue's expenses, and we're already $250,000 up from the July issue.

"Not great, actually. We're grossly overbudget. Although all Mimi seems to want me to do is track what comes in and what goes out, not make any actual changes based on the numbers. I'm like a Monopoly banker."

"Or an Excel spreadsheet."

"Very funny." Money matters were a different story with Louisa. Every year Corporate kept shrinking our budget, and we'd have to scrimp and scrounge and practically work magic to make the show go on. I scrutinized expense reports line by line—a midafternoon latte while on location was not a valid professional expense, I'd tell the staff—and I unearthed up-and-coming photographers who hadn't yet realized they could charge the going rate for shoots. It was a real challenge, but a gratifying one.

"So you're a big spender now?" Julia teases. "Hard to imagine from Target's number one customer."

"You know how it is, always living large at *Hers.*" I'm not being as facetious as I sound. The thirtieth floor mysteriously hasn't called us out on our new free-for-all spending sprees, despite no news of an expanded budget. I've heard rumors of this kind of thing: Corporate turning a blind eye when a new editor in chief steps in. I've learned to not push my questioning with Mimi, but it makes me feel inconsequential to have so little control over the finances, which I'm supposed to be in charge of.

Erin tiptoes into my office and sets a frothy drink down on my desk. "What's this?" I ask.

"Huh?" Julia says through the phone.

"Sorry, the intern just brought me coffee, but—"

"Oh, the pretty little intern has a thing for you?" Julia asks.

"Mimi thought you might like a Frappuccino," Erin whispers.

"Of course she did," I say to Erin, who smiles, then steps out.

"By the way, check your in-box," says Julia. "I'm sending you more profiles."

"All ambitious, sporty, and upbeat?" I ask.

"Triple check, and with green eyes, too." I roll my brown ones—I don't know what Julia's obsession is with having a green-eyed child. "Just read them, OK?"

"Yes, ma'am." Lately I feel like I moonlight as an examiner of sperm donor profiles. The process makes me uneasy, and I'd just as soon let Julia pick the guy, but she insists I be involved.

"You have to go, don't you?" she asks.

"How can you tell?"

"I can hear you fretting your brow from here. It's deafening. I've got a German shepherd waiting on me, anyway. Ta-ta, my love."

I hang up, then poke my head out of my office to survey the scene: I'm not surprised to see that the desks are all dotted with Starbucks' signature green straws stabbed through clear cups. I lock eyes with Mimi, who raises her drink in a toast. "It's hot as hell out there," she says. "It seemed like a nice treat, iced beverages for all."

Five-dollar iced beverages, I think, but I swallow my reprimand along with the sugary froth. It tastes delicious.

Victoria's shouts echo down the hall, and I assume she must be hopped up on all that Starbucks: "They're obviously pretending they didn't say those things because they're having second thoughts," she trills. But then I spot our research chief, Sylvia—oh, dear; whatever the situation is, it's likely due to more than caffeine. Victoria's voice escalates: "You have the transcripts, don't you?"

Deciding to intervene, I go hover outside Victoria's office (which I still think of as Leah's). I can see the back of Sylvia's head, that tight coil of jet-black hair. The woman is a dynamite fact checker, but she tends to bring out the worst in editors. "You guys OK in there?" I ask tentatively.

"We're discussing some alleged facts in the cheaters story," says

Sylvia. Victoria rolls her eyes. "Certain sources are claiming they're being misrepresented."

"That's because our writer is top-notch and she got the women to open up about all the horrible ways they screwed over their husbands," Victoria says. "Now they're panicking that they revealed so much. But it's all there in the transcripts."

"We don't have tape recordings of these so-called transcripts. And it's not just that. The expert quotes have been twisted to the point of no recognition. Let's see now: Dr. Masterson said that some couples, with a lot of hard work and in most cases counseling, can sometimes work to repair the trust in a relationship after an affair. You have him saying, 'Cheating is the new spat. Plenty of pairs go through it, but they get over it and move on.' I've looked through his book and, for starters, he would never use the word 'spat.' " Sylvia spits out the word, and Victoria recoils. The staff is constantly complaining about Sylvia, but most of her concerns seem valid to me. I admire how she stands her ground.

"The essential meaning is the same," says Victoria. "In both versions, he's saying cheating doesn't necessarily spell divorce. Obviously some liberties have to be taken for the benefit of the narrative."

"Some liberties!" Sylvia tosses up her spidery arms. "This is not your personal Web log, Victoria. You cannot simply invent facts and attribute them to people and then defend the action in the service of creating a narrative."

"You're being too rigid."

"OK, let's hold on," I interrupt. "Sex stories are obviously extra tricky because people's personal reputations are at stake. How's this? Sylvia, if something appears in the transcripts, let's go with it. To protect the women, we'll use first names only. And with the experts, we need to run the edited quotes by them and make sure they're kosher. All right with everyone?"

"Fine," they say in unison, both fuming like petulant children. I often feel like I'm the only adult around here.

* * *

It doesn't surprise me, later that day, when I spot Victoria and Sylvia in Mimi's closed-door office. Sylvia looks as if she's behind bars instead of glass.

Nor does it surprise me an hour later when I get a call from Suzie in Human Resources. An exit interview has been arranged for Sylvia. I sigh, mentally allotting myself an extra glass of wine for tonight. I make my way to Mimi's office and wait to be filled in.

"Oh, Christ," Mimi says. "Stop looking at me like I'm your teenage daughter who you just caught sneaking out to go blow my boyfriend. It had to be done. In fact, you should be kissing my ass. I'm saving you $85K in the budget." It takes me a moment to realize that is Sylvia's salary.

"But we'll need to hire another researcher."

"We can find someone fresh from college and throw her a starter salary—one of those freelancers we just brought in, for example," she says. In other words, someone Victoria and company can stomp all over. "How hard it is to fact-check, really? Plus, it'll mean fewer butting heads around here." During Sylvia's decade of duty, we haven't had to issue a single correction. I fear for the future.

"OK, I'll send word up to H.R. that we're looking."

"Oh, Abby, I wanted to see if you were free after work sometime."

"Sure. That would be perfect. We could stick around and go over the budget together in peace, with no distractions."

"Oh, no, nothing like that. I feel like you and I are on the same wavelength, and I see potential for us to be great pals, but we haven't had the chance to get to know each other. I'm thinking drinks, maybe at a wine bar or that cute Mexican place down the street. It'll be fun." This is somewhat surprising, considering Mimi just accused me of acting like her uptight mother, but not *so* surprising. People tend to think I understand them; I'm someone others always confide in.

"OK, how's this Friday?" I ask. "What's that, June fifteenth?"

"We're on." As I watch Mimi record my name in red ink in her planner, I have an ominous feeling that I'm being added to the wrong list. "You know what?" She looks up. "It's been a rough day. How about tonight—are you free?"

I shrug. Julia wanted us to spend the evening scrolling through more donor profiles, but I could use a break from that. "Sure, why not?"

"Yay," Mimi says, and shocks me by pulling me in for a hug.

My wife would say this is a flaw of mine, my tendency to make friends with everyone. She believes selecting an elite few to associate with is a sign of good taste. According to her, choosiness in friendship is a demonstration of loyalty and commitment to those who've made the cut. I, on the other hand, think many people are worth befriending, and that hanging out with a hodgepodge of people is a good way to broaden one's horizons. People say I'm easy to talk to. I suppose it's ironic that I find it difficult to open up about myself.

With an hour left of the workday, I run into Sylvia by the photocopier. She must be back from her session in Human Resources. "I'm sorry about how this has turned out," I say to her.

"I appreciate it," she says calmly. "I suppose it's time to move on. It has been ten years."

"For me too."

"You're looking to move on, too?"

"Oh, dear, no." My voice catches. "I meant I've also been working here for ten years." Julia regularly encourages me to scour the job boards, pointing out that the only way I'll make more money is to move on from *Hers*. She once caught me checking out a posting for *Brooklyn Ladies*, a Webzine for gay women in our borough; she got so excited, going on about how perfect it would be for me, that I immediately exed out of the listing. I never applied for the position. The truth is, I'm comfortable at *Hers*. Even amidst the recent chaos, it feels safe.

"What are you copying there?" I ask. Sylvia holds up a packet: *Hers'* research guidelines, which I happen to know she's painstakingly compiled and updated on a biannual basis for the past decade. They now fill eighteen pages.

"I know most people will probably chuck them out immediately," she says. "But maybe they'll at least glance at the contents beforehand. It's not popular or hip to say so, but the first and foremost duty of a magazine is to be accurate."

"Right on." It's so dignified, Sylvia's grace in the face of her firing. As a tribute of sorts, I decide I'll display her guidelines on my bulletin board. "We'll miss you."

"Not everyone," she says with a dry laugh.

"Well, I sure will." I take in the sight of her, spine straight as a yardstick, looking like no one could knock her over. I make an effort to stand a bit taller, and then leave Sylvia to her photocopying.

After work, Mimi and I head to a nearby Mexican joint. I feel like a bit of a traitor since it's the same place I used to go with Liz before her maternity leave, and Leah, too, before she had her triplets. Our monthly tradition consisted of pigging out on tacos and getting tipsy on margaritas, and then Liz would start in on mocking the models who mill about the Schmidt & Delancey building. Liz could perfectly impersonate their pouty lips and big alien eyes; even while she was pregnant, suffering through virgin cocktails and stone sober, she could pull off the impressions. I really miss Liz. I kind of hate it when my friends become moms.

Turns out, margaritas are Mimi's favorite—and she demonstrates it by sucking back three in the span of an hour. "I haven't had drinks this good in months," she says. "In fact, I haven't had drinks at all. My friends keep saying we should go out to celebrate my new job, but I'm too preoccupied with the actual job to make it happen. Ha!"

I'm not sure what the motive is for this explanation: if she's trying to prove to me her diligence at work or maybe the fact that she has friends, or if it's a rationale for why she's already slurring her speech. I nod silently. "You know who can mix up a mean margarita?" Mimi says. "My ex-husband. In fact, both of my ex-husbands! Ha!"

"Who doesn't love a delicious margarita?" I say, trying to keep the conversation innocuous.

"We should tour the city's offerings, you and me. We could do a bar crawl of all the *restaurantes Mexicanos. ¡Ole!*" Mimi winks and clinks her glass against mine, and I'm surprised to find myself thinking that might actually be fun. I'm realizing how it must be lonely in Mimi's position, all alone up at the top. "Hey, wanna do shots of Patrón?" Mimi asks.

"Uh, OK." I mentally note to make sure this tab doesn't end up on her corporate card.

I can hold my liquor, but after taking her shot Mimi demonstrates further that she cannot. She's mooning at the bartender, beginning to embarrass herself. "How about I call you a cab?" I offer.

Mimi shakes her head and comes dangerously close to toppling off her stool. "José and I are having fun." Oh boy, I'm fairly certain the bartender said his name was Joe.

"All right, you have your fun." I order a soda water and sip at it, scrolling through my BlackBerry.

"Hey, José, guess what? I'm the new boss in town."

"Oh yeah?" he responds, uninterested. He looks like my eighteen-year-old nephew—that young, too—and I'm mortified on Mimi's behalf. I pretend to be absorbed in my e-mail.

"I'm the boss," she repeats. "That means I'm in charge, and I get to say 'Yes, yes, yes' or 'No way, José!' Whatever I want. All it takes is a single nod, or one stroke of my red pen. But let me tell you, *mi amigo*, it's not all fun and games. Everyone looks at me like I'm gonna eat them alive. I'm a big girl, I know, it's a funny joke, ha! Really they should be kissing my big, fat ass because I am going to be the one to save this freaking magazine. *Jesus Christo*, you should have seen this piece of crap before I came in, trying to be all top-shelf when the drinkers—I mean, when the *readers*—wanted the shitty well brand, you know? I know exactly what I'm doing, and I'm going to make this brand some serious *dinero*." Oh, Jesus. "Hit me, José. Another Patrón for me and *uno* for *mi amiga* here."

"I don't think that's the best idea," the bartender says, eyeing me.

"C'mon, Mimi. He's cutting us off because I've had a few too many. Let's go, we're getting a car."

But Mimi won't budge. "Abby, does everyone at work hate me?" she mumbles, head suddenly in hands.

"What? No!"

"I can bring in people and pay them to like me, but it's not the same. My little puggle-wuggle Pookie likes me, but that's not the same, either." I sigh and start rubbing circles against the small of my boss's back, like I've seen Julia do to the stomachs of sick animals. I'm thinking how in all the years I worked for Louisa she shared perhaps a total of five sentences with me about her feelings.

Eventually, with the bartender's help, I manage to drag Mimi outside and into a cab. She immediately conks out, head pressed up against the window. I have to extricate her driver's license from her wallet to find out her address. She snores softly as we cross Manhattan and fly up Park Avenue.

The taxi pulls up to Mimi's building, a luxury high-rise on the corner of Seventy-fifth and Park. Mimi topples out, and the doorman catches her forearm. As we pull away, I spot my boss in the rearview mirror, removing the doorman's cap and running her fingers through his hair. Oh dear. I bury this nugget in the let's-try-and-forget-this-ever-happened portion of my brain, and then do my best not to imagine Mimi leaning over the lip of her toilet and vomiting for the rest of the night.

"Park Slope, Brooklyn," I tell the driver, and then start scrolling through e-mail. I open one from Julia, which contains a photo of her holding a hamster, her own hand uncurling the creature's tiny paw into a wave. She knows a hamster is my idea of the perfect pet, cute and cuddly, but also pocket-sized and manageable—no big messes or wild personalities to contend with. Julia has banned all animals from our home, her rationale being, I leave my work at work, so why can't she, too? A fair point, although I don't think she realizes how many middle-of-the-night hours I spend awake worrying about my job.

Just as I suspect, the hamster photo is a teaser for yet another sperm donor option. I scroll down, and this one reads like the dating profiles I sometimes see up on coworkers' computer screens:

He loves horror movies and crime novels, he appreciates a well-placed pun, and he rolls his eyes at all the gluten-free, farm-to-table, and caveman diet trends that seem to take hold of our culture for six months at a time. I laugh out loud at the last part (Julia is often imposing these fads on our home). I catch myself wondering when the guy and I can grab drinks, though, not whether I'd like his genetic material to make up half of my theoretical child.

I peer out the cab window and see we're soaring over the Manhattan Bridge. I take in the New York City skyline, the glistening East River, Lady Liberty. I enjoy the same sights every morning on my way to the office, and again each evening on my commute home—and amazingly, all it usually costs me is the couple of bucks for the subway ride. I often wish I could figure out how to translate this concept of "the best things in life are free (or nearly so)" to my job; it would be much easier to stick to the budget.

I'm feeling anxious, and I fear it's due to more than the four stiff drinks swirling around my bloodstream. I try to shake the image of Mimi slurring her words and slipping off her barstool, and instead focus on the familiar panorama. I am a creature of habit, and just as I depend on my elliptical-and-NPR morning routine and my very intricate, very effective filing system at work, I rely upon this twice-daily view of New York City to ground me and make me feel, if only for a glimpse, that all is right with the world.

7

Drew Hardaway, Photo Editor

Now that a new regime has begun, we're being extra careful, Mark and I. I make sure to put at least three seats between us in the art department's daily meetings. Mimi has taken to dropping in "for a listen," and then it becomes like a poorly acted play, all of us delivering stilted lines as we strain to sound dazzling and visionary. I avoid Mark's eyes for fear of breaking character and collapsing into giggles.

"Which stories are on tap today?" Mimi asks, propping herself on the table's edge next to Mark.

"We were talking about October, figuring out visual concepts for the features," says Mark. Mimi's ass is perched inches from his hands, which he usually flails around in large mad-scientist-like gestures, but now he's set them folded on the table. He looks like he's wearing a straitjacket. "We already nailed down the free stuff shoot. Drew's on it."

My niche at *Hers* has become still shots of products for the give-away and shopping pages. Pretty boring, but it also leaves me lots of time to zone out and think about my personal photo projects, or whatever else is on my mind. This gig has been great. Before *Hers*, I was sick to death of my starving-artist diet of Ramen noodles and dry cereal, not to mention my roach-infested digs in Bushwick. And ever since Debbie learned I like to cook, she sometimes sends me home with leftover ingredients from her recipes: half a pint of cherries, most of a wedge of Asiago, and last week a few ounces of truffle oil (I think the latter was just plain charity, since oil keeps). It's a pretty good deal.

Mimi picks up the list of October features. "Ooh, the cheaters story! What are you guys thinking for that?" I silently root for Mark to blurt out something brilliant. He's a genius in his sleek, minimalist way—I first fell for him when he showed me his series of stark black-and-white shots of suspension bridges—but it's becoming clear that his design vision does not complement Mimi's more-is-more sensibility. Rumors are flying about who's interviewing to replace him. This is something he and I do not discuss.

Mark is still stammering. I hesitate before breaking in: "How about we shoot traditional-looking portraits of each married couple along with the person one of them is having the affair with? Like they can wear matching outfits and pose in those ridiculous Sears kind of setups, and they'll all be smiling. But underneath the smiles you'll be able to tell, for example, that the wife is furious, and the husband is all tense, and the other woman is triumphant, or sexually satisfied, or something like that. If the real people won't do it, we can use actors." I'm not sure where this concept came from but, looking down at my hands, I'm thinking it might not be such a terrible idea. For the tenth time this week I promise myself to stop biting my nails.

"Love!" says Mimi. "She's got the plan. Mark, let's schedule the shoot." She slaps our creative director, and my secret boyfriend, on the shoulder; it's playful, but I happen to know he bruises easily.

This office runs on meetings. Meetings to set deadlines, meetings to pitch ideas, meetings to review ideas, meetings to schedule more meetings. On my first day at *Hers* about a year ago, I recognized a fellow sensitive soul in Mark, and to survive this onslaught of meetings with some semblance of our spirits intact, the two of us began exchanging glances; they translated to "When will she give it a rest already?" and "Think it's safe to take a little nap?" and "Please wake me up when this is over." It all began harmlessly, until six months ago, when I was going through a breakup and started noticing Mark's eyes: intense and smoldering, like a soap opera star's. Apparently Mark liked the looks of me, too. Eventually our intrameeting looks came to mean "Meet me in the supply closet—*stat.*"

It's a doubleheader today: After the art meeting is a full staff one to discuss the notorious November relaunch, when everything the *Hers* brand has been up to this point will be crumpled up and tossed in the trash, and we'll reinvent ourselves into a brand-new, suitable-to-sell-tons-of-ads magazine. At least, that's the idea. I've wagered a bet with Mark that the redesign will be nothing more than a handful of tweaks that Mimi will pass off as a grand revolution.

I arrive early to the conference room and position myself against the back wall, far from the thin pane of glass that's the only thing separating us from air, nine stories high. The seating arrangement is a clear marker of hierarchy. The top editors and directors all seat themselves at the table—the higher up in editorial, the closer to the front—and the art senior staff sits at the other end; we peons perch ourselves on the ledges around the perimeter, or hover in the back. Even those of us who find this pecking-order organization reminiscent of the middle school cafeteria have fallen in line.

At least we used to. Today the new guy, Jonathan, commits *Hers* blasphemy. (Ever since Mr. Powder Puff showed up I've been teasing Mark about his new male colleague, someone to talk football with. Mark, possessing perhaps even less knowledge about the sport than Jonathan, and sensitive about it, doesn't find this very funny.) Jonathan saunters right up to the front of the table and plants himself in Abby's usual chair. Victoria then seats herself next to Jonathan, surprising no one in her displacement of Leah. The rest of us file in, more or less in our appropriate places, until just one spot remains at the table. Laura and Leah are the last ones to enter, and Laura nonchalantly plants herself at the table—the first assistant who's ever dared such a move—leaving Leah, our co-second-in-command, seatless. Zoe gasps. I'm surprised at how shocked I feel, too. As inane as the seating politics are, I'm no fan of this Laura character, whom I overheard telling Mimi that she thinks the whole magazine looks flat. *It is flat, you idiot,* I wanted to blurt out. *A magazine page is two-dimensional.*

Mark glances in my direction, his demeanor stark. He's usually game to poke fun of the seating silliness, but today he looks staid sitting at the head of the art side of the table, proud to have claimed his position, however tenuous.

"OK, announcements first," says Leah, who's taken the seating blow in stride and is standing at the front of the room to reestablish her authority. (Mimi is absent, taping a *Today* show segment based on a *Hers* story about the best ways to prevent heart disease, a story commissioned and edited by her predecessor.) "Mimi has decided that the big feature for the relaunch will be about extreme plastic surgery." Leah makes no effort to mask her distaste at what she's saying.

"You guys," says Jonathan, "we found moms across the country who had at least ten procedures each. We're going to do a before-and-after kind of thing, and explain each procedure and whether or not you should do it, too."

"Actually, it'll be more along the lines of 'don't try this at home,' " says Leah. "These women are narcissistic freaks. The story will be a cautionary tale."

Laura jumps in: "Not necessarily, right? I bet some of our readers are eager to hear which surgeries might make sense for their lifestyles."

"I can manage the photo shoots," I blurt out. All eyes land on me, and I feel my skin sprout up with goose bumps.

"That's the spirit, Drew," says Victoria. Abby marks down the update on her clipboard, registering no reaction. Mark is less subtle, but I avoid his condescending stare. Something about photographing women with so many fake parts intrigues me. I picture shooting them like dolls, limbs stiff and expressions fixed, the backdrop a kind of real-life Barbie's Dreamhouse meets horror film set. Maybe we can find a crazy, plastic-surgeried man to play Ken.

"I have an announcement to add," says Abby. "I just got word that GladWare and Crystal Light are upping their advertising for November, so we'll be blowing out the Thanksgiving entertaining package into a ten-page feature, like a mini-magazine within the magazine. We'll supplement our usual coverage with leftovers recipes and low-cal cocktails for cold weather."

"Deborah says she'll have recipes to me for editing by end-of-week," Victoria says. I happen to be glancing at Leah just then, and in one flash I see her expression morph from outrage to hurt and back to neutral, then she fixes on a smile so bright one might mistake the water pooling in her eyes for a twinkle. I guess no one told Leah that Victoria was taking over as editor of the food coverage.

"Ahem, and for those of you who need a cocktail today," Debbie says, "and I'm guessing that's everyone"—she eyes Leah—"I'll be bringing down Hot Toddies and Dark and Stormys this afternoon for testing."

"Fun!" says Victoria. "Though let's push back the happy hour until after six, so everyone can get all of their work done beforehand."

Debbie nods, but at four o'clock on the dot she appears in the office carrying a large tray of drinks. Only Victoria and Laura remain at their desks.

I'm halfway through my Dark and Stormy when Jane approaches, wielding a page layout. "So I've only got room for about ninety-seven words here," she says, pointing to a text box that easily fits two hundred words. "Do we really need this enormous image monopolizing the page?"

"That's one of our standard layouts, Jane." Of course she knows this already; she's been producing the love and marriage section for years, and there's the same room for text that there always is on a one-pager.

"Can I please have space for just a few more sentences, or

maybe a teensy extra paragraph? Pretty please!" I know I'm probably being paranoid, but I imagine in Jane's plea the covert message: *You know what I know.* Namely, about Mark and me.

I cave: "Sure, no problem." As I rejigger Jane's layout, shrinking the photo to tiny and expanding the text box so that the page looks cramped and uninviting, I remind myself that at any point Jane could sabotage my relationship with Mark. A few months ago, after Mark had finally broken up with his girlfriend, and just when we were starting to relax out in public together, we had the luck of running into Jane at the movies, the two of us holding hands no less. I rambled on about who knows what—I can picture myself laughing too loudly and making a dumb pun about the film's title. And although Jane gave me the "lips zipped" signal when we parted ways, I've been nervous, and sucking up to her, ever since. Coworker dating is prohibited at Schmidt & Delancey.

When I present the new layout to Jane, I find myself complimenting her skirt. "Thanks," she says, all smiles.

I'm browsing the boxes of off-brand sandwich cookies and powdered milk, waiting for Mark in our postwork meeting spot, the 99-cent store in the subway station below the office. We're careful never to leave work together.

Mark barges in. "Fucking *Me-me-me*," he says, referring to our new boss by the nickname he's coined for her; he believes himself very clever.

"Well, hello to you, too." I peck him on the cheek.

"She calls me into her office to talk about the redesign. She shows me tear sheets from *Starstruck* and *Teeny Bopped* and *OMG*. The pages were so garish, I practically had a seizure right there at her desk. I actually asked if she was joking. Turns out, that load of garbage is what she wants us to aspire to for the redesign."

"Well, she did show us that data about how *OMG* is the other magazine *Hers* subscribers are most likely to buy. Our readers are not exactly *New Yorker* fans."

"Our readers are idiots, just like Mimi! *Idiots!*" He shouts it, making a passing woman flinch. Mark sighs and snatches a package of Hostess Sno Balls. I happen to know this is the reason he designated the 99-cent store our covert meeting spot. He would never admit it, much less let anyone else catch him eating the hyper-processed snack; after all, he prides himself on his rarefied diet of artisanal farmer's market fare. My eating habits are not nearly as virtuous, but just glancing at a Sno Ball gives me a sugar headache, that cloying pressure that permeates the brain.

"Let's go," Mark says, tearing open the cake's package. The cellophane squeak sends a shiver down my spine.

The next morning, Mark is fired. He emerges from Mimi's office fuming. I am technically his employee, so I hope it doesn't look remarkable that he immediately calls me into his office.

"That *Me-me-me* Walsh possesses a complete and utter lack of taste," he says. "And our readers are total morons who couldn't recognize fine design if it showed up and magically made over their living rooms." Mark sits there like a lump as he rants and raves, and meanwhile he has an hour to pack up all his belongings. "I am so happy, I am goddamn thrilled to be free of this fucking place, to never have to return to this shithole ever again."

I start clearing out Mark's desk drawers, zoning out the rest of his diatribe and saying not a word. I don't respond to his freak-out, nor do I point out that Mimi seems to be noticing and appreciating my taste. I don't mention that I am still employed at this so-called shithole, or that I have already filled three boxes to Mark's zero. Never mind the fact that now we can finally be open about our relationship. I keep my mouth shut then, and also an hour after Mark is gone when Lynn, the new creative director, moves into his cleared-out office, and also that night when I arrive home and Mark shouts out hello.

He's in the living room, slapping thick swaths of paint onto a canvas. Flecks of red and green speckle the carpet. The guy who will pick a fight over a lack of a coaster under a glass apparently hasn't laid down a drop cloth before deciding to pull a Jackson Pollock. An empty wine bottle rests atop the side table. Mark says something, but I can barely hear him over the music: Nirvana.

"What?!" I yell.

"I said, how was your day?" he shouts back.

"Fine." I wander into the living room. "Louisa's still gone, Laura's still a total ice queen, the coffee machine's still acting up, and the guy I love got canned." I leave out the they-hired-your-replacement part. "New day, same old crap."

"Yeah?" Mark puts down his brush and pulls me down onto the couch.

"We should crack a window," I say, feeling suddenly light-headed from the paint fumes, like my brain is filling with soap-suds. Mark's fingers are working at the buttons on my shirt. "And how was your day?" I ask.

"Shitty commute, boring meetings, bad coffee. But I scored a surprise afternoon off." He kisses me, his breath ripe.

"And then you got wasted, huh?"

"And then I got wasted." His hand inches up my skirt. "Now, no more talking, my sweet spice."

Mark's drunken snores are like the honks of an 18-wheeler, bellowing over the wheezing air conditioner. I give up on sleep and instead watch the night shadows shift from one menacing shape into another on the wall. When I moved into Mark's place three months ago, I painted these walls slate gray. I brought hardly anything with me besides my clothes, my cameras, and my TV, so the painting was my one special thing, the one marker that this space would become my home, too. It was a new beginning, a fresh coat over the pale yellow that Mark had shared with his ex. But now I wonder what I was thinking; the gray looks dreary and ominous, and I feel as if the walls might start closing in on me.

Anxious thoughts fling about my head like pinballs, jolting me further and further from the possibility of sleep. I forfeit exactly half of my salary to Mark each month, which comes to just over a third of our rent, and now I wonder how much Mark has saved up, and how much severance he'll receive; he is notoriously cagey about money. I hoped to stay at *Hers* for another few months, socking away enough to be able to quit and then refocus on my own art or try something else; but now I fear how essential my regular paycheck will be. I wonder if I'll have to dip into my savings, which are meager. I wonder how long it will take Mark to find a new job, and how much drunken finger painting he'll have to get out of his system before he even begins looking. I wonder how long before I'll be able to share anything substantial about my workday without considering how it will affect my boyfriend's feelings. I'm starting to tremble. For fear that I might emit a howling scream à la Munch, I grab my camera. I start snapping photos, first of the shadowy shapes on the wall and then of Mark sleeping, curled up on his side, mouth agape. Perhaps there's some artistic potential to this situation.

"I love this place because the waiters are all so darn fuckable and they humor you by pretending they'd actually consider taking you to bed." Lynn, Mark's replacement and my new boss, is treating me to lunch at Applebee's on her third day. "Look at that one's fresh buns," she says, tittering and peeking out from behind her menu at a waiter carrying a bread basket.

Lynn wears a gauzy floral dress that floats behind her when she walks, or, more accurately, glides. Gemstones speckle her boxy pumps, and delicate silver bangles climb up her forearms. Pendant earrings reach nearly to her shoulders, over which is draped a colorful knit scarf, and her shock of orange hair is slicked back from her head like a flame. Suffice it to say her look is not exactly standard Schmidt & Delancey.

"You have got to try the breadsticks," she says. "They're both delectable and abundant—finish one basket and another arrives without delay. Like magic!" Up until an hour ago, I was certain that no Manhattan resident had ever stepped foot in the Applebee's in Times Square. "This is my absolute favorite restaurant," Lynn says, and I can't tell if she's screwing with me. "I'm from Ohio, you know."

I didn't know. When Mimi introduced Lynn to the staff, she didn't go through the usual résumé rundown, and the rumors of Lynn's mysterious past are rampant: She taught graphic design to women prisoners at a correctional facility upstate; or she oversaw the catalogs for Bergdorf's back in the nineties; or she was selling her abstract paintings at a roadside farmer's stand in the Poconos when a headhunter from a major advertising agency discovered her; or she's an ex-con herself. Google has proved surprisingly reticent on the matter. That Lynn is not of the magazine world is as clear as the glass of water she's now tapping at with her spoon.

"Speech! Speech!" she announces. "OK, I know I'm new, and that life is a little wacky back at the ranch, what with folks getting the ax left and right." She beckons the waiter, keeping her glass held aloft. "We'll have the spinach artichoke dip and the classic wings for the table. We're just going to have to make like glue and ride out this storm and see where the chips land, OK?" The server looks confused, like this convoluted pep talk is part of our order, and Lynn shoos him away. "I'm not saying we'll all make it through the battle with all our limbs intact, but we've got to dig out our little foxholes and try. And that means choosing the most dynamic photos to go on page and designing the most wow-a-riffic layouts we can possibly create, OK?" I nod, and we clink our water glasses. "Don't worry, I'll order us a round of Bahama Mamas on the double," she adds.

Back in the office and both of us a little drunk, Lynn shows me the new, brighter palette we'll be working with for the redesign. I'm scrolling through the photos for the cheaters story—the shoot was yesterday—altering the color on the subjects' clothing and eyes so the pictures pop in a kitschy retro way, when my phone rings. My home number flashes up; it's a strange sight on my work phone.

"Hi. I can't find my magnet," Mark says. "You know, 'Earth' minus 'art' is just 'eh.' Last I saw it was in my office."

I roll my eyes. I've always thought that magnet was moronic. "OK. And?"

"Well, can you check if it's still in my office?" My stomach flips. I haven't yet told Mark that *his* office is under new management.

"Maybe later, love. I'm in the middle of something right now."

"I know, you're very busy with your long, important to-do list at your big, fancy job. Such a busy little bee." I can't tell if he's purposely being mean or if he's just drunk again. I hear the TV on in the background. Mark didn't own a television before I moved in, and I've never seen him pick up the remote, much less turn it on; I'm curious what he's found to watch. "Look, I'm sorry," he says, switching to the sweet, quiet tone that always gets me. "That magnet is just very important to me and I'd love to get it back."

"I'll see what I can do. Make sure you eat something today, OK?"

"I will. Bye, love."

"Bye," I say, then realize Jane is standing by my desk.

"*Psst*, was that Mark?" she whispers. "How is he?"

"Driving me crazy at the moment." I keep my voice low. "He's throwing a fit about losing a magnet with some stupid catchphrase on it."

"Oh, the one about art? I thought that was so clever." I remember that Jane's cubicle walls are plastered with inspirational quotes from important female journalists.

"He's transformed the living room into a painter's studio," I say. "I come home and he's working on these big, crazy art projects, stuff he never did when he was toiling away here. So that could be good, I guess. Though he's pretty much replaced all food intake with alcohol."

"I don't blame him, considering. When Jacob and I were dating, all it took was his boss shooting him a dirty look and he'd turn to a bottle of Jack and slip into a funk for the whole night."

"It's hard," I say, thinking it's a good thing Jane is no longer with that guy.

"And how are you doing?" she asks.

"Shitty, I guess. Or fine. I don't know. It's been kind of nice to not have to walk around hiding our relationship all day."

"I bet. Hey, can I ask you a personal question?"

"Okay," I say tentatively.

"I've never been into older guys myself. So what's the appeal—is it like a power thing, or a daddy thing?"

"Thank you for your astute Psych 101 insights, Jane," I say, feeling my stomach turn over despite myself. I think about how my father has always referred to my work as "your little pictures." Mark examines each of my photographs like it's hanging on the wall at the Met.

"Sorry, that was over the line," Jane says. "It's just that I'm editing a story about couple dynamics and what makes people stay in love. Jacob was six months younger than me, and I'm starting to think one of our problems was that I was older and somehow made him feel emasculated."

"Believe me," I say, "that can be an issue even if a guy's fifteen years older *and* your boss."

"The plot of like half the romances out there is some brilliant boss seducing his innocent little underling. Or a genius professor falling for his eager young student. It works because he's the one in charge, right?"

"I'm guessing those stories are all written by men, or at least *for* men," I say. "Notice how the brilliant boss never gets fired? If he did, the heroine would probably find him even more irresistible because he's all vulnerable and stuff. Utterly the stuff of male fantasy."

"Hmm. Well, if it's the power thing you're into, you could always shack up with Lynn now."

"There's a solution," I say, laughing at the thought. For the first time it feels like a relief to have a coworker who knows about Mark and me.

I knock on Lynn's office door, and she waves me in. "I'm hoping we can talk about the images for the shopping pages," I say, and then rattle on for five minutes, reestablishing the most basic points about optimal lighting and camera angle. Meanwhile, I'm glancing around furtively in search of Mark's keepsake. No dice.

On my way out I conjure up the courage to ask Lynn directly: "Oh, hey, did you happen to see a little green magnet in here, up on the shelf over there?"

"Yessiree, let me see if I can find it." Lynn spins in her chair. "Did your lover leave it?"

I freeze. Lynn laughs. "Oh, relax," she says. "Listen, I respect the tricky position you're in, and I commend the professionalism you've displayed in the face of it."

"Uh, thanks." *Who told her?* I wonder. *Surely not Jane.*

"Here's my advice: Break the toilet so he can show off his manliness by fixing it. And when you're cooking dinner, burn the potatoes or undercook the pasta so he can feel superior. Most important, keep buttoned up about your work achievements—of which I can tell there will be many. Ah, here it is." Lynn hands me the magnet, pats me on the shoulder, then shoos me out.

As I pass Mimi's office, she beckons me in. She has her shiny pink stilettos propped up on the desk, the phone receiver cradled between her cheek and shoulder, and a lock of hair twirling between her fingers. "Yes, darling," she says into the receiver, gesturing for me to take a seat. "Let me talk to her. Hello, my little-wittle Pookie bear. Did you enjoy your playgroup in the park and your big, special, yummy bone today? I know, Mommy will be home soon. I know. Ruff, ruff!" Mimi hangs up, and I try to mask my horror. "Oh, that was just Pookie, my dear sweet puggle-wuggle. She gets lonely at home with just the sitter"—*a dog sitter?!*—"so I have to call and let her know she's still loved by her mommy. Look at how beautiful." She hands me a photo: It's Mimi pretty much making out with a slobbery dog. The lighting is terrible.

"Precious," I say, wanting to gag.

"Now, I was hoping to touch base since I know you have a new boss all of a sudden. I see a great future for you here at *Hers*, and I believe Lynn will be a wonderful mentor."

"Thanks. It was nice of her to take me out to lunch." I'm not sure why I'm suddenly nervous.

"Yes, she's very into 'team building,' " Mimi says, miming air

quotes and rolling her eyes. "Anyway, she's a newbie in our magazine milieu, so please don't hesitate to let me know if you're having any particular problems, OK?" I think Mimi is suggesting I
should feel free to rat out my boss, though I can't be sure. I nod.

"Great, that's settled then." She hunches over to examine a layout on her desk, a fashion story about autumn accessories. I edited
the opener photo—a big, splashy image of a girl in a chunky scarf,
a crocheted bag slung across her shoulder; she's at a street fair,
holding up her red-gloved hands as if to show off her new purchase
and also wave to the reader. "Gorgeous shot," Mimi says, scribbling red notes across the page. "Oh, and I think it's better for
everyone that we're rid of Mark now. We can't have staffers in
management positions chasing after their underlings, now, can
we?" She looks up and fixes her gaze on me, just long enough to
see how petrified I am, then bows her head back to the layout.

"Hmm, this headline won't do," she says, seemingly to herself.
I watch as she exes out "Go big for fall!" and in its place scrawls
"Caught—red-handed!"

"Here, why don't you bring this over to Lynn?" Mimi hands me
the page, and I skulk out of her office, sweating through my shirt.

That evening, it's possible I'm trying to assuage my guilt when
I pop in the 99-cent store and buy a Sno Ball for my boyfriend. Although if it's true, or even partly true, that Mimi canned Mark because she discovered our relationship (who the heck knows how),
there's no way that plying him with snack food is going to right
that wrong.

When I arrive home, Mark glances disinterestedly at the cellophane package before turning back to his canvas. The Sno Ball sits
on the counter sealed and untouched for longer than I've ever
seen Mark ignore one of those things: one night, then a full day,
then a week, then longer. There are so many preservatives in the
snack that I think—*I wish*—it might outlast my feelings of blame.
In fact, I imagine it could outlast this whole work drama, and possibly Mark's and my entire relationship, and maybe even Mimi's

reign over the magazine. I picture the Sno Ball sitting on the counter years from now—when *Hers* will likely feel to me like a distant, blurry memory, when hopefully I will have moved on to bigger, better things—that plump, pink half ball still intact, its sweet, pillowy give still appetizing to a select few. It's creepy but also comforting to imagine, so I let the Sno Ball be.

8

Liz Walker, Beauty Editor

Baby Matilda has just awoken, and she's sleepy-calm after her late-morning nap. Only her big eyes stir. Watching them dart around to follow the sunlight dappling through the blinds, I find it doesn't matter that I haven't put on makeup in weeks or that my hair is a greasy mop or that I'm still stalling on the diet I said I'd start two months ago, a few weeks after I gave birth. I greet Matilda's return to the waking world like a miracle, and each of her coos and gurgles seems like a sacred message meant just for me. At this hour, my sleeplessness is like a wispy dream (as opposed to later in the day, when the crush of exhaustion threatens to bury me and makes me lust after sleep like I used to crave sex). As the sun reaches toward its crest in the sky, casting its warm spotlight upon my baby and me through the bay window, I'm open to any possibility. This is my favorite time of day.

I strap Matilda snuggly-close onto my chest and we drift from coffee shop to farmer's market to grocery store. We wander into boutiques where I dangle pretty trinkets in front of my baby's button nose, we observe the dog run and I whisper "woof, woof" in her tiny ear, and we sit in the community garden where I recite Mary Oliver poems to her.

Jake and I have lived in our Cobble Hill brownstone for more than two years, yet only within the past three months have I learned the names of the guys who man the deli and forged friendships with my neighbors. Mrs. Golden is a particular delight; she must be eighty-five, her face so shriveled that even her wrinkles have wrinkles. Trading conversation on our side-by-side stoops has made me understand how age isn't just something to be fended off with the right potions and powders, how the physical signs of growing older can actually indicate wisdom and even beauty. (When I shared this revelation with my husband, he responded that most seven-year-olds have figured this out; well, it's not my fault that neither of my grandmothers was particularly nice or that millions of Americans are desperate to buy the promise of youth that I just happen to be very good at selling.)

Occasionally I hear a faint echo in my head, the old me begging the questions: *What is happening to you, Elizabeth Walker? Whom have you become?*

When Jake reunites with baby and me at the end of each weekday, I set out a simple meal and we drink wine as Tilly lolls in her cradle at our feet. Though she rarely sleeps, she rarely cries, either. She is a happy, curious baby, and I am a happy mother, incurious about my bliss. The bottles of herbs and potions I preemptively bought to ward off postpartum depression remain sealed in the back of the kitchen cabinet. Next to motherhood, maternity leave is quite possibly the best thing that's ever happened to me.

I didn't imagine it this way—not at all. Throughout my pregnancy I was terrified, collapsing into tears as Leah gave me tutorials on how to work a breast pump, as I shopped endlessly for baby "essentials" that seemed to fill every nook of my formerly minimalist apartment, as my stomach ballooned along with the rest of me and my breasts and feet swelled up into pale, veiny monsters. Jake joked that I'd still be at the office turning in copy when my water broke, and that I'd have to be torn from my desk in order to give birth. He wanted to bet me that I'd return to *Hers* early from maternity leave, but I wouldn't shake on it, secretly fearing he might be right. I felt petrified by the idea of three months at home alone with a baby—no brainstorm meetings, no deskside makeovers, no product launch events.

What I never could have pictured was how pretty the light would look filtering through the nursery in the late morning; I'd never before been home for it. I didn't know the sublime joy of a quiet house, a soft lullaby, a baby just stirring awake. I didn't understand that late nights at the office reworking a story couldn't hold a candle to the sense of accomplishment and sweet relief of getting a baby to finally go down after a long day. I had no idea.

The phone rings. "Hi, cutie, just checking in." It's Jake. Although he's just ten miles north at his law firm in midtown, pleading cases and writing depositions, he may as well be a continent away. "What are my ladies up to?"

"Tilly's feeding," I say, "and I am planting a kiss on the top of her perfect fuzzball of a head."

"Send a hello to my sweet girl."

"Hello from Matilda. What's up with Daddy?"

"Oh, nothing. Did you hear Mark got canned from *Hers?*"

"I didn't hear that," I say. "How awful for him." But I don't really feel awful; I feel pleasantly numb. Whenever someone tells me about the upheaval happening back at the office, the usurping of power and the reign of terror that has begun in my absence, I have an urge to open Matilda's jewelry box and lose myself in to the tinkling tune of "Someday My Prince Will Come," to watch the ballerina spin and spin and spin. It's as if there's a blockage in my brain, something that stops all absorption of *Hers*-related news.

"I'm taking him out for drinks tonight," Jake says, "so I'll probably be home late."

"OK, I understand," I say, because I know it's what I ought to. I glance at the chicken I'd been looking forward to roasting for dinner and serving with sweet potatoes and salad; its raw sliminess now turns my stomach. "Pass along a hug from me to Mark."

I do feel sympathy for Mark. He's a quiet, sweet soul, and he and Louisa enjoyed a nice pas de deux. He doesn't seem cut out for the kind of battle I hear is now being waged at *Hers*. I actually owe my marriage to Mark: He first introduced me to Jake, his college roommate, at a happy hour event three years ago this fall. I remember feeling relieved to learn that our sensitive creative director had this guy Jake to look out for him, Jake who appeared to be so much sturdier and better equipped to navigate the world. Jake and I began dating immediately, we were married a year later, and ever since he looks out for me, and now Tilly, too. The thought brings me back to my lovely baby-makes-three reverie, and I lift Matilda into my arms and dance us around the kitchen, humming, "Someday your prince will come."

The call from Leah is inevitable. In one breath she blurts out, "Mark took the fall, and Mimi replaced him with this total nut from East Nowhere who was settling into his office within about seven minutes of him leaving." I hear the thud of the phone dropping, then Leah reprimanding a daughter, who apparently knocked something over. It must be one of her at-home days. Every time I talk to Leah I thank the universe that I have one baby, not three. Leah retrieves the phone and continues: "And now that I've ceded my office to that C-U-next-Tuesday—excuse my language—I'm seeing the new guy, Jonathan, eye your beauty closet, too. I'll bet he weasels his way in, supposedly just for the rest of your time off, but then gets to stay after you're back, too."

"Oh, Leah, I'm sure this Jonathan and I will get along fine. Drew sent me the stills from that jungle makeup shoot, and I thought it looked fun! He seems very talented."

"Liz, you have no flipping idea. Every day it's something new: Mimi's assistant, Laura, claimed the office Web cam was acting up so they didn't include me in today's planning meeting. Mimi tells me she's redistributing some of my pages to other people, with the justification that I have so much going on at home—"

"But that's true, isn't it? You do have a ton happening at home." Just then I hear something crash to the ground over the line.

"*Shoot!* Sorry. But that's not the point, Liz! It isn't Mimi's right, and it's certainly not Victoria's right, to call out what's going on in my personal life as a rationalization for shrinking my professional duties."

"Oh," I say, unsure if I'm grasping the nuances of the drama. I've never met any of these people.

"How much longer until you're back, anyway?"

"Um." I consult a calendar; my return date of "Monday, July 2" is circled in red. "A week. Wow, that flew by."

"You better get into fighting shape. It's a war zone out here."

"Thanks for the warning." We hang up, and Leah's words spark me to queue up the mommy yoga DVD she gifted me at my baby shower; she swore the workout made her feel like Superwoman after the births of her triplets. But as I bend and twist into the poses with names like Warrior and Eagle and Cobra, I feel the opposite: weak and vulnerable. Standing unsteadily on one foot, I imagine this Mimi character flicking me in the ribs and sending me toppling over. I retreat into child's pose, where I remain for the rest of the routine.

Exercise calls for a treat, so I strap Matilda into her harness and set out into the neighborhood, intent on a chai tea. When I used to pop into the corner coffee shop before boarding the subway for work, it was all rushing commuters, their bodies cloaked in professional attire and their faces a dead giveaway for the particular day of the week—downcast signaled Monday, fatigued meant Wednesday, impatient and hopeful was Friday. But late afternoon, the coffee shop resembles a postapocalyptic world where only women and babies have survived, not a baritone or bass voice within earshot. I season my drink with shakes of vanilla powder, and then navigate the stroller maze to find a free seat.

"Excuse me, is that chair taken?" I ask, spotting the lone woman without a baby in tow at her table. She turns to face me, and I gasp. "Louisa!" My old boss's hair is pulled back in a ponytail to reveal a bare, drawn face. Her cheeks have hollowed out. "What are you doing here?" I blurt it out before I realize what I've said. I stop myself from adding, "Is today a holiday?"

"Hi, Liz. I live in the neighborhood, remember?"

"Oh, right." I do remember. When Louisa bought her brownstone in Carroll Gardens a couple of years back, I ogled the online listing like porn—nine rooms, a giant backyard, all for a cool $2.6

million. I wonder how long her severance will cover the mortgage payments.

"I'm mortified to run into you while wearing flip-flops," she says, reaching to close her laptop; I glance a résumé on the screen before it darkens. "And who's this little one?"

"Louisa, meet Matilda. She's eleven weeks old today. Say hello, Tilly." I wave my baby's hand, and Louisa smoothes down the patch of peach fuzz on her head.

"She's beautiful. And how are you?"

"I'm great."

"Well, that's great." She eyes me warily. "You know, when I had my kids, I remember thinking I'd have a grand old time during maternity leave."

"I'm sure."

"But boy, was I miserable. I was so unsure of myself and crazy with cabin fever, covered in formula and rash ointment and all manner of bodily fluid. I think I held a countdown to when I could get back to work and civilization. You probably know exactly what I mean." I force a nod, recalling my dwindling time left at home with Tilly: just seven precious days.

"Last time I saw you, you were out to here," Louisa says, extending her arms.

"I know I haven't exactly shed all the weight yet." I'm suddenly self-conscious of the lingering belly fat that has hardly bothered me until now.

"Nonsense," Louisa says, although I imagine she was back to a flat stomach eight weeks postpartum. "All I meant was, a lot can change in a short time."

My former boss looks so pale, and I'm stricken with shame: to have thought Louisa would be tuned in to the progress of my post-pregnancy weight loss! "Shoot, I'm so sorry," I say. "I mean, about what happened, I would've sent a note or a card, but—"

"Oh, stop. It's all right, seriously. Listen, if you're an editor in chief, here are your options: you stick around till you croak, you move on up to the corporate suite, or you get fired. That's the nature of the business."

"Well, everyone misses you desperately, from what I hear," I say. "I confess I'm not looking forward to the return to the office. Do you want to just meet here every day instead and we can start our own writer-mom coffee klatch?" Louisa smiles, humoring me; I'm not serious, but this is her reality now. "So, I've got to get the little one home for naptime," I say. "If there's ever anything I can do . . ." I trail off, knowing how lame the offer sounds.

"Thank you, Liz. Congrats again on motherhood, and good luck on the return. Do me a favor and spit in Mimi's coffee once in a while." She has a glint in her eye. "I'm not going to say, 'Just kidding.' "

We exchange kisses on the cheek; hers is thin and cool like a Band-Aid. "Bye, dear," she says.

I bounce Matilda out the door, singsonging, "Good girl for not crying in front of the boss lady. Good, good girl."

Seven more good nights, seven more morning cuddles, seven more midafternoon jaunts to the coffee shop to masquerade among the stay-at-home moms, and then it's back to the grind. I buy a DVF wraparound for the occasion, since they're supposed to be slimming, and anyway I can't yet fit into the rest of my office wardrobe.

Everyone lies and tells me how skinny I look, even the mysterious new ones—Laura and Victoria and Jonathan and what seems like a college sorority's worth of freelancers—none of whom saw me pre-baby.

"Knock, knock." I enter Mimi's office to meet her.

"And she exists in the flesh! Hello, Elizabeth." Mimi reaches across her desk and lays her hand across my stomach before I even have the chance to suck in. "I always wanted to know what happens to that area after you have a baby," she says, as if that's an appropriate explanation for groping my midsection ten seconds after meeting me for the first time. "Not so bad, really. Anyway, I hope you enjoyed your extended vacation, and welcome back. Time to get to work!" We shake hands, and before I can respond, her assistant is ushering me out.

Midday, Jonathan appears in my office and hands me a business card. "I know motherhood can take a real toll on you physically." *He does?* "So I made you an appointment." I examine the card—a dermatologist. "Botox," he whispers. I'm thirty-one years old. Has it come to this?

Being back at work is like living in a dream, the one where you think you recognize your whereabouts, but key details and people are changed; the office seems both normal and not. We still use colored cover sheets to route our ideas and our first drafts and our revises, but all the colors have changed: pinks where we used to use yellows, blues for the old greens, a sort of magenta that looks like our former red but is for art notes not revises, as if to deliberately confuse members of the old staff. "Hey, Laura," I say, approaching her cubicle. "I know I asked you this before, but would you please remind me which color corresponds with first drafts?"

She sighs. "I'm superswamped right now. I'll review it with you later." I thought she was an assistant, but surely she wouldn't be talking to me this way if she were. I'm suddenly doubting everything I know.

Right as I'm about to raise a point in a meeting, my breasts begin to leak. I feel the milk drippy-cold against my skin, and it makes me shiver. "Excuse me," I say, as if I spoke up to ask for the bathroom pass instead of to contribute a thought. I escape to the supply closet with my pump, where I set about squeezing my breasts into ugly, unnatural shapes. A sob escapes my chest. Then I'm breaking down into tears, thinking, *I'm milking myself like a cow. I am a cow. A cow in a supply closet.*

When I relate this incident to Jake that night, he laughs. I'm outraged. "It's not funny. You have no idea what it's like!"

"You're right, I don't," he says. "But it *is* funny." The gulping tears return, as if they just retreated temporarily in my throat. "Oh, cutie. If it's that bad, why don't you quit? Or try to get laid off? We could make things work on my salary alone, that is, assuming you could ease up on your spa sprees."

"What do you mean exactly, 'try to get laid off'?" I ignore his dig at my penchant for pricey facials.

"This new boss is on a firing rampage, right? So just help her along. Make her decision a little easier."

"Like, sexually harass someone?" I say, still whimpering. "Or say something racist?"

Jake laughs. "No, my naïve dear, you don't want her to be able to fire you with cause, which means no severance or unemployment pay. Just, you know, do kind of a bad job. Give it your fifty percent."

"Huh." I've never before thought of this option, but it's not such a bad one. I've been at *Hers* five years, so I'd get as many months' worth of severance; and these days, unemployment benefits last nearly a year. And Jake is right—his litigator salary is more than enough to support our family. Still, I'm not sure the overachiever in me could pull off such a stunt.

The next day, Victoria calls me into her office. "Let's talk smooth skin," she says. "Mimi wants to do a six-page package on cellulite for the relaunch, so please drum up some ideas and we'll meet to talk about it at seven."

"Seven?" I ask. "As in p.m.?" Victoria nods, her face blank. That means I'll miss putting Matilda down. Also, it's July third, and Mark and I hoped to kick off our Independence Day celebration with some grilling and frozen drinks; back in Louisa's day, we had half days on the eve of a holiday.

"Oh, and please print out fifteen copies of the eco-friendly makeup story," she says. "Everyone in ad sales wants a copy so they can review the brands and ensure they're targeting the right advertisers."

"The story's posted on the shared server," I say, thinking I'm being helpful. "We could maybe save some trees by having them look at the eco-products on-screen. You know, practice what we preach?"

"Please pass me the fifteen printouts by end-of-day. In color, please."

"Will do." Leaving Victoria's office, I make my decision and set my goal: within two weeks I will get myself fired.

As I'm halfheartedly brainstorming ideas about cellulite, Jonathan enters the beauty closet with the week's worth of event invites. "I took the liberty of grabbing these from Ed in the mailroom," he says. "I'm sure you're still adjusting to the back-to-work thing, so just pick the ones you want to attend, and I'll handle the rest. Oh, and I got you this." Jonathan hands me a Starbucks iced coffee, a blatant suck-up move, but one that works. He seems to get how totally wiped I feel.

"Thanks." I page through the invites, trying to drum up some enthusiasm for the promises of a mascara to revolutionize my lashes' lushness, a skin-care system that will shave a decade from my face, and a pheromone-infused nail polish with the power to attract sexy suitors. These products used to make me gleam with glee; now I just wonder if the gift bags will include a cupcake.

Remembering Jake's suggestion, I channel a slacker: "Honestly, I'm not up for any of these. Why don't you just go to them all and bring back notes?"

"Uh, OK," says Jonathan, sounding concerned. "Would you like me to send your regrets or give an excuse of some kind?" I shrug, turn back to my computer, and log on to Facebook. Over the course of the day I call Matilda's nanny four times and ask her to put the phone up to my daughter's ear, and then I speak in baby talk until I'm bored of it. I don't bother closing the beauty closet's door.

"Hey, Liz-O." It's Zoe. Others complain about her busybody ways, but she's always left me alone, maybe sensing I wouldn't indulge her brand of baloney. But now her radar for fellow slackers must be buzzing and she's gravitated to me from across the office. "You know, you might want to rein in that gibberish mumbo jumbo," she says. "I can see Victoria giving you the stink eye. Rumor is, she's so desperate for a baby she'd steal someone else's. So FYI, between you and me, I'd think twice about bringing yours to the office."

"Thanks for the tip, Zoe."

"And since you put on a few pounds, which is of course totes understandable, you might take the opportunity to bond with our—how shall I say it?—somewhat zaftig new leader. She's big into dieting. Could be something for you two to do together, trade recipes and all that."

"That's excellent advice. I appreciate it." My instinct is to shoo her away and say I have work to do, but I force myself to make small talk for as long as I can take it—I'm supposed to be playing the deadbeat. Eventually I excuse myself to go pump. I hide in the supply closet and read back issues of *Starstruck*. So this is the junk Mimi produced before coming to *Hers*. The writing is appalling, and the articles contain outright lies; the singer they claim had an affair last year with her hunk of a drummer recently came out as a lesbian.

My real test comes with the November issue memo. I pride myself on organization and efficiency; never once in my career have I missed a deadline. Ideas are due by noon, and I'm brimming with them. To urge myself to stay strong, I look to my screensaver, a beautiful image of Matilda sleeping in my arms, and I believe I can feel my heart physically aching. *I'm doing this for you, kid,* I think. Then I set about watering down my ideas, and littering my write-ups with clichés and misplaced modifiers and the occasional "you're"-"your" mix-up. I sit on my memo all afternoon, feeling sick to my stomach. It's nearing the end of the day when I finally drop it in Mimi's box. Then I flee the office, half an hour early.

The morning after the holiday, Leah strides into the beauty closet. "I'm onto you, missy," she says. "I called you at your desk at five thirty-five on Tuesday and you were already gone. Then I overheard Jonathan saying you passed on the Sephora Summer Blowout, which I happen to know is your favorite event of the season. I realize you're new to juggling the whole working-mom deal, but this is not like you. What's going on here?"

I shrug. "Maybe my mind's a little muddled, you know, baby brain and all."

"Oh, come off it, Liz. You're a terrible liar. I didn't want to have to do this, but I happened to see your memo with Mimi's heinous red markups, and it's not good. Not good at all. This is serious. You need to get with the program—fast!—or you're going to be out on the street, lickety-split." I nod and wrinkle my forehead, trying to look very concerned.

"Wait a minute," Leah says, perching herself on my desk and positioning her face inches from mine. "Oh, my God, that's what you're hoping for, isn't it?" I do my best impression of looking shocked. All this acting is exhausting. "I'm right, aren't I? You're trying to get let go. Oh, Liz, don't do it! From one mom to another, I am begging you! You have no idea what it's like to be cooped up all day with a baby, having zero adult interaction, your mind going to mush along with the bananas and sweet potatoes in the food processor. It's bad enough that I have to work from home two days a week! I have stay-at-home mom friends who seem like they've had a full lobotomy. Three months of maternity leave is nothing. You knew all along it was finite, a precious little stint with a concrete end date. But when the days unfold in that shapeless, interminable way, you will come apart from the misery and despair. You will completely unravel. Believe me, after two weeks you'll be praying you had a job to dress up for and escape to each day. Liz, I'm begging you, as your colleague and your friend, please don't make this terrible mistake."

My stomach is fluttering like mad. "I think you're wrong," I whisper, trying to shore up my conviction. "It's different for Matilda and me. Now, shoo, and don't blow my cover."

Leah looks distraught. She sighs. "If this is what you want, I guess I can't stop you." She exits the beauty closet and I queue up Funny or Die, intent on laughing away the surge of ambivalence that's creeping into my thoughts. To succeed in my mission, I know I can't waver from my resolve.

"We have terminated your position" is how they word it. It's on Friday the thirteenth when I'm summoned to the thirtieth floor, which somehow seems significant. Mimi is there, along with

Suzanne, the H.R. representative who brought me on half a decade ago. Suzanne still wears her hair in two French braids, as if in five years she's never once glanced at the beauty content of any of the magazines she hires for. "Your skill set no longer matches the needs of the *Hers* office," she says. "We'll be doing some restructuring."

"But it's only been ten workdays since I've been back from maternity leave and working for Mimi," I reply, reciting the lines I rehearsed with Jake. "How can she have a real sense of what my skill set actually is?"

"We believe it no longer matches the needs of the office," Suzanne repeats, shooting a sidelong glance at Mimi; I wonder, did no one tell her I just returned from maternity leave?

"Right, you already said that. But I've turned in just one assignment since coming back, and if you look in my file you'll see I've always received glowing reviews from my managers. So I'm curious, why exactly am I being fired?"

I direct the question at Mimi, but she defers to Suzanne. "We're letting you go because the publication is moving in a new direction," she says, words without meaning.

"Is that right?" I ask, sounding calmer than I feel. "Well, listen, I happen to know you can't replace someone while she's out on maternity leave. In my absence, Mimi created a new beauty associate position—and for a man, by the way—and now, suddenly, although I've been given very little opportunity to prove myself, I'm getting the boot. This is all striking me as very sketchy. Very sketchy indeed. My husband is a lawyer, and—"

"Elizabeth," says Suzanne, the chipper gloss gone from her voice. "We're willing to be reasonable with you."

"If you don't want me to sue—and I think that's what you're getting at?" They seem careful not to nod, but it's clear they're listening closely. "OK. Rather than the twenty weeks of severance for my many years of service to this company, I believe I'm owed a full year."

"Liz—" says Mimi, but I cut her off.

"I'd also like two months' full pay for my nanny, whom I've

taken the time to hire and get the baby accustomed to. You know, I thought I'd be working full-time for more than a fortnight."

"Let's be serious. This is not an investment bank," says Mimi, getting riled up. "We are not made of money!"

Suzanne places her hand over Mimi's. "OK, we'll grant you one year's severance, and then we'll all sign a waiver releasing all parties of future rights to litigation." Joy surges through my veins. I suspect my breasts are leaking, but I don't even care. Jake speculated I'd get nine months' pay at most, never the full year. "And while we regret that you've gone through the trouble of finding a nanny, unfortunately we cannot offer you compensation for that."

"Deal." I practically shout it. Suzanne nods soberly, and Mimi eyes me as if she suspects me of stealing. "I'll be out of your hair immediately."

All the holdovers from the old team offer me heartfelt hugs, which make me cry—although everything does these days. "I promise to visit," I say. Half the staff offers their babysitting services. "Send me a postcard," says Ed, handing over my last batch of mail.

Only Leah doesn't get sentimental. "You sly fox," she says. "Now I can no longer be your friend. We're on opposite sides of the mommy wars, and each of us is required to believe we're superior to the other."

"Leah, you know I would never dare compete with you."

"God, can't you just be a bitch for once so it's easier to see you go?" She helps me carry out my boxes, and waits with me for Jake. When he pulls up to the curb, Leah leans in to the car window. "I hear you're responsible for this turn of events, you prick," she says. She's told me she'd sleep with Jake if ever I dared divorce him. "Take care of her for me, will you?" Leah lifts me off the ground into a bear hug, then sets me down and taps me on the butt. "See you around, Mama! Off you go."

From the passenger seat, I stare up to the ninth floor of the Schmidt & Delancey building, where I've spent the majority of my waking hours for half a decade. I can still recall the mix of pride and excitement I felt when Louisa first shook my hand, and said, "Welcome to *Hers*." Well, good-bye to all that, I think wistfully. Then I remember with a thrill that we're on our way home to sweet Matilda.

"Wait a second, love," I say to Jake. I hop out of the car, gather the six or seven magazines shoved into every crevice of my handbag, and toss the lot into the garbage can. I can't believe how light I feel. Tomorrow I'll stop at Barnes & Noble and buy an actual book. I'll read it slowly, savoring it like a prize. I love the idea: me, a reader of literature! (Halfway to Brooklyn, I'm already wishing I hadn't thrown out the newest issue of *Pretty*; it's the perfect thing to page through while nursing Matilda.)

Jake drops me off at home, then turns around to head back to midtown. I dismiss the nanny early and scoop up Matilda from her crib. She's gurgling softly and smells of sweet talcum, her eyes at half-mast. I spin the colorful mobile above our heads, and as it trills a twinkling melody, I invent a lullaby: "*Hers*, Mimi, move away. Mama and Tilly will share the day. Good-bye newsstand, good-bye desk. Mama loves Matilda, sweet God bless."

9

Leah Brenner, Executive Editor

When Laura schedules a remote meeting for Mimi and me, she usually cites a reason. So when she calls my home office and asks if I'm free to Skype at three, vaguely adding, "Mimi wants to chat," I assume this will be my finale. We've just shipped the final pages of the September issue, and Mimi is likely thinking she's kept me around long enough to glean all of my *Hers* wisdom.

As always, it feels like an invasion when Mimi's wide, white face appears on the screen of my home computer. "Hi there," she says, not quite looking at me, although it's admittedly difficult to make eye contact through a Web cam. "I'm doing some reshuffling, so let's talk change." I brace myself. Although I've imagined this moment many times, I still don't have a clue if I'll respond with the poise of a princess or the dumb hysterics of certain toddlers I know. Mimi continues: "I'll need you to take over all of the top-editing for October."

"The entire issue?" I ask, shocked. Victoria and I have been splitting this task half and half, and it's a massive one: It means constructing and deconstructing and reconstructing every story all the way from its initial big, messy concept to its final perfectly placed punctuation; it means acting as liaison between dueling personalities in edit and art as the text and photos come together on-page; it means being the first and the last pair of eyes on a piece, and sticking around until the wee hours of the night during shipping to usher each layout, error-free, out the door to the printer. Even in Louisa's time, this was never a one-woman job.

"Yessiree, the whole enchilada," says Mimi. A feeling of flattery is worming its way into my brain—could Mimi possibly have decided I'm a smart, competent editor, after all?—but a part of me knows to remain skeptical. There is, in fact, a catch: "Victoria is moving on to focus on the November relaunch," Mimi says, "and since you have such a fan-friggin-tastic handle on the old content, I thought it would serve us all best to pass the baton over to you for the last month of it." Wow. She does get points for bluntness.

The screen flickers to black—it must be the Web connection; even Mimi wouldn't end a conversation quite so harshly. As I wait for her smug mug to reappear, I hum in order to avoid any thoughts of my overwhelming new responsibilities. I peer up at my wall calendar, a reproduction of Seurat's *Grande Jatte*, and soon lose myself in the picture. Oh, to break free of my windowless office and become one of the fashionable women in the painting, promenading along the shore on a balmy summer day. I settle into the fantasy, imagining the delicate lace pattern of my parasol, the thin breeze against my face, the gorgeous French accent I've acquired by magic or divine intervention. It doesn't take long for the nearby squall of one of my babies to snap me out of my reverie and remind me how absurd it is to pine away for an alternate life while also feeling utterly terrified of losing the one I have. I narrow my eyes, and the calendar image turns into what it is: a bunch of dots.

An instant message from Laura pings up on my screen: "Mimi's having technical difficulties. Do u need 2 ask her anything else?"

Unbelievable. "Nope, message loud and clear," I type back.

I do the math: The October issue ships in the first week of August, which means I have at least—or more likely, exactly—three more weeks of employment.

The fact that my workload has suddenly doubled does not stop me from dimming my office lights and collapsing on the couch for a catnap. In Louisa's day, I would have felt guilty even extending a midday coffee break from five minutes to ten. But now, for what-ever reason, I'm not the least bit ashamed to call a time-out on my workday. I suppose it's a response to my helplessness. Still, I hardly recognize this version of myself. I wonder, *How the hell did I get here? How has it come to this?* My mind meanders back in time several months, back to when I felt confident about and certain of my exact role and purpose at work, back to when the name Mimi Walsh meant nothing to me.

Louisa and I were like yin and yang and, if you added the man-aging editor, Abby, I suppose you could say she was the yung, or something. Louisa was our strong, fearless leader, a bit removed, but always decisive, and I ran the day-to-day operations, managing the team and lending emotional support and gently nudging Louisa away from her more outrageous, out-of-touch ideas. Al-though I don't exactly blame myself for Louisa's demise, I sup-pose the beginning of the end was when I started telecommuting part-time. I was always available by phone or e-mail or Skype, but I wasn't always around physically, and that made a difference. Our delicate balance began to teeter.

Remotely, I couldn't manage to stop Louisa from running a lifestyle story about decorating a vacation home, full of two-hundred-dollar throw pillows and design ideas for gazebos and fountains; Abby did protest in her meek way, but Louisa wouldn't listen. The experi-ence was like when you trip and everything slurs to slow motion, but you still can't prevent the inevitable fall—I saw it all coming: the del-uge of angry reader mail, the flagging sales, the Corporate freak-out upstairs.

And the staff got edgy, too. Without being on-site day in and day out to moderate disputes and smooth out tensions, I'd return to the office and discover festering grudges and built-up resent-ments. Louisa would retreat, impatient with her restless under-lings and, left sequestered in her closed-door office, she'd cook up even more esoteric ideas: how to get your child into a top private school, what to look for in a personal trainer, and (God forbid) an editorial about how it was time our president followed through on his promise to reform the tax code to bridge the economic gap between rich and poor. She dismissed my concerns that our readers' median income was $64,000 and that half of them hailed from red states. Mark, though I love the guy, only made things worse; he egged Louisa on, fawning over her "ingenious" ideas and designing layouts more fitting for an Ayn Rand pamphlet than a middle-America parenting magazine.

We did try. On one of my days in the office, Abby and I teamed up to deliver a convincing presentation to Louisa about how *Hers* was on a fast course to disaster. Louisa heard us out, and then the three of us powered through a full day of brainstorming for a redesign with friendlier layouts, more welcoming language, and stories that would acknowledge our readers' realities—their finances and home lives and political views. Louisa delivered a brilliant speech to the staff about the changes, and then everyone pulled together and worked long hours to make over the next issue. I felt so proud of our team.

But it wasn't enough—that redesign, or the next one. Part of the problem was that Corporate had lost its faith in us, and kept slashing our budgets when what we needed was the opposite: an extra influx of cash, our own stimulus plan. It got so Louisa banned Abby from her office because she always came bearing bad financial news.

I tried to help Louisa get into the heads of our readers—I sent her on a road trip to a slew of megamalls across the Midwest to meet them—but her heart wasn't in it. For all her effort, she said she couldn't connect with the chubby women with bad hair and ill-fitting clothes, women who described their ambitions as just getting through the workweek and who said their dream vacations were Disney World or a cruise to Cancún, women who shook her hand heartily and declared her outfit "real neat." Louisa returned to the office cranky and despondent. Listlessly, she parroted back the concerns and interests of the women who had lined up by the food courts to get their copies of *Hers* autographed, but she couldn't abandon her highbrow sensibilities or ignore her natural instincts.

As a result, we couldn't deliver for her. By the time we rounded

up the staff in the conference room to discuss a third redesign in a
year, it was clear they were exhausted—and that some had lost
their confidence in Louisa, too. Our once invincible leader had become vulnerable and anxious. And I, as second-in-command, had
failed to prevent her meltdown. When the call came from the thirtieth floor, Louisa and I were both ready for it.

I lie supine on the couch, peering up at my basement's ceiling
tiles, possibly for the first time ever. I notice they're overlaid with
a pattern of tiny, concentric circles. As I stare, the circles seem to
animate into trippy swirls. I start drifting off into that hazy median
between wakefulness and sleep. At some point my eyes float shut.

*From somewhere I hear a phone ringing. The Human Resources num-
ber flashes up on the phone screen. So this is it, I think, inhaling what feels
like a hot air balloon's worth of breath.*

*"Hello?" I say, but it's a distorted version of my voice, like the one that
plays back from a recording and makes me wince.*

"Come to the thirtieth floor." A deep, booming voice, like a deity's.

*I ascend as if by magic. The carpeting in the corporate suite feels plush
between my toes, and I wonder why I'm barefoot. Someone who resembles
Suzanne, the H.R. woman, is standing at the end of a very long hall, beck-
oning to me. I feel as if I'll never make it to her, wading through the thick
carpeting that's like mud.*

*I'm seated across from this simulacrum of Suzanne in an office where I
swear I've been before. "Where's Mimi?" I ask, that same strange voice filtering through my mouth.*

"An appointment."

"Oh." I get the sense my boss is hundreds of miles away.

*"Well," says the Suzanne-ish woman, shuffling her papers and avoid-
ing my gaze. My heart is thumping. I feel bad for her. It wasn't her decision
to call me up here, and it's not her fault that the speech she's about to deliver is carefully constructed with euphemisms and corporate-speak. I suddenly suspect someone has a gun to her back. I search frantically for an
exit. Wasn't there a door around here? How did I get in?*

When sort-of Suzanne looks up at me with a smile, I can tell she feels bad for me, too. How totally wretched, this mutual pity party. I squirm in my seat. "Your position has been eliminated," she says, and then— poof!—I'm eliminated from her office and off far, far away, settling in on a blanket by the Seine, spreading Brie on a baguette, and basking in the mild light of late afternoon. It's all jolie and gentile and merveilleuse, until suddenly my snack disappears and I'm clutching at a packet labeled "Moving on and moving up"; the Seine dries up, the pretty women with parasols vanish, and I'm back in an office with Suzanne's clone, clasping her clammy hand with my own.

"Get yourself a lawyer," the Suzanne impersonator whispers, a tickle in my ear. I should ask her, "Who?" and "Why?" and "How?" but I'm utterly exhausted, desperate for a bed.

"Good-bye, Leah," I hear, or maybe just imagine.

I jolt awake, disoriented. Strands of my hair are matted with sweat to my cheek, and my left arm is imprinted with the nubby diamond pattern of my couch. Oh, right, I'm in my home office. I have no sense of how long I was out. The phone is ringing.

"Hello," I say into the receiver, my voice hoarse with sleep.

"Phew, you're still there." My mother's voice is like espresso; I clear my throat and snap to full attention. "I'm never sure when I'll call and your replacement will answer and pretend like she's never heard of you."

"Gee, thanks, Mom. You know you're calling me at home."

"Well, still," she says. I only let her get away with such talk because she's been through this kind of staff turnover herself, and in her case, she was the displaced editor in chief. My mother—the famous and brilliant Betsy Brenner—was one of the first women to head up a Schmidt & Delancey publication, back in the era when women's magazines were usually run by men.

"So, what's up?" I ask, now fully awake.

"I wanted to see if you're coming in for a visit this Sunday. Or do you have to work?" Of course my mother believes work is the only reason I might choose to not spend my weekend with her. I think she honestly sometimes forgets I'm a mother of three.

"I'm not sure, Mom. Why don't you come out to our place and we can inflate the pool in the backyard for the girls?"

"Oh, I'm not up for all that suburban revelry." I roll my eyes. She and my father have resided in the same Upper West Side floor-through since my sister and I were infants. She believes it's a tragedy I shipped out to New Jersey, and when I recently told her that Rob and I were mulling over a move farther from Manhattan, she simulated a stroke. "I thought we could work on the program for your sister's little play," she says.

What my mother calls Cara's "little play" is an off-Broadway revival of Chekhov's *Three Sisters*; the production's previews inspired the *Village Voice* to declare it the most hotly anticipated show of the year. "You're writing the programs?" I ask, incredulous.

"Sure I am. It should come as no surprise that they don't know the first thing about producing a publication—"

"You mean a program, not a publication. It's more like a pamphlet, right?"

My mother ignores me. "When I mentioned my decades of experience as one of the most preeminent editors in the history of the publishing industry, the producers practically fell at my feet and begged me to do it."

"So did you already set the deadlines for first drafts, revises, fact-checking? How's the copy flow coming?" My mother doesn't acknowledge my sarcasm. Maybe she's actually gone bonkers and believes she is back at the helm of a real publication, running the show.

"You may be interested to hear," she says, her voice turning sneaky, "that they're letting me include a crossword on the back page. We could theme it, like The Sounds of Sondheim, or Comedies, Tragedies, and Tonys." I'd prefer not to admit that this intrigues me; my mom knows how much I adore a word puzzle.

"I don't know, Mom. We've got a lot going on here. Rob wants us to spend the weekend looking at more house listings."

"Oh, don't be absurd. You belong in Vermont as much as a dairy cow belongs in Times Square." I bite my tongue. Asking my mother to explain this absurd comparison, or disputing it with something logical, would only lead us down a black hole of frustration. In fact, the thought of living 200 miles away from my mother has never sounded so appealing. I'm half-prepared to call Rob right now and, out of spite, suggest we gather our things and relocate north tonight.

"Oh, Leah, don't pout. How's this: I'll give you creative control over the editorial mix, and you can have final say-so on the wording of the actors' bios." This is her hard sell; we both know how difficult it is for my mother to cede control. "What do you say? It'll be fun to collaborate!" She sounds so eager and excited. This always gets me, my mom's devotion to the craft.

I'm remembering how I grew up worshipping my mother. I mimicked her bottomless ambition and dreamed of following in her footsteps. She ingrained in me like a religion the idea that editing a magazine was the best job in the world; you got to use creativity and business smarts, you were charged with the lofty mission of sharing vital information and inspiration with the masses, and every single month you created something real and tangible, a valuable object that millions of people across the country would race to get their hands on and pay actual money for. My mother made it sound like the most exhilarating and prestigious work in the world, and of course I did everything I could to make it just like she had.

And yet, after my mother fell from her pedestal a decade ago—she'd refused to figure out the Internet and was alienating her younger staffers with constant invocations of Betty Friedan and Gloria Steinem—it was as if she'd lost her entire self. Ever since then she's been puttering around her apartment, irritable and bored, having never developed any outside interests or hobbies, scoffing at my father's suggestions that she join a women's league or a book club. *Like mother, like daughter,* people used to say to us, and I'd beam with pride; now this maxim sends a shiver down my spine.

"Mom, I have to get back to my job."

"Of course you do, dear. I'll figure out the programs myself. You know I love you."

My chest wells up with emotion—is it pity? regret? affection?—and I stutter, "OK, I'll ask Maria if she's free on Sunday. If she can watch the girls, I'll meet you in the city and we can do Cara's programs." With my mother, I always end up caving.

The next morning, I arrive at my cubicle to find Lynn staked out, juggling a slew of layouts. "We're finalizing all the art for October, and I need your input," she says.

It occurs to me that now that Victoria has moved on to the more important month of November, for all matters October I'm not the executive divided by two, or a "co-"; I'm the actual executive editor. At least for a few weeks, I can maintain the illusion of wielding real power at work.

"Here's the 'Lingerie for your body type' story," Lynn says, spreading the sheets across my desk. "There's the 'How to talk to your kids about sex' one, and that's the essay by the woman who lost both her legs when a limo ran over her."

I point to a bunch of printouts of fruit. "What's all this?"

"I'm thinking for the lingerie story, let's construct life-sized pieces of fruit and then have them model the bras and panties, as if they were mannequins. That way, you match your body type to the fruit—you know: pear shaped; apple shaped; and banana shaped for long and lean—and then you pick your corresponding getup. Ta-da! See, I drew a mock-up."

A skimpy thong is stretched over a pear's bulge, lending the fruit a pair of fleshy love handles. "Interesting idea," I say. "Although I think when women realize they're, say, apple shaped, they don't want to think they look like an actual apple. Better to have a model with just the slightest curve of a tummy and call her apple shaped, so the readers will be reassured that it's not so bad to be round in the middle." I cannot believe I have to explain this to our creative director; this is Women's Magazines 101.

"Huh. But mmm, these pictures look so delicious. Don't you just want to eat them up?" When I don't respond, Lynn turns to the next board. "OK, so for the parenting story, how about let's recruit actual couples to have sex and we'll stage it so their kids walk in on them. A photographer will pop out to capture the looks on their faces. What do you think?"

I am working on a response along the lines of *"Are you flipping kidding me?!"* but somehow conveyed in a respectful manner, when Laura bounds over to my desk. "Copy flow meeting!" she announces, miraculously saving me from commenting on Lynn's plan to traumatize children and parents across America.

Lynn and I join Victoria and Abby in Mimi's office. "Exciting news," our boss announces. It's hard to believe that any aspect of copy flow could inspire excitement, but Mimi is clearly basking in whatever imagined brilliance she's about to share. "To save time, I've devised a new routing system. We'll send separate printouts of a story to all the different editors involved, everyone can make their notes, and then the main editor will scoop up all the files and integrate all the comments, easy-peasy."

Mimi is clearly delighted with herself, but her plan is preposterous. I picture all the editors scribbling conflicting comments on their personal printouts of a story, and the ensuing clash of egos as everyone debates whose insight is smartest, whose opinion counts most. Mimi's proposal will complicate what is well known as one of the simplest, most streamlined routing processes in the industry. This change can only be about the boss asserting her authority.

It's this pettiness, or perhaps my renewed (if deluded) idea that my opinion actually counts around here, that spurs me to speak up. Without masking my impatience, I blurt out, "We tried something similar with Louisa and it only confused things. This kind of so-called time-saver doesn't actually save time, and it isn't necessary for our small staff."

Abby puffs out her cheeks, her code for "Put a cork in it." I'm no idiot; I realize any reference to B.M. (Before Mimi) is blasphemy, as is any overt failure to fall in line with the current agenda. But it so happens I know what I'm talking about. And I have a hunch that, after dumping the whole October issue on me during our little Skype powwow yesterday, Mimi may cut me some slack.

"This will be different, you'll see," she says, in a strange tone that makes me question whom exactly she's trying to convince. She offers no follow-up explanation of how it will be different.

"Well, I think it's a wonderful idea," says Victoria.

"Great," Mimi says. "We'll implement the new system immediately." She clicks her red pen, and I'm left wondering if she actually has faith in the plan or if she's just pleased with her power.

"Knock, knock." Zoe appears on the office's threshold. Mimi has told the staff she's always accessible to them, but I can't imagine she actually meant it, and certainly not during a meeting. I can tell that whatever Zoe's planning to ask, she'll pay the price for it.

"Yes?" asks Mimi.

"I have a question about vacay?" Zoe has that awful habit of ending her statements in the higher inflection of a question, making her sound unsure of everything she says. I've pointed out this tic to many a junior staffer in the hopes of helping them sound more professional, but that kind of suggestion might come off as insulting to our Web manager. Plus, Zoe gets away with talking like a text message, with so many acronyms and abbreviations it makes my head hurt, so what do I know? "My besties and I are going to the Jersey Shore the week leading up to Labor Day? Just wanted to give you the 411, so you'd know when I'll be away?"

"Ooh, fun, what part of the shore?" This from Lynn.

Mimi releases a sibilant sigh. "We'll be shipping the November issue then, as you know. You don't actually think we can have people zipping away on vacations, do you?" Abby peers out the window, clearly not wanting to be involved in this public shaming.

"Well, we planned it months ago. I already laid down bank for the hotel," says Zoe. "It would be majorly inconvenient to cancel." *Shut up*, I want to yell at her. *Just stop talking.* At least she knows to stop short of saying, "I already cleared it with Louisa."

"Well, you should've realized it would be a bad time," says Mimi. She stares Zoe down until she leaves.

I wonder if Zoe too watched Mimi on the *Today* show last week bemoaning the fact that Americans use less than 50 percent of their paid vacation days. She meticulously outlined all of the health benefits of getting away, explaining how time off is the most important way to rejuvenate and refresh. "Look, vacation makes you a better worker," Mimi said, staring into the camera. "Your boss *wants* you to go away." I laughed at the television set, thinking, *She does indeed.*

When our meeting adjourns, I return to my desk and, rather than get going on the giant stack of October stories populating my in-box, I start planning my own pretend vacation. And not the long-weekend-upstate-with-a-slew-of-kids variety—in other words, the only kind of vacation Rob and I take these days, which is "vacation" in name only. I'm thinking of a real, true break. I envision fleeing halfway around the world to Asia; I wanted to honeymoon in Japan, though Rob ultimately talked me into Italy. I picture myself scaling Mount Fuji, slurping noodles in Bangkok, visiting the temples of Bali and Laos. I'm all on my own, unreachable by phone and even e-mail.

I keep up my daydreaming through the rest of the afternoon and into my commute home. I begin my walk down to Penn Station as I always do, utterly in awe of this incredible city where I work. Central Park is brimming with blooms, and the streets are energized and bustling, the swaths of faces lit up with that collective postwork glow. I conjure up the image of myself as a little girl strolling down this very block, hand in hand with my mother, all dressed up to spend the day with her "helping out" in that glittering high-rise where she reigned supreme.

It's a decent trek from my office to the train station, twenty-five blocks south along Eighth Avenue, and my guileless reveling fades fast. Within a few blocks, all signs of the park's greenery vanish and are replaced with crowds of stalls schilling cheap pashminas, knock-off sunglasses, and every variety of schlock. An occasional whiff of toasted pecans from a Hot Nuts cart reminds me of the city's irresistibility, but mostly it's a march of endurance. I power through the increasingly seedy streets until my journey culminates in the ultimate den of squalor: Penn Station.

Now I am desperate to board the train, flee the city, and settle in to a softer, suburban day's end. I crave a vodka soda in my backyard, where I often spot a blue jay zipping across the sky, whirring his "welcome home" whistle. I marvel at how, in the span of fifteen minutes, I've transformed into a dozen nuances of myself, from happy city girl to staunch suburbanite. How mutable, my mind-set. Maybe any setting—even rural Vermont—would suit me given the right mood.

The train lurches out of the station, and through the window I watch the cityscape of crowd and construction give way to green and sprawl. When our family expanded from two to five last year, the concept of space suddenly felt like a basic human necessity, and Rob and I fled from New York like refugees. I'm grateful for so much about our home in New Jersey: a basement storage space that's bigger than our former Brooklyn one-bedroom, a yard that doesn't mean a postage stamp of concrete but rather a vegetable garden and plenty of room to play, neighbors whose names I know and whom I actually like, having both a car and a place to park it.

The train speeds by a big park, and my mind moves on to babbling brooks, freshly cut grass, cows grazing in fields. I conjure up an oddly clear image of my three girls, a bit older, running around a blueberry patch; they fill up gallon milk cartons with berries, and then the four of us head home to bake fruity muffins.

It's only many hours later, when I'm in bed and wrapped up in sheets and Rob's elbows and knees, that I realize I've stolen this bucolic family image straight from a brochure. It's something Rob left out on my desk, an advertisement for an orchard located a mile from his favorite house in Vermont, conveniently dog-eared to a photo of three little girls picking berries. I'm embarrassed by my imagination's pilfering, its lack of creativity.

Despite the unoriginality of the image, I'm suddenly craving blueberry muffins, in particular the ones from a deli near our old apartment in Brooklyn. The woman who ran the place would split a muffin down the middle and nestle a pat of butter between the halves.

"*Psst*, Rob," I say, nudging my sleeping husband.

He rolls over, his eyes slits. "What time is it? What's the matter?"

"It's late. And nothing," I say. "Remember the muffins from Baxter's Deli?"

"Uh-huh." I'm fairly sure Rob is still in la-la-land, but then he comes out with, "So yummy."

"I know, right? You could go out till the bars closed, and then pop in and they'd have a batch fresh from the oven, ready for the next day." I'm thinking how, unlike back in Brooklyn, no store within ten miles of our New Jersey home is open at this hour—all's quiet on the Westfield front. I urge myself to feel comforted not bothered by the thought.

"Rob." I poke him again.

"Mmm?"

"Let's plan a house-hunting trip up to Vermont." My husband nestles me closer to his warm body, and I drift off to sleep, certain I'll dream of muffins, buttery and warm.

10

Jane Staub-Smith,
Associate Editor

Laura's frequent interoffice calls set off a Pavlovian anxiety in my chest, so my heart is already thumping when she says through the receiver, "Coverlines starting."

We gather in the conference room, where Mimi has posted the stories she wants to advertise on the October cover: the cheaters piece, the eleven-minute abs workout, the *Office Jungle* beauty story, Ravenous Rhee's guilt-free desserts. Louisa always had us tout the stories of substance: the personal essay from a prominent Brooklyn writer about the surprising joys of parenthood, the article detailing groundbreaking treatments for breast cancer, all the stuff that differentiated us from the dozens of other women's rags on the newsstand. I respected that Louisa wanted to educate the readers, to teach them to care about the weightier pieces, even if our newsstand numbers were often dismal. Mimi, on the other hand, is sticking with the reliably hot sellers: sex and dieting. It's smart, I suppose, but it makes me sad.

We start with the workout. "Stronger, fitter, firmer in a flash," Victoria suggests.

"The incredible ab flattener," Jonathan adds.

"Fit in eleven minutes: You've never looked sexier," Zoe says.

It's like an auction, the ideas shouted out spitfire, every editor competing to win Mimi's approval. With Louisa these meetings were structured and formal—each person given her turn to read out her ideas, everyone nodding politely.

"Slim down in just eleven minutes—six-pack, guaranteed," Laura says. Mimi clears her throat; even for us, it's a bit too much of a stretch to guarantee a perfect stomach in the time it takes to smoke a cigarette.

"*Psssht grrr shttt,*" comes through the phone; we've patched Leah in remotely, but something's amiss and her voice has broken down to gravel.

"Huh?" says Victoria, and Leah repeats herself. They keep this up through several iterations, until Mimi says, "Oh, good idea!" though the reception is no clearer. We move on with the meeting, and the line remains silent. I eye Laura, though I don't think she's quite smart enough to have tampered with the tech system. Part of me hopes Leah has hung up and is doing something more interesting with her time than standing by and listening to this garbage.

Though the truth is, I can spew out trash like the best of them: "Eleven minutes to a trim and toned tummy. Break out the crop top!" I suggest.

"Ooh, that's a great one," says Mimi.

"It *is* great!" Zoe chimes in. I see Debbie mime a hand job under the table, which Abby swats away. Zoe considers herself a coverlines expert; she believes because she works on the Web and has mastered the search engine optimization gobbledygook that she knows exactly what draws people in. But a headline that catches the eye of some idiot surfing the Web at two a.m. in search of cat gifs is not the same thing that'll work on a discerning customer at the newsstand. Besides which, there's the simple (and I'm ashamed to admit, gratifying) truth that not one of Zoe's suggestions has ever made it onto a *Hers* cover.

"Let's put that one on the top left," says Victoria. I shrug. The top left is the holy grail of the coverline. We in the business like to believe that if the four or five words we place in that prominent spot are brilliant and enticing and sparkly enough, they'll have the power to convince hundreds of thousands or, heck, millions of newsstand idlers to single out and grab our publication, to *choose us*. It's all very desperate, our eagerness to please, and it's reflected in our ideas—the promises more and more extreme, the oversells more and more outlandish. No one who does this article's variation on a sit-up thirty times, three times per week, will lose a pound, never mind be miraculously toned for a crop top. Before Sylvia got the ax, she'd sometimes drop in on the coverlines meetings, but then always leave soon after, looking like she was about to faint (Louisa began scheduling the meetings when she knew the research chief would be out at lunch). It's a matter of mystery why the magazine's cover has never been subjected to the same strict standards of veracity as the contents within.

Next up is Ravenous Rhee's guilt-free desserts. "Delectable treats, all for less than a hundred cals," Laura suggests.

"Have you guys tried those so-called treats?" Debbie spits out, clearly disgusted. "Delectable, my ass. And it's 'fewer than,' not 'less than' a hundred calories." The recipe creator pulls out her chair with a squeak, stands up, and walks out on the meeting, murmuring something about having real work to do.

"She's right, the cookies are totes gross," says Zoe. "But on the plus side, you can stuff your face with them and still not get fatso!"

"How about 'Indulge in sinfully delicious goodies—guilt-free!' " I suggest. "Or, 'Five *OMG—so amazing* desserts, you won't believe they're healthy!' "

"Fantastic," says Mimi. "That makes me hungry for an actual cookie, diet be damned. Laura, go catch Debbie and tell her to bring down some cookies. I'd love lemon cream, or ginger molasses, the chewy kind and preferably warm. Now, let's try the beauty story. Thoughts?"

"Look your prettiest: Seven makeup tricks for dewy skin, shiny hair, and eyes that pop," says Laura.

"I've got it," says Zoe. "Dare to go bold! The cast of *Office Jungle* shows off the season's hot new colors." When no one fawns over the idea, Zoe exhales a dramatic sigh.

"Your get-gorgeous *hmmmmpth, pop, pop* . . . best features," tries Leah over the spotty line.

"How about, 'Makeup so magical, you'll get carded again'?" Victoria suggests it, so everyone squeals their approval, never mind that the story has nothing to do with antiaging.

"Perfect," says Mimi. "Actually, let's do that one on the top left."

I wonder if Abby will speak up about the coverlines focus groups, the ones we ran with real readers last winter. One of the things we discovered was that beauty lines bomb on the top left. Participants told us they were sick to death of hearing about all the new products they needed in order to be pretty; they just wanted to be reassured that they're already gorgeous. They would've hurled rotten tomatoes at a line suggesting they'd need magical makeup in order to look young. Alas, this meeting has already consisted of lies upon lies. Abby, along with the rest of us who attended the focus groups, holds her tongue.

In the days following the coverlines meeting, something funny starts happening: First I'm invited to a senior staff meeting about the relaunch, and then I'm asked to join a committee on our social media update. When Laura calls to say Mimi would like me in on a future strategy brainstorm, I begin the long walk from my desk to the boss's office, and can feel everyone's stares like lasers burning through my dress. Some eyes are hostile and others are in awe—all seem to wonder why I, a lowly associate editor, have been chosen.

Honestly, I'm wondering the same thing. In Mimi's office, it's just Victoria and me. I don't even ask if we'll be patching in Leah from her home office.

"So who would you rather sleep with, Brad Pitt or Johnny Depp?" Mimi asks. She and Victoria turn to face me.

"Um, I guess Johnny Depp. Pirates are hot." *Jeez, where did that come from?* I feel ridiculous, but I'm coming to understand that these "brainstorms" are often just excuses to dish about Mimi's date last night, the progress on her kitchen redecoration, or celebrity crushes.

"Good point," says Mimi. "Captain Hook can take me any day. Ha! I think Johnny's stare is smoldering."

"Oh, yuck, he creeps me out with those buggy eyes," says Victoria. "Actually, I'm not a fan of either one. They've both had kids out of wedlock, which I think is totally immoral."

"I suppose that is kind of trashy," says Mimi, a surprise since her chosen November cover girl's sole claim to fame is getting knocked up at age seventeen and becoming a terrible mother. "But we're not asking whether you agree with the guy's life choices, Vic, or if you'd hire him for a job. Quite simply, who would you rather bang? Ha!"

"I guess Brad Pitt then," says Victoria. "But I'd only cheat on my husband if I was held at gunpoint." As this debate continues, I try to minimize my panic about the real work piling up back at my desk. I'm learning a rendezvous like this can last a few minutes or all afternoon.

"Well, our jury is hung, no pun intended." Mimi cackles, though the statement doesn't even make sense as a pun. "Jane, will you take a look at these résumés?"

I grab the stack. "Which position are they for?" I fear I already know.

"We haven't come up with an exact title yet, but it'll be a senior position, maybe features director," Victoria says, handing me one of Mimi's red pens. "Mark the ones you like. We're looking for someone really special." More special than Leah, I suppose she means. "Mimi and I plan to look through them, too, but we thought you might have some interesting thoughts." Her glance plays over me, questioning, *Whose side are you on?*

I scan the first C.V., a magna cum laude graduate of an Ivy League university, a dozen years of experience in consumer magazines plus another decade at newspapers, currently the executive editor at a major lifestyle Web site. I find myself comparing her résumé to one I invent for Leah: staff mentor for three years, best giver of birthday gifts, most cutting critic of dumb sitcoms. I wonder, if we hired this woman to replace Leah, could Leah then snap up the woman's old position? This feels like a total betrayal, and yet it is now my job. "I'll go through them this afternoon," I say.

Back at my desk, I try to subtly conceal the résumés under a stack of copy. "Any insider info for someone out of the loop?" asks

Zoe, who finds a way to nose her way into every piece of business that is not hers. "Or will I just have to rifle through your desk when you're gone?"

"Very funny," I say, reminding myself to start locking my desk at night.

"Coffee break!" Afternoon coffee is the newest event; Laura actually inputs the timeslot—4 to 4:20—on our calendars so meetings won't interfere. I used to grab my cup from the office machine, but last week Victoria said to me in her joking-but-not-really voice, "Starbucks runs are like, kinda mandatory." I feel like I've been trapped at a high school dance, with all the accompanying angst about who clusters with whom and, of course, the nonstop gossip.

I wander by Abby's office. "Coming?" I ask.

"I'm allergic to caffeine," she says, a slight smile on her lips.

"Lucky duck." I don't think a caffeine allergy exists.

Everyone gathers in clumps by the elevator, and the split is mostly obvious: one group of the old staff, one of the new, with occasional crossovers (Zoe sometimes edges her way in with the new crowd, and yesterday Jonathan announced he was "extending an olive branch" and headed out with Drew and Debbie). I'm the wild card—in the awkward gray space of being of the old guard, but suddenly co-opted by the new—so I remain passive and noncommittal. It's like the snowball dance, when the girls stand on the edge and silently beg a cute boy to single them out from the crowd, only in my case, I wish I were invisible and that everyone would just leave me alone.

In Starbucks, Victoria hands me an iced latte and pulls me over to a table with her and Mimi.

"I don't know how I managed it, but I resisted the scone," says Mimi.

"Good for you," says Victoria.

"Here, here." I raise my cup. Yesterday Mimi caved in to her scone craving and we had to reassure her it wouldn't go straight to her thighs. I spot Zoe a few tables away, likely bitching to Drew about Laura and dissecting Victoria's bargain-basement wardrobe. When I'm grouped with them, if pressed for input, I add something catty and then immediately feel bad. In fact, I know Laura's in a tough spot, and I sort of admire Victoria's unwillingness to unload half of her salary on expensive outfits.

At 4:20 I shuffle back to the office with the pack, my latte untouched. As usual, I'm too on edge to drink it.

As per Mimi's instructions, I've gathered everyone's final round of ideas memos for the November relaunch. It's clear some people have gotten with the program—pitching juicy stories about women who gained and then lost and then regained one hundred pounds; round-table discussions between reality stars in which we pick the fights, let them duke it out, and then declare a winner; and fashion stories based on celebrity kid trends.

Some of the names on the cover sheets are unfamiliar—it's those new freelancers, the potential replacements, I think. One proposes sensational real-women stories: a tightrope walker who's been in traveling circuses for forty years; a five foot one, ninety-nine-pound mother of three who's the most successful bounty hunter in Tennessee; a mail-order bride who's been hit by lightning; and a woman who found out on her wedding day that her fiancé was still married. Gold mine. I do favors for some people, correcting Zoe's misspellings and grammar mistakes, jazzing up Leah's wording, and subbing out an adjective from Debbie's memo that I've learned Mimi dislikes. But ultimately, not everyone can be saved. And although I didn't ask for it, I fear I will have a hand in who else stays or goes.

The night before the meeting to present *Hers'* fresh vision to the advertising sales team, I try on my new suit. "Spin around," says Jenny, who's come over to offer moral support. "Show me the full view."

I check myself out in the mirror. "I look like a lawyer. I don't feel like me." In preparation for the meeting, which I was invited to without explanation, Mimi sent me off to Saks Fifth Avenue with her corporate card and without a spending cap. I imagine Abby knew nothing about it.

"Well, I think you look fantastic," Jenny says. "And after so long of being overworked and underpaid, you're finally getting the recognition you deserve. It's a sign, I know it." Jenny, who still hasn't found work since Mimi fired her, seems to have transposed all of her career ambitions onto me.

"I'm still overworked and underpaid, as you well know. I just have a new outfit."

"Wearing a suit like that, Mimi has to give you a raise."

"She doesn't have to do a thing she doesn't want to do." Two and a half months removed from the corporate world, and Jenny has reimagined the whole business as a Disney movie. She has me cast as the underappreciated worker toiling away until one day the big boss miraculously recognizes her skill and talent, doubles her salary, and launches a parade down Fifth Avenue to celebrate the occasion. She may well be right, but I've always hated parades.

"The brand-new face of *Hers* will be fresh, vibrant, and appealing to today's thirty-something woman who's blazing her own path through modern adulthood," Mimi announces to the ad sales team, clicking her remote control through a series of slides. The women who appear on-screen are stylish and laughing; they're riding bikes, buying flowers, and picnicking with handsome men and cute kids. Victoria and I flank our boss's sides at the front of the room, and I'm trying not to fidget, nervous and itchy in my new suit. The sound system blasts "Party in the U.S.A." and then fades into "American Boy." The soundtrack is familiar, though I can't place it. It's very hot in here.

"An hour spent with the all-new *Hers* will be like a happy-hour dish session with your best friend," Mimi continues. "Through practical, can-do tip pieces, gorgeous beauty and fashion coverage, deep-dive features, and can't-put-it-down reads, we'll share with our reader all the joys, thrills, and complexities of what it means to be a wife, a mom, a career woman, a friend, a fashionista, a coupon clipper, and—most important—a woman."

Next, images of reality TV personalities flash up on the screen. Mimi goes on: "Today's reader is obsessed with stars, and *Hers* will help her get that fix. We'll expand our celebrity coverage, infusing it into our parenting, relationships, home, and food sections." Beside each reality star, a product she shills pops up on-screen. "Plus, this strategy will open us up to new advertising revenue streams." The nodding audience members look like bobbleheads.

"Each section will speak to the nitty-gritty reality of our readers' actual lives," says Mimi. "That means recipes you can prep in twenty-five minutes or less, fashion that's actually wearable, and juicy stories that will let the reader leave behind the dirty dishes and fights with her husband as she escapes to the bathroom, locks the door, sinks into the tub, and grabs a precious fifteen minutes with her favorite magazine."

Wait a minute, I think. *That's Louisa image: the woman in the tub stealing her precious moments with* Hers. As "California Girls" queues up on the speakers, I realize this is the exact soundtrack Louisa played in her last ad sales meeting; it was compiled by Leah, who incidentally wasn't invited to this meeting.

"We'll draw in the reader with fun entertainment and practical advice that's specialized just for her," Mimi drones on. I'm wondering how long this meeting will last. My heels are rubbing raw in my new pumps; I can feel the beginnings of blisters. "We'll give the reader the tools to live a life she can feel passionate about, and to make every day calmer, richer, and happier. We'll talk to her on her own level about the topics and issues she cares about most. And if that's plastic surgery and TV catfights, so be it." Polite laughter all around. My knees feel weak.

"Perhaps most important, the new *Hers* will be an advertiser's dream," Mimi says, emphasizing the last two words. "Our stories will be perfect companions to their products, which will give them every incentive to get in on the revival of a classic brand and to be integrated into the stories that will be the talk of mommy blogs, Facebook threads, and afternoon carpool chats and coffee dates. *Hers'* fresh editorial mission will usher in a new chapter of success for the brand and launch us into earning the big bucks. So who's with me?"

Half the room leaps to their feet, and the applause is raucous. If I weren't standing up at the front, a so-called ambassador to the brand, I would plug my ears.

"Now who has questions?"

Suit after suit stands up and spouts jargony nonsense, asking about projected growth and advertising base rate and other concepts I know zilch about. I do my best not to zone out entirely, to chime in here and there and toe the appropriate party line. But I'm struggling with an intense bout of déjà vu; each time I look over and see Mimi, not Louisa, running the show, I feel disoriented. These ad sales meetings have always called for a smoke-and-mirrors routine, as the editors sell the content to the folks who actually bring in the money (and that's why they're the ones who get the ka-ching Christmas bonuses, Zoe likes to point out), but this meeting feels extreme. All this talk of "the new *Hers*" sounds strikingly similar to how we talked about the old *Hers*, only now with the clothing price tags slightly dropped and the celebrity-to-real-woman ratio tipped. I look around the room and the faces are beaming, their eyes glinting up at Mimi like she's the second coming. Most of them were here under Louisa's reign, so why don't they see what I see?

I shift in my suit uncomfortably. My skirt feels like it's shrunk a size, and a slick sweat sprouts up across my back, sticking camisole to skin. I feel myself overheating. I'm struck with the realization that, standing here at the front of this room, I am serving as a key seamstress of our fair empress Mimi's new clothes. I peel off my jacket, but the feeling that it's choking me remains. Then, black.

When I blink awake, three faces are hovering over me in a huddle, three strands of pearls hanging from their three corresponding necks. The necklaces dangle so close to my face that I could stick my tongue out and lick them. "She's awake," says one of the faces. I blink again and realize I'm lying atop the worn carpeting of the conference room, a foot from the front row of chairs.

"What happened?" I ask. In my peripheral vision I glance shiny wingtips and slim ankles, vulnerable in teetering heels.

"You passed out for a minute there," says another one of the faces. A hand begins fanning me with a copy of *Hers*. "It was a very dramatic end to the meeting."

"She must've been wowed by all of the big changes to the magazine. Ha!" It's Mimi's voice from somewhere far off.

"She's OK now," I hear Victoria say, and then her face appears in my range of vision, her features pinched together like a prune. "You'll be OK, right?"

I nod, sitting up slowly. My head feels filled with helium. By the time I manage, "I think I'll just sit here a minute," Victoria has already turned away.

The voices fade, the people file out, and then I'm alone in the conference room. The white noise sounds loud and distorted, as if someone has amped up the bass and transformed the office into a deserted nightclub.

It's Zoe who eventually comes and finds me on the floor. "I heard what happened and ran over stat," she says. "So what's the dealio, they abandoned you and left you in here for dead? Way harsh."

"I told them it was all right. I'm fine, really. I just need to rest for a bit." I'm suspicious Zoe is here only to hound me for gossip, but she passes me a glass of water, which makes me realize how thirsty I am. I take in a long drink, the liquid like a salve. My blurred vision begins to clear. "Thanks, Zo."

"You should've seen Victoria. Her ears were practically spouting steam, like you planned this whole thing on purpose just to steal Mimi's thunder. I was ROTFL."

"Oh no, really?" The lightheadedness returns, and an image of a pink slip floats through my mind.

"Don't worry, it's NBD. I told Mimi you suffer from a rare condition that causes you to faint when you get overly excited."

"*What?*"

"She totally ate it up, believe me. I don't think she's steamed.

In fact, she seemed flattered to hear you had such a strong reaction to her presentation."

"Zoe, you're a trip."

"Come on, I'm helping you up and taking you home ASAP." She walks me back to my desk, then insists on accompanying me in a cab all the way to the Upper East Side, even though she lives down in Tribeca.

When we pull up to my street, Zoe leans out the window. "Hey, look, it's a bar." She points to a sign featuring a buxom barmaid holding a pair of hefty beer steins. "Out of the car, lady, we're getting you a drink."

"I don't think I'm up for that, Zo."

"Here's what I think, Jane S.S.: You're stressing about a job that's not worth the energy and you've spent way too long down in the dumps about some lame dude who stomped on your heart ages ago. In my professional opinion, what you need is a generous dose of booze and some flirty convo with a cutie-pie guy."

"Thanks for the diagnosis, Dr. Zoe, but I'm wiped."

"Nope, sorry, enough of this FML B.S. We're going in."

And then I'm being hoisted up, dragged into the bar, and forced to down a shot of bourbon. "OK, I've spotted our prey," says Zoe. "See those guys down there? Don't look now, but they are hashtag-adorbs." Suddenly Zoe is flipping her hair and batting her eyelids and laughing as if I've said something fascinating and hilarious.

After five minutes, the bartender approaches. "Excuse me, ladies. Two shots of bourbon, compliments of the gentlemen at the end of the bar." He points to the same guys Zoe zeroed in on earlier.

"Bingo, works like a charm," she says, raising a shot glass and nodding at the guys. "Bottoms up."

I tilt my head back, then come up coughing. My cheeks are burning. Jeez, I must be getting drunk. "That-a-girl," Zoe says, patting me on the back. The boys make their way toward us.

"Ladies," says the cuter of the two, sidling up to Zoe. She deftly shifts positions, so he's now next to me.

"Yum-o, we coulda used a double of that, right, Jane?" Zoe says. I nod like an idiot.

"I'm Jon," says the cute one, shaking my hand. "Pete," says the other guy, who manages a hand on Zoe's thigh for a millisecond before she swats it away.

"Jane S.S. here is a brilliant rising star in the super-glam world of magazine publishing," says Zoe. "And what do you guys do?"

"We're drifters, wanderers, nomads of the soul," Jon says.

"Interesting," I say, finding my voice. I notice Jon has the same dreamy chocolate eyes as Jacob, my ex.

"What does that mean exactly?" Zoe asks. "Are you unemployed?" I shoot her a look.

"More like, in between gigs," Pete says.

"Hmm," Zoe says. "Well, thank you, gentlemen, for the drinks. We actually have some work to do. We're in the middle of a business meeting. TTYL." They slink away, clearly stung.

"What the hell, Zo? They seemed nice."

She rolls her eyes. "Jane, listen, you've got to take care of yourself. It's all well and good to get a free drink, but with your crap salary—sorry, harsh, I know, but I've been there—it's important to find a guy who can make bank, not some so-called musician" (this is a dig at Jacob) "and not some lame-o who doesn't even earn a paycheck."

Zoe buys us another round of shots, doubles this time, which is when the room starts to spin. In retrospect, it's difficult to piece together the rest of the night, the various gestures and glances and decisions that led me from sloshing those several ounces of liquor down my throat to waking up in an unfamiliar bed with an unfamiliar boy lying next to me. What I do remember is rocking out to that terrible Helena Hope country song that's on every radio station this summer, first with Zoe on our stools and then later with some guy on the dance floor. I remember another round of shots—vodka? gin?—with a pack of guys out on a bachelor party. I remember Zoe telling me that Mimi wants me to write about my supposed fainting condition for the magazine, and then saying it was late and skedaddling before I could wring her neck. I remember a gust of night air in my face, and then climbing into a cab even as I was half-aware that my apartment was less than a block away. And . . . that's it.

I sit up in this strange bed, and it takes my head a moment to catch up with the rest of my body; when it does, the pounding begins. I observe that I am wearing a bra, but no underwear and that the mystery man next to me appears to be naked. I glance around the room that belongs to a guy whose name I cannot recall but who seems to have won the dubious prize of being the third person I've slept with (besides Jacob and my college boyfriend). I see a desk, a dresser, a butterfly chair, and—aha!—the various pieces of my new suit twisted up and tossed onto a set of golf clubs in the corner.

Careful not to disturb the unknown sleeper beside me, I vacate the bed and tiptoe back into the various pieces of my suit, feeling even more uncomfortable in the outfit than I did a day earlier. On the street, it takes me less than a minute to orient myself. I spot two falafel joints and a tattoo parlor, and then a pair of teenagers clad all in black, both of them lugging giant backpacks and looking and smelling as if they haven't showered in a week. I shudder, feeling unclean by association. I must be on St. Mark's Place. I hail a cab uptown.

Back in my apartment I chug three glasses of water, peel off each wrinkled piece of my suit, and stand naked before the mirror, blinking at the image of my nude self. Here I am, I think, the survivor of a one-night stand. Feeling half-amazed and half-ashamed at this turn of events, I search for physical signs of my transformation. But my skin neither beams a special glow nor breaks out in hives; it's as unblemished as ever, not a freckle marring the smooth, pale surface, nothing amiss to give me away. Mimi would probably love for me to blog about this experience; the thought brings on a shivery wave of nausea.

I begin to detect the cling of an invisible film, sticky and stinky on my skin, and I scratch at it, feeling even sicker. I try to convince myself that I'm imagining it. I simply feel icky from last night's random coupling, I reason; all I need is a cold shower to rinse off the foulness. But a part of me knows better. I flash on yesterday's meeting—Mimi's empty presentation, the meaningless corporate speak, all of the gleaming eyes and clapping hands—and just in time, I rush to the wastebasket.

11

Ed Comello, Mail Manager

Just for kicks, I decide to time the morning's mail drop-off: twenty-three minutes to sort and distribute the load into everyone's individual boxes. Damn, it used to take me sixteen. The names keep changing on the slots, and it's been like musical chairs out on the floor—this one going to that cubicle, that one moving into that office, another one booted out for good. I've been at this for a while now, but all this lunatic switching around and trying to figure out whose mail goes where, it's keeping me on my toes.

Used to be, it meant good news when the mail labels changed. One of the girls moving up to a better job somewhere else, someone new coming in, eager to take over the spot. But now it's like I work at a funeral home, only removing labels for tragedy and misfortune. I don't always know the story—what with all the new folks around I'm not as entrenched in the gossip—but I can feel it. It's in the atmosphere; it's frosty, makes me shiver.

I take a quick break to page through the *Post* and grab a cup of coffee. One of the new girls walks by and gives me a look like, *What's with the slacking?* As if I don't see the lot of them messing around on Facebook half the day. No one used to mind if I rested my legs now and then. The girls would strut by in their tall shoes, and ask me, "How 'bout them Mets?" like they knew anything about the team besides that I'm a fan. Just being nice. Even Louisa would stop to chat. I'd ask after her two kids, and she'd do the same about my Becky and Joey, wondering how they were doing in school. Small talk, but friendly. Real nice. The boss's assistant, Jenny, would bring me little knickknacks for Becky, sparkly nail polishes and rainbow socks. Sweet girl. Too bad.

Leah passes by and offers up a little smile, but doesn't stop to talk. Everyone's on edge these days. Probably would do them all a world of good to just wrestle it out in a good old-fashioned catfight. Some scratching, hair pulling, the whole works. But I've learned these girls are experts at the nicey-nice kind of fighting, the subtle digs and jabs that are hard to spot. Sneaky sabotage. Much nastier.

Laura appears before me and clears her throat. She's never asked me my name and, as far as I know, probably thinks I don't have one. "We're still getting mail here for Louisa"—she whispers the name, like it belongs to the devil—"and Mimi doesn't like it. I'll need you to change the envelope labels so they're addressed to Mimi." She barks it like an order.

"Oh, like print 'em out with my label maker?" I say, joking, as if I've got one.

Laura looks relieved. She was probably nervous I couldn't write or something. "Yeah, that's fine, whatever," she says. "Just make sure they're properly changed."

That's *your* job, I want to say. But I know how things work around here, so I keep my lips buttoned. Laura walks off. No "thank you," of course. So now I've got this new job responsibility, dictated by some twenty-three-year-old assistant who's been on the job all of a couple of months.

I hunker down to write out the new labels with Mimi Walsh's name, then I page through the mail and stick them over the letters addressed to Louisa Harding. As if a sticker can erase a legacy. It makes me wonder about the new boss. To feel so threatened by someone else's name on your mail, that's quite a case of the insecures.

* * *

Hers was a real get for me. It meant no more shuttling clothing racks all day to and from those snooty girls at *Teen Fashionista*, who would probably mellow out a little if they ate the occasional meal. And no more delivering mail to those sissy boys up at *Metro*, or lugging all kinds of heavy furniture onto the sets of *Home Sweet Home*. *Hers* is mostly small packages and shopping bags, like every day's somebody's birthday. All the girls get the papers, too, which means I can scan the headlines on my rounds before I drop them off. And their free table's the best. Plenty of Made for TV crap and self-help hardcovers that sell on eBay lickety-split. I finally swung the *Hers* floor last year after Manny retired and Christopher left to get surgery on his bum knee.

"Cheer up, honey," I say, delivering a large package to Jane at her desk. She seems the most worried of the bunch. She's also the prettiest—thick dark hair, glasses that make her look like one of those sexy librarians. Maybe most guys wouldn't find her to be the best looking. She's not what you'd call a classic beauty, but she's got a way about her.

"I'm OK, Ed. I just had a rough night and I'm hungover as can be." She scrunches up her pointy little nose—her sign that she's working hard, I've learned—then flips her hair in a way that leaves it all in a crazy mess. For some reason I find it attractive as hell. I try not to stare.

"Two days till the weekend, right, honey?"

"Amen to that," Jane says, then signs for the package. "Please tell me this is my Xanax."

They sometimes open up to me, the girls. "Aw, you don't need that junk."

"Oh, yes, I do. You've been around, you know what's up." She tears open the cardboard and fishes out a pill bottle, holds it up like a trophy. "Thank God. Want one?"

"Maybe next time." I head down to the mailroom to pick up the midday stack, which includes a cake box from one of those swanky uptown bakeries. It's addressed to Zoe, the Web manager. One thing I'll never understand, why all these companies are always sending the girls dessert.

"Ooh, lookie loo, cupcakes," Zoe says, cracking the lid when I deliver the box. "And they've got jelly bean nipples so they look like boobs! Apparently August is National Breastfeeding Month, says the American Maternal Health Association. Who knew?" Well, that makes a lot of sense, a pound of butter and sugar to promote the health of moms and babies. "Yum-o! Want one, Ed?"

I hope I'm not turning red; no way would I walk around this place eating a breast cupcake. "Nah, I gotta watch the old ticker. Doctor's orders. Hey, who gets Regina's mail when she's outta town, Victoria or Leah?" It's extra confusing now that there are two executive editors.

"Depends on who you're trying to impress. Maybe split it up halfsies, just to be safe?"

"Gotcha."

"Unless of course it's anything good. Then you can hand it right over to me, and I'll put it aside it until Regina's next visit." Zoe winks.

I weave the aisles with my mail cart, trailed by the *click-click-clicking* of high heels. It's such a familiar sound that I've come to think of it as the soundtrack of the floor, the *Hers* theme song or anthem. I watch the girls teetering around on those tall shoes, and I honestly feel bad for them. I did even before all this nonsense started. They're all so pretty with their nice, shiny hair and fancy outfits, but I'm always hearing them moan about how fat they look or how so-and-so fellow hasn't called them back. It breaks my heart, how sad they can be.

I swing by Drew's desk, since she takes the creative director's mail. I hand her both a bunch for Lynn and a bunch that's kept coming in for Mark. I brace myself. The first time I gave her Mark's pile after he got fired, she smiled at me in the most miserable way and then fingered each letter like it was from a dead relative. This time she sorts through his stack like it's no big deal. *Phew.*

Leah's now sitting where Liz used to be, and Liz is long gone, so I hand both their bundles to Leah. "Thanks, Ed," she says, flipping through the stack. "Ooh, what's this?" She holds up a package with the return address "The Putney Academy. Putney, Vermont," then tears it open. "How's it going with you, Ed? How are your kids?"

"Not bad. Joey's cleaning up on his T-ball league this summer, and Becky starts kindergarten in the fall. They grow up fast."

"Sometimes not fast enough, that's what I think. All the dirty dishes, all the poopy diapers, all the laundry." Leah laughs as she glances through the contents of her package. "My husband must've sent out for this. It's information about a school, a possibility for our daughters down the line. Look at this. They have all the students feed the animals and work the farm. They help harvest the vegetables that go in their lunches. So cute."

"Pretty cool," I say, though I wonder why in the world you'd pay to send your kids off to do hard labor, when they could be comfortable in a classroom, learning their math and history. "Your daughters are still real small, right?"

"Nearly eighteen months," she says, setting aside the materials. "Let me ask you something, Ed." Leah focuses on me, a serious look in her eyes. "How come you live in New York City? Why settle here?"

"Uh, I s'pose cuz I've lived here all my life. My wife and I have decent jobs."

"Yeah, but there are jobs everywhere, right? I mean, with all the other places you could choose to live in the world, why stay in New York?"

I'm not sure the reason for the sudden third degree. This whole place has seriously gone bonkers. "Our families are here, y'know? We're close. And they help out."

"Family, right." The way she says it, I can't tell if she thinks it's a good thing or a bad thing.

"I'll be honest," I say. "Sometimes I think about shipping off with my wife and kids out to the middle of nowhere, where groceries and rent are cheap and there's space to breathe and we don't have to be shoved up against a dozen other families, two feet away on top and below and on either side, everyone all up in our business." As soon as I say this aloud, I realize it's the truth.

"So do you think you'll do it?" she asks. "Pull the trigger and skip town?"

"Nah, probably not. I can't really picture leaving this place."

My phone rings: the wife, her usual smoke-break check-in. "Excuse me," I say to Leah. I slip off into the supply closet for some privacy. "Hi, hon."

"Hey, Eddy. How's the grand land of glamour and bullshit?"

"Same old. How goes it with you?"

"Rotten. Someone splashed clam sauce all across my shirt this morning, and I don't have a change. Why don't you shuttle me over something nice from the fashion closet?"

"It's a plan." It makes me laugh, the thought of my wife waiting tables in one of those ridiculous gowns they've got lining the racks here. "The August issues came in today. Want me to bring one home for you?"

"Nah, I'm through with that junk," she says. "All the pretty models and all those goddamned *tips*, reading that magazine just makes me feel like crap about myself. And you know I'm not crap."

"Not even close." I see my wife's point. I've flipped through *Hers* once or twice. Every story's about how to fix this or that, how to be prettier or skinnier or happier.

"Any sandwich spottings at lunch today?" she asks.

"Negative." My wife loves the office gossip. She thinks it's hilarious that the girls here all order the same salads every day, dressing on the side. Jane actually went for two slices of pizza today—hangover food, probably—but I don't like to mention Jane to my wife.

"Imagine if one of those girls ordered a double cheeseburger with a big old pile of French fries. I'd kill to see all the reactions when she walked through the office."

"You're making me hungry," I say.

"Probably get fired on the spot."

"Funny thing is, anytime the recipe lady brings down food from the test kitchen—French fries, cookies, you name it—they all pounce. You should see 'em. Like wild animals."

"Well, duh, calories in free food don't count. Everyone knows that."

"So that's how it works?"

"And what's Her Highness, Ms. Mimi, wearing?" My wife is always trying to get me to describe everyone's outfits—the materials, the colors, the brands—but I'm no good at it. The best I can do is "a purple dress" or "high heel boots."

"How about I find out for you?"

"Seriously?"

"Sure," I say. I figure, what the hell? I'm not scared of Mimi like everyone else is. She can't fire me.

I say good-bye to my wife, then I whiz past Laura's desk—I ignore her "Excuse me!"—and march right into Mimi's office, package in hand (the label says her name, I checked). "You can sign here," I announce, handing her a pen before she has the chance to say her assistant can sign for it.

I hesitate, then speak up: "Hey, I'm curious. What brand are those nice shoes you're wearing today?"

Mimi looks at me like she's seen a ghost. It's pretty funny, I've gotta admit. Then she shrugs and grabs her notepad. She writes out the word in ink as red as Mars and hands me the slip of paper.

Fendi, I tell my wife that night, sensing the power in the word. *Fendi.*

12

Leah Brenner, Executive Editor

With five minutes left before I need to skedaddle out the door, I'm racing around my home office grabbing folders while also trying to keep an eye on Rose, who's eked her way in and is now teetering across the carpet to my pile of *Hers* back issues. She picks up the most recent one, the first-bound version of August that just came into the office, a week before the final version will ship out to newsstands and subscribers. I don't have the energy to discipline, so I watch absentmindedly as my toddler rips the cover in two and then tosses the torn magazine halfway across the room. Good arm—my baseball-obsessed husband would swoon. The issue lands sprawled open to Mimi's first editor's letter. Rose peers at the page; it features a photo that appears to be a friendlier (and thinner) twin of Mimi, perching in an almost-too-short skirt against her desk. Rose begins wailing.

"Thatta girl, good judge of character," I say, although it's more likely she's reacting to her sisters crying in the next room. I hoist up my daughter and glance at the page. Mimi's hair blowout for the photo shoot was rumored to cost four hundred dollars, and when Lynn showed her the shots, she insisted on more Photoshop-cropping of her waist and arms. I can barely make my way through her note: It's all sunshine and happiness for the summer, her loopy "Cheers, Mimi" sign-off stamped at the bottom in red ink. A sidebar features staff quotes about all our fun warm-weather plans. Laura had to pry them out of us, because really, who's had time this summer to frolic about on the beach or picnic in the park while on Mimi's grueling watch? A blurb on the bottom tells readers they can buy Mimi's skirt from the Gap for 20 percent off by mentioning they spotted it in their favorite magazine—clever. I kick aside the issue and grab my briefcase.

Maria appears to fetch Rose. I wonder for the hundredth time whether I should give the girls' nanny some warning about the job search that's likely on her horizon. Surely she knows something's been off; for the past three months, as often as I've greeted Rob at the door at six, he's had to come and coax me out of my office and soothe me through my tears. Even the girls have been crankier. And on the evenings before my work-from-home days, Maria has taken to laying out clothes for me along with the babies' next-day outfits, a not-so-subtle message that it would be a good idea for me to change out of my ratty pajamas while I work.

I glance at my watch: 7:58 a.m., August 2. My weeks of relative safety finishing up the October issue are speeding by—two out of three now gone. Just one week until I'm likely out, I think. I resolve to break the news to Maria tomorrow. Then I'll pass along her information to Suzie in H.R., who can give out her phone number to whomever they hire next. Although at the rate the firing and hiring is going, it seems like women with children are discouraged from joining the staff of *Hers*. Mothers can't stay until the wee hours of the night to ship pages. Mothers have to go home and cook for their family, clean their house, assist with homework, and do all the other things *Hers* offers tips for and supposedly reveres. I've heard Mimi rib (or threaten?) Victoria that she'll need at least a year's notice before she gets herself knocked up.

"Maria, you're a saint," I say. I kiss the tops of all three of my daughters' heads, then race out the door, manage to catch my train, and—a miracle!—slide into my cubicle by 9:30.

"Tweet, tweet," announces Jonathan, floating through the office and flapping his arms. "Tweet, tweet."

"What in the hell?" I say under my breath.

"Isn't he adorable?" says Victoria, who apparently has the hearing of a bat and is now casting a shadow over my cubicle. After so many years in an office, I'm still alarmed at the lack of privacy of my new space. It's like setting up shop in the middle of a cocktail party, people constantly cozying up to chat, the only polite escape a plea for the ladies' room.

"T-minus two minutes until our Twitter seminar," Jonathan says. "Everybody flit on over to the conference room."

I bring my notebook, mostly to doodle. The term "social media" makes me want to hole up in the stacks at the library and bury myself in an ancient, dusty book. I do keep a photo blog of my girls, mostly because I'm not organized enough to actually make prints and also because I was always accidentally leaving someone off of group e-mails. Some mommy blogger friends have urged me to sign up for Twitter, but my brief forays onto the site have revealed a wasteland of self-promotion and inanity. I imagine it would take a dedicated digger a lot of effort to unearth occasional flashes of wit. I'd rather not take on the challenge.

Mimi calls us to attention. "Ladies and ladies"—this joke has become her standard fare and, never funny to begin with, it's given me a pang ever since Mark got the pink slip—"the man who has transformed Twitter into his personal playground, the get-your-self-gorgeous guru who's the toast of the Twitterati, the media maven who's wracked up, I kid you not, one hundred thousand followers, I present to you, Mr. Join Jonathan!" The back door of the conference room swings open and in runs Jonathan, a cape fanning out behind him. He's fluttering pieces of paper into the air like he's a walking fortune cookie. One lands on my lap, and I unfold it: "@JoinJonathan: Big night out? A dab of glitter 2 ur eyelid crease makes peepers pop, & preps u 4 the rockin after-party!" I dab at the bags under my eyes, suddenly self-conscious.

"Ladies," says Jonathan, jogging a lap around the conference room. "I am here to help you expand your social media know-how and unleash your personal flair in order to grow the *Hers* brand . . . to infinity and beyond! Prepare to get the lowdown on savvy strategies to engage your audience, brilliant techniques to deliver incredible value, and creative ways to maximize user content. Ready to get going?"

I hear mumbling from Zoe, who's sitting next to me. "What's that?" I whisper.

"I said, just because he has a gazillion sleazy workout buddies from David Barton and thousands of randoms from Grindr and Scruff following him on Twitter doesn't make him some kind of social media maven. I bet he pays for followers." I nod, though I have no idea what she's talking about. "I should be running this thing. Join Jonathan? Hells to the no." I shrug, though Zoe is right; this silliness does seem like it's solidly Web manager territory.

Jonathan hooks up his laptop to the overhead projector, and the screen reads "Ready to get going?" in Comic Sans font. God help us.

"Oh, and the hashtag for this meeting is #Hersjoinsjonathan," he says. Zoe rolls her eyes, but I'm just confused. I see Laura whip out her phone, and moments later Jonathan pulls HootSuite.com onto the screen and points out her tweet: "@LovelyLaura1989: Lovin Her's new Twitter plan! #Hersjoinsjonathan." Huh, what plan? And how humiliating that someone on our editorial staff can't properly use an apostrophe, and that it's being broadcast to the World Wide Web. On the plus side, it seems phones are fair game at this meeting, so I take out mine and discretely load up a game of Words with Friends.

The next hour reminds me of my brief stint as a premed student, a period put to an end by my first Organic Chemistry lecture that may as well have been delivered in Mandarin. Gibberish words like "bitly," "analytics," and "tout" flash across the screen as Jonathan fills us in on dozens of ways to get as many people as possible to acknowledge our brand's existence. I don't see the point of this manic race to collect followers, but I sense it's not a good idea to raise my hand and ask.

"From now on, twice a day Laura will be e-mailing the staff with suggested tweets about articles we're trying to promote on-line, plus goings-on about the office," says Jonathan. "And I'll be encouraging you to tweet *Hers* beauty tips and giveaways."

"As in, the stuff we already tweet on the official *Hers* handle?" Zoe asks.

"Yes, but a hipper, funner version of that." Zoe smirks; even she knows "funner" isn't a word.

Lynn raises her hand. "Here's the thing. I use Twitter to share news about my favorite artists and their gallery openings—like, which ones will have free wine and cheese, wink wink. And to chat about which sexy male singers I'd like to serenade me. You know, the usual stuff. So how exactly does *Hers* fit into that?" Jonathan looks perplexed.

Abby jumps in: "I think what Lynn's getting at is, How we can separate the personal from the professional on our Twitter accounts?"

"Aha, excellent question," says Jonathan. "That brings me to my next slide: Be human." The slide actually says this, next to a photo of two women who look as if they've spent a collective six hours getting ready; they're fake-laughing and huddled over their phones. It does not surprise me in the slightest that this is Jonathan's idea of "being human."

"I definitely don't suggest just posting whatever we send you like you're some sort of droid," Jonathan says, and then launches into a performance of a very impressive robot dance. I wonder how long he's practiced. "The point is to bring your own unique personality and flair to the tweet so that users will really connect with you and get a glimpse of what it's like to be in the glamorous world of *Hers*. If I just tweeted, 'Sephora now has neon lipstick,' would anyone pay attention?"

"No way!" says Laura. That girl has a tendency to answer rhetorical questions.

"Instead, I get folks' attention with something like 'Neon lipstick is the new Brazilian wax: Risqué, but *so* now—& the boys'll

luuurve it! Hit up Sephora to try.' I rock my Jonathan-ness, and followers respond. I infuse the professional with my personality.
See?" Lynn is nodding, but Abby's brow is furrowed. I wonder
what Jonathan would think of my husband's and my no-Internet
Brenner Unplugged nights.

"OK, activity time!" Jonathan accompanies his clap with a little
leap. "Everyone take a worksheet and pass. I've blocked out 140
characters—the length of one tweet. I'd like you all to define yourself using this space. Bonus if you can do it in 125, so followers can
retweet your answer."

Is he serious? How vapid must you be if you can be summed up
in 140 characters? Victoria winks at me, so I face the paper. *"Hers*
editor, mom of triplets, wife of Rob, lover of wine." Oh, God, I'm
not even halfway through the allotted characters and I'm already
drawing a blank. I read over my list and add in "Soon-to-be-ex" at
the start, but I manage to cross it off before Zoe peeks over my
shoulder.

"I have wine lover, too," she says. "Only I say 'pinot-phile,'
natch. Adorbs, right? That fairy faker may be at the front of the
room leading this thingy, but I will most certainly have the best
self-definition."

I try again. "Words and wine lover, bookworm, morning person
and nap enthusiast, head over heels for Daisy+Rose+Lulu+Rob,
yearning for pre-baby weight." There we go, that sounds a bit
more like me, but also like some twisted online dating profile: a
housewife on the hunt for an affair.

Jonathan asks for volunteers to read their self-definitions aloud.
Zoe's hand shoots up. "Livin the *Hers* life, luv celeb gos-
sip&beauty tips, pinot-phile, trying to balance home&work&play.
(Moonlight as TMI *Hers* sex blogger! LOL)"

"Love!" exclaims Jonathan. Zoe raises her eyebrows at me, as
in, *That's how it's done.* "See, folks, how she promotes *Hers*, but also
breathes her own personality into her description? Who *wouldn't*
follow her on Twitter? This is a perfect example of being human."

I excuse myself for the bathroom, where I splash water on my

face and have one of those ever-more-frequent out-of-body moments, wondering who the pale, haggard person is that's staring
back at me in the mirror.

When I return to the meeting, Jonathan is directing our attention to the screen. "Look, an hour ago I tweeted my followers asking if they thought bright red lips were sexy or slutty, and I've
already gotten thirty-two retweets, twelve favorites, and thirteen
new followers. This is called engagement, people!" *This is called
inane*, I think. I wonder how Rob would react if I started a Twitter
account with a handle like @momofthree and simply decided to
crowdsource the entire raising of our children: "Triplets R
18months, my boobs R worn out. To keep breastfeeding or to
switch 2 the bottle? (Or 2 turn 2 the other bottle?!) Please RT!"

"We want all your great ideas for growing *Hers'* Twitter followers," says Jonathan. "Kindly submit your memos to me by end of
day. And stay tuned for upcoming meetings on *Hers'* Facebook and
Pinterest accounts and our Foursquare and Instagram presence,
plus plans for expansion onto other social networking and Web
platforms." It's a relief to think I'll probably be out of here by
these follow-ups.

The next morning, I call my former coworker Liz for my daily
venting call. "Look, why don't you ditch your office and come
meet me for an afternoon date?" she says.

"In *Brooklyn?*" Pre-parenthood, back when we lived in Williamsburg, Rob and I spent many a boozy Sunday brunching and playing
poker with Liz and Jake at their brownstone in Cobble Hill. That
feels like a century ago.

"You say that like it's San Francisco. Yeah, in Brooklyn. Why
not? Your girls have Maria. Keep your phone on to field the crazy
boss lady's demands and come out here to yuppie babyville. You
can call it story research."

I meet Liz at one of those coffee shops that open at ten a.m. and
don't seem to offer the option of plain black. Off a menu of drinks
bearing the names of women writers, I request an Eavan Boland
Earl Grey tea. Liz is sprawled across a divan in the corner, sipping

a Lydia Davis latte and cooing at her baby, Matilda. We exchange a double kiss. "Sorry if I'm sweaty," she says. "Tilly and I just came from mommy-and-me yoga-lates."

I roll my eyes. "Of course you did."

"So what's new in Hell?" she asks, waving to a pair of women who walk in pushing strollers.

"Now Mimi wants us to whore ourselves out on Twitter."

"Leah, everyone's on Twitter. I follow this coffee shop's feed, and if you can match the tweeted quote to the author who wrote it, you get that drink for free. It's fun."

"Oh, spare me. Also, all these random freelancers have started appearing in the office. It's like we're hosting the Oscars and we've got seat fillers."

"The parade of new faces. It's inevitable, right? Believe me, you'll be thrilled when you're finally gone." Liz doesn't even pretend she thinks I won't be fired. A woman taps her on the shoulder and says she's looking forward to baby sign language tomorrow.

"What is this, a flipping commune? A cult?" I whisper.

"I know, I know, but it's great. Doesn't it feel isolating not to be around people who have babies your girls' age? Ooh, I know, you should start a club in Westfield for moms of multiples!"

"And when exactly would I do that, Liz? At four a.m. before the rest of my day begins? We could meet at one of those after-hours clubs where our screaming babies would fit in quite nicely with the wasted clientele."

"OK, I get it. All hail Leah Brenner, the busiest person in the world."

"You got that right. So, do you really like this new life, the whole no-job thing?"

"I do. I adore it, genuinely."

"Huh." Liz does look fantastic. She's replaced her prebaby full face of product with just a dab of blush, mascara, and lip gloss, and it suits her. She even looks like she's been sleeping. I wonder why I'm not dripping with envy. "No offense, but do you feel like your brain has gone to mush?"

"Hmm, it's possible. But to tell you the truth, I don't really mind. I'm high on the endorphins of motherhood."

"That's wonderful," I say, meaning it, although I've only gotten an endorphin rush from a long run. Certainly never from an afternoon with my triplets.

"Listen," I say. "Rob and I are taking a trip to Vermont this weekend, just the two of us. We're hoping to live out the illusion that we're still actual people, beyond just our identities as parents."

"So you'll hit the clubs and dance all night? Swig mimosas at breakfast?"

"Yeah, right, I hear there's a crazy club scene up in rural Vermont. More like, I can't wait to get eight hours of sleep and to take a shower without three separate interruptions while I'm working up a lather."

"This is it, huh? You're shipping out and abandoning all your dear friends in the tristate area?"

"Hey, you abandoned me first, remember? I'm down in the *Hers* trenches every day, while you, my supposedly trusty comrade, went AWOL to go sip lattes on the sidelines."

"Amen." Liz raises her mug. "Seriously, I think you'll love it up in Vermont. Send me some maple syrup. So, who's watching the girls?"

"Well, Maria's staying over on Saturday, and my mom, God help us, will be there on Sunday. Actually—"

"I know, you want me to come over and supervise so your mother doesn't get your daughters drunk on martinis or start reorganizing your bookshelves by degree of feminism, right?"

"Oh, would you please?" Liz is such a gem. "Just for an hour or two. And afterward, you can fill me in on exactly how much terror my mom's inflicted on her granddaughters."

"Tilly and I will be there, no question."

I throw my arms around my friend, whose chest is even more substantial than usual. "Wow, your boobs are huge."

"I know, isn't it great? Speaking of which." She whips one of them out and Matilda latches on. It looks sort of peaceful, breast-feeding just one baby. No one in the coffee shop bats an eye.

After Tilly is done feeding, Liz and I stroll through Prospect Park and visit the zoo. The monkeys entertain us with their un-abashed copulation, and Liz shields her daughter's eyes. Then we break for more drinks, this time at a teahouse where you can mix your own blend from a list of fifty flavors. It's all lovely and pleas-ant, and when it's time to go home, I board the train, wave through the window at my old coworker friend, and feel genuinely happy for her that she's in such a place of bliss.

I settle into my seat, and at first the buzz of overcaffeination is a thrilling rush. The train lurches forward, and I'm content to watch the scenery whoosh by and to half listen to the conversation of the couple behind me. But I quickly grow antsy, at once overstimu-lated and listless. I pull out my *Hers* folder and begin editing a story about limiting your kids' Halloween candy intake. I cut words to clean up the prose and tweak the structure to crystallize the service. The work calms and centers me.

"You must be dying to get home to your daughters," Liz said to me before we hugged good-bye. It somehow seemed shameful to admit that I wasn't, so I just nodded. I love my girls, of course, but I haven't missed them while spending the day with Liz and her kid instead of with my own. In fact, as a rule, by Sunday night, after two full days in mother mode, I'm usually itching for Monday morning—to get back to work and to using my brain.

The thought of not having a job strikes terror in my heart.

The preparation required for parents of three toddlers to skip town for twenty-four hours must be on par with orchestrating the invasion of a small country. I call on my own army of help: Maria has agreed to stay the night, but needs to duck out early on Sunday for a niece's baptism. My neighbors on either side are on standby for emergencies. And though my mother moaned plenty about it—she has Cara's play programs to finish, and tickets to a Broad-way matinee, plus she could use some peace and quiet considering all the stress I'm putting her through with my job insecurity (thanks, Mom!)—she's agreed to watch the girls on Sunday. Reinforcements will arrive in the afternoon in the form of Liz and her daughter.

I've bottled what feels like a lifetime supply of breast milk, written out a book's worth of instructions for the various caretakers, and even managed to throw a few things into a duffel bag for our trip. Finally Rob and I bid a weepy good-bye to the girls (the tears are ours, not theirs) and make our escape.

I'm not sure if it's the fresh country air or the fact that it's our first adults-only getaway in over a year, but after five hours in the car of rocking out to Radiohead, Talking Heads, and (though Rob barely tolerated it) Katy Perry, I am positively giddy. It's late afternoon—the sky cerulean and cloudless—when we pull into the dirt driveway of the first house we've arranged to look at in Windham County, Vermont.

"Hey, folks!" Our realtor is waiting for us outside, clipboard in hand. He proceeds to tour us through three so-so houses. The dullness of hearing about yet another set of stainless steel bathroom fixtures is mitigated by the fact that his spoken words are just as entertaining as the script he wrote for that PowerPoint he sent us. How he describes it, a house doesn't have two half-baths, a mudroom, and central AC, but rather "two additional cozy sanctuaries to steal away for some privacy," "a designated spot for the hustle and bustle of transition, a veritable way station between public and private life," and "a cool sense of comfort in every nook and cranny of these 3,400 square feet." You'd think he was selling enlightenment rather than real estate.

Just as I'm starting to think the house featured on the Power-Point was a fake, the kind of bait I remember Manhattan realtors would use to lure you in to the dumps that were actually in your price range, we pull up a long, winding drive, woodland all around, and there it is: the dream house, even more dramatic than it appeared on our screen. Inside, the decorating is terrible, just as I remember, but it smells like chocolate chip cookies. I know it's an old seller's trick to bake before showing your house, but I don't care; it smells like home.

Rob listens diligently as the realtor goes on about the post-and-beam construction that will give us a special historical link to the Ancient Greeks who first popularized the architectural style; meanwhile, I slip upstairs. I discover an alcove off of the bedroom, where floor-to-ceiling windows give me a spectacular view to the backyard, all hills and running water. The setting sun is a fireball hovering over the creek, and the sky's the color of ripe peaches. It's easy to imagine transporting my basement office hovel to this grandiose spot. I immediately cook up several coverlines I wish I'd pitched in our recent meeting. Here is a place I could be creative.

A moment later, I feel a pair of arms envelop my waist. "Hey, Ms. Vermont," Rob says in my ear. "Our realtor-slash-spirit-guide is taking a call. Remember the PowerPoint slide of the bedroom, the one with the couple?" He's kissing my neck.

Rob obviously wants to reenact that scene of copulation, but I'm preoccupied by the fact that this is someone else's bed, and who knows when they last washed the sheets. "We've got a B&B for later, sweetheart," I say. I lead him down the hall, hoping he doesn't get the idea to undress me on the staircase.

"This is double the size of our house," Rob says. "And half the cost. We could afford to send the girls to that fancy private school."

"Well, at least one of them. Maybe two."

"I read about this great cheese shop for dinner," Rob says, and I realize I'm starving.

After devouring three grilled cheeses between the two of us and buying two blocks of cheddar to go, Rob and I discover a general store that sells two-dollar pints of "reject" Ben & Jerry's, meaning the factory screwed up and put in a double dose of chocolate chunks in the Chunky Monkey. I think I could be forever happy here. Happy and fat, but who would even care so far from civilization? We browse a thrift shop, and all the skirts are long and flowy, all the tops empire waisted. Picturing the future fat and happy me, I buy a paisley-printed peasant blouse for twelve dollars.

On the drive to our inn, I spot a sign that reads MAGAZINE SHACK. "Pull over," I tell Rob, then hop out of the car. I'm on autopilot, scouring the racks for *Hers,* like I do in every airport and supermarket. It's usually front and center in the women's section (and when it's not, I take it upon myself to rejigger the display). But here, the title is nowhere to be found. "Excuse me," I ask the clerk. "Do you have *Hers?*"

"Uh, her what? And whose?"

I wave her away, not wanting to get mired in an Abbott and Costello exchange. I content myself with browsing through the titles about hiking and skiing and environmentally sustainable cooking. I'm sort of intrigued by a place where *Hers* doesn't seem to exist, where it might as well be a figment of my imagination.

"The new *Brattleboro Bulletin* came in yesterday, if you're interested," the woman says. I smile, wondering if I really pass for a local. She brings me a copy.

The cover image is beautiful—a pair of backpackers perched on the precipice of a waterfall—though the coverlines could use some work: "6 Tasty Microbrews of Summer" takes the top left spot. Apparently no one told the editors that even numbers don't sell on the newsstand. Or maybe they do here in Vermont; who knows?

It comes to me like a bolt: *I could be the editor in chief!* Before I even open the darn thing, I'm already dreaming of my future life in command of the *Brattleboro Bulletin.*

When I do crack the issue's spine, I'm appalled to discover—on the very first page, no less—a grammatical error of the most egregious sort: the presence of an apostrophe when none is needed. It's a blunder I'm barely willing to excuse on a sign for an immigrant-owned business (YUM YUM SOUP AND SALAD'S). I keep flipping pages. The editors' page features photos of haggard, makeup-free women: One identifies her hobbies as canning and bird watching, and another says she's a romance language enthusiast and full-time mother to Uno, Deux, and Tre, which is apparently not a joke. I flip back to the well. The features are a four-page story on how to start beekeeping in your backyard and a six-page profile on a local woman who's been championing an "If it's yellow, let it mellow" initiative, with considerable success. I gag, discarding the magazine.

"Do you want to buy it?" the clerk asks. I shake my head and flee.

In our room at the inn, Rob settles onto the bed with a stack of mortgage literature, and I'm rattling on about the *Brattleboro Bulletin*. "They would probably kill to have an experienced editor like me heading up their quaint little publication," I say, trying on my new top.

"You do know who you sound like, right?" Rob says.

"Don't you dare say it!" I shout, knowing he means my mother. I'm suddenly nervous about my daughters being alone with her for several hours; so much could go wrong. "So, what do you think?" I spin around, modeling my new purchase. Rob cracks up. "What, that bad?"

"Baby, you'd look gorgeous wearing a potato sack, but that is just not you."

I pout and go to check myself out in the mirror. I have that saggy-boob, bloated-stomach appearance of someone who has everyone wondering if she's pregnant or not. "You're right, I look awful." I flop back onto the bed, and hot tears start streaming down my cheeks. "I'd never fit in in Vermont. I don't even like maple syrup!"

"Baby, come here." My husband reaches out his arms, and I crawl onto his lap. "When we moved to New Jersey, did you start buying hairspray in bulk? Did you become a Bruce Springsteen fanatic?"

"No, I hate The Boss."

"Exactly, and hairspray makes you sneeze. Moving somewhere new doesn't mean you need to change your identity to fit some made-up idea of what the people there are like."

"I know," I say, whimpering.

"Come on, let's get you out of this ridiculous shirt."

"It smells like mothballs."

"You're right, it does. Here you go." Rob eases the shapeless piece of cotton over my head. He kisses me, and I kiss back. It makes me feel good to know my lips are the luscious hue of ripe strawberries and the glossy sheen of pearls, thanks to meticulous reapplications of my favorite Dior lip stain. I could never give up my makeup. "You're beautiful, you know," Rob says, before laying me back onto the bedspread.

I sleep so hard that I don't stir until the sun starts peeping through the blinds. It's disorienting to wake for the first time to the light, accustomed as I am to regular rousings throughout the night to tend to small people. Rob and I have planned on a morning tour of the Putney Academy, but I'm aching to be back home with my girls. I picture their tiny feet pitter-pattering across the kitchen linoleum, asking Maria about Mommy and Daddy. "Let's go home," I say. "We have years to go before the kids'll be in school." My husband kisses my forehead and nods.

In the car, Rob slips a CD into the player. "What's this?" I ask.

"Shhh, just listen." First it's a sweet, old-fashioned plinking of piano keys, and then the unmistakable voice of Ella Fitzgerald.

Rob drapes his arm around my seat back. I listen to the song and stare out the window at what's now generic highway. We could be anywhere. In her pure, smooth voice, Ella Fitzgerald is singing about pennies and falling leaves and moonlight in Vermont. She's describing the kind of breezy summer evening we had last night, and I'm surprised to realize my eyes are blurry with liquid. I hear a lyric about meadowlarks. "You know," I say, blinking my eyes clear and trying to compose myself, "I read an article in the *Brattleboro Bulletin* about the fifteen varieties of birds to look out for on nature walks. There was no mention of meadowlarks."

"Hey, smarty-pants, I didn't write the song. Would you like to enlighten me about the types of fauna of this fine state?"

"Well, I sort of skimmed the article."

Rob rolls his eyes. "You would kill someone who told you they just skimmed a story of yours in *Hers*."

The mention of *Hers* makes me squirm. "You know what?" I blurt out. "Let's put in an offer on the house."

"Really?" Rob's gape is so intent that I have to readjust his gaze to the road.

I feel suddenly certain. "Yeah, let's do it." We toast the decision with chunks of Grafton cheddar, and it's either my giddiness or the cheese's sharp tang that makes my tongue tingle. I spend the next four hours half-appreciating the peaceful quiet of the adults-only ride and half crazy with excitement to see my daughters and soon embark on this new adventure together as a family.

13

Zoe Lewis,
Web Manager

My to-do list: insane! I'm toggling between uploading our August content onto HersMag.com, gabbing with fans on our Facebook page, and reading the latest batch of Bedroom Test Drive questionnaires to pick today's culprit for the blog. My mind's racing like a maniac, but it's cool because there's nothing I hate more than being bored. Graham calls me hyperactive, but he's a freak of nature who can not only sit through a three-hour documentary about tree pollen but actually enjoy it.

I flip to Regina's questionnaire and read: "Acting out my husband's hot nurse fantasy was fun, but the dirty talk was AWKWARD! Cringe." I cackle, picturing our entertainment director all dressed up and ready to administer medicine.

I scan Leah's next: "I bought the sexy lingerie, but I'm ashamed to say I've been too exhausted for two weeks now to even try it on. In other words, f&*# motherhood." Jesus, I am never having kids. I'll have to bug Leah to get on it; my supply of responses is running low.

Lynn's questionnaire is nearly illegible. In chicken scratch she's scrawled, "I went out with the vibrator in my underpants and I gave the guy the remote control (on a second date, by the way!). Did I get off? Yessiree! But I swear everyone in the restaurant could hear the buzzing. It was honestly kind of a turn-on. Yee-haw!" I bowl over with laughter.

Badoop! I check my screen and see an IM from Regina: "Only noon here. Boohoo, you're 3 hrs closer to closing time."

"Ya, but I've been working my ass off 3 hrs longer," I type back. Regina and I IM all day long when she's out in Cali. "Gotta figure out the next sex test, brb."

Bedroom Test Drive was my brilliant idea that was really just a ploy to dig up dirt on my coworkers. Though that no longer includes Mimi; when she volunteered to try out the Ben Wa Kegels balls, she wrote up such a detailed play-by-play of the increased pleasure of her orgasms (ew!) that I've blushed every time I've seen her since. I've stopped including her on the call-out e-mails.

Everyone's anonymous online—I give them stupid names like "Linda Loves It" and "Wild Wendy" next to their "red hot" and "sweet and sensual" ratings of the products and experiments—but they all turn in their questionnaires to *moi*, so I know the real woman behind the write-up. If someone wants to bad-mouth me, they better watch out since I know stuff like how it turned them on to slather their partner's privates in key lime pie–flavored lube. I'm still working on Victoria to sign up.

Mimi calls me into her office. "I have your edited copy for the Kama Sutra positions," she says. "Weren't we planning to test out sex tapes this week? All the celebs are doing it and then leaking the tapes for publicity, so now the whole thing's gone mainstream."

"Apparently not that mainstream. No one's volunteered."

"Zoe, do you understand that it is your job to coax these people into participation?"

"Ya, but—"

"Think of yourself as Dr. Ruth minus the wrinkles. Ha! You're supposed to make your coworkers feel like their disgusting desires and lusty impulses are totally healthy and normal, OK? Get a sex tape tester, stat. I don't care if you have to invent her from thin air."

Mimi fixes her gaze on me and quickly proves to be more of a staring expert than I am. Then she barks out a shrill laugh that may or may not indicate that she's joking. This is exactly the kind of thing I would do, and I feel a funny sort of kinship with Mimi. Everyone's been bitching about the new boss like it's part of their jobs, but I think she's totes genius for pushing every story shorter, sharper, juicier. Louisa deluded herself that our readers wanted five-thousand-word, dull-as-dirt features on attachment parenting, and eight-page profiles on some random woman who started a charity. Yawn city. Mimi gets that we're competing with tweets and YouTube clips and hilarious gifs, not with Faulkner novels and college term papers. Duh. No one wants to sit down and read anymore; who has the attention span?

I approach the art department and set my sights on Drew. "Hey, lady, you haven't signed up as a bedroom tester yet."

"That is correct." She doesn't look up from her proof pages.

"Come on, take one for the team and videotape yourself doing it. How 'bout it, lady?"

"Get out of here, Zoe. I'm trying to work."

"Oh, chill out, Drew. It'll be fun. YOLO!"

"Excuse me, yo what?"

"You only live once! And Mark would love it." Drew shoots me a look, like somehow her relationship is still supposed to be a secret even though Lynn spilled the beans weeks ago. I'd actually love for her to submit footage of her and Mark. That guy is hella sexy. "Mark could art direct, and you'd know just the right camera settings to use. It would be a real porno masterpiece. What do you say?"

Drew sighs loudly and swivels in her seat. "Zoe, with what frequency do you think an unemployed male wants to have sex?"

"Um, I dunno, all the time? He's got nothing better to do, right?"

She laughs bitterly. "Try never. Now scram, seriously."

"OK, OK. I'll get back to you when I've got a solo project up for grabs."

Drew is a tough one. I scan the office for another potential target. I wonder if I can cajole Jonathan, and just change some of the "he"s to "she"s. I could ask Laura, but she seems more naïve than even your average twenty-three-year-old. I can imagine her recording ending up on some amateur porn hub and forwarded to everyone she knows. I'm feeling oddly benevolent, so I spare her the exploitation.

By six p.m. I still have no takers, but I won't let Mimi down. I have a feeling I'm going to go far in this new regime. I edit the on-line horoscopes, and last week our astrologer Miss Starlee said she sensed I was turning a corner in my career, which makes sense considering the current planetary alignment and my Gemini–Cancer cusp sign. I've figured out that Mimi values spunk and grit, and lucky me, I possess both of those traits in spades. I eye the office and spot Leah's vacant cube. She's working from home, but as soon as Mimi stops stringing her along, all her stuff will be cleared out, too, like she never existed at all. Then I'll be gunning for her spot.

"Hey, hon, I've got an idea." I've plied Graham with red wine and his favorite honey-glazed pork chops.

"Hmm?" He's got one eye on the Yankees, the other on the *Wall Street Journal*.

"It's a surprise," I say. "Meet me in the bedroom in ten."

"Sweetie, I'm watching the game."

"It won't take long, promise. I'll have you back to the couch by the third inning. Don't you want a little adventure?" I'm aware that Graham's idea of an adventure is sitting at his desk and bidding on a risky stock, or whatevs, but my job is at stake here, and the least he can do is help out his dear, sweet wifey. I've changed into an old baby-doll slip that a girlfriend gave me for my wedding shower and that's been shoved to the back of a drawer for the year and a half since. It's wrinkled and smells vaguely like dryer sheets, plus it's snugger around my ass now, but I can still pull it off. I've got the camera rigged up on a tripod in the corner, mostly hidden by the drapes. I blow myself a kiss in the mirror, then hop up onto the bed, and call out, "Graham-y!"

"What is it?" He barges through the door. "Oh, hello, sexy."

I start in on my best Marilyn Monroe impression, cooing, "Happy Birthday to you."

"It's my birthday, is it?" Graham sidles up to me. "Does that mean you bought me those cuff links I've been eyeing?"

"Cuff links, Graham?" We really need to work on his dirty talk.

"But seriously, it is my half birthday. You know we celebrate yours." It's true, but that's because I figured out early on that my half birthday falls a week after annual bonus time at Graham's bank. Ka-ching!

"We *are* going to celebrate," I say. "*I'm* your present." I peel off Graham's shirt and begin unhooking his belt buckle. As I lean in to his boxers, I do my best Jenna Jameson-with-a-dash-of-Betty Boop impression, thrusting my cleavage and hips, batting my eyelashes, and flashing sultry glances up at my husband. He's smirking at me, but I can tell he's excited. I throw him back against the bed, and the making out begins. I nudge Graham over to readjust our angle.

"What are you doing?"

"Nothing, just making sure we're in the shot." I point to the camera and purse my lips.

"Jesus Christ, Zoe!" He rolls off of me and reaches for his shirt. "What, did you hook us up to a live Web feed?"

"No, dummy, it's just for work." I slump back on the bed and relax my belly pooch.

"*What?!*" Graham has been sensitive ever since he discovered my *Hers* sex blog. Back when Jane and I appeared on TV to promote its launch, he demanded I pull out. But then Jane abandoned her post, and Mimi was like a puppy dog about my contributions, so we compromised and I began writing under two pseudonyms, Randiest Rachel and Married Mona. Well, *I* compromised. I figure the less Graham knows, the happier he'll be. In Mona's posts, I chronicle my actual married sex life: the quickies and shower nookie, my discovery of Graham's box of Asian Babe DVDs and the dry spell that followed, the mind-blowing sex we had the night he was promoted to a VP, the unspeakable act I agreed to do in exchange for his shelling out on $700 boots for me. Standard married-lady stuff. In Rachel's posts, I harken back to my single-girl glory days: the drunken one-night stands and early-morning headachy shame, the pregnancy scares, the occasional threesome—inserting a bit of sexting and dirty Snapchatting to make it all sound up-to-date. The blog has skyrocketed to two million hits a month, and Mimi tells me she's in talks to turn the posts into a *Hers*-branded romance novel and maybe even a sitcom on Lifetime. I'm cool with it as long as I'm played by someone like Jennifer Lawrence or Mila Kunis.

"That came out wrong," I say. "I'm not, like, hosting a screening of our rendezvous for my coworkers. Jesus, I'm not that cray-cray."

"Oh, you're not, huh?"

"I'm just testing it out, for the Web site."

"Hand me my pants."

"Graham-y, relax, will you?"

"Hand them to me now."

"So, what did you think? Red hot? Sweet and sensual? Major bust? Oh, come on, hon, I'm joking. Look, I'm stopping the recording." I pass him his pants and kiss him on his nose.

"You promise it's really off?"

"Yes, look, no red light."

"OK, then get over here, you naughty little minx." Graham pulls me toward him, and I'm giggling like a schoolgirl.

Afterward, Graham gravitates back to the couch to watch the rest of the game, and I nestle up beside him. In my dreamy post-coital state I don't even mind that my husband sounds more enthusiastic when A-Rod hits a homer than he did in the bedroom. I decide that later I'll make my own sexy little video and leave it under his pillow.

The sex tape copy is due the following afternoon. I don't have the usual completed questionnaire to consult, so I turn up the volume on my iTunes—it's that awesome Helena Hope jam, and Jane is too polite to tell me to turn it down—and I start writing freestyle:

> Theodora Thespian says, two thumbs-up. "At
> first we were camera-shy, nervous to shed our
> clothing and get down to business," notes the
> newlywed of the filming. "But after some awk-

ward fumbling, I began to think of that little red
dot in the corner as a spectator, and it was a huge
turn-on." Exhibitionists will identify with the joyful titillation of being watched, according to
Theodora, and those looking for a new thrill will
surprise themselves with what acting for the camera can stir up inside. And what about the next-
day screening? "I wish I'd had another glass of
pinot beforehand," notes the tester, who
squirmed through the viewing of her coupling.
"My hubby loved it, but I was fixated on my mortifying O face, not to mention my cellulite.
Yuck!" (Click HERE for the best cellulite-erasing
beauty treatments.) A rave review for the act itself, a pan for the follow-up. Rating: Sweet and
sensual. Click HERE for a link to the video.

I immediately erase the last sentence, cracking myself up.
Jesus, I should write erotica. I print out the write-up and drop it in
Victoria's in-box. I love to watch her editing the reviews, coughing
primly as she stumbles upon words like "oral" and "anal"—what a
prude. But today there's a sample sale at Alice + Olivia, so I let Victoria work without my lurking.

"Press event," I say to Laura on my way out. She eyes me dubi-
ously.

We shoppers are crammed like cattle into the mass dressing
room, but I don't even care because I nabbed the perfect skinny
jeans plus *the* season's wedges in 8, the most popular size. I occasionally fantasize about a reality show starring me as an expert
shopper. In fact, I've already written up the pitch and am just waiting to meet someone well connected in network TV so I can slip it
to them. I'm trying to squeeze into a size 4 pair of floral jeggings
when I feel my phone vibrate. "Hello?"

"Zoe, hi, it's May. I'm the new freelancer in the research department." I attempt one more suck in of the stomach, and eke the

zipper closed. Success! God, my ass looks amaze in these. I check myself out in the mirror, then lose my grip on the phone. Shit.

I eventually locate the device under someone's discarded bra, turquoise and lacy—*tacky*. "Sorry, sorry. What's up?"

"You weren't at your desk, and I had a question about the Bedroom Test Drive."

"Can it wait an hour? I'm at an event."

"Well, Victoria claimed this was urgent." Unbelievable—the person responsible for firing Sylvia and obliterating our research department in one fell swoop has suddenly decided that fact-checking is important. "I don't have your backup for the sex tape write-up," May says.

"It's *my* write-up. I tested it. I figured I didn't have to fill out a form. I promise I won't sue. Scout's honor."

"Well, what about your partner?"

She actually has a point there. "Graham won't care. He doesn't even read the site." It's true. He's faked it before: Once at a dinner party a colleague asked him his favorite article of mine, and he turned red in response and nearly choked on his cream of asparagus soup. I saved him with, "Graham particularly enjoys the posts on how to follow your passions and discover your true inner self," and everyone laughed—some a little too heartily, I thought—and then I gave my husband the cold shoulder for the rest of the night.

"OK, I guess that's all right," May says. Wow, that was easy. Mimi should hire more of these lightweights; it would make my job a cinch.

I buy the pants and stuff them into an old Digital Strategy Expo bag I saved from last year; this way, it'll seem like I'm returning from a work event. Back at my desk, I don't have anything pressing, so I reach out to P.R. contacts to get myself on invite lists to all the Christmas showcases. I do this every year to help out the swamped junior editors who write the gift guide. The gift bags are to die for, too; I haven't spent money on holiday presents for ages.

My sight is suddenly obscured by two hands. "Guess who?"

"OMG, Regina!" I shout.

"How'd you know?"

"Duh, you must've smoked an entire carton on your way here. You know everyone in NYC quit ages ago."

"Not you."

"That's true. Lemme bum one?" The entertainment director nods, and I yell, "Yippee!" Laura eyes me warily.

Regina and I head downstairs and sequester ourselves in the smoker's corner by the back entrance. "So what's the 411?" I ask.

"Did you hear we snagged the mean teen Janine from *Worst Moms* for the November cover shoot?"

"Oh, she's the worst!" Regina and I share a passion for terrible TV. The best part of my job is that I get to host the morning-after chats with the *Hers* reality TV e-club.

"Have you seen the *Real Housewives of St. Paul* yet?!" Regina trills, and I nod like a maniac. I was skeptical at first, but those women are clueless and catty all at once; it's amazingly juicy TV. "Hey, Zo, how about an off-site meeting?"

"Yay!" I clap my hands, thinking that's it for the day, since "off-site meeting" is Regina-speak for the bar. Regina is like my BFF in middle school: It's a party when she's around, and she's always got some mischievous scheme up her sleeve. I'm forever counting down to her next visit to New York.

We hoof it to the Mexican joint around the corner. "Laura sent me the notes from the Twitter seminar," Regina says. She throws back a shot of tequila, sucks on a lime, then scrunches up her face into a citric wince.

"Ugh, I hate to admit that it was really fab," I say. "Good thing Jonathan's ambitions seem to revolve solely around eye shadow and blush. I don't want him crowding in on my turf."

"Trust me, you're safe," says Regina. "If someone told him he could no longer spend half the day giving himself a makeover, I think he'd curl up in a fetal position and cease to function."

"But really, my Randiest Rachel handle has exploded. I've got forty thousand followers. And a billion brands have started following me and offering me free swag. Tomorrow I'm getting a massage from the guy who used to train that captured soldier guy on *Homeland*. Can you believe?"

"Good for you, working it." We clink beers. "Listen, I have an idea. I'm thinking we can drum up our own little scandal."

"Ooh! I'm in."

Regina laughs, a smoker's hack. "You haven't even heard the idea yet."

"I'm on the edge of my seat."

"Here's the deal, and no one else knows about this, so don't go running your mouth like I know you like to do."

"Who, me?" I say, though it's true that secrets have a tendency to leak out of me no matter how hard I try to prevent it.

"Everyone will be grateful in the end—and the press will be epic—but for now this has to be hush-hush, all right?"

"Check. Now tell me, before I pounce and rip it right out of you!"

"OK." Regina lays out the plan, and I toast her genius.

That night, after Graham has gone to bed, and I've ordered a blingy rose gold watch from a very convincing saleswoman on QVC, I log on to the Twitter account for my alter ego @RandiestRachel, and type in the message Regina and I planned: "Hey Kev. I'm totally hot for u, cutie pie. Come over stat. Thank Gd ur wife's away so we can play!" Then I attach the photo, the full-frontal one I downloaded from Xtube, a boobalicious woman with short blond hair and deep tan lines. Her face is blurred, but the rest of her—teeny waist, crazy curves—is on full display. I've blogged about a Kevin; Rachel is supposedly seeing him on and off. This is the first mention of a wife.

In the Twitter seminar, Jonathan was superclear about the difference between direct messages and those that get blasted out to everyone, in this case to all of @RandiestRachel's forty thousand followers. But apparently Mimi thought I was too ignorant about social media to lead the meeting; plus, maybe I was in the bathroom during that part of Jonathan's presentation. *Oops!*

I can't sleep all night, I'm so giddy with anticipation.

* * *

The first thing I do when I arrive at my desk, uncharacteristically right on time, is log on to Twitter. #RandiestRachel is a trending topic, my followers have ticked up to 56,000, and it takes me five minutes to scroll through all my direct messages. Amaze! My stomach flips as I imagine myself famous, a modern-day Monica Lewinsky or what's-her-name who slept with Tiger Woods and then got a newspaper column and all those TV gigs. *I knew I could do it!* My voice mail blinks with eight new messages, and I see that Laura has added a morning meeting with Mimi to my schedule.

"Jeez, Zoe, what did you do?" Jane whispers. "Everyone's freaking out. The *Post* has been hounding Mimi for a comment."

"You're kidding, the *Post*? OMG!"

"You don't seriously think this is a positive thing. It makes us look so sleazy. You better come up with a good story fast." This is exactly what Regina anticipated: first a bit of negative press, which would quickly fade into an excited buzz about the *Hers* brand, and then a bump up in subscriptions.

I step into Mimi's office, assuming an appropriate sulk. Victoria and Regina are already seated, and Mimi reads aloud: " '*Hers* blogger scandalizes the staid brand with racy Twitpic, plus home-wrecking to boot.' '*Hers* sinks to all-time low with nudie writer photo exposed.' " Mimi has underlined the headlines in red ink, and after she reads them out, she tosses each paper my way. "Oh, here's a good one: 'What's next for *Hers*? A line of pornography DVDs? A dating site for cheaters?' "

"Not such bad ideas," I say, smiling at Regina, who strangely won't meet my gaze.

Mimi looks at me with an expression of rage straight out of a cartoon; I'm half surprised steam isn't shooting out of her ears. It makes me want to laugh and cry all at once. "Do you think this is some kind of joke, Zoe?" she asks. "Advertisers have been pulling out left and right."

"OMG, you've got to be kidding me," I say.

"I saw you goofing off in the Twitter seminar," says Victoria. "Everyone warned me you weren't the sharpest tool in the shed, but I never expected this level of stupidity. Do you realize how your actions have tarnished this brand?"

"Come on, Vic," I say, my voice suddenly hoarse. I don't appreciate this ganging up on me. I just have to make them understand. "Listen, Regina and I—"

"Regina first alerted me to this scandal in the middle of the night," says Mimi.

"I happened to be awake," says the entertainment director, not looking in my direction. "Thank God for jet lag."

"And she's been working like a madwoman ever since, trying to talk dozens of publicists and advertisers off the edge of a cliff."

"But everyone's talking, right?" I say. "Won't that ultimately be a good thing?" I'm repeating what Regina laid out for me yesterday, and meanwhile boring a hole through the crown of her head with my eyes. She won't look up from her iPhone.

"Janine's rep isn't sure she wants her to do the cover anymore," says Victoria.

Oh, this is rich. "You're telling me that TV's worst mom is scandalized by one little nudie shot? Give me a break!"

"What I don't understand is, Randiest Rachel is a figment of your imagination, yes?" Victoria spits this out as if she wants zilch to do with my imagination. "So then who the heck is this Kevin?"

"Have you never heard of a little online flirting, Vic?" I say. "I thought we were trying to liven up this brand."

"But what's the deal with the photo?" she asks. "I mean, you're a brunette." Jesus, and she calls me dumb. Even Mimi gives her a look, like, *Are you kidding me?*

"Zoe, you can understand the difference between pumping in some fun new energy to the brand and alienating half of our subscriber base, right?" Mimi is wearing a scowl that reminds me of Louisa.

"So," I say, "you're telling me that the fifty-five-year-olds who flip through *Hers* between their freaking Bunko tournaments and their scrapbooking socials are signed on to Twitter and following Randiest Rachel?"

"That's a very flattering view you have of our readers, Zoe," says Victoria. "But guess what, those fifty-five-year-olds watch the *Today* show, which covered the story this morning." See, this is what Regina was talking about—*the press!*

"Several A-list celeb moms have unfollowed *Hers* on Twitter and put out statements condemning the brand," Regina says, finally making eye contact with me. I can see it in her pupils, the usual smirking glint replaced by a pulsing panic. I search in vain for the wink from last night that says, *Trust me, this will work out wonderfully.* Her blinks are anxious twitches.

The gravity of the situation hits me like a two-by-four. This has gone much further than Regina predicted. My mouth goes desert dry and my stomach gurgles with nerves. Until this moment I've taken it as a given that Mimi would go nuts for my charm and talent and probably promote me. Now I'm freaked out.

Regina continues: "It's not just celebrities who are taking a stand that they don't want to be associated with such filth. People are unfollowing us in droves and *Hers* is being taken off the shelves in Walmarts in two counties in Georgia."

My head's pounding muffles her words. My breath speeds up like I'm on crack. I gulp at the air, which seems suddenly absent of oxygen. I flash on an image of Graham's boring dinner parties with his coworkers: Mostly they leave me out of their debates about politics and the economy and other snooze-worthy topics, and when I do chime in I can see the dismissive looks they think they're exchanging so subtly. Graham always tells me I'm being ridiculous and paranoid, but I know what his colleagues think of me. Still, I've never really cared. I mean, every one of them would trade all that brainy babble for landing a fun job like mine. The thought of having to face those stuffy dinner parties as simply the unemployed wife of Graham—ugh, it makes me just want to give up.

"Listen, Zoe," says Mimi, "whether or not this happened accidentally—"

In a panicked rush, I cut her off. "You know who's blond? You know who that picture's of?" It's out of my mouth before I can stop it, and Regina whips her bleached bob around to face me. If she shows any indication of a truce, I tell myself, I'm prepared to back-

track and make peace. Just a flicker of a smile, or the tiniest gesture of compassion, and I'll halt what's coming, unite with my co-
conspirator and work to fix this mess as partners. But I watch as
Regina narrows her eyes. *What are you doing?* her look pleads, but
it's with contempt, not concern. And with that, she seals her fate. I
meet her steely gaze with a silent memo of my own: *You're out of
your league, lady.*

"Excuse me?" Mimi says. "Can someone please tell me what
the hell is going on here?"

"Why don't you ask Regina?" I say. She fits the profile: blond,
California tan, curvy but fit (I'm betting she's got a pair of perky
silicone sacks tucked under that cotton scoop-neck), and not so old
that it's impossible.

"I have no idea what Zoe is talking about," Regina says. She's
back to freezing me out, staring straight ahead. It's infuriating; I
hate to be ignored.

"Really?" I ask, indignant. "Then how about all the other shots
you sent me along with that one we posted? That rose tattoo on
your inner thigh?" Regina once told me about getting a tiny pink
flower inked after a breakup, how it made her feel sexy again. My
mouth is motoring faster than my brain, and I just keep chattering:
"Regina wanted to post a photo of herself in her birthday suit.
Who knows why? Probably to get some sort of sick thrill. I'll be
honest, I was skeptical. But she said it would get us loads of attention, and I went along because I figured when it comes to P.R.,
she's the more experienced one. After all, she's *so* much older than
me." At this, Regina's jaw drops.

"Plus, she threatened to report me for slipping out of work to go
to the Alice and Olivia sample sale yesterday. I admit it, I went!
Guilty as charged. I've got the totally cute pants to prove it." I can
sense the energy shifting in the room, and I stand up and twirl
around to show off my ass in my new jeggings.

"You took naked photos of yourself?" shrieks Victoria. Always
several steps behind, that one.

"Zoe is a liar and everyone knows it," Regina says, a tremble in
her voice. "Have you ever heard her tell the same story twice? The

details change so much you'd think she actually believed she could rewrite history." I roll my eyes.

"Ladies, I don't know what to say." This from Mimi. "Both of your Twitter privileges are suspended and I'll figure out what else by the end of the day. In the meantime, Regina, I'll need a press release responding to this debacle, and Zoe, try not to set any more fires. Now both of you, get the hell out of my office."

I saunter out. Regina catches my sleeve. "Zoe, let's talk about this." I hesitate, but I just can't shake off her betrayal, those slitty eyes fixing me with such condescension. Screw her. I brush past.

Back at my computer, I open my in-box and type Mimi's address into the "To" line of a new e-mail. First, I craft an apology— I know how unprofessionally I acted, and how inappropriate my part in this scandal has been. I got carried away in the character, and I've learned a big, important lesson from the experience.

I take a breath, start a new paragraph, and begin the list: "Snorting cocaine on set; spending whole weeks 'working' while actually sunbathing in Malibu; telling everyone within a five-mile radius that she'd jump at any opportunity to leave the hick, piece-of-crap magazine that employs her; and"—here's the kicker—"calling Mimi 'that fat cow in charge.' " I click Send, and it's done.

Within the hour, Regina is gone. Not back to Los Angeles, but canned. I saw her in Mimi's office, presumably trying to defend herself, but all the charges were true, so how could she?

Others take turns hugging her and issuing empty promises of how they'll keep in touch, blah blah blah—the same rigmarole that goes down each time someone's pink-slipped around here. But I remain at my desk, penning Randiest Rachel's next blog post, an apology for disappointing her fans, and an allusion to the fact that she did in fact meet up with Kevin. I figure I've got a whole new plotline as Rachel struggles to do the right thing and abandon the affair, but still makes the occasional shameful (and sexy!) slipup. I watch Regina gathering her things, and I feel a pang—I will truly miss her—but I remind myself that I was only doing what I had to do. No one dares throw me under the bus.

The next morning, I tally up the numbers. Randiest Rachel's new blog post is the most popular one yet. And after the initial hemorrhaging of *Hers*' Twitter followers, the numbers have ticked up to nearly 125 percent higher than two days ago. The magazine's Facebook fans have doubled, our Web site page views have spiked, and nearly eight hundred *Hers* references have appeared in other media outlets within the past day. I've checked in with the ad sales team, who tell me they've gotten interest from new advertisers; granted, the companies are sex enhancement manufacturers and lingerie retailers, but still. Armed with this info, I approach Mimi's office.

"Wow," says Mimi, examining the data. "You really managed to turn this situation around, didn't you?"

I walk out with a promotion to digital director. That night I toast with Graham, and we set up the video camera and go at it like gorillas.

14

Jane Staub-Smith, Associate Editor

Victoria plunks a pile of paperwork onto my desk, and it's enough to set my head pounding. I'm not sure what's with me lately. Though I only nursed two drinks through an entire *Worst Moms* marathon last night, I've got the kind of epic hangover that even a greasy egg-and-cheese and a monster latte can't touch. Maybe it's the sudden freeze-out from Mimi and Victoria—a result, I'm sure, of my fainting at the Corporate sales meeting a couple of weeks ago, mortifying everyone involved, and then failing to devote my entire existence to apologizing for the gaffe. (I did say I was sorry, but Zoe overheard Mimi and Victoria griping about how I clearly wasn't remorseful, as if I should fall all over myself atoning for what was an involuntary physical reaction.) Whatever the reason, these days I'm chronically tired, no matter how much sleep I get and how little I drink.

I flip through the papers—a W-4, an I-9, 401(k) forms, information on an introductory session, and a computer training. It's the welcome package for our new entertainment director, Johanna White. Laura used to handle this type of paperwork, but ever since my face-plant fall from grace, the responsibility has fallen on me. I don't totally mind, since it means I'm in the loop early on the new hire. And boy did they hire her fast: Within twenty-four hours of Regina's ouster, Mimi announced her replacement.

The word is, Johanna White made it to the final round of the United Kingdom's version of *American Idol*, but was voted off unfairly because the public resented her supermodel looks—this according to Zoe's research, culled mainly from back issues of British tabloids. Apparently Johanna writes a style blog and is buddy-buddy with a handful of B- and C-list celebrities, but has never before held an editorial job.

"This Johanna should be interesting," I say to Abby, handing over the completed forms.

But Abby doesn't take the bait. "She starts tomorrow," she says. "Will you double-check to make sure her phone is all set up?" Abby is nothing if not discreet. I'm sure she's pretending not to notice my under-eye circles. Bless her.

"Aye-aye," I say.

My cell phone buzzes. I wince—that number again. The vibrating makes my temples throb, so I press "reject." Poor guy. But my pity is fast replaced by stress when I discover a new pile of documents waiting in my in-box. I calculate how much I have to do before I can go home and bury myself under my covers: tons.

Victoria calls me into her office, gives me an obvious (and likely intended to be obvious) once-over. "Looks like you could use some relaxation," she says. I am skeptical. "I bet you'd have fun writing the debut of the '*Ahhh . . . relax!*' well-being section."

"I thought Laura was doing that one."

"She's working extra hard on November's new entertainment section," Victoria says. It makes me fume; that so-called section is one page, and Laura doesn't pull near her weight. Jenny and I used to divvy up the front-of-book evenly, but now I'm like a one-woman show, writing everything from home decorating items to relationship research. Flip through the first forty pages of the magazine, and you'd think someone's played a joke by stamping my byline under nearly every headline. "I'm hoping you'll be willing to step up and help out," she says. This is not really the optional request it sounds like.

I don't do as good a job as I think stifling my eye roll, because Victoria says, "I sense you're frustrated, Jane." My heart ventures a minileap, swelling with the hope that maybe Victoria really does get how heavy my workload is, that maybe she really is still on my side, that maybe she's about to say, *Oh, forget all this. Come and gossip with Mimi and me, just like we used to.* But her words snap me back to reality: "It's a busy time, and we're all overwhelmed. The thing is, most of us don't whine about it. Do what you have to do— push some of your work down to the intern and the freelancers— but you need to accept that this is the way things are now and adjust your attitude accordingly."

I stifle my desire to scream, and instead say, "I've heard about this new version of mindful meditation that involves dabbing essential oils on your temples. It's getting a lot of traction in medical circles as a clinically proven destressor. Maybe we could get three superbusy women to try out the practice and report on the results."

"That's the spirit," Victoria says. I turn to leave, silently cursing her.

The intern, Erin, drops off photocopied packets of the tentative November lineup for our update meeting. Unsurprisingly, the last three characters of each line are cut off. I make a note to administer a photocopier test to future prospective interns. In her interview, Erin told me she hoped to write features during her time at *Hers,* and out of politeness I did not laugh in her face. What she doesn't understand (and apparently Victoria doesn't either) is that interns can't write. They show up fresh from last semester's research papers, I assign them an item on how to get more vitamin A into one's diet, and they approach it like they're penning a term paper on the role of landscape in George Eliot's novels or a thesis on Pynchon's and DeLillo's use of postmodern symbolism—totally incomprehensible. No wonder English majors graduate so unemployable.

I'm growing suspicious of my in-box. I swear it's been sneering at me, taunting me with new documents every time I glance up. Luckily, I see that the latest addition bears the small, stylized marks of Leah's pink pen; it's my draft of the real women volunteer profiles back to me for revisions. I glance through the notes. Next to my write-up of the founder of a prenatal health organization: "Amazing story, but let's find a stronger way in." Alongside my stat rundown: "Scary numbers! Please tease out anecdote to show impact of what they really mean for moms." By my kicker sentence: "Lovely. Tone down sentimentality a tad."

Leah has the rare ability to critique a piece while also making me feel like I'm on my way to nabbing a Pulitzer. And unlike most editors, she doesn't edit just to put her mark on things. She adds three words to a sentence and it becomes doubly as clear or interesting or fun, or she asks just the right question to elevate the story. In the end, the pieces still actually sound like I've written them. I'm always proudest of my stories that have been edited by Leah.

I'm tweaking the piece's lead when Zoe interrupts. "Yoo-hoo! I've got your most embarrassing moments blurbs for the home page tomorrow. Let's chat." No asking whether I'm busy, of course. Since getting that bullshit promotion to digital director, Zoe has been acting even more entitled than usual.

"A super start," she says. "You scrounged up some supercolorful quotes. But I think you could give it a push, punch it up with more specifics. Let's make sure we have the right mix, too. We don't want too many old fart stories about how some grandma's cat did the cutest thing, know what I'm saying? OK, good talk."

I flip through the copy. Zoe's idea of editing is ticking check marks next to quotes she likes, exing out ones she doesn't, and writing "make better" next to those she wants me to work on. She stamps "duh" next to sentences she finds too obvious, which is actually helpful, because for Zoe to think something is obvious is saying a lot. At least she's easy. It takes me ten minutes to make the changes, but I hang on to the text for another hour to make her think I've worked hard on it.

I'm onto my last item of the day—the light at the end of the tunnel, my bed, is finally within sight; it's a revise of the "Your Healthiest Desk" story, slated for November. Victoria's the editor, much to my chagrin, since you can't bullshit health pieces as much as you can with, say, relationship coverage, and Victoria's recent comments require big heaping loads of B.S. In one section we've specified the best settings on ergonomic chairs to maintain the natural curve in one's lower back, with the help of Dr. Dunken, an orthopedist who specializes in spine alignment for office workers. Victoria has scrawled, "Can we get Dunken to say that this is extracrucial for women who are always lifting toddlers? Is there a different setting? Lots of our readers are young moms!!!" "Very true," Mimi has added in her signature red.

Beside the column about keeping one's desk free of germs, Victoria has written: "Dislike this expert—too stringent. Who's going to clean their keyboard every Friday?!?!"—this from the woman who eats two to three meals a day at her desk—"Can't really be that much bacteria! Find new expert!!"

Another note: "Think I read somewhere that desks are dirtier than toilet seats. Let's include!" Victoria considers herself an expert on every discipline; she should really just start her own magazine, call it something like *Dubious Advice by Victoria*.

I get Dr. Dunken on the phone for a follow-up. "Would you say maintaining your back's natural curve is especially important for young moms?"

"Well, it's important for everyone."

"But, you know, because they spend so much time lifting their babies?"

"Yes, it is key to maintain proper alignment while carrying a baby. One should bend at the knees and lift from the legs."

"But how about when they're sitting? Is there a special setting on the chairs that moms of babies should consider?"

"You mean if they have the babies in their lap?" He sounds perplexed.

"No, just in general."

"Oh, well, not really."

"OK, thanks." I'm mortified to have to initiate these exchanges.

I examine the text and think about how I can be accurate while still stroking Victoria's ego. "Maintaining the natural curve in the spine is crucial for those who spend their workdays sitting, even if you're running around with your toddlers the rest of the time." Maybe my next job will be writing evasive speeches for some dirtbag politician; I'm certainly qualified.

On the rare occasion when I leave work on time, I avoid broadcasting the fact by shutting down my computer; instead, I leave the monitor glowing and head to the restroom, bag in hand, then make a discreet dash for the exit, ducking familiar faces, some of whom will be toiling away for another two or three hours. It works like a charm, and my horrible, terrible, no-good, very bad day is officially over.

My apartment looks like it's weathered a hurricane—it's all wreckage and disarray. The usual clutter has recently edged over into turmoil territory since Mimi went and wreaked havoc on my life. I step over the tangle of last night's outfit and climb into bed. I wouldn't complain if I could hide out here for eternity.

I'm drifting off, half-encased in a dream where I'm giving Victoria a hack-up of a haircut, when my phone buzzes under my cheek and snaps me up. I answer without checking the screen. "Hello?"

"Oh, hey there, I've been trying to reach you for days." *Oh, shit: him.*

"I've been really busy," I say. "How's it going?"

"Great. I'm at that bar down the street from your place, you know the one. Wanna come out and play?" *Seriously?* I can't even remember this guy's name and yet he won't stop hounding me, each of his calls reminding me of the stupid, reckless decision I made that one night. I'm furious at my drunken self for giving him my number (though I actually don't remember doing so).

"I don't think so. In fact"—I bite my tongue, wondering if I'm really going to do it—"I got back together with my ex-boyfriend, so I don't think I'll be up for any more coming out and playing. Ever."

"Aw, bummer." The guy hangs up, no good-bye. I still haven't forgiven Zoe for getting me so drunk that night.

The following Monday, despite my go-straight-home-to-bed personal pledge, on my way out of the office I find myself asking Laura if she wants to grab a drink. As much as the girl irks me, I still feel a pull to befriend her. Laura looks shocked, as if I've invited her to accompany me to an S&M orgy. "I thought I'd stay a bit late and get a jump start on my November revises," she says. *Goody Two-shoes.*

"Come on, you can do them tomorrow. I know a place a block away with amazing nachos."

"I don't know."

"Three kinds of cheese. We can even expense them. Abby won't care." I wonder if I should've said that; I'm still paranoid that Laura reports everyone's missteps back to Mimi.

Laura nods, barely perceptibly. I think I'm safe.

I order us two beers and a heaping plate of nachos. "Cheers," I say. We clink glasses, and then I come out with it: "So, how's it going for you, being Mimi's assistant and all?" I've been dying to ask Laura this for months.

"I was doing it before at *Starstruck,* so it's not like I'm new to the job," she says defensively. "I've been assisting Mimi for two years now."

"Right, I know. I wasn't questioning your qualifications." Jeez, she needs this drink more than I do.

"Mimi is so wonderful. She is totally going to turn the magazine around." I nod. "Oh, I'm sorry. I know you were at *Hers* before." Laura looks flummoxed, like she's trying to figure out whose side I'm on, and why I went suddenly from boss's pet to just another stray in the pound.

"That's OK." I can picture Mimi's pitch to Laura, an invitation to join her on this big adventure to revitalize a tired brand, the thrill and glamour of it all. "It's not a secret what she's doing."

We both go silent, sipping at our drinks. Our food arrives, and

Laura hits the nachos hard. The sight of her chin slick with grease turns my stomach. I lose my appetite.

"I know what you must think of me," Laura says finally, her mouth full of salsa and guac.

"What do you mean?" My heart is pounding.

"Come on, I'm not deaf. Everyone thinks I'm this big bitch, as if it's me who's making all the staff changes."

"Staff changes?" I say. "You mean firings?"

"Yes, the layoffs." Laura digs in to another cheesy clump of chips. "Mimi is an amazing leader, and if any of you had known her before all this and had been given the opportunity to go along with her to somewhere new and to get a promotion and a raise"— I bristle at this, wondering if Laura is raking in a larger salary than I am—"you'd realize it, too. Why doesn't anyone see that?"

"Laura, how did you imagine people at *Hers* would treat you?" I'm genuinely curious.

"I thought they'd see how hard I work and evaluate me based on my performance at my job. I thought they'd give me a chance." She is so earnest and naïve, I almost feel bad for her.

"Laura, no one could care less whether or not you're good at your job." *And you're not as good at it as you think*, I want to add. "No one cares whether you're a talented writer or if you come up with brilliant ideas. The point is, you're safe, and most people aren't, and that makes them resent you. You have a power that they don't have. Don't you get it?"

"Well, it's not like I asked for it."

"Sure you did. You're the first editorial assistant in the history of the publishing industry who doesn't deign to debase herself at the fax machine or photocopier." Laura came on board and flat-out refused to perform administrative duties (apparently Mimi had promised it to her in the interview—I guess you move up that high and you forget how much lowly crap is required to run an office). So now all the grunt work has fallen to the intern and the new freelancers, with my supervision, of course.

I'm worried I've gone too far, but Laura frowns, and I can see she truly believes she's above such menial work. It may not even have occurred to her that she's lucked out. "I just thought it would be different," she says.

"Well, join the club." I raise my beer.

Laura is twisting a lackluster lock of hair around her finger and worrying her eyebrows, which could use a serious threading. I examine her outfit: The shapeless shirt, buttoned up all the way to her neck, does nothing for her broad figure. And her posture is a disaster. She could be attractive if she tried. I fantasize about being Cher from *Clueless*, giving Laura the ultimate makeover.

"You know what, I'm going to buy you a real drink," I say. "A martini."

"Oh, no, I don't drink hard liquor," says Laura.

"Come on," I say. "You don't go out to drinks with coworkers, either, but here we are." Jeez, I'm feeling tipsy from just one beer. I order the drink, and the bartender places it in front of Laura. She ventures a sip, and then a gulp, and then twists her face up into a grimace. "There you go," I say.

"Are you going to eat those olives?" The voice is male, and I'm thinking, if that's some guy's idea of a pick-up line, God help Laura. But when I swivel around to get a look at him, I'm surprised to see he's not so bad-looking.

Laura hands the guy her spear of olives, no questions asked, and he pops one in his mouth. "I'm Laura Maxwell. Pleased to meet you." She reaches out her hand like she's at a business meeting.

"Sebastian. How's it going?" He shakes with his right hand and places his left one around Laura's shoulder. He must have learned the move from a book, something like *Suave Pick-up Moves for Gentlemen*. "So, what do you beautiful ladies do?"

"We work for a magazine called *Hers*," says Laura. "It's directed at the thirty-something woman who wears many hats—career woman, wife, mother, friend—but who still wants to feel like she has the time and space to just be herself, with no label attached."

"Wow." Sebastian snickers. "You must be the number-one salesman. I mean, sales*woman*. You've got the pitch down pat."

"Mimi—she's the editor in chief—she says we should be representing and promoting the brand at all times," says Laura.

"Well, it's a good thing you ladies have carved out the time and space to just be yourselves tonight, right?" says Sebastian.

"It's important to take some me time occasionally," Laura says.

Now, I understand how Mimi convinced Laura to join her on the front lines and march gung ho into a war zone: She's not used to being seduced, and can barely recognize it when it's happening to her. And somewhere along the way someone forgot to teach her how to flirt. I sigh, considering whether I'm up for the job.

I realize I'm too exhausted. I predict three more minutes of her speaking like she's on an interview and this Sebastian will move on. I overestimate by ninety seconds: Sebastian announces he has to take a piss, and he's gone.

"He was nice," Laura says. I nod and say nothing.

Laura starts fishing through her purse and quickly grows frantic, removing every object—wallet, phone, keys (attached to a Minnie Mouse keychain), a musty hardcover stamped with "New York Public Library," cotton candy lip gloss, the same barrettes my four-year-old niece wears. She's still searching. "Oh, I'm mortified," she says.

"What's wrong?"

Laura leans in close so I can feel her hot breath in my ear. "Do you have a tampon I could borrow?" She laughs, then snorts. "Not borrow, ew! I mean *have*."

"Oh, sure." I grab one from my purse. I consider the date—August 13—and a dark thought flashes through my brain; I push it away.

Laura snatches up the tampon and shoves it into her pocket, then looks around suspiciously. "You're a lifesaver."

"No prob."

"One time when I was at a party"—*Yeah, right*, I think unkindly—"I got my period and didn't have tampons, so I just had to wad up toilet paper. I think you could tell through my pants. It was *sooo* embarrassing." Again the laugh and the snort, then a hiccup.

"I bet," I say.

"This is fun." Laura swigs back the rest of her martini. She's still laughing as she zigzags her way to the bathroom. I watch to make sure she doesn't teeter over. I order us two more beers, thinking I could use another layer of fuzziness over my brain.

"Jane!" I turn my head in the direction of the shriek. It's Jenny.

"Hi! What are you *doing* here?" I go in for a hug, then step back, realizing my friend is wearing a business suit and pumps. "And why are you dressed like you're ready to take over the world?"

"Don't I look fabulous?" She does a spin. "It's because I'm gainfully employed again."

"When did this happen? Please tell me you miraculously scored a gig at the *New York Times*." I've secretly been wishing Jenny would land an awesome job so she could come back and throw it in Mimi's face.

"Sadly not. The truth is, I've caved and gone over to the dark side. I started last week."

"No wonder you've been ignoring my calls."

"I've been meaning to call you back. I promise."

"So don't tell me," I say. "You're doing P.R.?"

Jenny nods. "It's horrible, I know. I'm repping diapers and cough suppressants."

"No!"

"Even more horrible is that I don't really hate it. They hired me as an account manager, and if I can land this deal on antiseptic wipes within the next month, I'll be promoted to senior account manager. Can you believe that? Three months after getting fired as an assistant, I'll have 'senior' in my title! I have a corporate card and my own office and I get to dress up in these incredible skirt suits for client meetings."

"And let me guess, you've doubled your salary?" Jenny looks down, guilty. "Well, I think you'll be covering our bill this evening, Moneybags."

I sense someone's stare and glance up. Laura is lurking. "Oh, hey. Jenny, this is Laura. Laura, Jenny, your predecessor."

"Hi," says Jenny. "It's nice to finally meet you. How's my old post going?"

Laura looks back and forth from Jenny to me. Her eyes well up with tears. "Do you think I'm some kind of idiot?" she says, speech slurred.

"Laura, she just showed up, I swear," I say, holding out a beer to her. "Here, I got this for you."

"It's true, I did," Jenny says. "I had no idea you'd be here." She means Laura and me both, but it sounds like she's singling out just Laura.

"Whatever," says Laura, ignoring my drink offering. "I knew I shouldn't have trusted you, asking me to go out like we're friends or something. You probably drugged that drink, just to make fun of me."

"Oh, come on," I say, feeling weirdly to blame for the chance encounter. Laura grabs her bag and storms out. "Laura, wait," I call, but she doesn't turn back.

"Just let her go. I can't believe you, hanging out with Whore-a," says Jenny, slapping at me with her clutch. "What a traitor!"

"Hey, I still have to work there. Might as well try to befriend the enemy. And as it turns out, your replacement is probably not the whore you imagine her to be. She's got zero game, I've recently discovered." I immediately feel bad and resolve to stop blurting out things that make me ashamed five seconds later.

"Oh, whatever. So guess what? I had lunch with Louisa last week."

"No way! How is she?" I ask.

"Really, who knows? We used to be straight with each other, but this time we were painfully polite until the third glass of wine. Only then did she mention she's interviewing for the executive editor spot at *Suburban Home*."

"Yuck," I say. "That magazine runs the same tacky Christmas cover every single year. That crackling fireplace and the gingham stockings."

"Yeah, and that dinky little menorah on the mantel, as if that makes any sense. Although, if Louisa gets the job, I'll have an in for all the products I'm repping."

"Jeez, you really have gone over to the dark side," I say.

"At least I escaped that hellhole. No offense."

"None taken," I say, thinking how little I envy her.

"Oh, and gossip!" Jenny claps her hands. "I went out on a date with my new coworker last night. He's dreamy."

"No wonder you look so good," I say, now slightly jealous. "You're working with hot guys." The only straight guy I've ever worked alongside was Mark, who was too broody and creepy to even count.

"Finish both those beers and I'll buy you another," Jenny says.

"You know what, I actually don't feel so well. Come with me to the bathroom?" I lock myself in a stall and lean over the toilet, willing my fitful stomach to empty itself.

After a few minutes, Jenny knocks on the door. "Are you OK in there?"

"Jenny, I have to tell you something."

"Is this about Jacob? Is he dating someone new?"

"What do you mean, *is he?!* Did you hear something?" I feel so frantic, my fingers are shaking.

"No, no, sorry. Stop freaking out! I don't know anything. What were you going to say?"

"My period is usually so reliable I can bet on a ten-minute window when it'll arrive."

"Well, whoop-de-do for you. So?"

"I'm ten days late."

"But . . . but how? You're on the Pill, right?"

I shake my head, though I know Jenny can't see me. "When Jacob and I broke up, I couldn't imagine ever being with another guy."

"Seriously? Oh, Jane. But anyway, *were* you with another guy?"

I flash on the phone calls, and waking up next to a boy whose name I still don't even know. "I don't want to talk about it."

"I'm sure you're fine, that it's just a fluke." Jenny is a terrible liar; she's raised her voice about an octave. "You stay right here, OK? I'm gonna run over to Duane Reade and buy you a test."

Waiting for Jenny, I can hear a crowd forming outside the bathroom. A gruff voice yells out, "Did you drown in there? Need a prince in shining armor to come rescue you?" I stay put, silent except for deep breathing, my head between my knees. Jenny returns after five minutes and slips me a small package under the stall. I read the instructions and take some comfort in being able to follow the simple steps: Hold the stick between your legs and let go. The trickle of pee seems to originate from somewhere other than my body. I shut my eyes tight.

"I can't look," I say, "You do it." I pass the damp stick back under the stall to my friend. When I finally shore up the courage to emerge, the expression on Jenny's face brands itself in my memory: her eyes like saucers, her mouth the smallest O.

Meandering home, I'm shocked I can remember the way. Jenny tried to put me in a cab, but I insisted on walking. She asked to walk with me, but I said I wanted to be alone. I duck into a deli and buy two Snickers. I tell myself I'll give the second one to Laura as a sort of peace offering in the morning, but it takes only two blocks for me to devour one bar and then tear open the second.

What am I going to do? I'll have to start eating healthy, I think, mouth full of nougat and peanuts. Nuts have protein, right? I'll have to save up money, and buy a crib, and get maternity clothes. Or not, I guess. *Oh, my God,* I think, remembering when Victoria went on about Jonny Depp and how the biggest moral failing was having kids out of wedlock. *Didn't Mimi nod in agreement?* I'm going to get fired, I'm sure of it. And fat. I'm going to get very, very fat. Or not . . . I suppose it's up to me. Even if I don't get bloated with baby, the pressure inside me feels like enough to fill my body and blow it up to burst. I break down and call Jenny. Within two minutes she's by my side. She practically carries me home, up my stairs, and into my apartment, and then tucks me into bed and sings to me maybe all night long.

15

Abby Rollins,
Managing Editor

I'm in the middle of my morning file organizing ritual when Jane appears in my office, looking tense. Oh, dear, it's only nine-thirty. Usually the problems don't start until at least eleven, when everyone's fully caffeinated and can muster up enough energy for anger or conflict. I brace myself.

"Johanna has a concern," Jane announces in that wobbly voice that's her signal to me of trouble pending. She holds out her arm to present our new entertainment director, as in, *Here's the trouble.*

"Good morning, Johanna." She hasn't even put down her purse. What could possibly have gone wrong within her first ten minutes of employment—a broken elevator? "I'm Abby. Welcome to *Hers.*"

"Yes, hello. I'm wondering when my office will be set," she says, her thick British accent competing for shock value with the words spoken in the accent.

"I'm not sure if you're aware, but there's been a lot of shifting around lately."

"Right, the mass exodus of the former staff. I've been told."

"OK, then you may also know that you will be our first New York–based entertainment director. Your predecessor worked out of Los Angeles, so there isn't an office in this space allocated for your position. We were able to arrange one of the largest cubicles for you. Did you notice the nice view of the park?" Johanna fixes me with a withering look. "It's the only spot we have for now." Still she waits. I cave: "I'll see what I can do."

"Lovely, thank you," she says. That's my job description, seeing what I can do. Whatever the problem, here I am to solve it. My wife claims I let people take advantage of me; she's always encouraging me to be more assertive. But I'm good at putting out fires and maintaining office harmony, and I relish the role. When everyone is getting along, all feels right with the world.

I shouldn't have mentioned the cubicle's view as a selling point to Johanna; everyone's seen grass and trees. I should've instead pointed out the etched chrome nameplate on the cubicle's edge. We all used to have cheap cardboard placards displaying our names and ranks in the pecking order, and I admit I was skeptical when Mimi unloaded this large new expense into our budget. But since the new nameplates went up, I've seen several staffers marvel at them, running their fingers along the slick surface and awestruck by their own stately looking name. It's an illusion, of course, that the professional carving of a name indicates any kind of permanence for that employee. Still, I believe it's been worth it for staff morale.

"So when's the official pop-around? When do I get to go meet and greet?" Johanna asks.

"Excuse me?"

"I'd fancy some introductions with my coworkers so they're not all wondering why this bonkers British woman has invaded their office. I've already been here fifteen minutes and no one has bothered to show me around. Where is my mailbox? Where is the coffeemaker? Where is the loo?"

"All right, I suppose a tour is in order." I smile, reminding myself that I will soon discover Johanna's many strengths and talents and will therefore be able to help integrate her into the team. For now, patience is a virtue.

I used to be entrenched in the hiring process, screening every résumé and greeting every potential candidate for a warm-up interview, or as Louisa called it, a character test. I never insisted upon or vetoed a particular choice; nearly every applicant possessed some trait I believed would be an asset to *Hers*. But I did find quieter ways to exert my influence, employing a gesture or a choice word to express my opinion, careful not to step on anyone's toes or ego. Of course now I have nothing to do with the firings or hirings. When Louisa's fate was handed down, I made a point of assuring her of my noninvolvement. "You think I'd actually believe you were behind this?" she responded, laughing. "You couldn't fire a killer shark." These days I simply get a call from Suzie in Human Resources about the new hire or the upcoming exit interview; she either assumes I'm already in the loop or offers up the small kindness of acting as if I am. So it was with Johanna.

"This is Jane, our associate editor," I say to Johanna. "She knows everything there is know about this office, so ask her anything."

"Pleasure," says Jane.

"So are you one of the newbies, too, or a holdover?"

"My three-year anniversary at *Hers* is next week. If you're wondering what to get me for a gift, I love chocolate." Jane winks.

"You think you'll survive till then?" Johanna asks. Jane's eyes grow wide. "Oh, I'm just joshing you, keep your pecker up. I'm Johanna."

Lynn's office looks like a dance club; a disco ball is affixed to the ceiling, spinning to the bass-heavy beat. I wonder if she charged it to *Hers'* account. "I like to embrace the mood of the story I'm working on," she says by way of introduction. "This fashion spread is seventies-style disco boots and miniskirts, which calls for a Studio 54 revival. You dig?"

I wait for a cutting remark from Johanna, but instead she starts undulating her limbs to the beat. Lynn gets up, and the two bump their hips against each other. Lynn reaches out to draw me in, but I resist. I only dance when there are specific moves to follow, like at the ballroom dancing events Julia and I attend. Plus, I'd prefer not to be caught gyrating between two women in the office.

We move on to Drew's desk. "A shutterbug, eh, mate?" Johanna says, handling Drew's Leica.

Drew nods warily, not masking her judgment of Johanna's outfit. I admit it's a bit over the top to wear a fur vest and leopard-print leggings on one's first day, especially when it's eighty-five degrees outside.

"Drew recently produced a photo shoot of kids' most inventive Halloween costumes," I say. "She staged it so the kids were standing in door frames, so it'll look like they're showing up at the reader's house to ask for candy. Drew always finds offbeat ways to bring our stories to life visually. She has a real eye."

Johanna shakes her hand. "Horrid, children are, right?"

"Um, I guess." Drew's whole cubicle is plastered with photos of her young nephews. I shoo Johanna away. As awkward as this introductory walkabout is becoming, part of me admires Johanna's candor. I can't count the number of times I've stood around staffers' desks oohing and aahing at their latest crop of baby photos, all the while feeling bored and impatient, plus frustrated with my inability to invent an excuse to walk away.

To Laura, Johanna says, "You know, you'd look absolutely smashing as a blonde." After meeting Ed, she insists on delivering his stack of mail—grabs it right out of his hand—as a test to see if she remembers everyone she just met. Zoe isn't at her desk, which surprises me not at all; she usually rolls in around ten-thirty with an excuse about stalled subways or a story about some work-related event. When I bring Johanna up to the test kitchen to meet Debbie, she remarks, "Pardon me, but food is so passé. *Hers* should hop on the liquid diet bandwagon. It's all the rage."

"Is it really?" Debbie asks, popping a butter cookie into her mouth and then offering me one. I shake my head, fearful of what Johanna might say were I to accept.

We pass by Leah's empty desk, and I explain her telecommuting situation. "Not very clever, is it?" says Johanna. "Very little face time with the big boss." I shrug.

Next up is Victoria. "So there's two of you executive editors, then?" Johanna asks. "But I see you've got the office, so it must be the other one who's in hot water." She's a fast study, I'll give her that.

Victoria titters nervously. "Nice to meet you."

"How long have you been on staff?"

"Just over two months. Don't worry, you'll learn the ropes pretty fast."

"So, this is a big, new job for you? Lots of pressure, I gather. I think you'll do OK." Johanna faces me. "Let's go see Mimi."

"She's at a meeting with Corporate," says Victoria.

"Are you her secretary, too? I'll take my tea with two lumps of sugars, hardy har har." Oh boy. To me, she asks, "Actually, who will be my assistant?"

"We're a small staff, so you'll be running your own one-woman department. I'm sure if you need help with something, Laura would be happy to pitch in. But we don't ask our assistants to fetch us coffee. Or tea."

I keep an eye on Johanna all afternoon. She'll sink or swim soon enough, although it's unfortunate I have to figure a whopping five thousand dollars into this month's budget for what we shelled out to move her overseas.

The phone rings. I assume Julia, but it's Leah's voice: "Did you hear the news?" Just like my wife, Leah also avoids pleasantries at the start of phone calls.

"No, what?" I'm hoping Leah will say she's found another job.

"Louisa's been appointed the new head copywriter for Bloomie's catalogs."

"Really? That's great!"

"Are you kidding? It's a *catalog*, Abby! She'll be writing about the way a certain scarf hangs across the shoulders or the flipping durability of a leather shoe."

"Louisa loves Bloomingdale's," I say. "She'll be perfect for it. It's a good gig for her. She'll get some more fashion experience before moving on to the next big thing." Louisa was always able to sell me on anything, which is probably why the fashion spreads under her reign tended to feature the same bland black and gray wardrobe each month. During the run-throughs, Louisa made the clothes sound glamorous and chic—you couldn't argue.

"God, if the brilliant Louisa is stuck at a catalog, what am *I* going to be doing in a few months? Reporting for SkyMall, probably. The latest power juicers and foot massagers. Oversized popcorn tins for every occasion."

"Oh, Leah, quit being so dramatic."

"Also," she says, "Mimi asked me to write the table of contents for November. The freaking table of contents! Isn't that Jane's job?" My stomach flips. I offhandedly mentioned to Mimi that Jane was overloaded and maybe we could shift some of her duties around. I meant to Laura.

"Well, at least you can write it in your sleep, or while you're playing with three babies."

"Screw you."

"Nice, Leah. I'll talk to you later."

The train emerges from the underground tunnel and flies up into the fading daylight to cross the Manhattan Bridge. I know I should spend my commute working, but it's my small rebellion that I instead peer out the window and lose myself in the surroundings: the sunset reflected against the river and the backdrop of gleaming buildings. Every ride, I'm amazed and humbled by the sight of the city I live in. The journeys across the river are distinct daily markers—leaving home for work, or leaving work to head back home—moving from one of my worlds to the other. My commute is the ultimate comfort.

At home in the front hall, I step over Julia's lab coat, dress, and sandals. This random tossing of garments drives me nuts, but it does mean she's showering, so at least she won't smell like a day's worth of animal fur.

"Hi, love," I yell out. I can hear her singing Billy Joel over the spray of water.

I dial Louisa and get her voice mail. "Congrats on the new gig—"

A click indicates she's picked up. "Hello?"

"Oh, hi. I was midmessage."

"I know, I screened the call. I wanted to find out if you'd sound fake happy or genuinely happy for me."

"Louisa, you're ridiculous."

"I'm paranoid, so sue me. But I'll tell you the truth, I'm a tad bit excited."

"You should be."

"All the free clothes I want, and for the whole family, too. Very little stress, it sounds like. Regular hours, that's the clincher. Can you imagine? Leaving your desk at five on the dot each day."

"I think it sounds perfect for you."

"Though my manager is twenty-eight. That kind of makes me want to shoot myself."

"Maybe she can babysit."

"True. I'm going to figure out how I can add some substance into the catalogs. I'll describe a trench coat as just the right piece of outerwear to don at your feminist revival march. Warm and sturdy, a smart shape for the thinking woman."

"Pair it with the perfect 'take back the night' leather pumps."

"Try on a skirt so hot your man will insist on handling dinner *and* the dishes."

"Well . . ." I say.

"You're right, that one needs work. This whole business will probably bore me to death in about three days. But hey, you gotta keep on keeping on. So . . ."

"You want to know how life is back at the ranch?"

"Yes, I seem to remember I've planted you there as my personal spy."

"Ah, so you're paying me, then?"

"The check's in the mail. Come on, any good gossip?"

"Here's something," I say. "The intern fetches us Starbucks now."

"Not very titillating, but I'll take it. Expensed to *Hers*, I presume?"

"Yep. Oh, and Leah's writing the TOC."

"Poor girl. Well, I've got some dirt for you. I was out to dinner last night and saw your new British tart of an entertainment director having drinks with one Helena Hope."

"First of all, how do you know about our new entertainment director?"

"I read the *Post* just like everyone else."

"Oh, right." I'm always amazed how quickly those reporters dig up all the industry gossip. "So Helena Hope, is she that terrible country-western singer?"

"The one and only. Famous for those eight-minute ballads about heartbreak and blushing virgins. She's got that one song they seem to have on repeat on every radio station these days. It's sickening, really. And what's worse is that I've actually had time to listen to the radio these days."

"What's she doing north of the Mason-Dixon line?"

"You tell me." Three months ago, Louisa would have been a bundle of nerves to happen upon a coupling like that at a restaurant. Now she just sounds tickled.

"Thanks for the tip, Liz Smith," I say. I feel a wet body press against my own and get a whiff of Julia's lavender shampoo. "Gotta go."

"OK, I'll be in touch about teaming up on a joint story in *Hers*: Ten essentials for your closet, brought to you by Bloomie's," says Louisa.

"Very funny. Congrats again. We'll talk soon." I drop the phone.

"Hey, babe," Julia says, spinning me around.

I kiss her blue-tinged lips. Julia likes to air-dry postshower. It makes me shiver to even look at her.

"Chicken's roasting in the oven, wine's chilling in the fridge, and I've printed out that stack of profiles for us to review over dinner," she says.

"You had me sold until the last part. Can't we pick out a baby daddy another time?"

"Don't be such a wet blanket. One of the guys wins surfing championships. Can you imagine, our future baby a pro surfer?"

"Where's she gonna go surfing, the East River?"

"Come on. I've done a complete vetting process to meet your every need. They're all tall, liberal, nonsmoking readers of serious literature, and there's not a native New Yorker in the bunch." So then she's been listening to me: my theory is that everyone who grows up in New York turns out kind of off-kilter. But it follows that I wouldn't want a kid of mine growing up in New York. And Julia and I both have good careers and good lives here; we're not going to just uproot ourselves.

"All right," I cave, already feeling my stomach churn. Our tendency to discuss this topic over food has left me with a serious case of indigestion this past month.

"Wahoo!" Julia scurries off naked to fetch the stack.

It's her idea, of course, the child thing. Julia says she can't believe I've spent a decade working at a magazine for moms and yet feel uneasy about becoming one myself. I point out that I've also spent ten years working at a magazine for women interested in men, and it hasn't turned me straight. In fact, I'm the one who often thinks up the best *Hers* parenting coverage because I'm the most paranoid about the myriad ways that you could screw kids up and that they could screw you up: *What if they're allergic to everything? What if they throw tantrums in the middle of traffic? What if you just plain don't like them?* My anxious what-ifs make for better story fodder than the actual mothers' dreamy "You just figure it out" dismissals. Like a mantra, I keep repeating to myself that the maternal instinct will kick in once an embryo starts growing in Julia's stomach, or at least once the baby arrives in the delivery room, kicking and screaming and shitting and . . . oh, dear. I treasure the order of our lives.

"Check him out." Julia passes me a photo of a blond guy with a toothy smile. I'm about to comment that his sweater looks like a Christmas present from my dad when I catch Julia's look: expectant. Oh boy, she's already expecting. I love her dearly, so I inhale and decide to apply the same optimistic approach I've been using at work with all the new staff members: Johanna seems like a pain in my butt, but maybe her connections really will be a boon to the magazine; this guy may have terrible taste in tops, but get a load of those big blue eyes.

"He's handsome," I say.

"Fertilize-my-eggs-with-his-sperm handsome?" Julia asks.

"I'm not sure." Julia is clearly disappointed, but I can't help thinking it's creepy to try to imagine a grown man's traits transposed upon a baby.

I flip through the stack between bites of chicken, and it's like a game: What nice thing can I find to say about each? Which good attribute can I highlight? Now I'm having fun, like I'm a first-grade teacher doling out progress reports to six-year-olds.

I turn to the next packet, and Chardonnay sprays from the sides of my mouth. Pictured is an orange-skinned body builder posing in a G-string, muscles fully flexed, florescent teeth flashing.

"He's perfect, right?" Julia asks, fixing me with a mischievous smirk. "Tall, check. Nonsmoker, check. Though we'll have to investigate his steroid use."

"Also, his origins," I say. "I believe he hails from Planet Self-Tanner." I chuck the rest of the profiles at my wife.

"Well, I spared you from an even worse one, so count yourself lucky."

"Who's that, John Boehner? Does he want to plant his seed to create mini-Boehners all over this great country of ours?"

"Eek, I hope not. No, it was that art guy you used to work with—Mark something?"

"No! Mark is donating sperm? Are you sure?"

"His profile talked about his love of black coffee, minimalist art, and cinema verité."

"That's our Mark, all right. How much do you earn from this kind of thing?"

"Who knows? Maybe a hundred bucks a pop."

"Oh, dear." I push my food away, no longer hungry. I wonder how desperate Mark must be.

That night I dream Helena Hope is perched on the edge of Julia's hospital bed, serenading her as she goes into labor. When

Helena strums the last note of a ballad about the circle of life in perfect synchrony with the baby's arrival, and we fail to applaud enthusiastically enough, she slams down her guitar and flees, leaving us to try to calm our screaming newborn. His cries pierce my skull—truly a splitting headache. Suddenly I'm wailing, too, yelling out, "Shut up! Shut up! Shut up!" Julia looks at me as if I'm a freak, the worst person in the world, totally unfit to be a parent. I fear she's going to leave me. Everything seems to be falling apart, like if I'd only kept quiet the screaming baby would disappear and Julia and I would be back to our old lives, just us two. Julia begins breast-feeding the newborn, and I watch as he sucks greedily at my partner's tit. I feel starving, too, but I'm careful to keep this information to myself. I know how inappropriate it would be to sneak out for a sandwich at a time like this. A trickle of fear invades my stomach along with the pangs of hunger: I fear I'll never be brave enough to speak up and say I need food, that I'll never be allowed to eat again.

I wake up with the sound of a baby's wails still ringing in my ears—which, in retrospect, feels like a fitting prelude to the day.

I'm midswallow, the day's first sip of bitter coffee halfway down my throat, when Mimi, Johanna, and Lynn barge into my office. Mimi flings aside a pile of folders I've just organized, planting her butt directly on my desk. The oxygen in the office seems to reduce by half. "Janine's publicist called," she says. "The worst mom in the world is out for the November cover."

"What do you mean?" I begin to sweat. "The shoot is scheduled for tomorrow!"

"It turns out they wrote a special deal with Regina into the contract," Mimi says, "and now apparently Regina is filling in at *Work It* magazine, so they've secured Janine for their November cover. What a traitor."

"Well played, Regina, right?" Lynn says. We all gape at her.

This kind of oversight would have never happened with Sylvia around, I think. "Were our readers all that excited about Janine, anyway?" I ask desperately. Those reality shows stress me out. I can't fathom the appeal of watching the total chaos of other people's lives.

"Oh, everyone loves Janine," says Lynn. "Every mom feels like she's the worst in the world, but then you watch a TV show where some moms are, like, feeding their kids ice cream for breakfast, or carting them along to illicit rendezvous, actually propping them up on the next bed in the motel room as they go at it like dogs with some random dude. Seeing that, you can't help but think, wow, at least I'm not *that* bad."

"You know what I'd like to watch on TV?" I say. "A show where someone sits all those moms down and teaches them about good parenting and proper nutrition. Then they could all go grocery shopping together for milk and eggs and vegetables, cook up a healthy meal, then sit down to eat it as a family."

"Something is seriously wrong with you," says Mimi. "The best part about *Worst Moms* is the way they decorate their houses. It's beyond." *Really?* I think. Just yesterday Mimi mentioned that she wants to run a home makeover in the magazine with décor exclusively from Walmart.

"OK, well, who are our alternatives for the cover?" I ask.

"I've already found us someone who's bloody brilliant," says Johanna. My stomach flips, the memory of the baby's cries from my dream still echoing in my head. "Helena Hope."

"She'll be incredible," says Mimi.

"I have a slight concern about her reputation," I say. I Googled the singer last night after talking to Louisa. "I've heard she travels with an entourage of twenty and that she recently sprayed mace at a reporter."

"Seriously?" says Mimi. "Ooh, scandalous!"

"Well, the readers adore her," says Johanna. "She's got that hit song this summer, and she's a huge star in all those states in the center of the country. What do you call it, the Midwest?"

"It's true," says Lynn. "Flyover country gold mine."

"It's already quite late in the game for November," I say. "If anything were to go wrong—if she bailed on the shoot or didn't cooperate with the writer—we'd be in a very tough spot." I can feel my armpits dampen; it's rare for me to go head-to-head with three other heads.

"She's a dear mate of mine, totally trustworthy," says Johanna. "And get this: She's in town and could be ready for a shoot *tomorrow*."

"We already had everything set up for Janine," says Lynn. "Drew says she can just do some rejiggering to make it all work for Helena."

"Wow, that Drew is a real rock star," I say.

"I say, let's do it!" says Mimi. "Ooh, maybe she'll put on a show for us in the office. Ha! Abby, please look into that."

"Blech, have you heard her music?" Lynn says. "Remind me to call out sick."

"Well, I guess we have no other choice but to go ahead," I say, sighing.

The three of them file out, leaving me alone with a pit in my stomach. In the past, as a rule *Hers* did not engage with difficult celebrities. Louisa's attitude was, there are plenty of famous people out there grateful for their star status and gracious to all the forces keeping them on top, so why not reward that behavior? The divas always cost more time and more money than they're worth. I could not agree more. But Mimi hails from *Starstruck*, where I imagine the opposite sensibility rules. To Mimi, celebrity drama is fodder for a juicy story, something to be milked for exposure and profit. I know it's a new chapter at *Hers*, so I'll have to revise my thinking and get on board.

I open my in-box and see a new e-mail from Leah, subject line: "Updated résumés! Which one's your preference?" At first glance the two attachments seem identical: her Columbia bachelor's, her list of editorial accomplishments, her fluency in French (huh, never knew!). A closer look reveals differences. One reads, "Top-edit monthly middle-of-book health, parenting, and relationships features"; the second, "Slave away at increasingly trashy stories about plastic surgery trauma, sex scandals, and reality show stars." The first, "Commissioned partnership with prominent TV networks for co-branded surveys, stories, and events"; the second,

"Sweet-talked my way to synergistic B.S. in efforts to promote 'the brand,' heroically triumphed over pangs of self-revulsion and worthlessness." The first, "Salary requirements: $125K+"; the second, "Please pay me enough to support my three rapidly growing, constantly hungry, horrifically needy children (and my fourth overgrown, adult-sized child), or—*gasp!*—we'll have to move in with my mother."

I type a reply: "The second one works better. I'll blast it out to all my contacts, stat." I press Send, thinking, I can't remember the last time I updated my résumé.

The twang of a banjo disrupts my concentration, and I peek out of my office. A group has gathered at Johanna's cubicle; she's popped open a bottle of champagne.

"Fancy a glass, Abby?" she asks. "Helena has officially agreed to pose on our cover for November, and to fast-track the photo shoot. We're having an impromptu party in honor of the occasion, listening to her brilliant new record."

"Sure," I say, agreeing to the drink out of self-consolation rather than celebration. I approach Debbie, who's scowling in the corner. "What's up?"

"Look," our food guru says, pointing to a platter. "That British bimbo put out Ritz crackers and packaged cookies,"

"Oh boy, culinary scandal. You can't be surprised, right?"

"I bet she's never even turned on her oven. No wonder she thinks food is passé. Probably she plays this garbage music on loop as some kind of appetite suppressant."

I survey the scene: Zoe is spinning herself in circles in a wheelie chair. Laura and Victoria are dancing awkwardly to the music until Laura bangs her hip against a file cabinet, and then limps back to her desk to nurse her wound. Drew is in her cubicle, where I notice her supplementing the glass of bubbly with a nip of something from a drawer. Lynn has shut herself in her office, from which I can hear the competing noise of Pink Floyd. Jane is offering a drink to Ed, who's nodding his head to the music's beat. It's a ragtag team we've got here, but it's mine. I feel a funny kind of pride.

"How about a packaged cookie?" I say, grabbing two of them

and passing one to Debbie. She sighs and takes it. We munch away and the crumbs rain down onto our shirts. "Not bad."

"Not bad if you prefer a cardboardy aftertaste with your sweets," she says. "You know, it's a good thing Mimi's keeping you around. What would we do without your steady stream of reasonableness?"

"I imagine you'd be just fine," I say. The question is, without this crowd, would *I* be fine? Hopefully I won't ever have to find out.

"I guess we'd all have to stop bitching and moaning so much," says Debbie. "But I'd really prefer not to. Pass me another one of those cardboard cookies." I take one for each of us.

"Cheers to Chips Ahoy and bad country music," I say. Debbie and I clink our plastic glasses and sip at lukewarm sparkling wine from New Jersey. It's not great, but it's not terrible, either. A light fuzziness begins to blur over my thoughts, and I swig back the rest of my glass. It tastes like relief.

16

Erin O'Donnell, Intern

One egg white frittata with steamed mushrooms; two ciabattas with tomato, basil, and mozzarella; five Diet Cokes; two large ginger cookies; one impossible-to-read-order-that-I-hope-isn't-Helena's; and one double cheeseburger with fries—which must be for the photographer, the only straight man on set. I'm dictating all of this to the server who clearly feels bad for me (this is a new low, the waitstaff taking pity on me), and when he asks, "Anything else?" I realize I better get something for myself if I'm going to make it through the photo shoot without passing out.

My phone is vibrating inside my pocket, and I play a personal Twister, readjusting the five large paper bags I'm schlepping in attempts to grab it. I give up and let the bags plunk to the ground, but the phone has stopped buzzing. The missed call is from the hospital's main line, so I can't call back, and cell phones don't work in there. *Damn it.*

I lug the takeout to the fountain in Columbus Circle, where the crew is set up for part three of the four-part shoot: Helena Hope's day of touring the Big Apple. She's already posed on the top floor of the Empire State Building looking wistfully out on the city's skyline, and among the throngs in Times Square carrying shopping bags from a dozen upscale brands (potential advertisers?)—

never mind that the stores are all actually located fifty blocks south in SoHo. I drop everyone's lunch by the staging area and watch Helena wade ankle-deep into the water, a pose I've previously only seen homeless men assume. The photographer yells for Helena to open her arms wide like she's embracing the whole of New York City, and she scowls. Earlier she threw a fit about the sleeveless shift the stylist suggested she wear for the Times Square shot, and now she's flying off the handle about arm jiggle, and how if anyone had read her rider they'd know she refuses to pose the very way the photographer is now suggesting.

"She does look about fifteen pounds heavier than she did on her last album cover," I whisper to the photographer's assistant, who gives me a look of scorn, like how lame am I that I know anything about Helena Hope's album covers? Whatever, the assistant's hacked-off hipster hair looks like a five-year-old cut it.

"Five-minute break, everyone!" I race to set up the battery-powered footbath that Helena carted to the shoot to warm her toes between shots, even though it's eighty degrees out. Helena stomps her feet in, splashing water up at my jeans.

"Ouchy! Not so hot next time," she says, more to the air than to me.

Jonathan swoops over to touch up Helena's makeup, and I'm his trusty assistant, handing over the eyebrow pencil, then the eyelash curler, then the bronzer, like they're surgical tools. One of the key things I've learned over the course of my summer internship is how to distinguish between items like concealer and under-eye powder, and cheekbone brightener and foundation cream. And while I'm grateful to Jonathan, whose personal makeup lessons have significantly upped my game on the bar scene this summer, I'm not sure his teachings are great fodder for the essay I have to write for school credit about my experience.

I admit I dreamed about writing feature stories for *Hers*, and not just that but raising the magazine's bar by filing hard-hitting investigative reports that would land me on CNN. Still, I was realistic enough to know that my intern duties would likely not include such groundbreaking assignments. But having just finished a year's stint as editor in chief of an Ivy League newspaper, I didn't quite anticipate spending my summer planted at the photocopier and now fetching props for a spoiled-rotten redneck who calls herself a superstar.

"Hey, Erin." Drew is plying me with her corporate card. "We need hot chocolate, stat. Helena refuses to get back in the fountain without a warm beverage, and apparently the set coffee won't do the trick. She's demanding Godiva. They have one in the shops over there."

"Okay, I'm on it."

"And while you're at it, please get me a chocolate-dipped handgun. Thank you!"

I race across the street and into the upscale mall that's crowded despite it being three o'clock on a Thursday. Don't these people have jobs, I wonder, and if not, what are they doing shopping? My heart is pounding, anticipating Helena's wrath if I screw this up, so I don't immediately notice my cell buzzing again. I manage to grab it just in time. "Hello?"

"Hi, darling." This is my father's impression of my mother's voice—sweet, soft, and gentle. For the past three months it's become his permanent act.

"Hey, Dad. How's Mom?"

"Sleeping right now. Snoring too!"

It's hard to picture the shrunken version of my mother having enough strength to snore. "How is she otherwise?"

"She's being a trooper, you know Mom. We're going to get out of here probably by tomorrow morning. Meanwhile, how are you faring at the illustrious internship?"

I remember with a jolt that I'm supposed to be looking for Godiva. I book it down one of the mall's arteries, scanning the shop names. "Great. I'm, uh, researching women who started their own education nonprofits, and later I'll be interviewing our contributing doctors for answers to readers' health questions."

I spot the store and dart in. I cover the phone's speaker to ask the clerk for one hot chocolate—extra whipped cream, please. "What's that, Dad?"

"I said, I'm just so proud of you. Keep up the good work!" I hear the random beeping of machines in the background, and I can almost smell that awful hospital odor through the phone line. I think of my father there all on his own, hands shoved into the pockets of his pleated khakis, trying to make small talk with the nurses to ease the tension, as if that's his responsibility. By now he probably knows all the names of their children and boyfriends.

"I love you guys. Tell Mom I'll see her this weekend."

"Only if you have the time, dear. I don't want you disrupting your schedule to keep coming out to check in on us."

I end the call without saying good-bye. Relief. I am constantly on edge waiting for my father's calls—I've even been dreaming of ringing phones—but then when he does reach me, my desperation to disconnect comes on strong and immediate, an urge as palpable as the metal contraption in my hand. Each time I discover anew that what I really want is my mother to pull me in to her formerly doughy chest; the sound of my father's voice is no substitute.

I look around at the mall shoppers and I hate them and their frivolous purchases. And fuck Helena and her dumb gourmet beverage, I think, stopping short at a trash can, where I consider tossing the drink. Someone jostles me and nearly knocks over the cup. "Careful," I shout, thankful it's remained righted.

"It's about time," Helena says when I hand her the covered cup. "This is skim milk, right?"

Drew nods at me frantically from behind her. "Of course," I say.

At Helena's request we've been listening to her own music all day long. Like everyone, I know that one song, and I think I've heard the Muzak version of a few others in Duane Reade, but a lot of it is new to me. We must've made it through her whole repertoire, because the last hour has featured repeats from this morning. At seven a.m., when her track about the power of emotions blared over the loudspeaker atop the Empire State Building, the lyrics rhyming "love" with "dove," and "pain" with "rain," I wondered if someone on set might feel compelled to jump. But now in the late afternoon, with the sunshine dappling through the fountain's spray, gilding the whole plaza in a sort of magical sheen, I find myself reconsidering the words. I listen as, over the recording, Helena sings, "I thought my love was a locked gate, our togetherness God's fate. We'd be bound forever, joined as one, the two of us so young and fun. We'd be lying in the sun, boy, I really thought we'd won. But, oh how I was wrong, how you strung me right along, told me I gotta be strong, left me with nothing but a song."

"Erin, are you OK?"

"Huh?" Drew hands me a tissue, and I realize tears are trickling down my face. I was picturing my mother on my last trip home, oohing at the constellation of freckles newly revealed on the side of her bald head, trying to convince us—and probably herself— that the chemotherapy was a source of exciting new discoveries about herself. I'm not nearly as strong as my mother. "Yeah, I'm OK," I say, embarrassed. "Cheesy music, huh?"

Drew smiles. "You've worked a full day. Why don't you head on home?"

"No, it's all right." I picture my quiet, sterile sublet like a pit of quicksand. "I'm fine, really. I get allergies."

"OK, well, next stop is the Staten Island Ferry. I'm warning you, it may be a rough ride with Miss Dixie Diva over there."

"I'm up for the challenge."

Drew's prediction is right on the money. Helena discovers they sell beer on the ferry, and by the end of the shoot she's slurring her words. She insists that Jonathan take her out on the town in Staten Island, where "town" seems to consist of one dusty thrift shop and a biker bar, and she begins weeping when her publicist tells her it's time to return to the hotel. The upside of this debacle is that it makes me feel better about my own waterworks earlier in the day. But everyone is in a foul mood, and even Drew snaps at me when I botch up the packing of the lighting props.

We divvy up all the gear and pile into cabs. Most people are heading back to the office, but my apartment is nearby in Battery Park, so I direct my taxi to my address and plan to bring my share of the stuff into the office tomorrow.

The next day Drew and Jonathan are out on a different shoot, so I'm stuck taking orders from the editorial team. Laura enunciates her instructions on sending out mailers like she's addressing a small, possibly slow child. I heard her mention that it makes her head hurt to read anything but the fashion and style sections of the newspaper, and sometimes it takes all my restraint to not yell out, "I'm smarter than you!" Johanna sends me to Starbucks with a dozen coffee orders, an errand I don't totally loathe because it means I can get something for myself, too. I like working with Zoe best, since she's the only one who gives me real tasks. It's clearly her own work that she's just too lazy to do—edit and format these blogs, write copy for those slideshows, respond to reader e-mail and tweets—but I don't mind since it means I get to use my brain.

What makes me start counting down the hours and then eventually the minutes and seconds until six o'clock is an assignment from Victoria. She's asked me to create binders that archive the last fifteen years' worth of *Hers* stories that cover abstract notions such as "hope" and "faith" and "adventure." There's a digital archive where you can search by keyword, but Victoria says she doesn't trust a computer system to net stories that may not include the actual word "faith" but may still embody the concept. So I've been flipping through hundreds of issues to create these binders that, Victoria explained, will give her a panoramic sense of the magazine's history and its coverage of these topics. She's told me she'd eventually like similar binders from all of *Hers*' competitor titles, too, though I hope she forgets about it until after I'm back at college in the fall.

I dump the completed binders onto Victoria's desk, with just five minutes to go until the weekend. "So what have you learned today?" Victoria asks, as she always does at day's end, with that I'm-so-clever smile plastered onto her face.

I want to say I've learned that *Hers* has run a version of the same superfoods story about a dozen times over the past fifteen years. Ditto with pieces about the "ultimate, best-ever" beauty tricks, and the most effective exercise to attain a flat tummy, and nine—or sometimes thirteen, or seven—ways to raise happy, healthy, polite kids. "I've learned that *Hers* has a rich history in covering these topics that are crucial to today's modern women," I say.

"Very true," Victoria says. "The cool part is that it's only going to get better. You're lucky to be here during such an exciting time." *And doing such exciting things!*

"I've also learned that paper cuts really kill." I've gotten about twenty of them in the past hour.

"You are adorable," Victoria says. She fancies herself my mentor, and believes I'm as devoted to her as she is to me, a notion I've done nothing to contradict. "You're just like me when I was your age. You know, I worked at the *Daily Sun*, too. I was the forefront reporter on student life." I know girls like Victoria at Cornell, the ones who wear velvet ribbons in their hair and talk mainly about upcoming sorority formals.

"Go Big Red!" I say, and then scuttle out to catch my train.

It's a reflex to feel a rush of relief and anticipation when the workday ends on Friday and you're suddenly freed from the confines of the office, free to . . . in my case, go home and visit my sick mother in Connecticut. It takes about five minutes for my elation to fade away into this realization. My seatmate on the train looks around my age; I wonder if she too has an internship in the city and is going home for the weekend, if her mother will be doing her laundry and taking her shopping and cooking her "a decent square meal," as my mom used to call it—all the things my mother did for me during past visits home. The girl catches me staring. Her "What's your problem?" glare hits me like a physical blow. I wonder when the world got so mean.

My dad has offered to pick me up at the station, but I save him the trouble and grab a cab. As we round the corner to my street, a familiar dread trickles into my belly: Every plot of land is the same as always: the Ludlows' lawn riddled with toys, the Kaplans' prize-winning garden in full bloom. The familiar sights seem to mock me, a reminder that life has plodded along like normal for all of our neighbors, even as everything has gone to shit in the contained world of our quarter acre. The taxi pulls up to the curb in front of our house, and I observe a lawn that's the color of weak coffee. No one has thought to water the grass this year. The driver has to clear his throat to get me to budge from the backseat.

I take deliberate steps down the path and into the house. I will myself into the dayroom, where my father has set up the hospital bed so Mom doesn't have to climb stairs.

"Darling, it's you!" My mother hugs me, her arms like wire hangers, and I blink away the moisture welling up in my eyes. As is always the case when I'm back in my childhood home, I feel the age drain from me, years and years slipping away; suddenly I'm a ten-year-old girl who's just skinned her knee, and I need my mother. But not this strange-smelling version of her who's still clinging to me.

I realize too late, as I do on every one of these visits, that I should have made plans. I should've packed more than ratty sweatpants and T-shirts; I should've brought my skinny jeans and rompers and cute tops so I could escape the fog of sickness and go out with my friends who are home for the summer. These visits are like my father's phone calls: I so much look forward to them, eager to pack in the moments with my mother, but the minute I step over the threshold of our beautiful old Tudor now overrun with medieval looking medical equipment, I want to flee back to my cramped sublet in lower Manhattan.

"How's it going, Mom?" I say, detaching myself from her hug. She smiles, but says nothing. I remind myself how happy she is to see me. My dad hands me a list of tasks. He needs me to go grocery shopping and cook dinner and clean the kitchen. These things I can handle. "Look, I bought an immersion blender," he says proudly, holding up the contraption like it's show-and-tell. I've never known my dad to prepare anything more elaborate than a turkey sandwich. "She's keeping down soups these days," he adds in a whisper.

My mom goes to bed early, and my dad and I stay up late watching terrible talk shows on TV. At some point I conjure the energy to stumble up to my childhood bedroom and pass out.

In the middle of the night I'm awoken by strange, guttural sounds, and before my mind can tune out or deny them, I understand it's my mother dry heaving. I half sleepwalk to the bathroom, where she's crouched over the toilet, a mop of someone else's hair askew on her head. I hate that she feels the need to wear that thing even to bed. Saying not a word, I trace the length of her back with the pads of my fingers, avoiding the jutting nubs of her spine. I soak a towel in cool water and lay it onto the back of her neck. I open a bottle of seltzer and feed her sips, pushing grim thoughts from my mind. I see in the mirror that, even now, my mother and I share the same profile, the same way of smiling with the edges of our lips curled up unevenly. Eventually my mother kisses my head and tells me to go back to bed. She has no energy for a speech. So I leave her. I feel guilty turning on my noise machine, but do it, anyway. I sleep deeply until eleven o'clock, which also makes me feel guilty.

Saturday morning, I'm grateful to flee to Pathmark. I weave the aisles of the store—so vast compared to the D'Agostinos and Associated Markets in the city. I pretend I'm a suburban mom, shopping for her husband and three little rugrats: I'll need juice boxes and macaroni and ground beef. That kind of life feels so distant from my own that I nearly laugh out loud. On my grocery list are Saltines and applesauce and ginger ale. Huh, funny that shopping for a cancer patient is pretty much the same as shopping for someone with a hangover.

So far I've managed just half of a Wikipedia article about my mother's condition. I'm a researcher by nature, usually driven by intense curiosities that lead me down long paths to yet more curiosities. But in the case of my mom's disease, the shallowest forays into Google have left me close to full-on panic attack. I don't know her prognosis or the functions of the army of pill bottles on her bedside table or what it feels like to endure a round of chemotherapy. I don't know how or where the tumor has spread, or where it might spread further still. My father issues palliative statements like, "I think she's really fighting this" and "She seems like she's getting stronger every day," and I take his words at face value. As much as possible, I think of my mother as a fun-house mirror reflection of her real self, like one day soon we'll all step out of the carnival and return to regular life.

I add to the cart one of those fancy grass-fed chickens, a bunch of specialty vegetables, and a box of Godiva chocolate–dipped strawberries (they're sold in the supermarket, too, apparently). At home my dad unloads the groceries. "What's all this?"

"I figured I'd make a nice meal for us tonight, a treat."

"Oh, all right, honey." I catch him checking the receipt. I bought everything organic, and I'm remembering now that he'd asked me to stick to the generic brands. But Mom has cancer, for God's sake; surely we can spare her pesticides or whatever.

Then I remember what my dad said about Mom and soups, and I cringe imagining her pretend to enjoy a big meal. So that evening I wait to start cooking until after she's nodded off. The chicken and vegetables are roasted just so—delicious. Still, with each bite, I can't help feeling I'm eating up funds that could have gone to doctors' bills or medication copays or whatever. Dad and I converse in stilted sentences, and I'm equal parts relieved and disappointed when he flicks on the TV. I forget about the box of chocolate strawberries. Several weeks later, when I'm up at night ravenous (apparently we've all started skipping meals along with Mom), I'll come across the strawberries rotting in the pantry.

I leave earlier than I should on Sunday. I mow and water the lawn, wash a load of laundry, and help my dad cook up a big batch of minestrone, then I invent a lie about having to get back for an acoustic concert in Central Park. It's the type of thing I'd planned to do when I decided to spend the summer in Manhattan, back before my mother got so sick. I board the train and immediately begin missing my parents.

I spend the rest of the day sprawled out on the bed in my rented apartment, watching episode after episode of a terrible show about the country's worst mothers. I picture the show's children growing up and their terrible mothers, aged by twenty years, getting diagnosed with cancer; I wonder, even though long ago the moms insisted the kids get ankle tattoos at age eight and howled at them when they chose to do homework instead of massaging their moms' bunioned feet, would the grown-up kids still feel sad?

Monday morning, Zoe dumps the stack of entries to the Mother's Day essay contest on my desk. "I was supposed to go through these back in May, when they came in, but they got lost in the shuffle when Mimi started, and I really can't stand this sentimental crap," she says. "Mimi's asked for my winner picks this afternoon so we can get them up on the website. In other words, it's über-urgent. Hopefully you're a speed reader."

"I can't," I blurt out. "Photo needs me."

"Oh." I see that Zoe suspects I'm lying, but calling me out on it would risk my calling her out on passing off all of her work to me.

Drew doesn't mind my hanging around in the photo department. She's in the retouching studio, and invites me in to watch. They've picked out several images of Helena Hope as options for the November cover—none from the ferry, unsurprisingly. A fountain shot is up on the projector screen: Helena is laughing and kicking up a spray of water, looking carefree and joyful—pretty much the opposite of how she actually seemed that day on set. I'm impressed the photographer was able to create this happy fantasy.

"We haven't retouched it yet," Drew explains.

Lynn, the creative director, is taking an inventory of Helena's body parts with a red-tipped laser pointer, dictating notes: "Erase crow's-feet and under-eye circles. Even out skin tone. Gloss up hair, particularly around the temples. Let's see. Brighten teeth, recontour bump on top front tooth, plump up lower lip. Fix folds along shirt collar, darken dress color to contrast better against sky and water. Airbrush underarm, define waist. I think that should about do it." Drew has been nodding and scribbling down notes as if Lynn were reading out a grocery list. I wonder how she can possibly make all those changes and still have the photo resemble the Helena pictured before us.

"Mind if I stay and watch?" I ask.

"No problem-o," she says. "Prepare to get supercynical." Drew begins tweaking, and it's amazing craftsmanship—how she can adjust the line of a cheekbone just the slightest bit so you can barely notice a difference, but also think, Oh, right, that's what we call beautiful.

"Newsstand sales spike in inverse proportion to a cover girl's wrinkles and weight," she explains. "But only up to a point. Watch this." She smoothes out the tissue-papery lines around Helena's eyes, but leaves the faint indents in her forehead. "She's got to look aspirational, but not totally out of reach. Women want to buy the issue and think, How does she do it, so I can do it too? The reality is, *I* do it in the retouching studio."

As Drew tweaks the colors—deepening the hue of Helena's dress, lightening a shadow here and darkening another there—I remember the set of paper dolls I had when I was little. I would sit on the living room floor for hours at a time with all the separate hairdos and dresses and accessories splayed out around me, and I'd work on assembling the perfect dressed-up doll. My mother would crouch beside me, pick up my construction, and very seriously consider whether to supplement it with a pillbox hat or heart locket necklace. I thought her final touches were genius.

Drew is gradually shrinking Helena's upper arm, and I flash on my mother's own arm. My family used to have arm wrestling contests, and she would triumph even against my father. "It must be from mixing all that cookie batter," she'd say sarcastically, flexing an impressive bicep. I picture a photo of my mother up on Drew's screen, her clicks of the mouse melting the muscles and fat, adjusting the rosy reds and ivories to greens and grays until my mother has become the new, surreal shell of her former self. I feel nauseated.

"I need to use the ladies' room," I say, and bolt from the room. It's a shock to move from the studio's dark to the office's florescent lights, and my unadjusted eyes distort the view. Everything looks like it's been retouched, overly bright and garish.

I'm sitting on the toilet, doing a deep breathing visualization exercise I read about in an old issue of *Hers*—an article about the surprisingly high prevalence of anxiety disorder in American women.

Someone enters the stall next to me. "She's supposed to be smart—in the interview she bragged about her perfect GPA—but she's a sloppy worker." It's Jane.

"I know, and she acts like it's all beneath her." Zoe's voice. "She totally bailed on a project I gave her this morning, like she couldn't be bothered to do something so lowly." Despite the deep breathing, my heartbeat lurches to a sprint.

"And this is awful, but—"

"I know what you're going to say. That dress, right?"

"What was she *thinking?*" Their cackling mixed with the angry grunts of a toilet's flush is one of the crueler sounds to have rattled my eardrums. I stare at the crack in the door in front of me as the editors gather by the sinks and then exit. Then it's just me and the whirring white noise.

I look down at my dress. I pulled it from my mother's closet this past weekend, a retro-print shift, pink and green polka dots, fringed on the bottom. There's a photo of my mom at around my age; she's wearing the dress along with big green sunglasses and steep wedged sandals—totally glamorous. It's true that I'm wider in the hips and a bit stouter than her, but when I looked in the mirror this morning and twirled around, I felt like I'd stepped right out of the photo. I guess I must've done my own spontaneous retouching.

It feels like half an hour before I can peel myself up from the toilet. I skulk back to the retouching studio, and Drew gives me a warning look. The entertainment director, Johanna, is perched over her chair, the veins popping from her forehead. "Never in a million years will Helena go for this," she shouts. "Her arse is the size of Texas! She looks like a bloody cow!"

"I shaved off a good inch and a half from her waist and practically performed a virtual tummy tuck," says Drew.

"Rubbish! Look at her arms, her thighs, her double chin, for Christ's sake! You've got to cut her down by at least another size or two."

"What did Lynn say?"

"Never mind Lynn. She'll understand that we have to appease Helena. We can't send her photos where she looks like bloody crap or she'll go off her trolley and call the whole thing off."

"But if we do more editing she won't even look like herself."

"She'll look like all the photos the whole jolly world sees of her, a slightly lovelier version of herself."

"Slightly?" Drew whispers under her breath.

"And oh, Christ, fix her giant earlobe—it looks like an alien's ear."

"If you say so," Drew says. "Let the games begin." As Johanna looms over her, I watch Drew perform what amounts to severe plastic surgery on the photo, until it looks like Helena's "after picture" if she were featured in one of those gastric bypass ads. It's amazing and disgusting both.

"Perfect," says Johanna, then exits.

"*Puuuh*-fect," mocks Drew. "For the record, Mark would never have OK-ed this kind of a hack-up." I remember Mark, the old creative director, vaguely from the first few days of my internship. He was knee-deep in boxes.

Zoe catches up with me in the afternoon and asks me again about the Mother's Day essays. I'm out of excuses, and I can't stop thinking about her words in the bathroom, so I let her unload the stack on me. I set it aside on my desk, ignoring it in favor of Facebook and celebrity gossip blogs. I scroll through people's dumb photos of their kids and pets and the stupid things they ate for lunch, and then celebrities "looking just like us," feeding the parking meter, hailing cabs, and cavorting in the ocean. It all feels so fake, like this can't possibly be what we all covet and crave and care about. I try to be a good citizen and click over to *The Economist*, but my eyes immediately glaze over. I resign myself to the drivel, and head to MAGnifier.net, the snarky blog about the publishing industry.

PHOTOSHOP CONTEST: **$10K prize!** the home page reads.
I click through to the post:

> Ladies, we all know that women's mags are noto-
> rious for computer artistry otherwise known as
> Photoshop: the red-pen-wielding editors are bril-
> liant magicians, er, airbrusher-retoucher-digital-
> alterers, so that the so-called photographs we see
> on covers are nothing less than remarkable (read:
> horrifying, unconscionable) re-imaginings of real-
> ity. (Mini-rant alert!) We buy the issues, desper-
> ately feeding on the articles about diets and
> workouts, hoping and praying that—*please, God
> have mercy!*—maybe just maybe we can look like
> these perfect pod people pictured on the pages,
> meanwhile hating what we look like now. But it
> turns out even the models don't look like the per-
> fect pod people, not to put too fine a point on it.
>   Well, we wanna expose this forgery once and
> for all. So kindly help us, mag insiders, by getting
> your grubby little hands on an unaltered, original
> cover photo and sending it our way. Pretty please!
> Our not-so-little thank you? 10 G's direct-
> deposited into your bank account. Spend it on
> diet pills or personal trainers or Spanx—whatever
> it takes to get you in tiptop cover-girl shape.
> We're talking to you, editorial assistants barely
> earning enough to pay the rent in your run-down,
> 300-square-foot studios in Crown Heights. May
> the most shocking photo win!

I immediately click out of the screen, peering over my shoulder
to catch any lurkers. My heart is beating madly and my mind is racing. I think of my father's insistence on buying the store-brand
food, the crazy-elaborate medical equipment in my mom's sick

room, and the bedside table crowded with pill bottles. My shitty $1,000 stipend for this internship. The loads of equipment from the shoot I've been meaning to return to the office.

"Did you pick your favorites?" Zoe materializes in my cubicle. I wonder if she can hear my heartbeat.

"I sure did," I say, the words rolling off my tongue. I hand her the top three essays from the pile. "These ones really moved me. The imagery, the descriptions—I felt like I truly know what it means to be in those particular mother-daughter relationships."

"Awesome, great." Easy, no questions asked. I care not one bit what will happen if Zoe reads the essays and discovers they're terrible. But I wouldn't be surprised if she handed them straight off to Mimi without even bothering to look them over. Of course she never gives me credit for my work. I smile, imagining Mimi calling her in to discuss the "winning" essays that were most likely penned by illiterates.

That night in my apartment, I draw the shades (as if the neighbors across the wind shaft have any interest in my activities) and I dig through the duffel bag from the Helena Hope photo shoot. Among the various tripods and props I find a container of duplicate memory cards and a card reader: *jackpot!* I stuff the items in my pocket and walk the two blocks to the local library branch, picturing myself the heroine of a film noir. I push from my mind the image of Drew, so kind to me—*would she be blamed?*—and instead think about Jane and Zoe, as cruel as classic high school mean girls. I think of my mother's medical bills. The unachievable standards of beauty and womanhood and self-hate that magazines like *Hers* perpetuate with their bogus, fraudulent images.

I meditate on these facts as I download the photos, and then find the copy of the one that was up on Drew's screen this afternoon: Helena frolicking in the fountain's spray with her arms at her sides, left foot kicking up a cascade of water. I open a new e-mail. Into the "To:" slot I type "tips@magnifier.net," add the subject "Photoshop contest: for the *Hers* November issue," upload the photo, and click Send.

Momentarily my mind's eye fills with cash—loads of it, stacks of dollar bills and mountains of coins, so much that it covers my entire bedroom and I can leap into it like a pile of leaves. Then the image recedes and in its place appears the black-and-white fuzz of a TV channel empty of programming. I find I don't feel a thing.

I wander the library like a zombie. I pass through an echoey alcove of weighty reference books that look as if no one has consulted them for a decade or more, and then I find myself in the children's section, brightly painted in pastels. I weave through the stacks, perusing books whose covers show cuddly kittens and puppies, voluptuous princesses and broad-chested princes, big imposing dragons and lions. *Are these images fakes, too?* I wonder. I crack the spine of a book called *Naughty Nan*. Turns out, Nan has done many things wrong: colored on the wall with crayons, shoved all of her stuff under her bed instead of putting it away properly, and stolen from her brother's candy supply. As a result, she's been sent to bed without supper. Denied her mother's pot roast, Nan pigs out on candy. The book implies that this is some sort of tragedy, all that sugar and artificial flavor instead of a decent meal, but if you ask me, Nan was smart to raid her brother's stash, and she looks pretty damn smug tucked away in bed, her stomach filled with sweets.

I leave the library and, inspired by Nan's antics, pop into the ice-cream shop on the corner. I splurge on a triple scoop of chocolate chip with whipped cream. I gorge on the sweet, creamy cold, taking in spoonful after spoonful until I've scraped the bowl clean, meanwhile ignoring my phone's vibrations in my pocket. On the way home, my stomach performs achy somersaults. Its flips become increasingly more treacherous, until I'm forced to lean over a trash can. The ice cream has barely had time to melt. "Sicko!" a homeless man yells out.

I'm hunched over the garbage, trying to catch my breath, when an anonymous hand rests itself on my back. I let myself be soothed, imagining my mother's warm touch. But then the person speaks—"Are you OK?"—and the sound is unfamiliar, the voice nasal and wrong. I flinch, right myself, and hurry away, my mouth sour with acid.

I consider calling in sick the next day to work. But instead, when the alarm sounds my wake-up call, I get up, take myself through the motions of getting ready, commute, sit down at my desk, and turn on my computer. I feel calm and cool and ready to photocopy.

17

Leah Brenner,
Executive Editor

Mimi looks uncharacteristically upbeat, standing at the front of the conference room before the whole staff. "You guys have worked your butts off all summer long," she announces, "and now we're in the final stretch, heading into the November ship. Just two more weeks until the first issue of the relaunch is totally, completely, 100 percent out the door. Let's hear a round of applause for everyone in this room."

A chorus of claps fills the space. Laura queues up an iPod, and as pop music pumps through the speakers, Mimi thrashes her limbs about in a way that vaguely resembles dancing. I exchange across-the-room eyebrow raises with Debbie.

Next comes the slideshow. A series of pictures projects onto the wall: women blowing at dandelions, women sipping at cocktails, women lifting children up onto their shoulders. Bold words stamp themselves onto the pictures: "vibrant," "daring," "joyful," and "fun." This inspirational fare is interspersed with screenshots of *Hers'* new pages and sections. This slideshow may actually be a clever brainwashing trick, because with the flash of each new image I find my skepticism fading further. Soon I'm sitting there spellbound, rapt with the visual evidence of all our team has accomplished this summer. Four months ago, none of this existed.

Even more miraculously, the October ship came and went, and here I am two weeks later, still gainfully employed. Maybe Mimi is keeping me on staff after all. I let myself feel proud of the summer's work: We created all of these concepts, all of these pages; they're ours.

A buzz in my pocket snaps me out of my revelry. I open my phone and see five missed calls from Rob. I slip out of the meeting and dial him back.

"They accepted our bid," Rob shouts into the receiver, in lieu of hello. "The dream house is ours!"

"No!" I truly don't believe what I've heard. Maybe he misspoke, I think, or maybe I misheard. This can't be real. It's all too fast—we just put in our bid two days ago.

As if he can read my mind, Rob says, "It's really happening, baby. Aren't you thrilled? Say something!"

"Wow" is all I can manage. I'm not thrilled, actually, although I'm not upset, either. I simply can't get my brain to process this turn of events. I suppose this is what they call shock.

"Listen, I have to call our realtor immediately and get things going on this end. Love you. We'll talk later!"

I hang up and stand dumbstruck, gaping at my surroundings: The office is a ghost town, with everyone gone from their desks and crowded into the conference room for Mimi's praisefest. I feel as if I'm on a movie set of my life, the shooting wrapped for the day. I begin weaving the aisles of abandoned cubicles without pattern or direction. I don't suspect myself of a motive until I notice that I've stopped in front of Laura's computer and that I'm suspiciously checking my peripheral vision. Her e-mail window is right there, open on her screen—and below Laura's in-box is Mimi's (Laura has full access to keep track of her boss's schedule). *It doesn't matter,* I tell myself, as I reach for the keyboard. *I'm out of here, moving to Vermont.*

And then it's happening. It doesn't feel like it's me making the decision or like it's my own hand launching Mimi's in-box and conducting a search for my name, then wading through a flood of meeting invites and all-staff notes in order to locate something interesting. I feel one step removed, like an actress is playing the role of me.

A header jumps out: "Staff changes." *Aha!* Under this subject line lies a string of e-mails between Mimi and Mrs. Winters, Schmidt & Delancey's editorial director (her signature actually says "Mrs. Winters," as if she doesn't even possess a first name). Their exchange reaches back to Mimi's first day on the job, May 2, when the new editor in chief sent Mrs. Winters her first impressions of the then-members of the staff. I scan for my name: "Leah Brenner is deeply entrenched in and loyal to the old vision of *Hers*. She seems smart, more or less."

More or less? I'm fuming, but I'm also aware that I have to work fast. At any moment someone could emerge from the conference room and catch me, head bent over the wrong computer. Fingers keep guiding the keys, eyes keep skimming the back-and-forth. Shortly after Mimi delivered her snap judgments of the staff to Mrs. Winters, the latter e-mailed a lengthy spiel on the best ways to bolster staff morale during a time of upheaval. She writes about scheduling group brainstorms and providing opportunities for feedback so staff members are made to feel valued, like their opinions count. (Notably, Mrs. Winters's stated goal is to give the staff the *impression* that they are thought well of; she offers no advice on how to *actually* value your staff or listen and respond to their feedback.) I skip over a series of bullet points on the blah blah blah of establishing authority.

The next section is entitled, "The importance of timing." In the dense paragraph that follows, Mrs. Winters lays out the thesis that, when a new editor in chief is rejiggering a staff to build a revised team, it is crucial for her to move quickly, but not too quickly. While she shakes up the old way of doing things, Mrs. Winters goes on to say, a new boss must maintain a certain semblance of stability. An easy way to do so is to temporarily keep on two to three members of the old establishment's senior staff. Still, a new boss must be careful not to drag out the layoffs over too long a period, so as not to create a culture of fear and distrust among the remaining staff. According to Mrs. Winters, a window of three to four months should be sufficient.

After this manifesto, Mrs. Winters ends with a section labeled "Big Blowout Party!" The gist is, Mimi should notify Corporate once she's completed all of her staff changes, and then they'll arrange and fund a fabulous party. This will serve as both a celebration of the magazine's relaunch and an assurance to the remaining staff that they're solidly and safely part of the new team—that they've survived.

I stare at this last sentence, feeling wholly back to myself, knowing full well that I am violating my boss's privacy and perhaps even breaking the law. Not only do I not care, but at the moment neither do I care about the house—*our* house—in Vermont; all that concerns me is that Mimi has not yet scheduled this Big Blowout Party. She's closing in on four months at *Hers*, and there's been no mention of such an event.

I'm about to ex out of Mimi's in-box when a new e-mail pops up on the screen. It's a one-liner from Suzanne in Human Resources: "Meeting is on the books, 8 a.m." I scroll down to find out what Suzie's responding to, what this meeting is that she's put on the books. The original e-mail from Mimi reads: "Please schedule an appointment for us and Leah Brenner on September 4, the earlier in the day the better." The day after Labor Day, two weeks from today. My knees give out, and I plunk down into Laura's seat.

I still haven't moved when I hear Abby's voice. "Leah, is that you? What are you doing?"

"Borrowing a Post-it," I say on reflex.

Abby eyes me warily. "Come on back to the meeting, OK?"

She leads me, the walking dead, back to the conference room. Maybe it's just paranoia, but as I enter the room I sense my coworkers' looks of pity like spiders on my skin. I imagine this is what it would feel like to be bald and underweight after chemotherapy. (I immediately scold myself for the comparison.)

Mimi is raising a glass of champagne. "In case you haven't figured it out yet, I am so enormously proud of what this magazine is becoming, and I can't wait to keep up the momentum we've started. Cheers!" Someone places a glass in my grip, and I feel my eyes blur with tears as I raise my champagne to the thing I've been fearing and dreading and half-hoping for all summer. I toast what I now know for certain will be my last ever issue of *Hers*. As the bubbly liquid slides down my throat, I think about how every single month for the past fifteen years—my entire working life—I have been instrumental in putting out a magazine. That's nearly two hundred issues that I've used to measure the progress of my career, and more than that, my life. I wonder, next month and the month after and the month after that, how will I mark the passage of time?

I arrive home bursting with the news of my official end date, but the moment I open the door and discover my house in the cleanest state I've ever seen it, the information flees my brain. The front hall, usually a disastrous wreckage of shoes and coats and toys, looks like the set of a *Hers* lifestyle shoot, all clean surface and calm. The sight of a vase with actual fresh flowers poking out nearly moves me to tears. I step into this alternate universe of my home, and there is my husband in the living room, dressed in slacks and a button-down instead of his standard uniform of jeans and ironic T-shirt, splaying out my magazines in a fan on the coffee table.

"What the hell is going on?" I ask. Maria emerges from the kitchen carrying two platters of catered cold cuts. My mother trails behind her, stealing a slice of Swiss from one of the trays. "Mom? What are you doing here?"

"Your husband called me to come help out." She plops down onto the couch and grabs a magazine, disrupting Rob's stylized design. He swoops in to rearrange.

"Help out with what? Rob, hello, can you hear me?"

"Hey, baby." My husband leans in for a kiss, then grabs a broom and sets about sweeping around my feet. "Sorry, I've been running around like a crazy person. The realtor was able to pull together a last-minute open house for tonight. She said to expect at least a dozen people. She also recommended we clear out, but I thought it would be fun to attend. So Maria's going to take the girls out driving—let's pray they fall asleep in the car—and your mom offered to do the appetizers."

"I ordered from Zabar's," she says. "It's my not-so-secret scheme to get you to stay near Manhattan. Fix yourself a sandwich and you'll realize what morons you are to move. What kind of bagel do you think you can get up in Vermont, in the middle of nowhere?"

I roll my eyes. "I love you, too, Mom."

I squeeze Maria's arm. "Thank you for staying late. The girls tend to nod off at twenty-five miles per hour." Our nanny's nod is gracious, like I'm enlightening her with information she doesn't already know. Last week we finally told her about the probable move. We invited her to come with us—wherever we ended up, we knew we'd have room to spare—and she said she'd think about it. I consider Maria to be family; still, I know her real family all lives here in New Jersey.

I turn to Rob, trying to tamp down my panic at this sudden turn of events. "Why didn't you call me? I would've come home early. How can I help?"

"I didn't want to bother you at work. Everything's under control here. Just try and relax."

"OK." But I can't relax when everyone else seems to have a job to do. Rob and Maria buzz around like it's their calling to transform the house into a pristine museum of itself. Even my mother looks like she's on a mission, though in her case it's to lounge around on the couch with her boot-clad feet propped up on the coffee table. I loiter, still clutching at my work purse, feeling like I've already been displaced from my home.

"What time are people coming over?"

Rob checks his watch. "T-minus ten minutes. Prepare to be one half of the charming couple who owns this charming house."

"Aren't I always?" I say, thinking I better rush to kiss the girls good night if I'm going to have time to chug a glass of wine before the home invasion.

*   *   *

Ten minutes is not nearly long enough to prepare myself for the pockets of strangers gathering in my living room, peeking into my private spaces, and sizing up my home. Rob insisted our presence would be a selling point for the house—we're a young, attractive couple that others will aspire to be like, he claimed—but now I'm seeing why people generally hit the road for their own open houses.

From my hideout in the kitchen, I can hear Rob in the next room parroting our Vermont realtor, singing the praises of our light fixtures and original moldings. I'm shoving my eighth slice of turkey into my mouth—my mother is right, this stuff is addictive—when I sense a woman at my side.

"I hate to say it, but you've got a beautiful home," she says.

"Excuse me?" I ask, mouth full.

"Sheesh, I'm sorry, that came out wrong. I'm Isabella." She sticks out her hand, and I wipe my own greasy one on my shirt before reaching for a shake. "I figured you were the owner, since you've been standing around looking so wistful and uncomfortable."

"Oh."

"Plus, the décor in here is to die for, and you're the best-dressed person in sight. It all just added up."

"Thanks," I say, thinking maybe I like this woman. "Picture the place covered with toys and dirty dishes and you'll have a more accurate idea of what it's usually like."

Isabella laughs. "We live in SoHo. I'm here with my husband, Jim. He's the one talking square footage in the other room with the guy I presume is your husband."

"Fascinating." I roll my eyes.

"Can I let you in on a secret?" Isabella reaches over me for a bagel, then tears into it. "I'm absolutely petrified of the suburbs. Jim dragged me out here kicking and screaming."

"God, I know what you mean. I grew up in Manhattan, and Rob and I were in Williamsburg before we transplanted out here."

"So are you guys moving back to the city?"

"With triplets, are you crazy? No way. I wish, though. I miss all the restaurants and the 24-hour delis. All the people. All that energy."

"The truth is," Isabella whispers, leaning in to speak, "I'm pregnant, ten weeks along. Jim thinks we'll need more space once we have the baby."

"People in the city manage OK with one kid, right? Are you in a studio or something?"

"No, we have an extra bedroom."

"Oh, then you'll be fine. Are you planning on staying home?"

"Lord, no. I'm an attorney. I do litigation, mostly mergers and acquisitions, some bankruptcy cases. I'd rather shoot myself than become one of those moms who quits her job and is so bored she becomes president of the PTA and starts running it like a Fortune 500 company." I'm cracking up and nodding; I pass those women in the supermarket all the time. "So what do you do?" she asks.

"I'm an executive editor at *Hers* magazine." I'm about to say, *for now*, but Isabella gasps.

"That is incredible! A job where you get to be creative, and where you probably don't have to wear a suit, wow. I'm seething with envy, honestly. I always wanted to be a writer, but I never had the guts. Hence the boring, sensible lawyer track. You must absolutely adore it." I smile, which seems like the simplest response. "But wait, you're moving away."

"Yeah, well, it's a long story."

"Ah. So tell me, how brutal is the commute? My office is in midtown."

"It's pretty bad. You get used to it, but it's kind of like *Planes, Trains and Automobiles*, only with you it'll be Car, Train, and Subway." Just saying the words is enough to overwhelm me, to set into motion a tidal wave of exhaustion—the back-and-forth from suburb to city and city to suburb, day in and day out, the attempt to be everything and everywhere at once, the spreading of myself so thin that sometimes it seems as if I've disappeared entirely, the impossibility of it all. I feel like I'm drowning, and I grab Isabella's arm to steady myself.

On a whim, I start spewing my thoughts: "Isabella, don't do it. I'm telling you, stay where you are. Live in SoHo, take a ten-minute train ride to work, go out to dinner at the cool new spot on the corner, and bring your baby to the hip bar where they allow kids. Live that illustrious Manhattan working mom life. Whatever you do, do not buy this house and move to the suburbs."

"Um." Isabella is looking at me like perhaps I need to be institutionalized.

"Hey, ladies." Rob sidles up to me, eyeing me warily, and Isabella's husband is at her side now, too. It's clear they've overheard my tirade. "I take it you met Jim's wife," my husband says. "I was just telling Jim here about the Westfield neighborhood association, and how responsive they are to complaints."

"Yes," I say. "Very responsive."

Rob goes on: "They were saints helping us with that rabid raccoon we had up in our oak this spring." I smile and nod, but I'm zoning out, imagining a different sort of neighborhood association, one that could respond to other kinds of complaints: *I want to work and be with my family and also get seven hours of sleep each night. Why is that too much to ask? How can you work so hard to build a big, ambitious career, only to have it all come to pieces at the whim of a single person? How will I figure out a new life?*

After all the strangers retreat from the house, my mother walks around with a garbage bag and collects the half-filled cups and paper plates with scraps of food. Maria pulls into the driveway and carries our sleeping babies, one by one, upstairs and into their cribs. I stand at the sink, washing dishes, and Rob stands beside me, drying them. He doesn't scold me for begging that woman not to buy our house. He doesn't insist that he had the husband sold. He doesn't say a word. When the dishes are all clean and dry and tucked away in the cupboards, the two of us go upstairs, lie down in our joint bed, and each think our own separate sets of thoughts until weariness overtakes us, and we both sink into sleep.

18

Jane Staub-Smith, Associate Editor

I'm emptying another pack of ballpoint pens onto the tidy but growing pile in my apartment's storage nook, when Jenny appears in the doorway. She's invited herself over to help me, in her words, "buckle down and make a goddamn decision." I, meanwhile, would rather revel in my brand-new stash of office supplies—so much shiny, functional stuff. I've never been much of a hobbyist, and I'm amazed how satisfying it can be to grow a collection, to set my sights on certain specific things and then acquire them.

"Ready yet to take out Staples?" Jenny asks. I don't respond. "Well, it's up to you. You can fill this space with a pile of pens and paper, or you can have a nursery. I found you a great crib, half off, in case you're interested."

"Thanks. I've got loads of time, you know."

"Not as much as you think. Time flies, as they say."

"Oh, is that what they say?" Jenny's strategy has been to push, push, push me. She's started bringing me Babies "R" Us catalogs with pages dog-eared on what she considers mommy essentials, as if such inspirational fodder will magically shift my desire for office supplies into a desire for onesies and bibs. Or maybe her theory is, learning about all the gear and gizmos required for motherhood will be enough to repel me from the whole idea and get myself to the clinic. Jenny believes, if I can actually visualize what it will be like to have a baby, I'll be able to make the best-informed decision about my situation. Her whole earnest campaign, as if my pregnancy were one of her P.R. accounts to manage, makes me want to curl up into a ball and take a nap.

The next morning I get to work early and plot my path to nab three new staplers. I do a mental calculation of my winnings from the past two weeks: twenty-one ballpoint pens, two reams of paper, a calculator, a clipboard, four pairs of scissors, a dozen Post-it pads, and six one-inch binders. I've built up my stash carefully but quickly, placing small orders through the company's Web site, ducking into the supply closet to swipe extras and, only when I'm feeling desperate, snatching items from other people's desks. I don't have near enough, and though I'm not quite sure what "enough" is, I'll know it when I see it. The important thing is to be prepared.

I duck down to the cafeteria for a wedge of frittata, and when I return to my desk, Zoe eyes my purchase. "Didn't you have a bagel an hour ago?" she says. "Is this some kind of strategy: fatten yourself up so Mimi will look skinny in comparison and bring you into the inner circle again?"

"Lay off, Zoe," I say, digging into the eggs. "I'm just stressed."

"OK, whatever." Of course it's this creature growing inside of me that's driving me to eat and eat and eat, sapping my energy, and reducing me to tearful fits of anxiety at the slightest provocation. Morning sickness is not supposed to start for several more weeks, according to a book Jenny's forcing me to read, so it must be my nerves twisting me with nausea. I pray I can keep the whole debacle a secret for as long as possible. At least until I decide it's what I want. I fear an impending baby will give Mimi yet another reason to cut me loose, so she won't have to pay out my (admittedly paltry) salary during a maternity leave.

Stay sane, Jane, I say in my head. It's my new mantra, one I've been repeating ever since worry has become my main emotion, permeating everything in my life: It's crept into the pixels on my computer screen, it's appeared as stubborn itches between my toes, and it's spread itself onto my peanut butter sandwiches—*ooh, peanut butter sounds really good.* I worry about all kinds of things big and small, but the real doozy is, I worry a goblin is growing in my womb. It's ridiculous, I know, especially since I read my embryo is currently only the size of a pen's tip. But what started as a silly, outlandish hunch has recently crystallized into pure white fear.

I get to work editing a Q&A about women's health concerns— Does sunburn really cause skin cancer? Is it risky to sit in a wet bathing suit?—but I'm easily distracted. These run-of-the-mill worries seem so benign compared to the fear that I'm incubating some kind of a monster in my womb. I'm rational enough to realize that voicing this concern aloud, even to Jenny, would make me seem certifiable. Plus, who *wouldn't* fire a person who believes she's harvesting an alien? Perhaps more important, who would choose to issue a biweekly paycheck to the future mother of a creature capable of serious destruction?

Another part of me fears I've cooked up this delusion so it won't feel so awful to just end the whole ordeal. I mean, what kind of normal person *wouldn't* do everything she could to prevent a monster from entering the world? And yet, somehow I sense that if I visited Planned Parenthood, I'd leave my appointment with something even more terrible in my gut: a dark pit of regret and guilt. Ugh. I'm suddenly itching to get my hands on a pad of graph paper.

"Jane, will you join me in my office?" It's Mimi, interrupting my spiral down into the depths of anguish. I comply, and she hands me a printout. "Take a look at my notes."

It's the final draft of my allergies story, and I see she's slashed up every line with her notorious red pen, branding sentence after sentence so that the page looks like it's bleeding. "As you can see, I'm not a fan of this expert's advice." Of course she didn't think to mention this on the first or second draft. "All that business about the endless rounds of shots required and all those medications, it's so depressing!" She's crossed out whole quotes and scribbled down new ones; she has one of the nation's top allergists saying,

"You wouldn't believe how effective the power of positive thinking can be!"

"So you'd prefer me to include this advice instead?" I ask. Mimi tilts her head in a way that indicates my question is absurd. With our fact-checking department reduced to one clueless freelancer, there's practically no barrier to these out-of-thin-air inventions making it to print. This story is supposed to ship to the printer tomorrow.

"Listen," Mimi says. "My puggle, Pookie, used to be allergic to his kibble. He'd break out in these horrible hives after meals. It was wretched. But I was reluctant to switch brands since the one I fed him was organic and locally sourced. So at the suggestion of his doctor, I posted a ton of positive images and affirmations around his food bowl, and that was all it took! No more allergy! I'm happy to put you in touch with the doctor."

"Your dog's veterinarian recommended affirmations?"

"Sure." Mimi hands me a card with the name "Dr. John 'Doolittle' Crawson, DVM" printed on it. *Is it my sanity that's slipping away,* I wonder, *or everyone else's?*

"My point is," she continues, "see to it that we get stronger experts next time, ones who are more on message with the *Hers* mission."

"Right on." I truly have no idea what she's talking about.

"Also, I was talking to my niece Dahlia, who's a total card, the most popular girl in her fourth-grade class. She thought it would be really fun to have an advice column from Mr. Mom in *Hers*. A genius idea, right?"

"What exactly do you mean by 'Mr. Mom'?"

"We'll find a man with the last name 'Mom' and get him to answer readers' parenting conundrums, obviously. So please get on that."

"OK, will do."

I stick around until late that night, scouring WhitePages.com for Mom last names and fantasizing about looking up Mimi's snotty little niece and wringing her "genius" neck. One of my new initiatives to look like a diligent, competent employee, and not the half-crazed, monster-bearing maniac I know myself to be, is to never be one of the first people out the door at night. My rule is to count fifteen exits—half of the staff—until I dare shut down my computer. It's already nine-thirty p.m. and I'm still held hostage in my cubicle, waiting for one more person to take off before I'll budge. In the meantime, I imagine calling my ex, Jacob. Perhaps he'll take pity on my situation and want to be my boyfriend again. Better yet, maybe I can convince him to meet up with me and be seduced into my bedroom where we'll—oops!—forget to use a condom, and then I can drop the pregnancy bombshell on him; we'll get back together and raise the kid as ours. Happily ever after.

I must be staring off into space because I don't notice Mimi's approach. "Jane," she says, startling me. "I wanted to check in to make sure you have enough to do."

I blink up at her, flabbergasted. It's almost ten p.m. "Yes, I believe I have enough to do," I say, as calmly as I can manage. "But if there's more you need from me, just say the word."

When I finally make it home and climb into bed, I dream a twisted, reverse version of Sleeping Beauty: Jacob is under a spell, asleep in a glass case and awaiting a princess's kiss, but when I find him and lean in for the crucial smooch, he keeps right on snoozing. I suppose he's been waiting on a different princess. When I bolt awake I'm alone in the thin morning light, the creature in my belly sending shivery shock waves of worry through my body.

The next morning, I start a countdown: one more week until Labor Day weekend, and one more day after that until the end of the November ship. Ascending the Schmidt & Delancey elevator, I scan the ten-day weather bulletin on the digital screen: It'll be eighty-three and sunny for Labor Day. Jenny and I are heading out to Montauk for the long weekend, a trip she idiotically keeps referring to as my "maybe-baby-moon." I imagine my friend and myself settling in to our beachy digs and mixing up Bloody Marys (mine possibly a virgin), *Hers* magazine the furthest thing from my mind.

Before I even boot up my computer, Abby approaches my desk, looking apprehensive. "I'm sorry to say, but it looks like you're taking over the prize pages." I guess this is the result of Mimi questioning whether my plate was sufficiently full.

"You're kidding. What about Laura?"

"Mimi decided Laura wasn't sophisticated enough to handle the responsibility." Abby knows enough to deliver this news without an entirely straight face. "She thought you'd have just the right expertise to take over the section."

I've worked on prize pages before, so I know there is zero sophistication required to beg public relations people to give away the products they represent, then to run a computer program that randomly selects winners from the entrant pool, and finally to send e-mails informing the winners they've won. I had this duty a decade ago, back when I interned at a teen magazine as a college freshman, and even then I could listen to the radio and maintain a conversation all while I worked.

"I'm not going to lie, your first order of business is a toughie," Abby says. "Splendid Soaps promised to gift a dozen decorative bath baskets worth a hundred dollars each, but the company went belly-up after when we featured them in the magazine."

"And I'm guessing we can't just eat the cost and cut checks for all the winners from the deep coffers of *Hers*?"

Abby shakes her head. "Not quite."

"So what you're saying is, now I have the pleasant task of rounding up $1,200' worth of stuff to make up for the prizes?" Abby nods, arching her eyebrows into a pitying kindness. "Oh, goody."

I spend the rest of the morning scrounging around the beauty closet in search of expensive lipsticks and scouring the giveaway table for hardcover books (I briefly consider including in the prize packages copies of *How to Finally Leave an Angry, Abusive Man* before ultimately deciding against it.). I feel my brain softening to mush. It makes sense, since my body will soon be moving along the same trajectory. I suppose I could send the winners my office supply collection, though I doubt they'd feel the proper amount of appreciation. Only I seem to grasp the wonderful comfort of a tall stack of crisp, clean paper.

It takes me several hours, but eventually I manage to assemble what liberal calculations would add up to $1,200 worth of stuff: a mishmash of makeup samples, gag gifts from P.R. firms, and fashion shoot rejects. I distribute the items among twelve boxes and deliver them to Ed, thankful to have the task off of my hands.

"Everyone into the conference room," Laura calls out, announcing a story pitch meeting. I situate myself on the room's perimeter and begin rapping my fingers against the glass. I don't say much lately at these brainstorms. Ever since Mimi and Victoria did a one-eighty on their opinions of me, I've been second- and triple-guessing my every thought. Plus, I suspect my alien embryo is not only suckling on me for food and energy, but also feeding on my brain for smarts. I've been feeling dumber every day.

After ten minutes, I force myself to speak up: "How about we run a story on women who have higher sex drives than their partners?" I'm more confident than usual about this idea, since I'm speaking from experience; toward the end of my relationship with Jacob, I was always raring to go and he was never in the mood. I add, "Several recent studies have found that this kind of mismatch of libido in relationships is very common, much more so than you'd think." My hormones have been raging these past few weeks, which I suspect is one of the monster's evil schemes. This horrifies Jenny. Last night when I saw a hot guy on the street and whispered to her all the things I wanted to do to him, she looked at me as if I were insane, as if she believes impending maternity should snuff out sexuality.

Victoria cackles. "Every woman I know practically has to fend her partner off with knives."

"Tell me about it," Leah adds, in a rare moment of solidarity with Victoria. "I've become an expert at pretending I'm already asleep. I'd be thrilled to never have sex again." *Yeah, but you have triplets under the age of two,* I want to scream. *And can one of you please lend me your husband for the night?*

"Exactly," says Victoria. "Return from la-la-land, Jane."

The meeting moves on, my idea left on the chopping block and me left feeling mortified. Panicky, I excuse myself and make a beeline to the supply closet. I swipe a two-inch binder, then run to the bathroom, where I lock myself inside a stall and methodically clench and unclench the binder's rings. If I can't handle a little dissent in a meeting, there's no way I'm cut out to be a mother. That's it, I think, my heartbeat churning like an overheated engine: I'll call the clinic today.

When I eventually calm down, I return to the conference room, resolved to keep my mouth shut. "I'm still not happy with the personal essay options for November," says Mimi, "and we're down to the wire—one week until the entire issue is out the door. We need a strong voice with a strong story, and we need it fast. Let's all think along the lines of grand triumphs over adversity, massive flops, bizarre and incredible occurrences. Come on, people." For a split second I consider suggesting I write about the weird creature growing in my stomach, but then I remember: *Stay sane, Jane.*

"I know of a group of women who were abducted by aliens," offers Johanna. I eye her to see if somehow she's read my mind and is mocking me. Apparently not. "They're from this town in Nevada, and they all disappeared one cool summer night. The authorities searched high and low, but after a few days and no sign of them, everyone assumed they'd been hacked to pieces by some murderous maniac wanker. Then one day, a farmer was up at dawn milking his cows, and he discovered all seven lasses lying in his field, buck naked, looking as if they'd stuck their fingers in sockets, their hair all frizzed up and their eyes all crossed and mad."

"Bullshit," says Debbie. "Where did you hear about this, in line at Wendy's?"

"No, I swear," Johanna says. "One of the women wrote a rock album about the experience, and I know her publicist. She'd sure fancy a profile in the magazine."

"That's an idea." Mimi sounds suspicious, like perhaps she shouldn't have invited the entertainment director to a story pitch meeting.

"I know," says Victoria. "How about we find a mother who was at the tippy-top of her game, just flying high and killing it in her career, raking in the big bucks. But then suddenly it all came crashing down. Everything just fell apart out of the blue, like poof! We'll have her sketch out the rise and the fall, the whole trajectory."

"That would really resonate with readers, considering the economy's still in the shitter," says Mimi. "Anyone know a writer who's been through something like that?"

We're all silent, until Abby coughs. I can see Zoe smirking behind her notebook. I drop my pen. "Oops." I wonder if everyone can feel it—our former boss's presence hovering over us, haunting the conference room like a ghost. In order to resist shouting out, *Louisa, for God's sake! Get Louisa to write the stupid story,* I repeat my mantra under my breath like a madwoman: *Stay sane, Jane. Stay sane, Jane. Stay sane, Jane.*

"Well, let's all think on it," Mimi says.

"How about we run a roundup of essays about the measures different women take to hide their pregnancies in their first trimesters," I say, praying no one will dismiss the idea as idiotic. "You know, like bringing their wineglass into the bathroom and swapping out the alcohol for grape juice they smuggled in, or talking up the great new sushi place they supposedly just tried. Or making a big show of taking their birth control, but really only popping the sugar pills." I brace myself for the response, hoping no one again accuses me of living in la-la-land.

"OMG!" Zoe squeals. "Jane, you're not knocked up, are you?" Before I can tamp down my panic and pull myself together to respond, she practically pounces. "I knew it! I could've sworn you've been acting all weird lately. Congratulations, you sneaky little snake!" When I still don't deny the accusation, I watch as the faces all around me contort into excitement and shock. And then I am being molested, a dozen perfectly manicured hands groping my belly, anxious to feel the imp underneath.

"Oh," I say, cursing my stupidity. I didn't realize my pitch would be a default pregnancy announcement. "Yeah, I guess you guys figured it out. Clever you." I flash a smile at Mimi, thinking, *Please don't fire me.* Jenny has told me it's actually trickier to fire a pregnant woman, since she could sue for discrimination. But I don't trust Schmidt & Delancey to play by those kinds of rules.

"I have plenty of other ideas along the lines of best remedies for morning sickness, savoring your last days of freedom, and how to shop for a bigger bra size every week." Everyone laughs, and I breathe a sigh of relief. Is it possible I can just let this be my decision, now that the cat's out of the bag? I can already imagine Jenny's disappointment in me, her insistence that I think this through in a mature, reasoned way and come to a genuine choice that's right for me. I have a sudden urge to steal someone's full-on computer.

My coworkers start treating me differently. Mimi insists I take a chair during meetings, and the view is different seated among my superiors. At my desk I'm opening a new pair of scissors—the fifth for my collection—when Zoe says, "Want me to get that for you?"

"What do you think I'm going to do, accidentally slip and stab my stomach?" I ask. Zoe raises her arms defensively.

"Hey, Jane. How's it going?" It's Abby popping by to chat, a first. She's usually not one for casual banter. "So how have you been feeling?"

"I'm good. Starving all the time, but otherwise fine."

"Is it strange to know you'll be a mom next year?"

"I guess. I try not to think about it."

She laughs, like she thinks I'm joking. "And what do you sense it is, a boy or a girl?"

A monster. "Um, I'm not sure."

"I'd want a girl, I think." I can hear Zoe giggling. I'm not sure why she finds it endlessly amusing that Abby is a lesbian.

"So how did you know you were ready to be a mother? And do you think most people will judge you or admire you for doing it on your own? Are you worried you won't be able to manage it all?" This torrent of personal questions is strange, for sure, but somehow it doesn't bother me. Abby isn't a judger, and it doesn't feel like prying. I suspect she's just fishing for whether I'll come back after maternity leave.

"I love my job," I say, a totally inappropriate response. Apropos of nothing, I add, "My mom's gonna help out with the baby." Not true. In fact, I'd prefer to permanently put off telling my parents about this turn of events. But I want Abby to know I care about my career and don't plan on tossing it aside to change diapers. And I don't.

But wait, if she thinks I'm leaving for good, then Mimi wouldn't have to bother firing me (and shelling out for my severance), which means I'd be safe for at least seven more months. "Well, my mom said she *might* be able to help," I say. "She does have her hands full with my father, who's on a very strict diet and whose memory has been going. Plus, she's very devoted to her bridge club." *Where do I come up with this stuff?* Abby looks puzzled. I should just tape my mouth shut with one of my four rolls of masking tape.

What I want to say is, "I'm terrified and I'm not even sure I'm going to go through with it." What I actually say is, "I'm excited, but also scared. I'm not sure if I'm ready, but can you ever really be?"

Zoe, meanwhile, has stopped ribbing me about getting fat. When I start polishing off entire calzones at lunch and then visit the vending machine for Kit Kats an hour later, I see her pretending not to notice. Bless her. But as if to make up for Zoe's discretion, Johanna approaches one afternoon just as I'm tearing open a second candy bar; in her dumb British accent, she offers the following unsolicited advice: "Pardon, but you know you only need three hundred additional calories per day when you're pregnant. That way, you won't blow up like a blimp and forever be known as the mum with the giant arse who couldn't shed her baby weight. Cheerio!" My mouth is full of chocolate as she walks away.

Debbie appears with a tray of cheese and crackers. "Five more hours until Labor Day weekend—three whole days of freedom!" she says, holding out her spread to our cluster of cubicles. But when I reach for a piece of Brie, she snatches my hand away. "No soft cheese, Jane," she snaps. "Do you want your kid to be born with two heads? Jesus!"

"Not fair," I say, sulking empty-handed while everyone else samples the offerings.

Victoria is a fountain of syrupy sympathy: "You just relax, take a seat," she says, loading up a cracker with a wedge of cheddar. "It's probably going to get harder and harder for you to move around, right? It's a good thing we don't have the time to take lunch breaks these days, so you can just stay put at your desk!"

I want to throttle her, but I remind myself of what Debbie just mentioned: only five more hours to endure until my weekend at the beach. "Staying put at my desk sounds great," I say. I can't resist adding, "Can I count on you, Victoria, to deliver my meals?" Debbie snickers.

Instead of responding, Victoria hands me a stack of proofs. "These pieces still need some work."

I sigh and return to my desk, cheeseless. As usual, the stories are marked up to the gills with that curlicued penmanship Victoria should have grown out of by her early teens. I toss the pages aside and decide to Google my name instead. This habit doesn't deliver the same fix as accruing office supplies, but it'll do in a pinch. I expect the usual posts about the other Jane Staub-Smith, a successful stockbroker in Cincinnati who's always doing respectable things like making donations to open a new branch of the local art museum or winning third place in her age group (thirty-five to forty) in her church's 10K. I've learned her husband is a hand surgeon, and from her picture I can tell she's tall and slim with these impossible boobs that are both large and perky. I rely on the other Jane Staub-Smith to continue racking up accomplishments as my life plods along mundanely.

When the new posts pop up on the screen, my first thought is, *Oh no, what has Cincinnati Jane gotten herself mixed up in?* There's a message board called "Winners' Circle," and the teaser shows our shared name beside a series of expletives. I click through to the site, which displays a long string of messages. It's not until I see the word *"Hers"* that I realize the posts are in fact about me. One says, *"Hers* sent me a load of crap! I was supposed to win a big beauty basket, but all they mailed me was a bunch of useless JUNK!!! Screw them! Associate editor Jane Staub-Smith handles prizes. Send complaints to Jane.Staub-Smith@Hers.com." I'm shocked and indignant. As if this commenter worked so hard to win her goddamned soap basket instead of just filling out a three-line form! I scroll down to the next one: "I've never won anything before, and boy was I disappointed when I opened my package to find three XXL T-shirts all with the slogan 'This Bitch Votes.' " (A fair complaint, actually.) I read another: "So unfair for you guys! Thanks for sharing the e-mail for the evil *Hers* prize lady. I plan on giving her a piece of my mind!" *Evil* Hers *prize lady!* Shit.

I'm trembling as I check my e-mail, and sure enough, a torrent of notes have poured in during the past half hour. They're all variations on a theme: *Hers* rips people off and I'm a terrible person. It's not just the prizewinners writing; they've got dozens of supporters, too. The messages keep arriving, ping after ping of vitriol delivered directly to my in-box.

I start to sweat. I wonder if the angry e-mailers have dug up *Hers*' physical address, too; if they've organized a protest group; if any minute they'll burst through the elevator doors and charge at me with burning torches, or at least very sharp pencils. Will they find out where I live and come stalk me at my home?

My palms go clammy and I'm gasping for air. I feel desperate to scavenge. A hole punch would really do the trick. I race to the supply closet. I sneak through the door, and then—smack!—bump into a body. I scream.

"Hey, calm down," says a deep voice. "It's just me." The light flicks on.

"Oh, Ed. Jeez, you scared me."

"Sorry, honey. I was just grabbing an extra bin." The mail guy puts a hand on my shoulder, and I take a deep breath, finally able to take in oxygen. "Oh, hey, congratulations on the big news," he says. I notice his eyes are emerald.

"Oh, thanks." Apparently even the mail guy knows I'm knocked up. He reaches to place his palm on my stomach, and unlike with the rest of my coworkers, I find I don't mind the touch. His hand is warm, his fingers long and calloused. My breath slows, and I imagine even the creature inside me is soothed, pausing its persistent campaign to make me panic.

"Isn't that nice," Ed says, smiling down at me. I suddenly realize how small the supply closet is. Ed and I are inches apart. He smells like Old Spice.

"I'll be sure to save you some goodies from the mailroom," he says. "Someone's wife is always baking us something or other. I'm sure you're extra hungry, eating for two now."

"Thanks," I say, feeling utterly grateful. I don't think it's just because Ed is the only straight man in our office that I'm so attracted to him. Unlike most of the wispy, skinny jean–wearing men I encounter in New York (my ex included), Ed has the sexy brawn and ruggedness of someone who hauls things for a living. He could star in a commercial for Home Depot or Budweiser.

"You're glowing, you know." He's looking at me in a way that I remember Jacob used to. Maybe Ed is one of those mythical men you hear about who actually finds pregnant women sexy. A flood of desire surges up inside of me. I step over a pile of legal pads, lean in, and press my lips against Ed's.

He stumbles backward. "Whoa there, hang on a minute, Jane."

Oh, shit. The words from the e-mails start flooding my mind: *You should be ashamed of yourself. You're an awful person to screw over decent people. What is wrong with you? Evil* Hers *lady.* I will the supply shelf to come crashing down upon us, to shower us in envelopes and binder clips and red pens, to free us from this cramped nightmare.

"You're a very beautiful woman, of course, but I'm a married man." I nod stupidly, paralyzed in place, tears starting to stream down my face. The newsreel of the inevitable is unrolling in my head: Everyone finds out about this kiss, the rumors of my slutty stupidity spread like wildfire, I'm shamed in front of the entire staff, then fired, then sued a million dollars for sexual harassment and blackballed from the industry, so that I go broke and can't make rent and have to declare bankruptcy. Fast-forward eight months, and I'm all alone, raising a newborn on the streets.

It feels like minutes later when I manage to snap out of my stupor. I bolt from the closet.

The entire office is in a frenzy. I wonder if I'm imagining it. *Could they possibly already know? Is there a hidden camera in the supply closet?* I start hyperventilating. My hands are trembling like crazy.

Zoe rushes to my side. "Hey, it's OK. Really, it's not that bad." She swings an arm over my shoulder.

"It *is* that bad. It's humiliating."

"I know. Shhh, calm down."

"I mean, I'm pregnant, for God's sake."

"I know, I know. But I really don't think it will affect us."

Huh? I look up and see all the bigwigs huddled in Mimi's office: Victoria, Abby, Johanna, and Lynn. The door is closed, and all four look as if they're in the principal's office, awaiting suspension. Mimi's shouts carry through the glass, and though it's difficult to make out the words, the sentiment is clear. I hear, "Who the hell—" and "Major scandal . . ." and "Totally fucking screwed!" I'm not positive, but it doesn't seem like they're talking about me sexually harassing the mail guy.

"What's going on?" I whisper to Zoe. Laura shoots me a look of disgust.

"Seriously, where have you been for the last fifteen minutes?" asks Zoe. "Come here." She pulls me over to her desk, and types "MAGnifier.net" into her Web browser. A photo of Helena Hope loads up on the screen, the image that's planned for our November cover.

"What is this? How did they get that picture?"

"Watch," says Zoe. Just then the screen flashes and another image appears: It's nearly the same photo, but in this one, Helena looks different—puffier and older, her eyes rimmed with crow's feet and bags. The coloring is off, too, and her dress is mussed in an unflattering way. Another flash and the screen reverts to the prettier photo, the November cover.

"Seriously, what is this?!"

"OMG Jane, really? Just read." I scan the post:

We Have a Winner: *Hers* Destroys Our "Hope" with Major Hackup of Singer Helena Hope

Women's magazines have a habit of making us feel terrible about our weight, our hair, our skin, our clothes, our relationship, our social life, our career, our finances, the conflicts in the Middle East, etc., etc., etc. Then they make us feel bad about feeling bad about those things, y'know? You may remember we put a call-out for submissions of pre-Photoshopped covers of lady mags (with a not-too-shabby reward of $10K), so we could *uncover* yet another reason these mags give us to feel bad about ourselves. Nearly a dozen photo assistants, production interns, and whoever the hell else lurks around at photo shoots and digital alteration caves heeded our siren call, and the day has come for the big reveal. Drum roll please! And the winner, the worst offender in women's magazine land, the parent production of the photo most heinously airbrushed is (OK, we know the header was a spoiler) . . . *Hers* magazine!

Granted, *Hers* faced quite the conundrum with its November cover girl, popular crooner Helena Hope: On the one hand, at age 39, the country-western star is squarely within *Hers*' demo, plus a hugely successful singer whose last two albums went platinum and who therefore has the potential to sell millions of magazines (yeah, we know you've only ever heard of that one earworm of a song, but you're not exactly the coupon-clipping midwestern soccer mom *Hers* is targeting, are you?). Helena's kinda hot, too. But on the other hand, Helena is only *kinda* hot, she's pushing 40, and we're guessing she's ingested her fair share of chicken-fried steaks on her recent tour across Dixieland. In other words, she's probably not gonna squeeze into those size-2 stonewashed jeans that stars like her seem to favor. And really, who would buy a magazine with an über-successful but only average pretty, slightly pudgy, slightly aged singer on its cover?

Hers' apparent conclusion: NO ONE! So let the airbrushing begin! For those who don't know, the November issue marks the grand reboot from newly minted editor in chief Mimi Walsh—her big, splashy, highly anticipated redesign! This Helena Hope hack-up sends a strong message about the new direction of the magazine, don't cha think? The revamped team at *Hers* is upping the airbrush ante, ladies. Find the fakey-fake issue on newsstands in six short weeks.

After the jump, check out our airbrush-by-number look at just how far the *Hers* miracle workers went in transforming heinously fat, ugly, old (read: not supermodel-anorexic-20-something) Helena Hope into standard cover girl fembait.

"Wow," I say. I can't bring myself to click through past the jump.

"Uh, you think?" says Zoe. "There are already parodies up all over the Web, too. Someone posted a YouTube video pretending to be our photo editors in the digital studio. They have a pic of Kate Moss up on screen and they keep moving around her body parts until she looks like a Picasso. They claim she'll sell more issues that way."

"That's actually kind of funny." I start giggling and find I can't stop. The monster performs somersaults in my stomach, as if in relief. Here is a scandal that no one can blame on me. I am not responsible. I am not involved. The truth is, I pretty much agree with the Web site's post, and I feel a small thrill that someone within our ranks took a risk to expose the kind of unrealistic standards of beauty we promote. Still, I could not be happier that that person is not me.

The taste of Ed—cigarettes and Swiss cheese—is still faint in my mouth, but no one saw, no one knows. The whole office is flipping out, phones ringing like crazy and at least one person crying in a cubicle. *Stay sane, Jane,* I say to myself, relishing the opportunity to seem like one of the calmer ones. And I actually feel sane. I rub my belly and whisper, "Hey, little guy, my secret scandal's safe with us." What I'm going to do about this other scandal, the one currently growing in my stomach, is not at all certain, but for the moment I don't feel panicked about figuring it out. Whatever I end up deciding will be all right—I'll make sure of it. I return to my desk and, amidst the mayhem surrounding me, I set to work with laser focus. For the first time in weeks I feel confident I will survive the storm and still have a job come tomorrow.

19

Drew Hardaway, Photo Editor

I never call in sick. As a policy, I don't get sick. I believe that once you've made a commitment to show up, you show up, no questions asked. I once photographed a Bar Mitzvah cruise ship party in December while running a 103-degree fever and delirious with the flu. The pictures turned out gorgeous.

Today, for the first time in my career, I'm copping out. No, I didn't spend the night upchucking into the toilet bowl, and I don't have some hacking bronchial cough. And it isn't because of the very real fact that I was awake all night waiting for Mark to come home or at least call (I've pulled plenty of all-nighters), or that I'll likely be out both a boyfriend and a home in the very near future (I've always been fast to adapt to new circumstances).

Rather, I'm lying in bed consumed with fear, actually sick with it. The various accusations Mark hurled at me last night—that I'm not a real artist, that I've sold out to corporate America—keep resounding in my head. But although it's troubling that my boyfriend would put me down with such disdain, I'm not actually scared that what he said is true. I *know* it's true, and what terrifies me is that this knowledge doesn't bother me. If I'm brutally honest with myself, I'll admit I feel more passionate about what Mark calls my "bullshit corporate job" than I ever did about my personal photo projects or gallery shows.

Working at *Hers* was originally supposed to subsidize my real work, but as it turns out, the former may just be my real work. Never mind that I kind of love going to a chic office every day where I get praised for my talents and hard work. Is it such a crime to enjoy all the trappings of a glamorous job with a fairly prestigious title and to aspire to climb the ladder of corporate career success? Is it really so bad to turn my back on the struggles of the true, starving artist? And so what if I have to put up with a few meetings now and then?

Despite, or maybe because of, these discoveries, I am freaking out—hide-under-the-covers-and-avoid-the-chic-office-at-all-costs kind of freaking out. I'd like to indulge myself with the belief that this spontaneous sick day is the result of a full-on Identity Crisis, though a part of me knows it also has something to do with the fight with my boyfriend and his subsequent disappearing act. I sigh and reach for my laptop.

I e-mail Lynn a lie about a stomach bug, and then pull myself out of bed. I avoid glancing back at the twisted, abandoned sheets for fear they'll make my heart ache. Mark split hours ago—who knows to where?—and the apartment feels dark and echoey all by myself. I pull on clothes and wander outside to Riverside Park. It's prime commuting time, and the promenade is packed with people. I pass hordes of smartly dressed workers rushing to their respective places of employment (I will not find Mark, still unemployed, in this crowd). The air feels fizzed with anticipation of the long weekend ahead.

Mark and I were supposed to go away for Labor Day, our first real trip together. It was his idea to surprise me with the destination. I tried to get him to leak some intel: I shared news of coworkers heading to the shore and friends' camping plans in the Adirondacks, hoping Mark would spill something of our plans. But he would only respond elusively, saying, "Isn't that classic for Labor Day?" or "Fun, fun, fun!" Then he'd put on a wry little smile, as if to imply that whatever plans he had up his sleeve were far more interesting, far more whimsical and exotic. The secret made me crazy with anticipation.

Last night marked the big reveal. I uncorked a bottle of sauvignon blanc, and Mark ceremoniously handed me an envelope. I felt like a presenter at the Oscars, holding in my hand the answer we'd all been waiting for. The envelope clearly contained tickets, and I imagined Venice or Madrid. I dreamed of rich culture, richer food, and roll-off-the-tongue romance languages. Of course I knew my fantasies were just that; Mark hadn't earned a cent since he got pink-slipped from *Hers,* so Europe was not exactly a realistic guess for our getaway. More likely my boyfriend had booked us a cozy weekend at a bed-and-breakfast upstate. "Go on, open it already," Mark pleaded.

So I did. What I found were two New Jersey Transit tickets to Trenton. At first I assumed it was a joke, which is why I smirked at Mark. I thought, he couldn't possibly have psyched me up for days and days in order to swoop me away—surprise!—to a city known best for its boarded-up storefronts, its rampant blight, its poverty and crime.

Mark grinned back at me, and his words—"So cool, right?"— made me understand this was not some hilarious antic. Poof went my fantasy Academy Awards gown, my glamorous updo, my neck and wrists glittering with jewels; I pictured myself falling from the prestigious podium right back down to Earth, here in the cramped apartment I shared with my boyfriend, a guy who was ecstatic about a romantic getaway to Trenton, New Jersey.

"You would not believe the deal I found at this motel, for a holiday weekend no less," he said. I could in fact believe that he'd gotten a deal at a motel in Trenton. "I can start working on my project at the train station."

Ah yes, Mark's project. Whenever I'd asked him about his work prospects—whether he was scanning the job boards or leaning on his network or doing anything at all to reenter the community of paycheck-earning adults—he'd start up about the project he was planning: to photograph all the major train stations in the tristate area, to capture on film these sites of decadence decayed, of glory rusted, of commerce and prosperity collapsed. *That's a great, if not particularly original, idea,* I'd think, *but what about a* job? Yet if ever I expressed an ounce of this skepticism, Mark would flare up and accuse me of not caring about art or about him, of abandoning my own artistic sensibilities, of ignorantly succumbing to capitalism and corporate greed and the status quo.

At first I took these accusations to heart. I'd feel guilty about how well I was thriving at *Hers* and start to wonder if I was doing myself a disservice by neglecting my own photography. Worse, I was ashamed that I didn't feel the kind of void real artists are supposed to experience when they neglect their art. Producing photo shoots for articles about cheating spouses and Halloween costumes felt strangely fulfilling, or at least quite fun, and I internalized Mark's disappointment in me. And so, ironically, at the same time that I felt happiest and most competent in my professional life, I'd never felt so lacking and miserable about myself.

I realized Mark was still talking: "And I'm certain you'll find inspiration on the gritty streets of Trenton, too. How could you not? It's a mecca of stories, with so many people struggling to just get by, to do all they can to keep their homes and their jobs."

"Their jobs, huh?" I blurted it out before I could stop myself. "You find it inspiring that they're making an effort to hang on to their livelihoods? That's quite interesting." I examined the train tickets, innocently stamped with information. Who knew a couple of city abbreviations on a slip of paper could cause such consternation?

"Oh, come on, Drew. This is our kind of adventure! Don't tell me you're not happy for me to pursue my passion. Don't tell me you're not excited to venture out and explore this pocket of our country together."

Mark's soulful, pleading eyes were so full of hope and maybe even love that it was almost enough for me to cave. But I took a deep inhale and said it: "That is exactly what I'm telling you, Mark. I'm not happy, and I'm not excited, and I'm not going with you."

I exhaled the rest of my breath, feeling like I'd shrugged off a backpack full of boulders, one I hadn't even known I'd been lugging around. Somewhere along the way I'd stopped feeling guilty for not being the artist—or the person—Mark wanted me to be. Even more, I'd started letting myself be pissed off that my boyfriend was not living in the real world that requires income, and that in a few short, severance-dwindling weeks he'd have zero means to earn his keep.

Then Mark turned mean: "Oh, so you're going to stay in town and work all weekend like the good little Me-me-me ass-kisser you've become? Or will you go to the beach with your pack of silly friends, all of you in your skimpy bikinis to fry in the sun and eat ice cream?" He pronounced "ice cream" like it was the most detestable thing he could imagine.

"Yes," I said sadly, only then understanding that the conversation was marking an ending. "I will probably eat some ice cream this weekend."

With that, Mark jumped up, tore the tickets from my hand, and fled from the apartment—off to who knows where, to Trenton, or to wander the streets of New York, or to somewhere, anywhere far from me.

Meandering over to Riverside Drive, I detect the faint jingle of a Mister Softee ice-cream truck. It reminds me of a photo show I put on back in college: I took shots of the meatiest kinds of meat— big, bloody steaks; pork chops glistening with fat; lamb shanks the size of my head—and at the gallery opening, I cued up the Mister Softee jingle to play on loop. The idea was, how would the pairing of those photos of so-called pleasurable foods and the melody that we all associate with the simple pleasure of ice cream change people's perceptions of what they were seeing? I was a vegan at the time, of course, and had a very specific idea of how viewers should interpret the work. The whole thing feels so silly and naïve to me now that I shudder at my former self.

The catchy tune draws me to its source. I spot the iconic cartoon of the smiling ice-cream cone, and I order myself a chocolate shake. The sweet, cool liquid slides down my throat smooth as butter, and my mind starts motoring about all the novel ways we could shoot a *Hers* story about milk shakes. We could treat the ice-cream flavors like paint colors, and show them pouring out of paint cans and swirled with brushes onto bright white surfaces. Or we could meld a food and beauty story, and shoot fingers clutching at tall glasses, the nails polished to match the flavors of the shakes that the hands hold: "Match your dessert to your manicure."

I'm now sucking at the dregs of my milk shake, having devoured the whole thing in about four minutes. The sound snaps me out of my brainstorms. I can hear Mark's voice in my head: "This is what you're wasting your thoughts on, coordinating your nails with your ice cream?" He wouldn't be wrong—I admit it's silly—but it also makes me laugh. I'm sitting on a park bench guffawing like an idiot, so much so that the woman next to me gets up and rolls her stroller to the next bench. But I don't care. I realize that Mark may come off as belittling and judgmental, but he really just wants the best for me, even if he doesn't understand that his idea of the best doesn't necessarily match my own. The thought spreads over me like a soothing balm. My boyfriend has been trying to take care of me, just as I've been trying to take care of him. The truth is, neither of us can give the other the right kind of care. It makes me a little sad, but mostly I feel all right.

And then I'm dialing Lynn's number. "Drew, is that you?" my boss answers, her voice more frantic than usual.

"Yeah, I wanted to tell you I'm feeling a lot better, so I'll come in this afternoon."

"Oh, thank you, sweet Jesus. Shit is hitting the fan up in here, and Mimi is demanding to see you on the double. I was about to beeline it to your apartment and ply you with ginger ale and Saltines until you felt well enough to haul ass out of bed and make an appearance in the office. I'll see you soon—*run* if you can." She hangs up before I can ask her exactly what kind of shit is hitting the fan.

Still clueless, I enter the Schmidt & Delancey building, ascend the elevator, and cautiously make my way toward my desk. Laura blocks my path and redirects me to Mimi's office. "You are wanted immediately," she says, the glint in her eye suggesting I should be worried. I can't possibly imagine what I've done wrong.

Stepping over the threshold to Mimi's office, I discover a group gathering. All eyes land on me, each pair projecting a different attitude: those of Mimi, Victoria, and Johanna are different shades of predatory; those of Lynn look apologetic; and those of Abby appear both agitated and sympathetic.

"Well, what do you have to say for yourself?" barks Mimi.

"Let's all remember that Drew was home sick this morning," says Abby, "so she probably doesn't know what's going on."

"Oh, rubbish. As if!" It's Johanna, fixing me with a glare. "Here, eat it up." She plants a laptop in front of me, and the screen flashes up two images of Helena Hope: the first is the original from the photo shoot, and the second is the one I massaged and tweaked and practically alchemized into what will be our November cover. I think I'm looking at *Hers'* internal server until Johanna scrolls down to what is clearly a blog, meaning it's published on the Internet, available for anyone and everyone to see. I quickly scan the post. *Oh no.*

"Who did this?" I plead, searching the faces around me for an answer. But I read the looks in their eyes. Oh.

"See, I told you Drew had nothing to do with it," Lynn says. "She didn't even know about the blog post."

Johanna rolls her eyes. "What, you fancy she'll up and admit she's responsible, like it's no big deal? Bollocks!"

My mind starts racing. Who could have leaked the images? The way Johanna's attacking me, I wonder if it was actually her—a backhanded publicity stunt to drum up more press for the big relaunch, kind of like what we all know Zoe did back with her Randiest Rachel Twitter account. On the other hand, Lynn is acting awfully sympathetic; maybe she feels bad that the blame for something she did is falling on me. Lynn came to *Hers* out of nowhere, and it wouldn't totally surprise me if she took on a job in women's magazine with the express purpose of exposing our not-so-noble inner workings; this kind of subversive act would definitely do the trick. Then again, there were a dozen people on that photo shoot, and Helena Hope was categorically awful to each one of them. Every single person involved would have a motive to swipe the film and expose the singer for her true, ugly self.

"I'll ask it again," says Mimi. "Do you have anything to say?"

"I suppose I'm meant to defend myself," I say, with a strange measure of calm. Part of me feels like this is all a charade, like even Mimi knows I would never commit this kind of betrayal and that they just need a scapegoat. "I'm not sure what I can say except that I'm sorry this happened. It's true I was in charge of that photo shoot, and in that sense I bear some responsibility for the fact that the film was clearly not as guarded as it should have been. I would be happy to draw up some ideas for how we can run a tighter ship in the future, and I am more than willing to participate in any investigation you wish to conduct. Beyond that, I can assure you I played no part in the leaking of these photos. I love my role here at *Hers*, and I would never intentionally do anything to jeopardize it." Voicing these sentiments aloud makes me realize how genuinely I feel them. I find myself sitting taller in my seat. "I hope my word is strong enough to convince you."

Johanna again rolls her eyes. "Look, it doesn't take a genius to figure out you're ticked off that your bloody boyfriend got fired. He's out of a job, with bugger all cash flow, and you could use the easy money. Just confess already!"

At the mention of Mark, a lump forms in my throat. "I don't have anything more to say."

Abby turns to Mimi. "You sure you want me to do this?" she whispers. Mimi nods resolutely. "OK, well, here goes. Drew, thank you for your statement. As you said yourself, you were in charge of the shoot where the photos were leaked. We are asking that you voluntarily resign, and in appreciation we would like to offer you what we consider to be a generous severance package: three months' paid salary."

I look from face to face. It takes me a moment to realize this is a serious proposal. "Wait a second," I say. "You want me to fall on my sword and effectively admit I was the one who did this, to give in to your nonsense accusation?"

"If you care so much about *Hers* like you say, you'll understand that this would be a significant help to the brand," Victoria says. "We will do everything we can to help you find a new position. It might be difficult in magazines for a while, but we all have many connections in other industries." I guess she's attempting to play good cop to Johanna's bad cop; it makes me feel sick.

"If you're so sure I did it," I say, "then why don't you fire me?" I see Victoria glance nervously at Mimi. "Aha, I get it. You don't have a real case against me, do you? Where's your evidence, huh? If you fire me, you're worried I'll lawyer up and sue. Well, you're right."

"Four months' severance," says Mimi. "How about that?" I gape at her incredulously. "Five," she says.

"Mimi," Abby says, placing a hand on her arm.

"Screw your severance," I say. Abby's lips curl up into the smallest smile. "I didn't leak any photo. I am good at my job, and all of you know it. Kindly direct your witch hunt elsewhere." I storm out of Mimi's office, totally shocked by my own gumption.

My heart is still pounding when I return to my desk. I pick up the phone to dial Mark, but then stop myself. Even if he did answer, he wouldn't tell me how proud he is that I stood up for myself; he'd say I was an idiot to not take the money and run. I can hear his words exactly: "You had the opportunity to hurl a big 'F you' to the world of commercial quote-unquote art, and better yet, to take responsibility for an incredible act of corporate treason, and you totally blew it!" I replace the phone in its receiver, and for a moment wonder if Mark would be right. I glance at my to-do list, which includes color-correcting the images for the "Dress Like Your Fave Celeb" spread and sorting through the shots for the "5 Minutes to Hotter Sex" story. I feel a swirl of confusion in my gut.

"Yoo-hoo." I jump. Lynn is crouching next to my chair, her face inches from my knees. "I sneaked down here. I didn't want anyone to see me chatting to the office's Public Enemy Number One."

"Gee, thanks."

She waves me away. "Don't worry, in no time this will all pass and then we'll be on to the next scandal. Mimi knows you didn't do it, anyway. I just wanted to let you know, I'm superproud of all you said back there. You've got real guts, girlfriend!"

Despite the fact that my boss looks ridiculous squatting next to my chair, I'm truly touched by her words. "Thank you," I say.

"And as I've told you before, I think you're doing a fantastic job here. Once we all move on from this hiccup, I'm going to see about getting you the raise and promotion you deserve." Lynn pats me on the knee, then skulks away in a crabwalk, which makes me giggle.

I shake out my shoulders and feel the day's pressures peel away. I lean back in my seat, close my eyes, and imagine the perfect photograph, that elusive one that's nearly impossible to get: the composition crisp, the lighting honeyed, the image magically capturing so much more than appears before the lens. The picture in my mind's eye is not yet in clear focus, or even developed, but I believe it's getting there. It feels like maybe I'm picturing my future.

I cue up Craigslist apartment listings and Google "Upper West Side moving companies," and then get to work.

20

Laura Maxwell,
Assistant to the Editor in Chief

I'm on autopilot, repeating "No comment," "No comment," "No comment" into the receiver before the callers even identify themselves. I haven't visited the ladies' room in hours, terrified that a call will make it through to Mimi unimpeded. I prepared her favorite chai tea with two shakes of cinnamon just like she likes it, but she hasn't touched the mug; this is unprecedented.

The maintenance office called about a spill in the kitchen and said they were sending up a couple of janitors, but only once the so-called janitors burst through Mimi's office and revealed themselves to be undercover reporters from the *New York Post* did I realize the incoming call hadn't contained Schmidt & Delancey's signature three-digit code. The weasels have parked themselves beside Mimi's desk, unbudgeable. I've asked Mimi several times if she wants me to call security, but she keeps saying no. Apparently kicking them out will only make for a more disastrous story in tomorrow's paper. Mimi has even stooped to answering their questions.

"Look, a magazine cover is an art object that plays into women's fantasies of the celebrity lifestyle," I hear her say, her voice tinged with anxiety. "It's an invented image, not a photograph. Everyone understands that when they're at the newsstand." One of the reporters emits a guffaw that pierces through the office's white noise and carries down the hall. I would like to chuck my computer in his direction.

All the interoffice calls route through my phone, so I see it when Lynn dials Drew. The photo editor doesn't betray anything as she walks into the creative director's office and closes the door behind her. If I had any friends around here (I gave Mimi my college roommate's résumé last week, a not-so-subtle hint that she would be an excellent replacement for Jane), I'd share my conviction that Drew is definitely the leaker. It's obvious. And even though she's one of the few holdovers who doesn't seem to harbor a massive grudge toward me, I'm still in favor of letting her go. I know Mimi is obligated to conduct a full investigation, but if it were up to me, she would've canned Drew on the spot this afternoon. If Mimi can convince those smarmy reporters that one rogue staffer was responsible for all the Photoshopping, then hopefully everyone will shut up about the whole thing and just get back to enjoying the amazing new version of the magazine.

I tilt my computer monitor away from Mimi's office and clandestinely click through the comments on MAGnifier.net. Women are blathering on about antifeminist depictions of models in magazines, the fact that the average American woman is a size 14, and how the media is responsible for the epidemic of eating disorders in this country. *Oh, cry me a river.* The truth is, no one would buy a magazine that had a big fatso on its cover with acne scars and an ill-fitting dress, or even if the cover model were a normal-looking person. When I was at *Starstruck*, the best-selling issues featured celebrities' new diets and how they dropped the baby weight and got back to looking amazing. That's what readers want, even if they claim otherwise. Everyone loves hearing about how celebs are prettier, thinner, and richer than the rest of us—it's what makes reading magazines so fun. Working in publishing, it's our job to play into those fantasies, simple as that. The fact that Mimi is savvy enough to understand this, and therefore to produce and sell a buttload of magazines, apparently makes her a target. The mediocre are always trying to bring down the superstars, which is something I remind myself on a near-daily basis in this office.

The phone rings, and I'm about to spout another "No comment" before I realize it's the mail center on the line. "Ms. Maxwell, your food is here."

Darn. I forgot about the party; we're supposed to be celebrating our intern, Erin's, last day. "I'll send someone down." I call Jane over; Mimi needs me to stay put at my post.

"Can you please grab the champagne and cupcakes from the loading dock for the party?" I ask. Jane sighs loudly. Ever since that girl announced her pregnancy, she thinks she's at the top of the masthead.

I Google "*Hers* magazine." The latest hit is an editorial decrying our tactics and urging readers to cancel their subscriptions stat. I think maybe it's a joke, or merely the ravings of some two-bit blogger typing at home in his underwear, but when I scroll to the bottom I see it's jointly signed by the heads of the National Organization for Women, the Feminist Majority, and the Girl Scouts of America, syndicated for dozens of newspapers nationwide. Rage bubbles up in my throat, and I'm tempted to comment: Don't these groups realize this kind of digital alteration goes on behind the scenes of every single magazine on the newsstand, that *Hers* is no worse than the rest? But I resist, knowing that engaging in the conversation will only stoke the flames of their outrage.

I will come up with a solution for this, I know I will. I dig through Jenny's old files to find the phone number for Subscriber Services. My predecessor's system confounds me—every folder the same manila, every label written out in boring ballpoint blue. I wonder how she ever found anything, and why she never took advantage of the top-of-the-line label maker I gleefully discovered in the back of a desk drawer on my first day. I would honestly label my cat if I knew she wouldn't bite.

I come across the phone number after ten minutes of searching (which is nine minutes longer than it would've taken if I'd been the one to file it), and dial.

"Jenny, long time!" trills a woman with a thick midwestern accent. Subscriber Services is based in Ohio. "Got any big Labor Day plans? How are you?"

"Oh, no, Jenny doesn't work here anymore. This is Laura, the new assistant to the editor in chief."

"Oh, hello, Laura. I'm Margene in Subscriber Services." That accent is an assault on my eardrums. I'm thankful I managed to lose my West Virginia drawl during my freshman year at Wellesley.

"Can you give me the latest subscriber numbers, and any recent activity?" My heart is hammering away at my chest.

"You know, there actually has been some funny business today. We've gotten a 3,000 percent jump in cancellations, nearly 24,000 just since this morning. It keeps picking up, too. Strange, huh? Usually this is the time of year folks really want to just sit back, relax, and hunker down with a magazine, on the beach or in the tub or—"

"Thanks." I cut off Margene's rambling, unable to stifle the tremble in my voice. "Would you be so kind as to send me hourly updates for the remainder of the day?" I'll hide them from Mimi until I can come up with an idea for how to reverse this catastrophe. Maybe some sort of two-for-one promotion for former subscribers, with exclusive access to a *Hers* weight-loss program. Or something like that.

Meanwhile, we have a party to throw. I pen an e-mail to the staff: "Please gather in the conference room to toast a job well done by our summer intern, Erin, and to celebrate her send-off!" I attach the animated balloon banner I picked out for the e-invite, but then I second-guess the degree of cheer and remove it just before hitting Send.

I overhear Jane telling Zoe how tone-deaf my e-mail is. As if I could have anticipated that such an unfortunate turn of events would coincide with the intern's scheduled good-bye party, as if I can just send back all of the food and drinks we've ordered. Scandal or not, Erin deserves recognition for all her hard work. I'm sure Mimi would agree.

The party's turnout is paltry, the conference room sparse with staffers. I pour twenty glasses of champagne, but half remain untouched, the bubbles left to deflate in the plastic flutes. Mimi doesn't even bother to make an appearance. Zoe is causing a scene, as usual: She downs her drink like a shot, then reaches for another. "Who wants to go halfsies on a s'mores cupcake?" she announces to the room. All afternoon she's been her usual flippant self, as if we're not in the middle of a crisis. I want to stick her face in a s'mores cupcake.

I escape to the kitchen to gather a gallon of milk and a stack of cups, and when I return Zoe is nestled in the corner with one of the *Post* reporters, piercing his cupcake with a fork and laughing idiotically. I march over. "Excuse me," I say. "This gathering is for *Hers* staff members only."

"What, am I too fat and imperfect to grace the *Hers* staff with my presence?" says the man, who actually does have quite a substantial gut. "I guess I better lay off the cupcakes, or you can just airbrush away my flab." Zoe beams up at him.

"Please leave before I call security."

"OK, OK." On his way out, the reporter grabs another cupcake from the platter and scarfs it down. Repulsive. I dread the story that will appear in tomorrow's paper: "*Hers* editors celebrate amidst the scandal, fancying themselves above the nation's harsh judgment," or worse, "*Hers* editors react to media brouhaha by feasting on cupcakes to demonstrate that they're not the wicked anorexic freaks everyone suspects them to be," then some silly reference to Marie Antoinette.

Drew slips in to the party. She takes a flute of champagne and clinks a plastic fork against its side. "Attention, everyone," she announces to the room. "Look, I know it's been a rough afternoon for all of us, but I'm glad we can take the time to acknowledge that today is Erin's last day here at *Hers*. Please bear with me while I make a little speech." She casts an arm around the intern's shoulder. "Thanks to Erin's talent and hard work these past three months, snafus like this one have been a bit easier to handle. She's had a lot on her plate this summer, but throughout it all she's maintained her cool and stayed poised and professional. Cheers, and good luck for your final year of college!"

We all raise our glasses. I wonder if Erin is aware of what's going on in the office, although she has Internet access like the rest of us, so how could she not?

"It's been a great summer, and such a privilege to work with all of you," Erin says in a trembling voice, contorting her face into a queasy smile. Her complexion is ashen. *Oh no, is the intern drunk?* I realize I don't even know if she's of age, and I reprimand myself for not being a better monitor, for not living up to the level of professionalism I expect of myself. As I leave to fetch her a glass of water, I see Abby, flanked by our company lawyer, pull Drew out of the conference room.

An hour later, the managing editor's office is still sealed shut, and no one has emerged. I wonder how long this silly investigation will be drawn out for before they cut loose the obvious culprit.

I do respect how carefully Mimi has proceeded with staff changes throughout the summer—she's given everyone a real chance before making decisions—but I think it might've been better if she'd ripped off all the Band-Aids at once, right at the start. On one of my first days at *Hers*, I happened to glance at an e-mail up on Mimi's screen, addressed to someone in Corporate; she planned to keep Leah on staff through the summer, it said, because the old staffers liked and respected her and because it would have looked bad to immediately fire a mom of three little kids. But by now surely more than enough time has passed, and I think it's weird that she and Victoria share the same title. Plus, Leah is the biggest slacker; she hardly does anything anymore. And, though I know it's selfish, I can't help thinking that the more the old staffers get the boot, the less the remaining people will view me as some kind of Grim Reaper.

Margene from Subscriber Services e-mails me the latest update: 13,000 more subscriptions canceled. I re-Google *Hers*, and it turns out the *Post* isn't waiting until tomorrow's paper to tear us apart: There's already a 1,500-word story up on their Web site, including detailed descriptions of staff members in the write-up. I suppose I'm "the huffy assistant-slash-hall-monitor who worked her damnedest to protect her turf but still took twenty-five minutes to get us ousted from the building."

"Laura!" Mimi calls me into her office, and I worry I'm in trouble. "Hi, Mimi."

"Jesus, are you OK?" she asks. "You look like you just ate a pound of jalapeños."

"I'm fine. How are you?" I ask idiotically.

"Listen, I need you to be my eyes and ears this afternoon, to really try to figure out who let this photo leak, OK? Corporate is on my ass and wants information by the end of the day."

"As in, *an hour* from now?!"

"I know, it's completely impossible. But anything you can do would be an enormous help. I'm desperate. We've interviewed Drew, and I think she's being honest when she says she has no idea who's responsible." *Yeah, right.*

Abby, Victoria, and Johanna scurry into the office. Abby smiles at me uneasily, but the others seem oblivious to my presence. Sometimes I wonder if they consider me just a piece of furniture.

"So I'll come right out with it," says Johanna. "I've talked to Helena's publicist, and she wants to pull out of the issue."

"*What?!*" Mimi opens her drawer and extracts a package of Oreos. Uh-oh, Code Oreo, as we used to say at *Starstruck*. At the old office, Mimi would bust out the snack food every time a celeb threatened to sue. One by one she pops the cookies into her mouth, then appears to swallow them whole. "But Helena can't do that, can she? We have a contract."

"Well," says Abby, "Sylvia always used to handle our contracts. Since we haven't hired a full-time researcher to replace her, the final version of the contract with the lawyer's notes has just been sitting around collecting dust, unsigned by either party."

"No way. Get Helena on the phone right this minute."

"It's no use," says Johanna. "She's bloody furious and totally humiliated. Her publicist says she's taken to bed with a family-sized bag of barbecue crisps. As if that's the solution to her big, fat arse." Johanna laughs. No one else joins in.

"It's hilarious to you, is it?" says Mimi. "All of this is some big joke?"

"Lord, calm down," says Johanna. "I'm going to try to talk some reason into her tonight. We're meeting for drinks at her flat."

"Her *apartment!*" yells Mimi, cookie bits flying from the corners of her mouth. "In the United States of goddamn America it's called an *apartment,* not a fucking *bloody flat!*"

"Mimi," says Abby, steadying our boss with a hand on the shoulder. "Johanna is doing all she can."

"She better be. Her job is on the line. Now everyone scram this instant. I can't take any more bad news for the day."

I skulk back to my desk and survey the rows of cubicles. How can I get some relevant information, and from whom? I wander over to Zoe's desk. "Hey," I say.

"That was not cool earlier when you kicked out that reporter from the party," she says. "I was working on swaying his opinion in our favor."

"Oh yeah, by performing some kind of kinky sexual rite with a cupcake? Clearly very effective."

Zoe rolls her eyes. "If nothing else I was delaying the inevitable fact of him getting back to his desk and writing up that total skewering of us."

"Zoe, we can't have *Post* reporters fraternizing with the staff during this kind of crisis."

"Did you just say 'fraternizing'?"

"Also, did you see he ate three whole cupcakes? He was disgusting."

"Whatevs. TTYL." Zoe turns away from me and begins filing her nails.

Well, that was a total failure. I decide to try Jane, and sidle up to her cube.

"Hey, Laura, what's the scoop?" Jane asks, not looking up from her screen. "You were just inside Mimi's office, right?"

"Nothing much, they were, um, discussing final tweaks to November pages. So what's new with you? What kind of gossip do you have for me?" I'm trying to sound casual, but it comes out wrong, like I'm both interrogating and chastising her.

"Uh, nothing," she answers, sounding defensive. "I'm just sitting here, getting my work done." Ugh, I'm hopeless.

I meander over to Jonathan, who's buried in the beauty closet trying on lipsticks. "Hey, how's it going?"

"Listen, I feel as morose as Little Miss Muffet," he says. "Why hasn't anyone written anything yet about Helena's makeup?"

Seriously? "I guess because it's not really relevant, right?"

"In the before *and* after shots, that coral lipstick is beyond hot—and it was my pick! It's going to be the next big color, thanks to *moi*, and no one has even deigned to mention it. I've been trolling the blogs all day."

"Wow, I'm sorry," I say, completely confused.

"Yeah, well, I'm cheering myself up with a makeover." Useless. I return to my desk, defeated, and dip into my own Oreos supply.

Mimi is still at her desk at seven p.m., when I see a call come in from the thirtieth floor. I let her pick it up. Her voice is as singsongy as ever, punctuated by her signature laugh, but through the glass of her office I see her larger-than-life features straining to stay sunny. She looks tired. Old. I find I can't bear to keep watching the conversation, and for the first time since I began working for Mimi two years earlier at *Starstruck*, and nearly four months ago at *Hers*, I shut down my computer and leave the office before she does.

Back home, even though it's the Friday of a holiday weekend, I decide to stay in. I partake of my usual evening-in diet of E!, TMZ, and celebrity blogs, but after a couple of hours my stomach begins aching from overindulgence. I click off the TV, set aside my laptop, and grab my purse. From its special safekeeping pouch, a side zippered pocket, I remove and unfold the printout of Mimi's November editor letter. It's just an old draft, one she crumpled up and tossed out last week when she decided it was too earnest, but

I adore it. I smooth out the paper and read it over for the tenth time:

> Dear *Hers* readers,
>   During this time of year when we mull over all the things we have to be thankful for, I feel most grateful (and honored! and humbled!) to have taken the helm at this incredible brand so steeped in history and tradition. I've been told you readers are a superpassionate and superbusy bunch, and that you wear many hats: mother, wife, professional, friend, sister, daughter, and (here's my favorite!) magazine lover. I can't wait to get to know you and to hear all about what you want from your favorite magazine—so please do let me know! I'm here to serve you, of course, and I plan on giving it my all. Happy late autumn, and here's to turning over a new leaf!
> XO, Mimi

When I overheard Mimi read this draft to Victoria and ask for feedback, Victoria said she thought it would open a big can of worms, encouraging readers to write in with all their silly opinions; they'd insist we run stories about their kittens and their favorite brands of laundry detergent. The current version of Mimi's editor letter announces the redesign and promises readers flashier, more forward-thinking content. I prefer the original.

My clock flashes 10:00. I wonder if Mimi is still at her desk, working furiously or passed out across an empty package of Oreos. Perhaps she's out at a bar surrounded by friends and throwing back round after round of shots. Or maybe she's made it home and is sitting on the couch with her beloved dog, zoning out to the Home Shopping Network. Or she could be tucked into bed in a deep, restful sleep. I resist the urge to pick up the phone, and I will my boss to call me instead. It's like we went out on a first date and now I'm trying to appear aloof. My phone doesn't ring all weekend.

*   *   *

On the Monday that honors laborers nationwide, on the day when everyone who has toiled so hard all year pauses for a collective, well-deserved rest, I do not partake in the celebration. I do not hit the beach or attend a barbecue. Instead, I mark the occasion by staying holed up in my bed and paging through back issues of *Starstruck* and *Hers*. I admire the photos of the stars who have inspired me to eat more veggies and to get my butt to the gym several days a week. I examine their perfectly sculpted jaws and cheekbones, their shiny hair and eyes, and the expensive dresses that hang just so on their trim hourglass figures. I don't care how much the photos have been altered; they're beautiful, and I am in awe.

Tuesday morning I'm the first one to the office, as usual. I love the quiet buzz of white noise, all the sleek surfaces, and the decades of big, glamorous *Hers* covers lining the walls. I admire the breathtaking view of early day lighting up the trees in Central Park and the office pristine and pretty before the inevitable bustle and complications of the coming workday. I pour my first cup of coffee and plop myself down in Mimi's chair, spinning around my ritual three times, briefly masquerading as editor in chief.

When Mimi texts me, "I'm on my way down," I assume she made a typo and meant to write, "I'm on my way *up*." Knowing she likely downed a few too many glasses of wine last night, I set out on her desk two aspirin; a strong coffee; and a bacon, egg, and cheese I picked up at her favorite deli around the corner. I've already erased all the hate mail from her e-mail queue, turned down the volume on her phone, and arranged her set of red pens in a neat row on her desk. She walks in wearing big black sunglasses, her skin pale and clammy.

"You are such a lifesaver," she says, sinking her teeth into the sandwich. "What will I do without you?"

Will. I swear she says "will," not "would." My arms perk up with goose bumps and I find I can't catch my breath.

Mimi, however, looks calm. She kicks her feet up on the desk and I see she's wearing loafers—beat-up, worn-out, moss-colored loafers.

I begin to cry. It's mortifying, but I can't stop the fat tears from plopping down and depositing dark stains onto my silk shirt.

"Oh, Laura," Mimi says, removing her sunglasses and scrutinizing me with pity. "Here, share the sustenance." She hands me half of the breakfast sandwich.

"Thanks." We sit there in silence, chewing and swallowing, the grease and salt and fat lulling each of us into a sullen stupor. "Listen, Mimi," I finally say, but she holds up her pointer finger.

"Here's a life tip, my trusty assistant. You win some, you lose some, and then you win some again. Ha! *C'est la vie.*"

Mimi dabs a napkin at the corners of her lips, then swivels in her seat to face her computer, where she begins typing rapid fire. Willing the floodgates of tears not to reopen, I smooth out my skirt, gather up the trash from our breakfast, and tiptoe out of my boss's office, careful not to disturb our editor in chief at work.

21

Leah Brenner, Executive Editor

I'm willing the stalled A train to get its act together and book it uptown, to not make me later than I already fear I'm going to be for my appointment on the thirtieth floor. I hopped on the subway in the first place, forgoing my usual walk uptown, to speed up my commute, not to get myself stuck underground in transit limbo, packed armpit-to-nose with hundreds of other passengers, plus the cat-sized rats and a decade's worth of garbage beneath us.

God, I'm a wreck. It baffles me why I should care about arriving late to a meeting where the sole agenda will be to fire me—especially when they scheduled it at eight in the freaking morning, making me jump through hoops to get Maria to the house at the crack of dawn. Still, when the train conductor repeats his announcement about more delays ahead, thank-you-for-your-patience, I groan.

My body is so heavy with exhaustion that simply standing still in kitten heels makes me feel as if someone is tugging at every one of my muscles, daring me not to keel over and collapse. I fear I may not be able to keep myself upright. So I make a decision. I glance around to make sure I don't recognize any of my fellow commuters, and then I pull my trick: I place one hand on my belly and begin rubbing big, heartfelt circles, then I literally gaze at my navel as I purr sweet nothings to my belly button. So ashamed am I of this deception (and the fact that I've been relying on it semiregularly ever since becoming a severely sleep-deprived mother), that I haven't told a soul. The thing is, it works: Usually it's thirty seconds or less before someone in my vicinity offers me his or her (usually *her*) seat. But now I'm going on one minute, two minutes, three minutes—the train is still stalled midtrack—and no one has noticed, or perhaps cared about my delicate (if phony) condition. Forget it, I think. I halt my hand's circling and suck my stomach back in its semiflat state. God, am I achy.

In addition to my usual I've-got-three-flipping-toddlers exhaustion, today I am sore from an entire long weekend of packing up boxes. After the antics I pulled at our first open house, Rob took the initiative to schedule the next one during one of my onsite workdays, on an evening when he knew I had to stay late; then he conveniently "forgot" to fill me in. The house sold in half an hour (Rob wouldn't give me any details about the buyers, I think for fear I'd call them and convince them to pull out).

"Baby, the timing's perfect," my husband declared when I arrived home and saw the picked-over platters of cold cuts on the counter. "You're getting fired next week, you'll pick up your severance check, and then we can skip town the moment all the sale details are finalized. Bing, bang, boom."

I don't think he expected me to burst into tears.

The truth is, no matter how long I've worked to prepare myself for the inevitable, no matter how many times I've assured myself (as has Rob, and Abby, and Liz, and even my mother) that this situation is totally political and not at all personal, and that I'm just a victim of circumstances outside of my control, deep down I know I am not ready to be fired. Despite all my posturing and flippant joking, I am not cool with it. I am not accepting of it. I am not blasé or Zen or go-with-the-flow about it. What I am is scared shitless. In fact, I think, maybe if this train flew off the rails and toppled all of us passengers into a disastrous, injurious heap, then I wouldn't have to face Mimi or Suzie in H.R. or anyone at Schmidt & Delancey ever again, and they could just messenger over my pink slip to my hospital room. Bing, bang, boom.

Just as I start getting into this trauma fantasy, trying to decide whether my hospital gown should hang in a sympathetically baggy or flatteringly fitted way, the train jolts forward. Three minutes later, it screeches to a halt at Columbus Circle, the doors swing open, and suddenly I'm being spit out into the world along with all the bankers, teachers, and whoever the hell else starts their workday this early. Climbing the stairs from subway platform to street, I see the Schmidt & Delancey building rise before me like a leviathan, its shadow stretched two blocks long. I peer up at all its thirty storys and feel myself getting sucked in and—*sigh*—succumbing to its powerful pull.

I decide to pit-stop at my desk to change into my Louboutin pumps. I expect the office to be empty, but as soon as I spot Laura at her station, dutifully typing away, I think, *Of course*. I wonder if she keeps a sleeping bag under her desk. "Hey, Laura."

"Hi. You're here early." She looks surprised to see me; I would've expected she knew about my morning meeting. She also looks like she hasn't slept in a week; the dark circles under her eyes give me a glimpse of what she'll look like at my age. Scary.

"Are you all right?" I ask. I'm about to place a palm on her shoulder, but her withering look stops me short.

Like a cartoon thought bubble popping up over my head, I flash on Friday's photo debacle. I'd rebelled that day, spending the majority of my at-home workday not in my basement office, but packing up my home, so I was barely tuned in to the situation. I did open an e-mail from Liz with the subject line, "What the hell is happening there?!?" and then glance at the MAGnifier.net link in the message's body. But I was immediately called away by a crisis involving Lulu and a roll of packing bubbles, and I never remembered to follow up with an Internet search or to check in with Abby about the fallout. Part of me figured, hey, it was no longer my problem, anyway. The bags under Laura's eyes tell me all I need to know about the effects of the incident.

"How are the troops faring after Friday?" I ask tentatively.

"Fine, everyone's fine," Laura snaps in a way that convinces me not one bit.

"That's good," I say. "I've got to skedaddle up to Corporate. Can you believe it, an eight a.m. meeting? I don't think I've ever been in the office this early. It was a huge pain in the butt to coordinate with my nanny. Though I suppose she could use the extra hours while she has the chance. I figure they're finally getting around to giving me the old ax." I make a gesture like I'm chopping off my neck. I must be more nervous than I thought, rambling on like this to Laura, of all people. "Well, wish me luck," I say.

Laura offers me nothing but a blank stare. God, what a snot.

In the elevator, ascending the twenty-one flights to the corporate suite, I whip out my phone and scroll through my e-mail, hoping without hope that Suzie has canceled our meeting. No such luck. Instead, I see a "BREAKING NEWS" alert from the *New York Post*, which I promptly open and read:

> **In the wake of last week's Photoshop cover scandal, exposed by magazine watchdog blog MAGnifier.net, Mimi Walsh is out after a brief stint as editor in chief of *Hers* magazine. Speculation abounds over which brave soul will next take on the editorship and navigate what are sure to be some very choppy waters.**

My jaw goes slack. I find I can't clamp it back shut. I feel my tongue hanging loose like I'm an overheated dog. I gape at the screen until the text looks like gibberish, a mishmash of symbols that can't possibly contain any meaning.

"Good morning, Leah." I look up and there is Suzie greeting me from the other side of the elevator doors, now open onto the thirtieth floor. She's holding out a coffee, which is apparently for me. In my entire career no one has ever brought me coffee. I grab it, grateful for something to do with my hands, and gulp it down.

Even the scald against the back of my throat can't snap me out of my shock. "Come with me," Suzie says, all smiles. Somehow my legs carry me down the hall beside her. I am numb.

We enter a space that cannot possibly belong to the H.R. rep: It's twice the size of Mimi's office, with floor-to-ceiling windows that afford even grander views of Central Park; it boasts not one but two separate sitting areas.

"Welcome, come on in." The voice is familiar, but all I can see of the speaker is the back of a head, and a thick gray bun balancing atop it. When she swivels her chair away from her computer, I discover it's Mrs. Winters, the editorial director of Schmidt & Delancey. I haven't laid eyes on her since way back in April, when she visited *Hers* to deliver the news of Louisa's demise. I'm starting to wonder if I misread that *Post* news alert.

"A pleasure to see you again, Mrs. Brenner," she says, extending a hand. "I've heard so many things about you." It's just like Mrs. Winters not to modify "things" with "wonderful" or "terrible" or some other telling descriptor; the phrase "so many things" could mean so many things. I accept the handshake, my palm clammy; Mrs. Winters's is dry and cool.

"Take a seat," she says. The chair's cushion is plusher than my living room couch. I sink in about a foot, so that I feel like a child looking up at Mrs. Winters from across the desk. Suzie plops herself down in the chair next to mine, letting out a small yelp when she too sinks into its softness. Despite what I read in the *Post* e-mail, I keep waiting for Mimi to walk in and deliver the official "We're letting you go" spiel (after Liz was fired, I made her repeat the speech to me over and over again until the words were etched into my brain like the Pledge of Allegiance).

"As you know," Mrs. Winters says, which is when I start trembling. There is so much I know, and I fear for which sliver of that knowledge she's going to select to repeat back to me and somehow wield against me. "*Hers* has gone through quite a shake-up these past few months. Louisa Harding struggled to keep the publication afloat during what was admittedly a difficult time, economically speaking. When she couldn't hack it, of course we brought in Mimi Walsh, a wonderfully talented editor with a standout track record and stellar reputation in the industry. We had high hopes that Ms. Walsh would pull in newer, younger readers and revive the *Hers* brand to its former glory."

To hear the past year of my professional life summed up into this tidy little trajectory—the demise of my former boss meriting a mere sentence fragment—makes me understand just how powerful Mrs. Winters is, reigning from her throne on the thirtieth floor. Powerful and ruthless. I know what's coming next, and I wonder if Mrs. Winters realizes she's already been scooped by the *Post*. I feel a bizarre urge to defend Mimi, to say that the leaked photos could not have been her fault, that no single person can control every little action of her whole staff and all the random hangers-on at any given photo shoot. It's such a heartless industry we work in, and so hard to be at the top, and how fast any one of us can topple from glory. "Have you guys seen the redesign?" I blurt out. "It's beautiful." Because as much as I hate to admit it, it *is* beautiful. Still, I'm not sure what I'm doing.

"Yes, the pages have turned out very nice," Suzie says, smiling nervously.

Mrs. Winters looks puzzled. "Well," she says, shifting in her seat, "it's my job to face up to some hard truths. In this case, the devastating impact of Friday's debacle with that pop singer on your cover. I'm not sure if you're aware that *Hers'* subscriber base has fallen by fifty thousand in just the past three days." Wow, I'm actually kind of impressed that our readers are so plugged in to media news, and also willing to take a stand against the Photoshopping of cover images. I feel a strange surge of girl power. Mrs. Winters is still talking: "And fairly or not, nearly the entire blogosphere plus about half of the talking heads on TV have rallied to have Mimi burned at the stake. Something had to be done. We really had no choice."

"I understand," I say, although I'm not really sure I do. I'm distracted by the thought that I could never stomach having Mrs.

Winters's job, and also the question of why she's offering up this whole explanation to me.

"Which brings me to why you're here," she says. I try to sit up straighter in my cushiony seat—to no avail. "Mrs. Brenner, you have demonstrated exceptional talent through your years at *Hers*, rising in the ranks to the prestigious spot of second-in-command and acting as a rock to the staff during these recent bumpy times." My mind goes fuzzy. *I'm being praised, aren't I?* After an entire summer of putting up with all the backhanded compliments and hits to my pride and harassment both subtle and blatant, it's hard to trust my ears. But if I'm not mistaken, I am sitting here before the Schmidt & Delancey editorial director, in the largest office on the building's top floor, being applauded for a job well done. "So, what do you say?" Mrs. Winters asks.

I realize I've zoned out. "Excuse me, can you repeat that?"

Mrs. Winters and Suzie both laugh. "I said, will you do Schmidt & Delancey the honor of accepting the position of the new editor in chief of *Hers* magazine?"

Everything stops. All is white noise. I am alone at the top of this mammoth of a building, not about to get thrown off, as it turns out, but to be exalted. I look from one face to the other—are they serious? Is this for real? *It must be.* Suddenly the events of the past fifteen minutes sprint to catch up in my brain. It's a pileup of images and thoughts and sentences, until all that's left is a solid feeling of certainty. *Of course* this is what would happen. *Of course* after all my hard work and dedication and experience, *of course* after enduring the kind of summer that even Job would cower at, *of course* I am finally being rewarded.

"Well, what do you say?" asks Suzie, which makes me realize I haven't yet said a thing.

"Of course!" I exclaim. I sense my daughters' *we're-getting-ice-cream!* look of glee spreading across my own face, and I immediately dial it back. I affix a pleased-but-demure expression that I imagine would be fitting for an editor in chief. "I would be honored," I add in my best professional tone.

Seemingly from nowhere, Suzie whips out a bottle of champagne, and I think, good for her. After all she's been through, delivering terrible news all summer long, she deserves a drink. She pops the cork, which soars in a perfect upside-down parabola before landing squarely on top of Mrs. Winters's bun. I brace myself, imagining a swift end to the party, but Mrs. Winters just shrugs and lets the cork sit atop her head until it eventually topples off on its own. She pulls out three plastic champagne flutes from a drawer.

"To the woman of the hour," she says, raising her glass. "God willing, you'll turn this publication around into a grand success." Though I sense a vague threat there, I remove it from my mind, knowing there will be plenty of time later on to discuss facts and figures. We clink glasses.

The champagne goes straight to my head, and my thoughts flit about like fireflies: I think of little old me sitting in that big corner office, my name printed at the tippy-top of the masthead, my photo stamped at the front of every issue. I am awed by my new power to yay or nay every single decision, and—oh, my God!—the clothing, makeup, and hair allowance. Little ions of happiness are performing somersaults in my head, and as much as I try to be cool, I'm certain a stupid grin has all but tattooed itself across my face. After two refills of champagne and more handshakes and congratulations, I must look as blithe as Bozo the Clown.

It's not until I'm back in the elevator that the reality of my life hits me—Rob! Our entire home packed up in boxes! The new house in Vermont! My heart starts to sink as I plummet the twenty-one floors. All summer, I've been working so hard to feel OK about leaving behind my career in magazines, to feel at peace about moving to the middle of nowhere and starting over. But now that this golden, new opportunity is glittering before my eyes, that sense of peace feels like a cheap, plastic consolation prize. I cannot turn my back on the job I've been dreaming about since I was a child playing office at my mother's feet.

But, of course, there is Rob. Rob, whom I love deeply. Rob, who is deeply in love with both me and the idea of our beginning again in Vermont. Still, one of the reasons I first fell for my husband was his beautiful, open mind, his willingness to consider and reconsider a scenario and to readjust his views accordingly, without reservation or resentment. Like the best editors, Rob always sees the potential for revision. Hopefully that outlook will prevail now, and my husband will recognize the Vermont plan for what it was: simply a rough draft. Surely when he hears about the new plan, he'll see it as a vast improvement over the original, a revise that's been tweaked and edited and perfectly polished—the final.

This reasoning does not prevent my stomach from catapulting into my throat as I reluctantly dig out my phone and dial my husband's number. Before I know it, I've dropped past the *Hers* floor and I'm speaking into a recording: "Rob, sweetheart, hi! I have news. It's big. And it's going to sound scary at first, but don't worry. I love you. We're going to make it work, I just know it. And even better, you'll soon have the benefit of being married to the happiest version of me I've ever been. And I love you. Did I already say that? Well, it's still true, I love you. Call me when you can. Bye!"

To halt the panic I sense creeping into my head, I adjust my focus—to *all the money!* When Mrs. Winters slid across her desk a piece of paper containing my new salary, the number made me gasp. I'll be earning more than double my current income. I picture never again waking up in a cold sweat, wondering how the hell we'll afford tuition times three for twelve years of private school plus college for the girls; now I'll sleep soundly through the night, happily ever after. I'll finally be able to spend and splurge and squander as I've always dreamed. I imagine tearing up the horribly restrictive budget Rob and I hammered out for Vermont, and then immediately hitting Barneys. It'll be just like that show our nanny likes where the contestants race through the supermarket with unlimited budgets, loading up their carts willy-nilly, only for me instead of groceries I'll be loading up on buttery leather handbags and gorgeous calfskin boots.

My phone's ringing jolts me out of my shopping spree fantasy: It's Rob. I step off the elevator into the building's lobby, inhale deeply, and pick up the phone.

"Sweetheart," I say, then before taking a breath or giving him a chance to respond, I blurt out my news.

"Wow." His tone is undecipherable. I remember offering the same one-word response when Rob told me we'd gotten the Vermont house.

"I know it's a lot to take in," I say. "I've been thinking, and I suppose you and the kids and maybe Maria can settle down in Vermont, and I'll get a little studio in SoHo and commute back and forth." I picture my weekdays: I'll be unattached, living that illustrious Manhattan working-girl life of catching the train for a ten-minute hop up to the office, popping out at lunch to shop at a boutique, hitting up the trendiest new restaurant for dinner (with an assistant to book the reservation!). "I'll spend my weeks in New York, and then each weekend I'll vamoose up to Vermont and dive into our wholesome new country life. Think about it, we'll never get sick of each other. You know how they say how distance makes the heart grow fonder. It'll be great."

My husband says nothing, so I continue my rambling: "Or maybe we'll stay in New Jersey, get another house—a bigger one!—in the same neighborhood, and Vermont will become our quaint, little summer place, for hiking and blueberry picking and baking bread from scratch. It'll be the best of both worlds! We can make it work. Right?" I'm willing my husband to say something, *anything*, and meanwhile thinking, I can have it all, right? *Right?*

"Right," Rob says, finally. I exhale, my heart pounding; I didn't realize I'd been holding my breath. "I guess we'll make it work. Congratulations, baby. This is a big deal."

"Thanks," I say. "Sweetheart?"

"Yeah?"

"How exactly will we make it work?"

"Hey, who the hell knows?!"

My laugh is a snort. "Oh, how I love you."

"You're lucky I love you, too, babe. Otherwise I'd probably kill you."

"I suppose that's fair."

"OK, well, I have to go rework the icing on the 'You're Fired' cake I got you. Got to change the 'F' into an 'H.' "

I giggle. "Good idea, sweetheart. I'll see you tonight."

My eyes are still on my phone's screen when I start back toward the elevator, so I'm not surprised when I smack right into someone. "I'm so sorry," I say on reflex, and then look up to see Mimi. "Oh."

"Had to get in a final blow before I left, didn't you?" she says, smiling slyly.

"I'm so sorry," I say again, not sure of what else to say or do. Mimi and I look at each other eye to eye. It's because she's in flats; without her usual sky-high heels, Mimi and I are the same height.

"I hear some congratulations are in order to the new editor in chief."

"Thank you," I say. I wonder how this news has possibly already spread, if maybe Mimi has rigged up some kind of wiretap in Mrs. Winters's office. "I was sorry to hear what happened to you, and with the Helena cover. Really. That could've happened to anyone."

"Well, you weren't the one to leak the photo, were you? Come on, fess up! Ha!"

"Honestly, I would never have the guts."

"I know you wouldn't." I suppose she couldn't resist the dig. "One thing about you, Leah, no one could ever deny how much you care about *Hers*."

I nod. It's true. "I know you cared, too, Mimi."

"Yep, and now I'll find something else to care about. That shouldn't be so hard."

"Any chance you want to get away from it all, leave the crazy city life behind? I've got this great house in Vermont I'm looking to unload. It comes with live chickens."

"Chickens, ha! Lord help me. The day I decide to leave Manhattan is the day I put a bullet in my head. No offense."

"None taken, although New Jersey really isn't so bad."

"Sure it's not."

"So, as a seasoned pro, do you have any advice for me in my new job?"

"You're in charge now, so act like it. You want them to be a little scared of you. I say, fire someone immediately."

"Hmm, I'm not sure I'm going to be that kind of editor in chief."

"You may just surprise yourself, Ms. Leah Brenner. Also, there's a package of Oreos in the bottom right desk drawer. For emergencies—and believe me, there will be emergencies."

"Thanks, Mimi. It means a lot."

"All right, let's not get too schmaltzy. Here, we'll hug it out—I promise I won't pull a knife—and then I'm out."

"All right."

Mimi pulls me in for a hug, holds on for exactly one beat, and then pushes me away. "Now, off you go, back up to the wolves," she says. It's bittersweet, watching my former boss walk away and out of the Schmidt & Delancey building.

As soon as Mimi is out of sight, I refocus on my own situation, on this impossible fantasy that has become my reality. I suppose I'll soon find out if this new job, this new life, will work out. In the meantime, I've got the November issue to finish shipping to the printer. I board the elevator and press 9.

When I step out onto the *Hers* floor, it's eerily calm. It's like the hush after a hurricane, when everyone's relieved to still have a roof over their heads, but shell-shocked that the skies, now clear and blue, could have unleashed such rage upon the world. I survey the damage. Laura appears. "Can I get you anything?" she asks, a submissive smile plastered onto her face. So then everyone must already know.

"A coffee, skim milk, one sugar," I say, surprised at how easily the answer rolls off my tongue, and how confident I sound. This will be my second coffee delivery in one day, and already it no longer fazes me. I retreat to my new office, turn on my new computer, and start typing up ideas, plotting and planning. It's thrilling to see how quickly the pages fill—one, then two, then three. Here we go.

* * *

"Everyone into the conference room, please," I announce. I stand front and center, posture perfect, until the troops have gathered. When the room falls silent, I unveil an image on the screen: the unretouched version of Helena Hope.

"Folks, get a load of our new November cover," I say, using my pink pen to draw attention to the singer's various flaws and blemishes. "It'll be a grand statement. A big 'F you!' to all those snarky blogs calling us names. *Hers* will become the first-ever women's magazine to print a completely unretouched photo on its cover. Inside the issue we'll give readers an intimate look at Helena's struggle with her weight, her aging, and her tumultuous career. It'll be the story of a true survivor. I predict this will be our highest grossing issue in years."

I scan the faces before me; they look attentive and intrigued and a little scared. *So this is what it's like to be in charge,* I think. A fiery satisfaction flares up from my belly and energizes my whole body. It's a feeling that could be addictive.

"It's genius," says Zoe. "Good for you, Brenner." She looks genuinely proud.

"Hear, hear," says Abby, flashing me a smile.

"If it works for Helena, it works for me," Lynn says.

"She really doesn't look half bad," Jane adds. "It's less creepy than the super-doctored picture, that's for sure." Even Debbie doesn't look displeased at this scheme.

"You guys are totally right," says Victoria, her tone thick with honey, stripped of all its usual scorn. She seems nervous. "This will be a wonderful fresh start to the brand-new face of *Hers,* a revolutionary take on women living their real lives, wrinkles and all."

I nod curtly. It's just a tiny tilt of the head, but I believe it's enough to convey that she now answers to me—that they all do— and that if I were as vindictive as some might be in my place, I could easily move certain office-dwelling employees to certain out-of-the-way cubicles, but that I'm probably (*probably*) above that kind of retribution.

"But what about Helena?" Laura blurts out, clearly horrified.

"Johanna spoke to Helena," I say, "and she loves the idea: it'll keep her name on the tip of everyone's tongues, plus it'll give her that touch of edginess she's been dying to project for ages."

"It's a win-win," Johanna says. "Those were the exact words out of her mouth, the bloody wanker."

"OK, everyone," I say, "we've got about two hours to get this new cover and the revised Helena interview out the door. Let's get moving."

"Well, I think it's an awful idea." Laura says it, perhaps louder than she intended.

"Is that right?" I fix my eyes on her. In that moment, I remember Mimi's advice, and I understand. Everyone wheels around to face my new assistant—the features editors, the beauty and fashion departments, Web and production, art and photo. The entire staff is singling out and staring at the one loyalist to the old guard. It's all versus one. They watch as Laura blushes a deep red, and I can feel a shift in the room. Everyone understands the girl's fate, and the fact that I have just decided it. And then I can see it in Laura's eyes: the slate-gray irises somehow darkening to the precise hue of defeat. She understands it, too.

Laura storms out of the conference room. I imagine her retreating to her desk, trying to deep-breathe her way into the picture of calm, even as she begins to unravel inside. I imagine her going through the rituals that just hours ago I believed I myself would perform today: scanning her Post-its and business cards and all the things that have shaped her days at *Hers*, trying to commit everything to memory, already feeling the nostalgia of returning to a place where she used to belong. I feel a pang for her, but I will myself to dismiss it. I jot off a quick e-mail to Suzie in H.R., and then add an item to my mental to-do list: collect résumés, entry level.

I rush past the rows of cubicles of everyone who works for me (*me!*), and take my position behind my desk—a sleek, solid number made of gleaming mahogany, special ordered for a small fortune by a certain predecessor of mine whose name will no longer be uttered in this office, a desk that is now mine, mine, mine. I hear the faint ringing of a phone: Laura's. The sound resounds like an announcement of my command.

As my assistant reaches to pick up her receiver, I slide the glass door to my office closed, shutting out all that's outside. The space hums with white noise, a pseudosilence I find even more comforting than the real thing. It's precisely the peace and quiet I need. I survey my surroundings, this grandiose space that now belongs to me, and I marvel at just how much I love *Hers*, how much I believe in the group of people who sit working just beyond my office door, and how much I'm going to do to make this magazine the best version of itself it can be. I click open my pink pen, and I get started.

Acknowledgments

I would like to thank the following people: Max Apple, my treasured teacher and friend, whose Writers House classroom I often conjure up in my mind for inspiration and motivation. Tom De-Peter (in loving memory), who first taught me to revere semicolons and to be wary of adverbs, and whose graceful teachings I will value always. All of my former cubicle comrades-in-arms, who made the magazine madness mostly a delight—and whose wit and good humor helped compensate for the rest of the time. Diana Spechler, whom I met by happenstance in a hair salon and who has since become a valuable mentor and thoughtful first reader. Zick Rubin, for his generous counsel, both legal and otherwise. My wise agent, Joelle Delbourgo, whose insight and savvy have shaped and sharpened this story. My editors, Audrey LaFehr and Martin Biro, and the rest of the team at Kensington, for transforming my scribblings into this beautiful book (and trusting me with the next one, too!). My mother, father, and brothers, for their endless love and support. And Damian, who joins me for coffee, shores me up with confidence and a kiss, and then leaves me be to write. I couldn't be luckier.